HIGH VALLEY

High Valley

by **CHARMIAN CLIFT**
and **GEORGE JOHNSTON**

THE BOBBS-MERRILL COMPANY, INC.
Publishers
INDIANAPOLIS   NEW YORK

COPYRIGHT, 1950, BY THE BOBBS-MERRILL COMPANY, INC.
PRINTED IN THE UNITED STATES OF AMERICA

For

TWO MOTHERS

ACKNOWLEDGMENT

HIGH VALLEY was awarded the first prize of £2,000 in the Novel Section of the *Sydney Morning Herald* Literary Competitions, 1948. The Competitions are held under the terms of a grant of £30,000 set aside by the proprietors of the *Herald* for the encouragement of Australian literature and art.

HIGH VALLEY

Prologue

HE had the appearance of one of those comical Chinese carvings in old ivory as he sat morosely amid the latticed shadows. It was a tavern even more squalid than the average West China inn. The afternoon was tedious, and the old peddler was bored.

In the first place, the heat was absurdly unseasonable for March. Three days before it had been interesting, a subject for comment and conversation. But three days and three nights had exhausted its novelty. Now it was merely irritating. It squeezed against the city of Ch'eng-tu with the clammy redundance of a soiled blanket on a summer night. No breeze stirred the bamboo awnings. The jasmine leaves sprinkled into the weak tea could not disguise the tepidness of the beverage. The sunflower seeds were without flavor. Those tavern patrons who had come in search of a reasonable measure of coolness were slumped at the tables, their clothing undone and their heads lolling amid spilled tea and overturned wine cups.

The peddler stared at the slack, rumpled figures with repugnance. Irritably, he wished that at least one of them would awaken sufficiently to be engaged in conversation. He was a lonely old man, and garrulous when he could find an audience.

Nobody stirred. But somewhere, not far distant, the stupor of the day was punctuated by a sudden strident outcry. The peddler shuffled quickly to the door.

In the lane the dried leaves lifted a little, as if disturbed also by the clamor, scratched aimless grooves in the dust, and then succumbed to the hot burden of the air. The dulled foliage of the plane trees crackled into stillness.

The peddler, momentarily brightened by the promise of excitement, sighed as the brief hubbub dissolved into the drowsing monotone. The city had stirred, restless beneath the heat, only to fall back again into its sweaty torpor.

He was about to return to his table when he saw the boy enter the lane, hesitantly, looking behind as if fearful of pursuit.

The boy's feet scuffed the dust, and now his head was bent, perhaps in dejection, perhaps merely because of the heat. A thin boy this, and with the face and frame of a northern man: nothing of the flat features of the Szechwan people: nothing of their squatness. Yes, the peddler decided, a Chinese boy who yet—and for other reasons also—certainly did not belong to this city or this province. For the thin, hardy-looking body was clad in the cumbersome garments of Tibet, and the flat felt hat that crowned the equally thin, hard-looking face was very different from the circle of straw that any self-respecting Szechwanese would wear, particularly on a day of such appalling discomfort. Now this was something that could not be related to the monotony of a stale and heat-stinking city that was at least a thousand years too old for its own good—since why should a Chinese boy wear the thick weaves of the snow country when a sun like a temple gong of bronze reduced all the province to wilting languor? Now this was a question that held a promise of conversation.

The peddler hooked a finger at the approaching youth and called to him. "Boy!" His voice was thin and dry as the dust that coated alleyway and trees and hung like a mist in the air.

The boy halted, and the dust twirled for a moment about his legs and fell in a fine powder upon his clumsy boots of felt. His attitude seemed puzzled and defensive. The peddler observed also that his face was not really hard, and that his eyes were lonely and bewildered with more than the loneliness and bewilderment of youth, and the old man's curiosity was increased.

He called again, this time in the thick tongue of Tibet: "Boy!" His tone was more wheedling. "Come, take tea with me. I am lonely for companionship and starved for talk."

The boy hesitated for a moment, eying the peddler warily, and then he shrugged and followed the old man into the shadowed inn.

"Sit, boy. Sit there." The peddler teetered excitedly, and then he clapped his thin hands and called for more sunflower seeds and another dish of tea. When these were placed before the boy, and he had haggled for a moment regarding the payment, he smiled disarmingly and said: "You are a stranger to the city?"

He spoke in good Mandarin, and yet this youth, who had the look of one from beyond the Yellow River, shook his head uncomprehendingly, and in his brown eyes lurked the still-hunted expression that one sees sometimes in the eyes of an animal newly caged.

"You spoke in the tongue of Tibet before," the boy said slowly, but only after a troubled silence. "You must speak in that tongue, for I understand no Chinese."

"But you are Chinese!"

"I do not understand the tongue of China," the boy repeated sullenly.

"Now this is a thing!" the peddler murmured. "I would have staked this worthless life of mine that you were a northern man, for I know the Tibetans well and you do not have the look of one from that land, although you wear their garments and speak their tongue. This is indeed a new thing!"

"Then you will laugh as the others did, eh?"

"Now, my son, who in this fine city was uncivil enough to laugh at you?" Suddenly his eyes snapped brightly as he remembered the outcry just before the boy had entered the lane. "Ah, then you were the cause of the disturbance I heard? Now why should that be?" He gestured impatiently toward the tea and sunflower seeds. "Come then. Refresh yourself, and when you are ready then tell me your story. I will not laugh. I am an old man, and I save my laughter for humorous tales and droll happenings. I do not use it as a weapon against an honored guest."

"You are kind, old man," the boy said awkwardly. He scooped the white sunflower seeds into his cupped palm. "And I am grateful. No other in this city has been so courteous."

The peddler bowed slightly at the boy's compliment. "You have been here long?" he asked.

"A day." Some of the suspicion had gone from the boy's eyes. He smiled nervously. "It is a wonderful city, this one! I had never imagined . . . the walls so high and so thick, and . . ."

"Yes, yes." The peddler's politeness was surrendering rapidly to his curiosity. "A splendid city! A magnificent city! But what was the disturbance, my son? Why did the people laugh at you?"

The boy's hands clenched, and the hunted look was in his face again.

"I did not understand," he said softly. "I think I do not understand yet. I was staring at the marvels of your city, and at first I did not notice that people were pointing at me and laughing. It seems you are the only one in all this place who has no wish to laugh because I wear these clothes and use a strange tongue . . ."

"Then you *are* Chinese?" the peddler interrupted quickly.

"Yes, I am Chinese. That is why I came here. To see my own land and my own people. But my people looked at me and laughed." His mouth twisted bitterly. "And urchins tripped me into the stink of a canal. And harlots simpered at me until they found I did not wish to buy their wares, and then they hurled clods at me, and screamed, and chased me from their booths. That was the disturbance you heard. I did not expect such treatment from my own countrymen, but then I did not know that I looked comical. These clothes are all I have. I have always worn them. I did not know . . ."

"What name do they call you, boy?" the peddler asked. His voice was very kindly.

"Salom."

"It is a name of Tibet."

"I know no other."

"There is no need; it is a good name. But did you never have a Chinese name?"

"Once, perhaps," the boy said sadly. "Once I must have had a Chinese name, and Chinese parents. But it is all so long ago. I . . .

I cannot remember. It seems that I have always lived in Tibet, and all I know before that time are the things I have been told."

The peddler plucked impatiently at the sparse white beard that straggled from his chin. Why did not the boy get on with his story?

"And what were the things you were told?" he prompted gently.

The boy sipped at his tea and stared beyond the old man, beyond the peeling walls and the faded scrolls made mysterious by stain and mildew and the activities of insects. He made a small gesture of deprecation. "But my tale would bore you. You have been kind, and I do not wish to make your day tedious with a stupid story that———"

"No, no. Tell the story, boy. I *wish* to hear it. There is nothing I love so much as a good story."

Salom smiled. "Then I will tell you," he said. "For fifteen years I have lived in Tibet, with two old ones who have always treated me as their own child. They said they found me at the edge of a peat bog after the evil Chinese army had gone."

"Chinese army?"

"Yes. It came up through Tibet on its way to the north when I was———"

"Of course! The Communist Army. Yes—it *would* be fifteen years ago!"

"I suppose it was that army," the boy continued. "The people up there said it was a rabble of murderers and plunderers, and it was only because I was a child, and starving, that they succored me. They said I was wrapped in a few rags of cotton, so they took me to their house lest I be killed by other Tibetans who hated this Chinese army. They hid me for many months, and then, when something of the people's anger had died away, they brought me out and dressed me in Tibetan clothes and named me Salom. They could never tell me much about that army, but some things I remembered. There was a tall man who carried me on his shoulders and sang as he marched, and many men in vests of padded green cotton who laughed and played with me. Then there were other things less clear." He paused and stared thoughtfully at the littered seeds. "Still, such things do not matter, I suppose. Anyway, I forgot my own tongue, and I lived as a Tibetan. I helped tend the flocks and herds. I combed the fleeces, and scythed the grain, and winnowed it. I rode with the yak caravans to Litang and Batang and Derge and Gantze. But always there were these other things in my mind, and always I knew that one day I would have to leave the old ones and come to China, because I belonged to China. You see, I knew I could only find my beginnings if I came to China." He shrugged, and the bitter smile twisted his mouth again. "So I left the old people, even though they wept, and I came to China. And China laughed."

In the blackness almost lost within the pouches and furrows of the old man's eyes there was a brighter gleam. It was turning out to be a very interesting afternoon after all.

"And do you remember nothing else about this army, boy? Think hard now."

The boy smiled hesitantly. "Well, there is a thing," he said. "Sometimes when I rode with the caravans I would close my eyes and see this thing. I would see the men in the padded vests of green cotton. They were clawing at a cliff, and beneath the cliff a river ran—a broad river. And there was rain. I could see that quite clearly, like fine lines drawn across the men on the cliff. The men wore fiber capes, some of them did, and they looked like bats. And I could hear guns and see the red flash of them. The guns chattered quickly, like an abacus. And I could hear the noise of the river. Somehow the noise of the river seemed to be mixed up with the smell of blood and with a knife cutting into flesh. But I do not know . . . Oh, it is all so stupid!"

"Go on, boy."

"Well, I cannot remember any faces, except that of the tall man who carried me on his shoulders. And I cannot remember my own tongue, except three words that tell me in some way of a bridge. Liu Ting Chiao. They are the words. And somehow I have always thought that the tall man was my father and the words——"

"The words are of a bridge, my son," the peddler said softly. "It is likely that your father died there. For there was a great battle at the bridge built by Liu. A great battle! And the bridge was won by thirty heroes. Yes, I think it is likely that your father was one of those heroes."

The boy pushed forward. His eyes glittered in his sweat-streaked face. "Then you know of this army! If you know, then tell me!"

The peddler jiggled on his seat. He had forgotten the heat, his own petulance, the tedium of the day. This was a subject dear to his heart. He clapped his hands and called for more tea, and this time he did not haggle over the price. He drank deeply before he spoke. It was tea of superlative flavor!

"Now I will tell you a story, boy." He wiped his mouth on the back of a hand almost as fragile as porcelain. "Regarding this army of your father's. An army of heroes, my son! They call it the Red Army. In the north, beyond the Huang-ho, it fights still."

"*Still?* But . . . but it is fifteen years since . . ."

"It still fights, my son."

The boy shook his head stupidly. "But I do not understand this thing," he said. "It was so long ago. It is such a long time for men to be fighting."

The old man pursed his mouth. His lips were broken into many fine lines and were devoid of color. "Listen to me, boy. Fifteen years ago the Red Army marched and fought its way across the plains of West Szechwan, these very plains. Women marched with it, too—fighters, some of them, and wives, and camp followers— and children also. You must have been one of those children. Now I think your father must have died at the battle for Liu's bridge. It took place a little before the Red Army was forced to retreat before the forces of the Yunnan and Szechwan conscripts. Yes, the army retreated. But it clambered across the mountains of Tibet and fought its way across the grasslands of the plateau—even taking women and children with it until it could support them no longer— and it went north fighting and dying that it might live."

"But you say it *still* fights!"

"That it still might live, my son."

"And it really was an army of heroes?" the boy pleaded. "The old ones were wrong? It was not an army of evil men, a rabble of plunderers?"

"Well, it is all in the viewpoint." The peddler smiled. "My crops were not despoiled by it, nor my daughters ravished by it, nor my sons killed in fighting it. And, since I have suffered no injuries that might blind me to its merits, I say it was an army of heroes. Perhaps if I had lived in Tibet I would think otherwise. But the facts are there. It marched more than ten thousand miles, that army. Whatever you think of its politics you cannot deny its fiber. It marched through all of China and it climbed over those mighty mountains and it put all Tibet behind it so that it could win freedom in the north. It plundered. Certainly it plundered. A man who does not plunder does not live. All life is plunder."

"And it was not evil?" the boy insisted.

"No. I think it is wrong to regard this army as evil. For it was an army of men made unconquerable by the very fact that it could not live with the thought of defeat. And, whatever their failings, men who are unconquerable are worthy men. When a man dies he should seek but a single word to be brushed on the tablet above his grave. Undefeated. That is the word, boy. *Undefeated.* This army to which your father belonged was an army of stalwart men who were undefeated. The killing, the rape, the plunder—all these things, besides the other, are not important. The importance is the word, my son. The simple word."

The boy called Salom nodded his head very quickly. His eyes were fixed intently on the old man's face. His mouth smiled as he shaped the word. Undefeated. All the loneliness and bewilderment and bitterness had gone from him. He felt as though he had been given some incalculably precious thing.

"Yes," he whispered. "Yes, I knew they were wrong. I knew my father was a good man. I am glad I came to China."

"Now, what thing is this?" The peddler cackled. "You have been tripped into a canal. You have been chased with clods of earth. You have been jeered at. And you are *glad* you came to China!"

"Those things are nothing! You must understand. This is my country! This is where I belong! And perhaps in time I will meet other wise men like yourself, and they will add some other pieces to this story of my beginnings. And then I will become powerful in my own right, and gain a name and a position and all the things."

The peddler cracked a white seed between his black and broken teeth. "Go back to Tibet, my son," he said gently.

"To Tibet?" The boy looked at him blankly. The light went from his face as though a candle had been snuffed. "But I have just come from there. Ever since I can remember I have longed for China, and dreamed——"

"You no longer belong to China."

"But I am no Tibetan! I am Chinese! I seek my own land and my own people!"

The peddler's thin finger traced a pattern in the spilled tea. "Listen, my son. Tibet is both your land and your people. You have lived for nineteen or twenty years. The first few were spent merely in giving you a brain and a body. But the other years have given you your life. You must return to Tibet because it understands you, and you understand it. Here you will have no understanding—and you will find none."

"But it is *you* who do not understand! I have *never* belonged to Tibet! I do not like many things about Tibet—the religion, the priests, the squalor of the people's lives, the way the world is packed inside two green fields!"

"Those who are young are always rebellious against simplicity," the peddler murmured. "Only the aged value it at its worth."

"But I do not want simplicity. I . . . I want life and adventure. I want my own country, my own people. I want a place where I can belong!"

"Well, you can find life and adventure here, certainly. But you will find other things also. Some of them you have found already.

Ugly things grow quickly where there are many people to fertilize the plants. How long have you taken in riding down over the great mountains?"

"Two months."

"Then you will have been in China for several weeks of that time. Have you felt that you belong here?"

"No. But——"

"Listen to me. I will tell you a thing. Already in this city you have been subjected to indignity. That, you say, is nothing. But do you know that you could be persecuted and perhaps even killed if you spoke with any pride of your dead father? These people are the enemies of your father's army, and they have long memories. Here you will find such men—tortured by old hatreds, twisted by desire for power; men covetous, intolerant, malicious; men lustful and jealous and greedy. If you would have a life of misery, my son, then stay here. Ignore the senile droolings of a silly old man. Stay here! But if you would find yourself, and a place where you can belong, then take your horses and turn their heads back toward the eastern mountains. Only when you return to Tibet will you find what you seek. It is not to be found here."

"You speak as if you know the country out there." His eyes were hard. "It is no land of easy traveling. If I go back I have had four months of hardship and nothing to show for it! Why should I go back?"

"Because there is no place in China for a Chinese without ancestry, without land, without a birthright, without a name—a Chinese who cannot even speak his own tongue." The peddler stroked his beard and looked at the boy quizzically. "Of course you could go north to join that army of your father's which still fights. Certainly you would be killed, but——"

"I have no wish for killing—or being killed."

"Then go back to Tibet."

"To Litang? To Batang? To the lousy towns of Kham?" The boy looked at him unhappily. "To live always among flea-bitten yaks in villages of mud and stench?"

"There are other places in Tibet—better places than Litang or Batang."

"How do you know so much of Tibet?"

The peddler smiled, not at the boy, but at something far distant in time. "Because when I was young I, too, longed for life and adventure. And I sought it—not in China—but beyond those mountains which you have put behind you. For many years I roamed the grasslands and the valleys, selling herbs and simples to peasants and nomads. I learned much of your country. I learned also to love it."

"Then I wonder you did not stay there," the boy muttered.

"So do I. I should have stayed. Once I had the chance to stay." He shrugged. "I had not enough courage."

The twisted smile was at the boy's mouth. "What courage does it need to stay in Tibet?"

"It needed courage to stay in this valley, my boy. It is a valley for hardy men. *Only* for hardy men. The price of living in that valley is endless toil, and a winter so harsh that only those can survive who will not be defeated."

"Then why do people live there?"

"If you saw the valley you would not ask that." The peddler mused for a time, and the boy grew uncomfortable.

"Is it beautiful, this valley?" he asked finally.

"Very beautiful. But it has more than beauty. It is locked away from the world beyond the barrier of the Ta Hsueh Shan. It means nothing to the world, and the world nothing to it. It has known no change for hundreds of years. It is a valley such as the storytellers spin into the fabric of their magic tales."

"Then who lives there? And where is it to be found? I have never heard of such a place."

"There is no reason why you should have heard of it. It lies far to the south of Litang, and the trail that leads there is a trail that few men take. A lonely trail, and a hard one. You would need to be uncommonly adventurous to set your foot on that trail." He looked at the boy slyly. "Who lives there? Only nomads, my son.

And peace. And happiness." He scooped up the last of the sunflower seeds and looked at them reflectively.

After a long moment of silence the boy coughed. "What is this valley called, old one?" he asked.

"Why, even its name is poetry, my son. It is called the Valley of the Dreaming Phoenix."

"And how long would it take to travel to this place?"

"From here? Four months' hard riding."

"Four months!"

"If you rode hard and did not dally by the way—four months."

"It is a long journey."

"It is worthy of a long journey. If you left now—let me see—yes, if you left now you would reach it by mid-July. That would be a good time to see it."

The boy laughed uneasily. "It sounds a wonderful place, oldster. But I have not four months to spare from my life in seeking an old man's dream."

"Not an old man's dream, boy. The dream of a young man now grown old. There is a difference."

A newborn breeze rustled at the bamboo screen. One of the figures that had been slumped at a near-by table stirred and yawned, and then looked sharply across at the oddly assorted pair. For a moment his flat face was blank, and then laughter tugged at his mouth and he nudged his sleeping companion and pointed at Salom and whispered behind his hand. Laughter cackled in the dismal room.

Salom flushed. "You see?" the peddler said. He stooped over his leather pack, and began to arrange his bottles and packages and boxes on the table. "I must leave you now, for there is business to be done," he said. "It has been a pleasant afternoon, and I thank you for it, boy."

The boy nodded dumbly. The hunted expression had returned to his eyes.

The peddler smiled down at him, and his old dried-parchment skin seemed to crackle. His hand fell softly on the thin shoulder.

"The Valley of the Dreaming Phoenix is a fine place in July," he said.

The boy fumbled at his clothing. Others in the tavern were sniggering now.

"Your beginnings would not matter up there," added the peddler. "There would be a wall five miles high between you and . . . and this."

"I do not care about your valley," Salom muttered defiantly.

"I will tell you a thing." The old eyes were shrewd. "For almost sixty years I have lived by selling things to people. These things I have talked about. Elixirs I have called them, and panaceas and unguents and balms and cure-alls. In my calling one cannot waste time. As I talk I look into the eyes of men to see whether they will buy or not. If I do not see this thing in their eyes then I stop talking and fold my bag. Now as I talked to you about this distant valley I looked at your eyes. My boy, had I been selling you a package of herbs I would not have folded my bag."

Salom looked away uncomfortably.

The peddler nodded. "Four months to the southwest," he murmured. "Ask your directions along the way. You will find the valley—if your heart beats high, and if you are not afraid of hardship." He sighed. "And now there is business to be done. It would be good to buy and sell stories, instead of herbs. Ah, well, you have been kind to honor an old and worthless hawker with your company. There is nothing I love so much as a good story."

Salom watched the shabby figure shuffle across the inn, stopping at some tables and bowing obsequiously as he displayed his wares. He felt an overwhelming desire to follow the old man, to plead with him for more conversation. There were so many things still left unsaid.

But the peddler had gone. Salom moved across to a table half-hidden in the shadows of the bamboo screen. There was nothing to do now but to await the coming of dusk to cloak his incongruous costume while he slunk back to the place where his horses were stabled.

BOOK ONE

Chapter One

I

FOR all its turbulence he knew the stream was young. The horses moved with high, precise steps. Salom peered over the arched neck of his mount. Each hoof went down with a nervous agitation, like an injured finger dabbing at hot water, and nerves fluttered in the animal's shoulder. The water sucked at its hocks, simmered across the stones, seethed at broken twigs, swelled dark over graveled crevices. The pebbles had none of the roundness that marks the caress of patient waters: they were uneven and broken along sharp angles, and they twirled tentatively in brown fans of disturbed sand. This was ice in its impetuous infancy as water. Salom knew he was near the river's beginning—and his journey's end.

His eyes looked ahead for the glacier. The shy people, in the forest where the mosses had hung from dripping trees like damp gossamer, had told him that he would ride along the river bed for two days—and this was the morning of the third day.

As the bend folded back he smiled and shouted "Chu!" to the horses. He could see the snout of the glacier. The birth of the river was a puny spring no larger than his wrist. He looked quickly to the left, remembering what the forest dwellers had told him:

"Then on the left bank you will see a forest of azaleas, and you must strike up through them to the lip of the high pass. The plains of Tibet are beyond. After the glacier it is a hard climb, but it is the last climb."

For an hour he rested the animals on the soggy turf beneath the ice wall. He lay on his stomach, flexing his legs with the idle luxury of a man freed from his saddle. He plucked a stick of wild rhubarb, flicked off the yellow flower between his thumb and forefinger, and chewed on the stalk as he listened to the hissing and grunting from within the static mass of the glacier. Occasionally he would squint across the boulders and beyond the flame of the azaleas. His eyes, creased into a brown contemplation, measured the far slope in terms of hours of labor and the stamina of his two beasts. He spat the shredded rhubarb from his mouth and nodded as if satisfied.

For a moment he experienced a quick stab of sadness. Would this journey, too, end only in a broken illusion? But the sadness passed. He was young, and the end of his journey was in sight. There would be new things at which to marvel, and the talk of men and the laughter of women, and the wide-eyed listeners to the tales of his travels. The sun had caught the rim of the pass now and he could see the smeared black edge where late snowdrifts had charred the grass. Already the sun was warm on his body. He took off the heavy cloak of sheepskin, and in his patched and faded suit of blue coolie-cloth his body was slim and hard and eager. Travel had grimed his skin and scarred his hands and frayed the fabric of his clothes, but there was pride in the set of his head and the rigid line of his back, and his youth existed only in his eyes.

He called to the animals. For four months he had journeyed alone, and now he talked to the horses or to himself, to rivers and rocks and trees, without embarrassment.

"Come, my skinny friends," he called. "You will be fattening too swiftly with so much rest. One more climb—and this the last. And sweet grasses beyond, and sleek mares to make a wanderer forget to wander!"

Salom laughed, and his teeth flared white in the sun.

It was a stern climb up the far wall of the cloven gorge. There was no trail and the animals had to be led and rested frequently. It was after noon by the time he reached the spur, and he took the saddles from the jaded beasts and allowed them to wander in the harsh grasses. From a wooden bowl he carried inside his jacket he took a hard white ball of kneaded dough and as he chewed on it he looked back across the ravine to the line of snow peaks. The peaks had been his companions for weeks, yet only now he saw them consciously. They had been a blink in the sky ahead, a shoulder of snow and ice thrust above his trail, a summit of significant shape recurring in his mind as some distant landmark. Now he could see the entire range of the Ta Hsueh Shan, still high above him, and suddenly he was afraid. These were the old gods of the world, the great white gods whose thrones were silence, and it seemed to him that a gate had clanged behind him.

The pass upon which he sat was a low spur which made a saddle in a ridge of alarming crags and cruel walls of black rock that were almost perpendicular. It formed one wall of the narrow ravine up which he had climbed. The opposite wall was the majestic snow range itself, stretching in a glittering wave crest of everlasting snow and ice into the snow blink to north and south, rising far above its buttresses of swirled glaciers and broken cliffs of basalt. Far to the southward he could see an icy triangle like a rent torn in the blue fabric of the sky; this he knew for the highest peak of the range, the sacred mountain of Minya Konka.

The shaded depths of the ravine between held a murmur of waters which served only to accentuate the silence, and then another sound came to him. It was the song of the skylarks, rising from below, like thin bells rung in a deep well. Across from him a fragment of life was whirled against the white giants. It was a bird, climbing to the zenith of its flight, flaunting a curved wing as a taunt for all this majesty. Salom watched until the fragment had curled away and down into the cavern.

His fear had gone. He looked toward the peaks. It had taken him four months to fight his way around that glittering wall, and for four months he had been afraid. But he had not been defeated. He had challenged the mountains and he had not been defeated— and now he was no longer afraid. They could not reach him now with their blizzards and avalanches and the stinging whip of their winds.

The horses were straying too far, cropping and wrenching at the snow grass. He hurried toward them across the blackened stubble. And then he stopped and his breath caught in an involuntary gasp of wonder.

On either side the mountains folded down—bare red mountains, vivid green mountains, distant ridges like pieces clipped from bright blue paper, nearer hummocks almost black with spruce woods—fold after fold as far as he could see, in an ever-receding pattern of gentle curves, and between them the sunlight was trapped in a valley so vast that its limits blurred into an opalescent haze. Threaded through this beauty a broad river glistened in the sun, fed by the many silver streams that twined down from the mountains. Both sides of the river were flanked by broad pastures that possessed a curious luminous brightness that could come only from many flowers.

It was unlike anything he had ever seen before, anything imagined. There had been big valleys in China, but not so big as this; and in any case in China the green acres were carved into farmlands and terraced by paddyfields and specked brown by villages. There had never been anything like this: nothing as big, nothing as empty. It was almost as if there were a bewitched quality about its loneliness: as if it lay sleeping under a luminous net, waiting for the sound of human voices to waken it. Even the sky seemed bigger here, and closer; if he reached up his hand he might almost touch one of the thin white clouds that trailed so languidly above this enchanted scene.

For a long time he stared down into the spreading bowl of light and color, half afraid that if he closed his eyes, even for a moment, the valley would vanish, and he would find disenchantment in austere snow and harsh winds and a half-obliterated trail that climbed and climbed unendingly.

Salom kicked at his horse. "Chu!" he shouted. He rode down into the Valley of the Dreaming Phoenix.

II

Seven hundred years before, a wandering tribe of Tufans had found it in a moment of hopelessness. Driven from the heart of the Tibetan plateau by the invading hordes of the great Kublai Khan, they had scurried eastward like leaves blown by a wild wind until their flight had been stayed by a wall no man could climb. This was the outer bastion of Tibet—silent peaks of snow and ice, gorges that glaciers had throttled, dark chasms shunned by all life. The humid plains of China lay beyond—but five miles below the fanged glitter of the ice wall. There was a way through, but this the Tufans had not known and so they turned away, despairing and afraid, and in turning they looked down into the haven of the valley.

There they had lived for as long perhaps as three families could be raised, and then a disheveled rider came to them with news that the foreign soldiers were leaving their old lands. The boldest among them had at once ridden off to the west, and others straggled after them in timid groups, less terrified of the long and hazardous journey than of the bleak cruelty of the valley's winters.

Only a few, more hardy or more feckless than the rest, together with some Mongolian deserters from the Grand Khan's armies, stayed to mate with the comely natives of the outer hills. It was their seed, sifted and crossed by seven centuries, that peopled the Valley of the Dreaming Phoenix—a dozen families of nomad cowherds and shepherds who unknowingly shared the legacies of all those yesterdays.

They possessed Mongol hardiness and nomad laughter and the tough bigness of seven hundred implacable winters. They rode small and sturdy horses that still retained some of the spirit of an ancestry that had drummed its hooves from the Gobi all over Asia.

In the beginning the valley probably had many names, varying with the seasons, with generations, with the moods and whims of headmen. Finally, with the occasional poetry of inarticulate men, it had come to be called the Valley of the Dreaming Phoenix.

The valley was perhaps eighty miles long, and fifteen miles broad at its widest point. It sloped away to the westward along its entire length, so that the highest extremity in the east, abutting the snow peaks of the Ta Hsueh Shan, was at an altitude of sixteen thousand feet, while its lower end was no more than twelve thousand feet. This lower end was the wintering quarter for the nomads.

Here a nameless village of square stone houses huddled beneath a knoll made untidy by the ragged banners of prayer flags. In summer the breezes pushed lazy ripples across high fields of barley and peas and corn. Water wheels creaked slowly in the brooks, so that the milling stones, turning on unoiled spindles, squeaked in harmony with the shrilled song of the cicadas. The few old people who remained behind to tend the crops spent much of their summers seated beneath the willows to escape the heat, while in the dusty sunshine village curs snapped tiredly at insects.

It was a village without a name, unplanned and unlovely, and yet without it no single nomad would have been able to survive the clamp of winter. It was here, during six months of frozen stillness, that the nomads back from the high pastures would grind and bake the harvested barley, prepare corn meal, spin from yak hair the black threads from which their summer tents were woven, patiently ravel saddle rugs and blankets from the unscoured fleeces of their sheep, and engage in the multitude of preparations necessary for another summer.

At first thaw they would stir from their houses. When the snow was only a dusting on the lesser hills they would move the thin-shanked sheep and snuffling yaks from odorous mangers deep in a winter's mud and urine to taste again the wet sweet of new grass. As the days lengthened they would wander eastward, moving their flocks and herds and squat tents to newer and higher grasses exposed by retreating snow.

By June they would reach the eastern end of the valley. This was the richest thang, or flat pasture, in their domains. It was known to them as High Valley, and it was almost three miles above the world.

In June and July they would camp there: in the insect-heavy weeks when the sheep, fat and lethargic, waddled through pastures bright with many flowers; when the yak cows, sleek and milk-swollen, cropped the glittering fields with the fastidiousness of repleted gourmets; and the bulls gouged their hillside pits with lashing tails and swinging horns in roaring, truculent testimony to an insatiable virility.

But August would bring portents of another summer's death. In the mornings there would be a laziness in the river, and across still pools a glaze that crumbled like gelatine beneath probing fingers. The night wind would mumble its fret at angled tent poles and thrumming ropes. Each dawn would find the snow crisper in the gorse and packed higher against black tents. Desolation would grieve across the brown and brackish tarns; the southing geese would honk above; and evenings would share with the winds the long gray loneliness.

The day would come when no birds sang and the brooks no longer echoed the infectious laughter of the river. The high peaks would plume ragged veils of blown snow against a shredded sky, and the nomads would know that the blizzards were reaching down. The people of the valley would muster their livestock. But as they rode away on the sullen trek to their squalid houses, they would look back often to the empty loveliness of High Valley, and their hearts would be heavy.

Such was the pattern of life in the Valley of the Dreaming Phoenix, year after year, century after century. Each year there was a summer. And each year the snow would whisper and the flakes fatten and contours and trees drown slowly in the white flood, until all the valley slept beneath the shining silence of another winter.

But in July such questions of transience were rarely considered. The warmth of High Valley was the caress of a woman who loves. The river, still chuckling its release from the manacles of winter, had mosaics of flowers along its scarred banks, and the fish were deft shadows flirting with the sun dapples. The sun came hot through the thin air. There was fragrance, and the murmur of diligent insects, and voices singing, and the dance of butterflies, and the chime of bells. The valley had a frail beauty that seemed then to defy the cold giants that stood above. But the high watching peaks brooded perhaps over an older wisdom. Summer to them was merely a lessening of the blows of blizzards, a brief falter in the screaming of an old wind. They waited.

And while they waited the boy Salom came. He came in the middle of the month of July, when the nomads were camped in the fat pastures of High Valley.

III

The valley sloped away quite sharply in front of him, as if the earth were set at a tilt. As the animals lurched down, sliding and stumbling in the loose stones, he threw back his head and sang:

> Long since I have ridden a Litang pony
> And sat astride the golden saddle.

The uneven ground gradually developed into a vague path that meandered through a forest of stunted trees deformed by the winter drifts, and down past an untidy cairn of round, smooth stones. Life swarmed below the sickly shrubs at timberline. There were rabbits and hares and marmots, choughs and snowcocks, and once a pheasant rocketed its brilliance across the sky. As the upper timber thinned, the ground vegetation grew more luxuriant, and he was riding down and still down through fat-stalked grasses and tall blooms of blue iris. The horses wrenched impatiently at the reins. Salom laughed.

"And did I not promise you sweet grasses?" he cried, and rode on singing.

As the descent began to slacken, he saw a high stone building half-hidden in a pine grove to his right. He rode across to it, only to find it a ruin—the weathered shell of some old watch tower rising gaunt and lonely from a tangle of briar and nettle and blue poppies. There was no way of telling how long since it had been inhabited. It added to the valley's emptiness.

Still the trail led down. Now he rode through a grove of birches enmeshed in sunlight that was thinner and clearer and more golden than he ever remembered sunlight to be. The slim trees rustled mysteriously around him, and his feeling of enchantment grew stronger.

He was increasingly conscious now of the sound of waters, and several times his horses splashed across the streams that romped down the slopes to unite into the beginnings of the river he had seen from the higher ground.

It was mid-afternoon before he reached the floor of the valley.

Only then did he look back. The massive range was beautiful now—remote and serene and quite without menace. He rode on.

The ground had become marshy, and choked with reeds, but ahead of him the river emerged young and vigorous from the puddles and streams, and rushed impetuously down valley, cleaving high red banks into the flower-studded grasses and foaming around upthrust rocks.

In the soft wind the grass flowed with the rhythm of a great sea, in which stood islands of cedars and willows and stands of slender birches. He listened for a time to the small and gentle sounds that for so long he had forgotten—the rustle of small creatures in the undergrowth, the call of birds, the murmur of insects, the cheerful gossip of the waters, the sigh of the wind in grasses and leaves.

But again he was conscious of the valley's strange, bewitched emptiness. What if no people lived here? It had been many years since an old peddler had wandered this way. He reined in the horses and looked back for comfort to the old watch tower, but he could no longer see it, and he recalled, with a stab of misgiving, its appearance of old decay and abandonment.

His face was troubled as he rode ahead—and then suddenly his pulse quickened.

High on the green slopes to the right a herd of yaks was grazing. Beyond, in a field of purest yellow, were several black lumps and around them numerous smaller specks, like a swarm of insects. Salom knew the black lumps for the tents of nomads, the specks their flocks and herds.

The song came again to his lips as he rode forward.

IV

In the high, untainted air distances were deceptive, and the declining sun was directly in his eyes as he reached the edge of the yellow field. He knew that this was the home thang as much by the trampled pastures as by the comforting drift of smoke hanging above three squat tents widely spaced along the curve of the river. It was a broad stream here, running through wide marshes and backwaters choked with reeds, and the air throbbed with the roar of its waters. The tents were larger than he had expected, taut and close to the ground and surrounded by a lattice of tangled poles and stay-ropes. Tethered to heavy stakes outside the nearest of the tents were two Tibetan mastiffs, shaggy and big as calves, and already leaping ferociously at the approach of a stranger. He rode toward the tent, skirting his horses to take them respectfully out of reach of the savage animals whose barking now was a strangled frenzy as the ropes cut into their thick necks. Even the inhospitable beasts were a comfort to him. For he had come back from loneliness into a world of people.

Two of them he could see already—a girl and a child patterned bright and still against the somber tent.

They were evidently the daughters of a wealthy nomad. Their bulky skirts were cut from good cloth, and they wore an abundance of rings and bracelets and neckpieces, all of heavy silver crudely hammered and set with turquoise and rock coral and rough bright gems.

As Salom prepared to dismount, the round-bellied child edged back behind the older girl, and the boy felt a quick pleasure. Ah, but this one was well worthy of a man's gaze!

She was small for a Tibetan woman—wiry and copper-faced and with a mouth as rich and red as a peony. Her wolfskin jacket was rolled down over her skirt so that her breasts and stomach were bare, and here her skin was the color of melted butter and it shone like satin. Her skirt was red, braided and banded in blue and yellow, and her clumsy felt boots were blazoned in the mystic colors—red, blue, green, yellow and white. Her thin wrists and fingers were weighted with bracelets and rings; her leather girdle was clasped with a curiously wrought buckle of dull jade, and suspended from it was a small knife in a carved silver sheath and a string of prayer beads. Silver dragged at the soft young lobes of the girl's ears, and a massively carved and jewel-studded band of metal supported the slender stem of her neck. Her face and body looked clean, and the heavy black flag of her hair was glossed and dripping. She looked perhaps sixteen or seventeen, but with a maturity of form that belied both her years and her small stature.

Salom raised his hand. "Go gently, little sisters," he called.

The girl's mouth curled up smiling from small, sharp teeth, although her eyes remained wary.

"Go gently," she replied, and tugged at the child's skirt.

The fat little girl darted from behind her, suddenly bold. "Go gently," she piped, and giggled, her teeth startling in their whiteness in the dirty little face.

"Is this the valley called Dreaming Phoenix?" Salom asked. He looked at the girl. She has the eyes of a gazelle, he thought.

She nodded.

"And you?"

"I am called Veshti," she whispered, lowering her eyes before the stranger's intent stare and twisting at her bracelets.

"I am Renzi," the child squeaked suddenly, and grinned at him. Her timidity had gone. "Our father is headman. He is very wealthy. And now what is your name?"

Salom laughed, pleased both with the child's boasting and her breathless curiosity, although he observed that the girl seemed distressed and grimaced a reproof at her sister.

He slid easily from the saddle.

"Men call me Salom," he said.

Renzi's eyes puckered. "Then your name is Salom. If men call you Salom your name is Salom."

"Whatever it is," said the boy, "it is not Salom."

The child showed her bewilderment, and her sister spoke for her: "This is strange talk of yours."

"Salom is a name of Tibet," he explained. "And I am no Tibetan. My birth was in China—" there was a quick, proud lift to his voice—"but the name they gave me has been lost and so men call me Salom."

"But how can a name be lost?" the girl called Veshti asked, curiosity overcoming her shyness.

But before he could answer Renzi gasped: "From China! Then that is why you wear such funny clothes!" Her eyes were wider than ever with new wonders.

He was suddenly conscious that the faded blue jacket and baggy trousers of coolie-cloth—the clothes he had purchased so proudly after leaving Ch'eng-tu—looked drab indeed against the brilliance of the Tibetan garments. So he ignored the child and answered her sister.

"It is too long a tale—and one not for women, or for children. They would not understand."

"But I still do not see how a name can be lost," the girl insisted.

"It was lost." He shrugged and bent to the straps of the pack saddle. His face was earnest with concentration, and the girl stepped back a little, as if conscious of the rebuff and vaguely hurt by it.

She turned away from him and felt for the soggy strands of her hair and began to squeeze out the water. The fat child chewed on a stalk of grass, her black eyes darting from Salom to her sister.

He grunted as he heaved the saddles from the horses. For a long time he stared down at them as if the complex lashings posed an insuperable mental problem. And then he looked across his shoulder and said: "You say your father is the headman?"

The girl nodded.

"Then I wish to talk with him."

"He is up there—" she gestured toward the foothills—"with the sheep. There was talk of wolves."

"Oh." Salom nodded and peered along the valley. The flatness of the immediate surroundings gave an illusory impression of a low altitude, and the valley stretched into the darkening hazes, rolling back endlessly. He reached down toward the harness.

"You . . . you will wait for him?" the girl asked quickly. "He will return soon. Before sundown . . . very soon." She braided her hair nervously. "You will take tea with us? You will take tea while Renzi goes to the flock for our father. Yes, that is best." She turned to the squirming child and snapped in her embarrassment: "Go then, Renzi! Why do you stand and stare with such rudeness? Go for Muhlam!"

V

Salom stood uneasy inside the doorway of the tent. To cover his discomfort he swung his bridle against the tent pole with monotonous nonchalance, and glanced from under lowered lids at the birdlike movements of the girl.

First she stacked hard cakes of dung on the fire, and then at the edges, where the coals glowed, she pushed clumps of sagebrush; and knelt and blew through a long pipe of bamboo until the brush roared. Finally, she hooked a black cauldron on the bar stretching across the flames.

She did not look at him, and the muted silence was only the more pronounced for the discordant clash of her bangles and the dull, rhythmic thump of his bridle. The fire spat.

Several times Salom was about to speak, for he felt the silence pressing in upon him, but each time something in her darting hands and the rippling cream triangle of her back made the words sound foolish in his head, and he thumped harder at the tent pole and looked around him.

He had seen nomad tents before—but in the mountains that reached down to Litang and in the northern valleys the tents were small and squalid; this had almost the spaciousness of a house and something of its permanence.

Beyond the square pit of the fireplace were piled wooden saddles for yaks and horses, oblong containers of brick tea still with the crude paper stamps of West China peeled against the cracked leather, heavy bags of barley meal, grass-encrusted spheres of yak cheese and a stubby churn of varnished wood flaked with congealed butter. Toppled on to the floor of the tent—trampled grass pulped and smeared with flowers—was a Tibetan bible, its oblong sheets of parchment clamped within wood slats that had warped and split. On the far side of the fire stood a dozen wooden pails and churns—long three-foot churns for buttered tea, neat cylinders for butter, squat-bellied tubs for cheese. From hooks driven into the twin tent poles dirty robes and sheepskins hung, and broken harness, and a set of copper ladles burnished to the ripeness of apples, and coils of rope, and a flintlock rifle with an exaggerated barrel and a bipod tipped with ivory and curved upward so that it resembled the tusks of some mythical beast. A small table of wood grimed almost to the color and texture of ebony stood on the other side, and upon it a group of small brass butter lamps contained the congealed white of fat and the blackened stubs of wicks. A battered prayer wheel and a string of prayer beads were tossed casually beside the lamps. From a fat rope slung between the poles hung five swollen yak bladders, transparently amber in the light that lanced down from a square opening in the center of the tent roof. The opening admitted air and light and was supposed to encourage the smoke to escape, but the light struggled with the fumes and reached the floor only in moving splodges, like sunlight on the bed of a fast stream. Against the wall circular cakes of dried yak dung, each disc imprinted with the mark of the splayed hand that had driven it against a sunny wall to dry, were piled neatly to a height of two feet. Against the opposite wall was a more untidy stack of dry sagebrush. Salom knew that the fuel was a reserve against sudden storms, the dung for creating warmth and the quick-flaming brush for kindling and cooking; and that the little walls formed of timber and excrement also served the valuable purpose of repelling cold night winds that probed beneath the tent cloth. On one wall was pinned the pelt of a fox, a frigid fiction of an animal flattened and elongated and with the stringy fragments of its flesh whitely brittle.

The tent was perhaps twenty-five feet square, and it was stayed against the winds by forty tall poles caught to an intricate cat's cradle of yak-hair ropes. But these were seen through the coarse weave of the tent only as a shadowy and involved pattern. The floor was littered with separate bundles of bright rugs and drab blankets, and among them, almost iridescent in the palpitating light, was one voluptuous rug—black and white and luminous orange—the skin of a fine panda. Salom knew this would be the headman's rug.

He looked back at the girl. She was crouched directly in the probing shaft of light, and smoke swirled about her as she bent over the fire and stirred chips and sticks of coarse tea into the simmering cauldron. Water still dribbled from her hair and fell, plunging, into the coals. It reminded him of a thought he had had earlier.

He started at the sound of his own voice: "I would ask you about your hair," he said, and laughed nervously. "Is it then the custom in this valley to cleanse the hair? I have not seen it before—not in Tibet."

Veshti turned her burning face to the cauldron, stirring at the mixture with a sudden violence. She made no answer. He stared down at her and saw that her face was sullen.

"There was a question asked," he said softly.

"No," she said, and the boy was astonished to detect tears in her voice. "No, it is not the custom."

"Then why do you—?" he asked, not bothering to finish the question, but again the girl was silent.

Her eyes smarted in the steam from the cauldron, but she crouched into it.

"There is no need for shame in this," he said gently. She looked at him quickly. He was sharp enough. Although she had said nothing he had sensed her feelings. "To be clean is one of the virtues," he was saying. "But in Tibet I seldom see it . . . and . . . and that is why I asked."

The girl was warm now, and grateful, and her words came with suppressed pleasure and an eager friendliness: "But is not your home in Tibet then? If your home is not here then how is it you have a name of these parts and speak our tongue?"

"My home was in Tibet for thirteen years. But I saw little of cleanliness. I thought here it might be different from elsewhere."

"And in the Han country?"

He nodded. "In the Han country it is customary to wash the hair," he said quietly, but amusement glinted in his eyes. Only once before in his life had he heard China referred to as the Han country. "It is customary to wash all the body," he added.

Her eyes were round. "The whole body?" she gasped, and her bejewelled hands clutched at her firm, pointed breasts and moved down to the polished flatness of her stomach.

He smiled. "Yes. In other parts it is also done——"

"I know nothing of other parts," she interrupted hastily. "My life has been only in this valley. And my father's also."

He was acutely conscious of the girl's vividness, of her eager shyness, and he stumbled for an answer, seeking one that would convey his tolerance for those who were untraveled and yet add emphasis to his own standing as a man of another world, as the man from the Han country. But by the time he had selected the words it was too late to say them, and so he said nothing, and the girl was silent.

She lifted the cauldron from the fire. It looked too heavy for her, but Salom made no offer to help, nor did she expect it. Expertly she tipped the big pot, and the tea hissed into the long wooden cylinder of the churn. She scooped up a handful of yak butter and a lump of salt and threw them into the mixture, and thrust down into the cloud of steam a wooden rod with a plunger attached.

Stooped over the churn, she drove the rod up and down while the steam beaded her face and her shoulders were glossed and light played over her in murky patterns. Her breasts were agitated from their curved tranquillity and quivered and swung with a rhythm of their own, until Salom felt a tightness in his belly and his throat was dry, and he could not look away.

"Is it not churned enough?" he asked thickly, and when the girl smiled across at him with candid eyes and blew a strand of hair from her forehead and shook her head he felt ashamed and brutal.

He heard with relief the jangled melody of horsebells. The mastiffs were barking, but this time an excited clamor, shrill and without ferocity.

"It will be my father," Veshti said, and put down the plunger.

Renzi hopped into the tent, absurd with importance. Behind her was a tall, thin woman. Her face was kindly, but she moved nervously, beringed hands fluttering at her flamboyant garments.

Then the doorway was blocked by a gigantic shadow, and Salom felt himself shrinking as he stared at the shaggy giant who looked at him with level, almost contemptuous, pride.

"I am Muhlam, headman of the valley," he said, and Salom had an odd fancy that somewhere cymbals clashed.

Chapter Two

THEY had eaten well. There had been a thin soup made from chopped nettles and small peas and leathery gobbets of dried beef, laced heavily with yak cream. And there had been the inevitable tsamba—made by mixing with buttered tea a quantity of barley meal and then kneading it with the fingers until it was a hard round ball to chew on. But still they sat before the fire and drank more tea from wooden bowls.

Smoke spread above them like a spongy blanket, splotched with ruddiness when the fire leaped, and the smoke smelled pungent and fusty and good. Salom waited not quite comfortably. He watched the fire—where long darts of light spurted pallid, and the copper ladles blinked sleepily. Outside he could hear the first whisper and pause and seethe of summer snow, and the snuffling and grunting of the yak calves inside their protective palisades of sagebrush. The dim tent walls moved in closer to the fire.

Muhlam, his great legs crossed on the lustrous panda skin, sucked up the last of his tea and belched his content.

Salom had not spoken since the meal began. He sat quite still, conscious of his extreme unimportance in the eyes of the giant. It would be for Muhlam to speak first. Outside, the plaint of a dog throbbed in the distance.

The more the boy looked at the headman the more his own feeling of insignificance increased. It was not only the immensity of the giant's body; it was the massive face that seemed like a brown rock upon which the pattern of a hard lifetime had been drawn thickly with charcoal. It was the authority of the curved nose and the deep clefts that dragged the thin mouth down into a rigid arch.

It was the dirt-choked parallels scarring his brow; the knotted hands covered with wedge-shaped mats of black hair. He had pulled his robes around him but Salom knew that beneath their shapelessness the body of the man was iron-hard and yet with an animal's litheness—and Salom felt a child, a weakling of no character, a nonentity without a past and with no foreseeable future.

Through the weaving smoke the headman's wife, Kelinka, was seen only dimly. She, too, waited for her husband to speak, although Salom had an odd feeling that her eyes offered him an encouragement she dared not voice. He liked the woman's thin, tired face, eroded by more troughs than her age warranted and beaten to swarthy hardness by wind and sun. She took a spindle bound with red wool and held it vertically in a wooden bowl. Veshti moved closer and began to wind the wool into a ball. The girl was in profile and the smoke clung to her. He was no longer certain of her timidity. Her burnished head was submissive over her task but she darted occasional flicking glances sideways at him, and sometimes she whispered to her mother and giggled.

Her actions had a curious effect on him, warming and yet unsettling, and he tried to study her without making his interest too evident. It pleased him that she was small, although he wondered that her delicate molding and quick color could be the result of a union between the bulky giant and his wife, who, for all her thinness, was big-boned and gaunt. It was pleasant to watch the girl. How long had it been since he had really seen a woman? Four months? More. One could not count the whores teetering in the wine shops of Ch'eng-tu, nor the harpies along the Litang Trail with their broken teeth and coarse laughter and the stink of the barley beer on their mouths. No, these could not be considered. Perhaps he had never before seen such a woman. It was pleasant to look on her. She had a curious effect upon him, as though the color and form and texture and smell of her seeped through his eyes and spread right through his body. Although he had lived long enough to have seen much traffic in the flesh of women, Salom had never had a woman. But now he remembered the ache of the long loneliness, and it came to him that he wanted a woman. He wanted this woman.

"So you wish to work?" Muhlam's voice ripped harshly at the silence. Veshti's hands were suddenly carved still in the wool. The woman and the child were motionless.

"I wish to work, yes," Salom said. "Already I have——"

"Yes, yes." Muhlam brushed the words away with a disdainful gesture. "I know you have worked with flocks and herds. You have told me this already." He picked at his teeth absently.

Salom waited. This was the moment. One of two things—either he would be accepted or he would saddle his horses and ride elsewhere. He was not looking at the girl but the image of her lingered, and he had no wish to ride elsewhere. On the other hand, if he was accepted there would be all the questions to answer. He wished to talk—for too long he had been starved of talk—but not to answer questions. There were some questions that could not be answered.

"There is room for an extra man among the herds," Muhlam said finally.

The tension breathed out. Kelinka smiled across at him and Renzi hugged the barrel of her chest. Only Veshti gave no sign that she had heard. Her hands were busy with the wool again, and the spindle spun in a dull red blur.

"There are questions to be answered," Muhlam said.

Salom smiled wryly.

"What is your age, boy?"

"Twenty."

The headman nodded as if the answer had been expected. For his years the boy's face was lined. Muhlam knew that it would look even older when the eyes were puckered into the sun glare or the blink of high snow. But the weathering had done little to obliterate his youth, because his years were in these eyes.

"There is a thing I do not understand," the headman continued. "You say you are a man of Han, yet your name is of Tibet. You were born in the Han country?"

"Yes, I was born in China." Already the questions were coming.

"Then is it the custom for Chinese to give their children the names of Tibet?" Muhlam asked.

"No. I think it is not the custom. But for most of my life I have lived in Tibet. North of here—not far from Litang." He paused but he saw that the name of Litang meant little to the nomad. "A Tibetan family cared for me. They gave me the name." He shrugged. "It serves. I have known no other."

Muhlam pondered this information. "I still cannot understand," he persisted. "If your birth was in China how is it you come to live with a family of Tibet and to be named by it?"

"I was abandoned as a child. These Tibetans found me."

"Abandoned?"

Salom nodded.

"You were unwanted?"

He nodded again. When would the man stop asking these questions? How could he give reasons that he himself had been unable to find? But the headman seemed to have lost interest in the interrogation. He was peeling off his furs, examining for lice his muscular upper body. From the silence that persisted in the immobile group Salom sensed that the others knew there had been only a postponement in the headman's inquiries. He tried again to think of that clogged memory of a child tagging and stumbling at the heels of a ragged army in flight, but then he shrugged it away. He had tried so many times before and he knew its futility. There was nothing that came to him. Even the tongue that once must have been familiar to him had gone—all but a smattering of gibberish and a half-recollected song.

Muhlam broke into his reverie: "What impelled you to make the journey here—to this place?"

"I had gone back to China, but I . . . I found little friendship there."

"In your own country?"

"In my own country. I looked like a Chinese but I spoke nothing of their tongue. They laughed at me."

Muhlam spat into the fire. His expression indicated that such conduct was to be expected from barbarians of the Han country.

Muhlam knew little of China, little enough of anything beyond his own isolated valley, but he was contemptuous of things he did not understand, and therefore all people beyond the immediate surroundings of the Valley of the Dreaming Phoenix were bundled into a loose category of unenlightened savagery.

"And so?" he said.

"Then I met a wandering peddler of medicines. He was very old and kindly enough, and he knew the tongue of Tibet. I talked to him and he advised me to return to Tibet."

Muhlam nodded. He relapsed again into silence, but his face was troubled. The others looked at Salom with interest, but still showed no disposition to enter the conversation.

The headman's cough rasped. His brow was heavy and his hard fingers stroked his chin.

"I still do not understand why you came to *this* valley," he said. "I see why you come back to Tibet. It is a good land—better than the Han country—and it has been your home for many years. But why come here? This is far from the people who fostered you—and few travelers come this way. So why?"

"I suppose it was an impulse," Salom said. "When I left Ch'eng-tu—that is the city of China which I visited——"

"We are not interested in that," Muhlam said impatiently. "Why do you come here?"

"The peddler talked to me of this place and——"

"What would a peddler know of this valley?"

"He had journeyed here. Many years ago——"

"He lied. I know of no peddler who came here."

"It was many years ago. He is a very old man—much older than you. He told me of the fine people who lived here, and of the valley's peace and beauty."

He observed that this time his answer had given pleasure to the giant, but the flicker of softness passed and Muhlam began again to scour disinterestedly the black and tangled forest beneath his arm.

Would he tell the headman of the challenge that had prompted him to come here, of the birthright he had received from his forgotten father, of the words the old peddler had used: *You would need to be uncommonly adventurous to set your feet on that trail?* Well, it had been a challenge, and life was worthy of a man only when it was a challenge. But would this grim, gaunt man understand? The journey had demanded a high price in endurance and fortitude; a price that this man who had probably never traveled beyond his own valley could not assess.

He remembered when he had reached the hem of the high country. It had been the first day for weeks that he had encountered other men. They were members of a band of mountaineers, wild-looking with their furs and their matted hair. They were hunters of the panda and the musk deer, but for all their barbarism they had possessed the quality of friendliness. They had shared their meat with him—and they had advised him to turn back.

They had warned him that the trail ahead was desolate and without pity and beset by perils; that it was nowhere wider than half the height of a man; that it was used infrequently and only by those whose calling was the commerce of gun and knife.

But Salom had laughed and gestured their fears aside.

"I am," he told them, "the son of a great fighter—one of the heroes of Liu Ting Chiao."

The mountain people, of course, had understood nothing of this statement, but they understood courage in a man, and clucked their admiration as they looked after the slim, straight figure that plodded upward until it was a trivial, wavering silhouette against the snow blink.

Nevertheless, in the lonely weeks that followed there were many times when Salom regretted that he had not accepted the advice of the mountain hunters. There was the sting of blizzards that screamed their rage at clammy mountains. There were river crossings where the melted snows were lathered in the gorges and the anger of the rapids wrenched at endurance. There were summits to climb that only the high clouds knew. There were snow-girt passes where a man's lungs were too big for the meager air, and each breath was a fight.

Many times he had almost admitted defeat, but always he had

thought of a father whose name he did not know—and he had ridden on.

There was a harder line to his mouth as he looked up from the fire. Muhlam was staring at him appraisingly.

"You understand," the headman said, "that it is *hard* work here—*man's* work?" There was contempt in his quick glance at the boy's thin, pliant chest and shoulders.

Salom flushed, but pride straightened his body and held his head high. "My father was a hero with the Chinese army," he said. "One of the heroes of——"

"Yes, yes. We have heard what we want to know of your past." The taut pride of the boy had not been lost on Muhlam, and he was pleased. "As long as you understand that life here is far from easy."

"In China there were soft pillows and couches of silk," Salom said, suddenly irritated by the older man's contempt. "I could have stayed in China had I sought comfort."

There was no relaxation of the hardness of Muhlam's expression, but again he was pleased. For all his slimness and youth the boy had fiber, strength. There was nothing Muhlam admired more than strength. But it would be injudicious to signify any such approval to this newcomer. He reached for his long pipe of bamboo and into the tiny bowl tamped a few shreds of coarse tobacco and closed his eyes as he lighted it with a brand from the fire.

And now the silence was broken for the first time by the child, Renzi.

"Was your father a headman, Salom?" she piped, but Kelinka grunted her disapproval, and Veshti snapped a curt rebuke, and he noticed that it was not by these things that she was subdued to squirming silence but by the measured stare of her father.

Then Muhlam smiled—a great moon of white in the burnt leather of his face—and his eyes sank into the furrows as he jerked his head toward the child.

"She is greater trouble to control, that one, than twenty calves in a meadow," he said. He shook with laughter, and Kelinka laughed, a sound that seemed mostly to imply gratitude to her husband, and Veshti, after a moment of indecision, laughed also, and her laughter was a ripple high in her throat. And Salom knew, as if the words had been measured out to him, that he had finally been accepted into the family of the headman.

Kelinka looked toward her husband to assure herself that he desired no further part of the interrogation, but he was scowling down at his body, utterly absorbed in his search for lice.

"Was it hard then—your journey here?" she asked.

Salom smiled his gratitude. Of such questions he had no fear. "Four months I journeyed, good mother," he said, with more than a hint of youthful braggadocio. "There were rivers fierce as wolves in a bad winter, and blizzards at the high passes, and once——"

Muhlam looked up quickly. "It is not good for a man to be restless and wishing always to saddle his animals," he said harshly. "Only the fool thinks there is prosperity at the end of aimless roads. Although—" he softened his rebuke—"you did well to come to this valley. It is a good valley. A fine valley. A man would be greedy to ask more than to be headman of such a valley." He looked hard at the boy, as if daring him to contradict.

But Salom looked at him evenly and said, "It is a fine valley."

"You saw no other as rich?" It was a statement rather than a query.

"No other," agreed Salom.

"And on the way—was there good hunting? Perhaps bear?"

Salom caught the flicker of Veshti's eyes, red in the fireglow, and for a moment a lie trembled at his mouth, but he shook his head.

"No," he said. "It is a country of desolation beyond the pass and game is not plentiful. I shot enough to supplement the food I carried."

"But no bear?"

"No bear. Once there was a good spoor, from a bear of great size, but the sky was already darkening, and so——"

"There are no bears of such great size as the beasts which threaten the herds in this valley," Muhlam interrupted. "Nowhere."

"Yes!" Renzi nodded excitedly. "Huge and terrible bears! Why, once there was——"

Kelinka frowned. "Quiet, child," she said, but with no severity. "And, Veshti—why do you not attend to your duties? The fire fades. Is it hospitable to allow our guest to be chilled in the night?"

She smiled at Salom, and his happiness warmed him, and he wondered if his own mother had been thin and kind like this one.

Veshti rose in one fluid movement. Her body flowed oddly in the smoke and her ribs and breasts were outlined with a soft, rich glow. The fire smoldered in her jewels.

For another hour the talk was desultory and of little consequence and largely concerned with the day's rural and domestic affairs, but Salom listened attentively, for this was to be his life. Moreover, he sensed that Muhlam's interest in the outside world was limited, perhaps even tinged by a latent hostility. Salom accepted the role of listener. Only at the end of the night did he again attempt to reassert his ego by the narration of his own exploits. The headman had been talking boredly of a hillside washaway in the lower pastures, and Salom's mind spun back to an incident of his journey—the incident which, more than any other, had almost forced him to retrace his steps.

That day a blizzard had spent itself and the sky had the dull sheen of old pewter. The trail had corkscrewed below the face of an overhanging glacier. Somewhere within the mass of rock and ice a pebble no larger than a walnut succumbed at last to the nagging of a water runnel that for centuries had been a vein of hard ice in winter and a rippled sigh in summer. The movement of the pebble was a breath in vastness. But other pebbles scurried after it. A trickle of water was diverted. A boulder quivered. Of these things Salom knew nothing. He saw only the last of a chain of movements that had perhaps been inevitable since time began.

He saw the ice precipice shudder and reach over into its final obliteration, saw a million tons of rock and ice hurled into the river bed ahead, heard the waves of thunder reaching above the world.

The earth writhed. Flung from his horse, Salom had clutched at the shuddering rocks and sobbed out the confession of his own puniness. For a long time he had lain there. His eyes were closed, his body twitching. For a long time he had lain there and even when he knew that he was safe he had listened to the silence creeping back. And when he looked up the mists of destruction were still rising against the high white peaks . . .

"On my way here," Salom said, "there was a great avalanche. On the trail ahead——"

Muhlam yawned, his mouth stretching to a purple cavern, and without a glance at the boy or at the others he rolled himself into his sheepskins and threw himself upon the panda rug.

The rise and fall of his breath that told them he was immediately asleep created a pulse in the silence. Kelinka, with an apologetic glance toward the boy, reached for her sleeping rugs and curled herself beside her husband.

Renzi's unblinking stare had gone and the child was a sprawled shape in the outer darkness of the tent. Only Veshti remained by the fire opposite him, prodding with a twig at the smolder of the coals, not looking at him.

There was an immense weight upon his eyes and his head throbbed. He moved into the corner of the tent and arranged the rugs about him. But before he stretched himself into the skins he looked again toward the girl.

The fire spurted and her shadow leaped above her, black and grotesque. Her nakedness seemed to be covered now by red silk, shining silk, transparently woven. The glow of the pale butter lamps stroked her hair, and he toyed with the thought that its sheen was the lustrous blue-black of the raven's wing. Her hands were gently stroking the curve and fall of her own breasts, and in the firelight her eyes seemed haunted by a troubled dream.

Salom watched the soft, almost unconscious, caress of the girl's fingers, and for a moment his blood coursed thick and quick, but then the image blurred and he slept.

Chapter Three

I

IN THE morning it was as if time had meant a changed pattern of color and texture rather than a progress of events. Skeins of smoke were still twisted beneath the sagged roof of the tent, but the smoke was cold and comfortless, as if the grayness, rather than being a visible product of heat, was a chill mist lifted from a chill sea. The panda fur had become drab, and upon it the same two bundles, without form or hue or evident life, were huddled in the rugs. Muhlam and Kelinka still slept. Veshti crouched beyond the fire, wide-eyed and rigid. Frail light guttered in the brass bowls. Beyond the tent the calves sniffed and grunted and a dog yelped.

The dry crackle of the flames lacked the comforting spit and hiss of snow dropping through the roof aperture, and the bladders above the fire had become opaque and dingy in a pallid light that bleached the tent fabric and faltered through the doorway and sucked away color.

Salom dragged his shoulder from the rug and when he leaned upon his elbow he flinched at the sharp bite of the air.

Veshti turned at the movement and smiled at him. She, too, had changed. The luster had gone from her hair and the color from her skin and the gloss of her body was concealed by lumpy furs. She wore the furs Tibetan fashion, with the softness against her skin and the cracked parchment of the hide outside. It was stained by blotches of dried blood and the shreds of fat and sinew had become ragged and grimy. It was an unlovely garment. The mystery that she had possessed in the night had vanished, and with it her allure.

She thrust a handful of tinder into the coals and the fire snarled.

"There was snow," she said evenly. "In the night there was snow."

He nodded and chafed his hands and arms and clambered to his feet stiffly.

"There is not snow every night?" he said.

"No. Only some nights. If there is no storm in the afternoon it snows in the night. Yesterday there was no storm." She smiled again. "It was a bright day when you came. Perhaps it was an omen, eh?"

"Perhaps," he said shortly. He pulled his furs tight about his body and walked outside.

He was suddenly uncomfortable in the girl's presence. She disconcerted him—under the placid survey of her eyes he felt uncouth and immature.

The snow was spread thinly across the fields and powdered on the sage and against the tent it was crusted and hard. The dogs were whitened, semicircular humps. They moved a little at his approach and shuddered the snow from them and lifted their noses, steaming from warm loins, and glared at him. He halted doubtfully, but the animals had accepted him now and they slumped back, sniffing, into the whiteness.

Beneath the low fog the valley was nebulous, undimensional and unimpressive, but already the veil was shredding in the east to reveal damp sunlight fingering the frosted shoulders of hills and trees.

Down near the noisy river he could see Renzi, tumbling naked in the snow and hurling pebbles at the apathetic yaks, and he savored the shrieked laughter of her childhood. He was glad to watch her, and after a time he walked slowly through the snow toward her.

Veshti nodded to Kelinka to signify that the buttered tea was ready, and propped the long churn against the tent pole. Kelinka nudged the bundle beside her, and Muhlam levered himself from the rugs and yawned and blinked and scratched himself, and reached a grimed hand toward his food bowl. Kelinka ladled the greasy liquid into it. He sucked at it noisily and belched.

"Go, Veshti, and get the boy," Kelinka said.

"He will come. Renzi will bring him."

Kelinka shrugged.

"He is puny, the Han man, but he will be useful," Muhlam mused to nobody in particular. He drained the bowl and walked outside.

In the grayness he was gigantic. While he relieved himself he stared up at the whirl of mists, and then he nodded and looked toward the low brush palisades behind which the calves huddled.

There had not been sufficient snow to harm them, and he knew that within the hour the valley would be hot with the summer sun and the night's precipitation would be only another loudness in the brooks. He looked toward the river and he could see the stranger darting with quick movements through the gorse in pursuit of a blundering yak while the naked Renzi shrilled her delight at the game. Muhlam's face softened, and he moved across and kicked the mastiffs to their feet and roped them to the tilted stakes. Then he trudged to the palisades and loosed the calves. They came to their feet with stiff, uncertain clumsiness and trotted down to the herd bleating their hunger. Muhlam dusted the powder of snow from his knees and stared again toward the river. The boy and the child were seated on the bank tossing stones into the stream.

Muhlam turned away and looked toward the ghost images of the hills and thought of the time when he had been twenty. That had been nineteen summers before, in the year he had taken Kelinka for wife. She had cost his father a yak bull and two cows and ten of the black-faced sheep, but she had been worth it. She had been a good wife for a headman. He knew that Chunor, with his slobbering, demon-ridden idiot wife, envied him his possession of Kelinka. That was why Chunor, for all his sly servility, seldom missed an opportunity to point out Kelinka's one great shortcoming. She had failed to bear the headman a son. And Chunor's fool of a woman had borne not one son but five! An old bitterness stung Muhlam's throat and he spat heavily into the snow.

It hurt him more savagely even than Kelinka realized that the next headman of the valley would possess no seed from the loins of a family that had ruled the Valley of the Dreaming Phoenix for four lives; that the Muhlam blood would not reappear for another generation and then only through Veshti. His face clouded. Veshti, for all her loyalty and industry, was undersized and delicate and timid and in many ways quite unworthy of the rich heritage of her family. She was lacking in purpose, often listless, a weakling and a dreamer. Where in this child of his was the fiber of Muhlam, where the strength that could give her dominance in any liaison between the families of Muhlam and Chunor?

He had no doubt that there would be a liaison. There were not many more summers before he would be compelled to relinquish the leadership of the valley. And Chunor was the next strongest man, and at the appointed time Veshti would become the wife of Dochi, the first son of Chunor—a lout and a simpleton who had inherited the strength of his father's body and some of his cunning, and far too much of the idiocy of his mother. Any woman but Veshti would be able to twist the clown around her finger and make him dance to any tune she called. But not Veshti, with her dreams and weakness.

Muhlam's face set hard. He did not deceive himself. The leadership of the valley, whether he liked it or not, would pass ultimately to the family of Chunor. And for all the brutish strength of the dolt, Dochi, there was no man yet in all the valley as strong as Muhlam. He stood wide-legged in the snow, and, almost without knowing what he did, shook his great fist in the direction of Chunor's tent.

"Why do you do that, Muhlam?"

The words came softly, but he jumped as he turned.

Kelinka's boots had made no sound in the soft snow. His mouth was open and the bitterness had not drained from his face.

"Why, Muhlam?" Again the words came gently.

"Why was not Veshti a boy?" he rasped, his anger coming unchecked to cloak his embarrassment. The shadow that tightened his wife's face sickened him because he had not wanted to hurt her, so he turned away and glowered at the hills and spat his impatience: "Why, woman?"

For a long time Kelinka did not answer, and he was uncomfortable in his anger and turned back to her. She seemed oddly smaller, more fragile, almost with something of the delicacy of Veshti, and with Veshti's dreams in her eyes. His face relaxed into kindliness and he touched her hand awkwardly. As she looked up at him a fragment of a smile curled at her mouth. She saw the massive head with its crop of straight hair falling square to his shoulders, the deep lines encrusted with thirty-nine years of dirt and toil, the taut molding of the hard mouth and the flared arrogance of the nose, and the deep-set eyes that had thawed now into a puzzled affection and regret.

"Perhaps it is not yet too late, Muhlam," she said, and there was a yearning with the query.

He shook his head without answering. Her face twisted.

"And you forget," she said abruptly.

"Forget what?"

"If Veshti had been a boy. He would have been sent to a monastery. It would have made no difference then."

"No son of Muhlam would have become a babbling priest!" he snorted.

"Muhlam!" She reached for her prayer beads and glanced over her shoulder apprehensively.

"Bah! You and Veshti are the same. To hear you talk one would think the priests were gods themselves. They are men. Nothing else."

"I wish you were less contemptuous of the holy ones."

"I am contemptuous of any man who is not so strong as I. Look at Yanong. He is merely a man, like the rest of us."

"He is a good priest. He is——"

"He is a man." Surprisingly, he grinned down at her. "According to the tales that men tell he is more of a man than many of us!"

She knew that his mood had dissipated itself as suddenly as it had gathered.

"It is time to eat," she said.

He walked into the tent. For a long time Kelinka looked toward the river, and then she walked very slowly down to Salom and the laughter of Renzi.

II

Muhlam's hooked finger scoured the last of the tsamba from his bowl. He reached for his bridle and walked from the tent. He made no sign to the boy, but Salom took his own bridle and followed.

The sun had broken through the mists, and the earth steamed and the flowered grasses were jeweled with thawed snow. Once outside, Muhlam seemed to have abandoned his intentions. The bridle was tossed into the grass; his head was bowed, his hands clasped behind his back. Salom looked at him in some uncertainty and then began to walk toward the edge of the thang in search of his horse, but he turned as Muhlam called to him and hurried back.

"It is well," said the headman, "that you know certain things about this valley."

Salom nodded. The older man looked toward the slow-moving beasts of Chunor's herd.

"For a time," Muhlam continued, "you will live in my tent. Until you prove yourself unworthy of my hospitality you will live with me. You will be as one of my family. You understand it is the headman's family? It is important you understand that."

Again Salom nodded.

"There are thirteen families in this valley. I am the leader of these people. Do you know why I am the leader?"

"I suppose it is because——"

"I am the leader of these people because of many things." He ignored the boy's words, if indeed he noticed them; his question had been pure rhetoric. "I am stronger than any man here. I have the heritage of leadership because my father and his father and even *his* father were headmen before me. Moreover, my wealth is greater than any man's. My yak number forty, my sheep sixty-seven. Chunor's herds and flocks are fewer—" he stared down-valley contemptuously—"and the beasts puny by comparison."

Salom kicked at the wet grass and waited for the headman to continue.

"There are fifty people who acknowledge me their head. They have respect for me, and they depend upon my judgment. From them I ask no tribute and demand no tolls. I am firm with them—you will find some who call me Hard Muhlam—but I am just."

"Where . . . where are all these people? I do not see———"

"Four families are here, on the high pasture. Mine and Chunor's, and down beyond the curve of the stream are the tents of Kaman and Lotor. There are three more families encamped at the end of a day's ride to the west, and ten miles beyond that three more tents. Three families remain. They are old couples, and childless. They are in the houses at the far limit of the valley. We leave them there through summer to tend the crops and harvest the grain, and to begin the winnowing and grinding and storing."

"But are they not capable, all these people, of living their own lives, without the need of authority?"

Muhlam glanced sharply at him.

"Why do you ask that?"

"Because outside, in China, there is———"

"I am not concerned with outside." Muhlam's words cut. "Only this valley interests me. And there is much that a headman must do." His words had chilled with his displeasure. "Who is to allot the pastures? To decide which flocks and herds are to have which grasses? Who to plan the movements to new grazings? Who to conduct the barter with peddlers who sometimes come? Who to arrange the selling of the wool when there are fleeces to be sold? Who to approve marriages and settle disputes and punish those who stray from the laws we set? Who?"

Salom was silent, aware that no answer was expected of him.

"Then who is to protect our cattle from the claws of wolf and bear? Do you wonder that my tent is pitched at the highest point of the valley? This is because the most savage of the beasts that threaten us frequent the Pass of White Watching." He flung his arm in an arrogant, encompassing gesture. "I, Muhlam, am the nearest to such dangers. Chunor's tent—you see?—is farther from peril. Why? Because Chunor is not headman. And because Chunor is neither so strong as I—nor so brave."

Salom did not know that on the gaunt, grooved face was the same expression that had come earlier when Muhlam had shaken his fist toward Chunor's tent.

As if suddenly irked by such wasteful loquacity, the giant turned his back on the boy and began to walk away. But after he had taken only half a dozen paces he stopped and turned.

"Remember," he said deliberately, "that while you live in the tent of Muhlam you are of the headman's family. And now you can talk with the women. I am not yet ready to ride." His heavy boots swished the wet grass as he strode away.

III

Veshti and her mother were still in the tent. He could hear the pleasant clatter of domesticity, the hum of talk, the chink and thump of utensils. The fat child Renzi was sprawled in the wet grass. She had donned her jacket and bright boots and skirt, and her sharp teeth were biting into the stems of buttercups from which she was threading a garland. She beckoned him imperiously:

"Come, Salom. Tell me of China."

He grinned as he sat beside her: "We are not concerned with China now, child. We are concerned with the valley here." He took a flower and dabbed it against her chin and the bright pollen gleamed in the sun.

Veshti came out from the tent carrying two pails. She glanced gravely at the boy and the child and walked away toward the herd.

She was wearing her gaudy boots, but it seemed to Salom that she walked with bare feet. In the sunlight she had regained the elusive magic she had possessed in the flare and gloom of the tent at night. He saw that for all her delicacy she was lithe and possessed of a taut strength. A small black tuft of hair had escaped from her red braiding and it curled crisply at her neck.

"Do you think Veshti is beautiful?" asked Renzi, watching his face with eyes that were wise with nine years of life.

"Why . . . why, I had not thought . . . it is hard to tell with strange people . . . at first it is hard."

"*I* do not think she is beautiful. She is too small." She cocked her head critically. "Muhlam says she is too small. Muhlam says she has the body of a baby. But he says I will be big and strong."

"In China the girls are small, like Veshti. In China for a woman to be small and thin is considered very good."

"And beautiful?"

"Yes. Often beautiful."

"Then I hope I am *not* big and strong." Renzi looked at her plump arms and legs with sudden distaste. "Perhaps I shall grow small and thin like Veshti. Eh?"

"Perhaps." Salom laughed at her drooping mouth. "But now, child, you must tell me of the valley."

"The valley? You see it." Her arms waved. "It is here."

"Yes." Salom stared up toward the pass. He remembered the exultation with which he had first looked down upon its immeasurable beauty and serenity, and how he had known that the journey had been worth while, that the reward had been sufficient. "Yes," he said softly. "It is very beautiful."

"Why do you say it like that, Salom? You speak as if you say something very sad, and yet all you say is that the valley is beautiful."

"That *is* sad."

"How?"

He plucked a stalk of grass and chewed on it, and then he grinned at her. "You are a child," he said. "When you grow up you will find that the picture of real beauty always brings some sadness."

"Why?" She was hungrily intent, her eyes fixed on his mouth about to shape new words, words which she could store away and examine at leisure. The boy sensed this, and was pleased.

"Because it cannot last. Because it dies, like a flower; it withers, like the grass beneath the snow; it is swept away, like the trees standing in the path of the avalanche."

"I know." There was an odd wisdom in her serious, chubby face.

"How can you know?" He was amused. "How can a child know these things?"

"The valley is beautiful," she answered him with direct and disconcerting simplicity. "The valley is beautiful and then it dies. Each snow it dies and there is *nothing* beautiful. It is cold and cruel and it howls like a beast. I hate it! *I hate it!*" He was startled by her vehemence.

"But even in China, child, there are winters as well as summers." His voice was gentle. "And winters are good. You have the shelter of your house, and fires, and talk, and laughter. You have many things, Renzi."

"*Bah!* I hate the house! And the talk. Talk! It is all of summer—of the summer that died, of the summer to come. Only summer. And outside the wind cries and the demons batter at the doors—and I am frightened."

"Of the demons?" He laughed. "There are no demons, Renzi. They are——"

"No. It is not the demons that frighten me. Well, not *only* the demons. There is another fear. *It* is the bad fear. One day the snow will go on and on, higher and higher, and there will be no more summer. Only the wind and the snow and the noises of the night." Terror, genuine terror, lurked in the dark pools of her eyes. She shook her head quickly. "And sometimes summer does not come. Not for all people..."

"Summer always returns, Renzi."

"Not for all people," she insisted. "Not for Chantek."

"Who is Chantek?"

"My grandmother. Two snows ago she died in the house. One night she was seated by the fire with us, stitching at clothes, and then she coughed and fell forward and she was dead."

"Yes, but she was old."

"Very old. We took the stones down from one of the windows and then Muhlam threw her body outside into the snow, to wait for summer."

"Even death waits for summer," Salom said, almost as if he were speaking thoughts aloud.

"Yes. She waited there under the deep snow, and when Yanong came in the thaw her spirit was taken away and she was gone."

"But she greeted many summers before she farewelled the last of them. You will see many summers come and go, Renzi." He smiled at her. "And in any case it is idle to be worrying of winter when the birds are loud and the sun warm. Now, child, tell me of your house."

He stared past the black slice of the river to the interminable marches of the valley. "Perhaps I will share your house in the next snows, Renzi. So tell me of it."

"It is larger than any of the others. *Much* larger. And we have six daggers over every door. And *twelve* Buddhas!"

He smiled into the grass. Her picture carried all the distortion of a child's vision, but he had lived before in Tibetan houses, and as she talked he found a clear image forming in his mind, and he was happy that this would be his home in the winter to come.

Renzi might begrudge every hour spent within its walls, and yet without that house none of them, not even Muhlam himself, could have survived one full turn of the seasons. None could have lived through the wrath of winter without the shelter of those thick stone walls and the warmth of fires never allowed to languish.

Moreover, Renzi was too young to realize that it was only the dreariness of winter that made summer possible. Only then could the barley meal be ground and roasted; the thread spun from yak hair and woven into stout cloth for the summer tents; the tents themselves repaired and frayed ropes spliced; the bullets for hunting cast; the wool spun from fat fleeces and woven into clothing and blankets and saddle rugs; the furs dressed and stitched; the garments repaired and harness mended; the cheeses made and packed and the meat smoked.

He twisted on to his back and looked east toward the sun. He understood as well as if he had been born in the valley the sadness of Renzi, the sadness with which all the people would watch the flaming sphere sidle each day farther to the southward, while desolation fingered at the valley.

"Salom!"

He jumped, and looked at the child inquiringly.

"You did not *listen*," Renzi pouted. "You were staring away, not hearing."

"I listened, child. But then I was dreaming. Often I find myself dreaming."

"Oh-oh, then you and Veshti are a fine pair! She, too, dreams in the day. Muhlam sometimes scolds her and says———"

"It is often good to dream, Renzi."

"Then do not let my father hear you talk like that. Do you know what he says to Veshti?"

"What?"

"He says that dreams are for babies and fools and crones. Salom—what is a crone?"

The boy laughed. "I do not think you will ever need to know, child. It is a fret you can leave to others."

Her eyes sparkled. And then a great shadow spread across them, and Salom turned and looked up at Muhlam. He flushed and scrambled to his feet, and instantly felt more foolish when he saw that the giant was leading his horse, already saddled.

"Your horse is not yet ready? You must stir yourself, boy."

Salom nodded miserably, but then the other man laughed. He jerked his head toward Renzi and his face was bright with good humor.

"I know—it is this one. If she talks too much she must be cuffed. Often she must be beaten because her tongue prattles like the water in the streams."

Renzi gasped. "It is *wrong!*" she protested. "Never, *never* have I been beaten!"

But her father exploded again, and then he reached down and ruffled his great hand into her hair.

"Come, boy," he said. "It is time to go."

They walked together toward Salom's horses.

"You like Renzi?" Muhlam asked.

"Yes. She is so joyous and———"

"Whoever takes *her* to wife will never lack for entertainment." Muhlam chuckled. "But, by all the Buddhas, he will need a will of iron to keep her in her place! She will be a true Muhlam. Yes. A true Muhlam." He pursed his mouth appreciatively. "What did you and the child find to talk about?"

"Your house—and about beauty, and dreams."

"Dreams?"

"Yes. Renzi says that Veshti and I are a fine pair, because we have dreams in the day."

"Bah! Veshti is a little fool!"

There was no more conversation as Salom saddled the horse and they rode together toward the uplands.

IV

Veshti knew what her mother would do even before she set the brimming pails down beside the fireplace. For a long time now mannerisms had entangled Kelinka's duties in a web of banal remarks and gestures. As always, she peered into the pails and dipped one dirty, beringed finger into the creamy fluid, still steaming from the cow's udders. As always, she ran her tongue along the dripping finger with great deliberation, and cocked her fur-capped head sideways, considering. And, as always, she murmured her formula of satisfaction. "Ah! It is good milk, this. Muhlam has fine herds. The best in the valley."

The girl turned away. It was a statement she had heard so often that it deserved no comment. Kelinka looked toward the girl. Her tired eyes were dull and unfocused, and her head was still tilting and nodding in that unconscious habit she had developed lately. The ponderous earrings of silver and jade shook heavily.

"Your father is a fine man," she said, but her eyes were opaque. Veshti turned. The stiff jerking of her mother's head made her feel uncomfortable. It had a stupid look, like the loose gestures of Dupken. She looked away.

"A fine man," Kelinka repeated flatly.

"Yes." Veshti drew patterns in the grass with the square toe of her boot. "He gave work to the Chinese . . ."

"That one is a nice boy." Kelinka was released from her trance. She began to fold the sleeping rugs. "A puny one, and probably of no wealth, but with courage in him. His mother should be proud of such a son. Four months he journeyed across the mountains. He will have tales to tell, I know. I hope he pleases Muhlam." She ran her callused hand across the panda skin, and the fur glowed through her fingers. "Muhlam is not easy to please," she added.

"Muhlam will be pleased," Veshti said, and flushed because her tongue had betrayed her wish.

Kelinka stared at her curiously. "No man is easy to please, Veshti. As you grow older you will see the truth of this. The more the gods give a man in strength and power the less they give him of tolerance for those neither so strong or so powerful as he. You will find that is true. It is better not to expect too much from a man in return for your labors. Then there will be no disappointment when you receive little. Wait until you have a husband of your own. Then you will understand these things." She bent again to the blankets and there was a flattening in her voice. "Although I dare say Dochi will not be so difficult as most."

Veshti considered Dochi—the way his hairy arms hung wide and forward of sloping shoulders, and the way his hands were thick and puffy, and somehow formless, like a kneaded cake of tsamba. She considered his massive head, and his mouth always hanging slightly open; and his little black eyes, peering, peering... and then another picture eclipsed the image of Chunor's son. A slim boy, delicate of color and movement; a boy in a blue jacket leaning with unconscious grace against the tent pole, slapping at it with his bridle, and watching her with warm brown eyes.

She felt a revulsion, outraged and unreasoning.

"Why must I marry Dochi?" she asked with sudden sharpness.

"Because, my daughter, since Muhlam has no son it is certain that one day Dochi will be headman, and Muhlam desires that his own blood should still flow in the headman's family." Her hand touched the girl's shoulder. "My child, the wise woman does not question her destiny. She accepts it, and earns merit for herself by her humility. And besides—" her voice lifted with pride—"to be headman's wife is to be something that every woman in the valley will envy. That, child, is something."

"I . . . I do not want other women to envy me."

"But it is something," Kelinka insisted.

"Yes," Veshti murmured. A girl accepted the decisions of her parents. It had always been so. She did not know why—except that parents were naturally wiser than their children. And yet when one desired the benefit of this wisdom there was no way of asking for it. There were many times lately when she had wanted to talk to Kelinka, but when the time came, as it had come again now, there were no words to say. For three years there had been the things in her mind, the thoughts that went spinning and bursting every time the thaw came, and although she tried to grasp at them they were gone before she could examine them. And there were the things unspoken in the eyes of men, and unsaid in their words as they sprawled around the night fires and talked of pastures and beasts and the details of harness. Sometimes she thought that she could discuss these things with the priest, Yanong, when he came upon her at work in the fields. But he would only praise her slyly for her industry or talk in unnecessary whispers of the fatness of the calves, and always her eyes slid away from the unknown thing that crouched in his, and her heart would jump like a snared bird.

Today her bewilderment was deeper, and she knew that it was the coming of the boy that had unsettled her, but again no words could be found for such things, and so it was best to leave matters to her parents and accept their decisions with meekness. In any case, what would happen if one did refuse to accept? She grappled for a moment with the unprecedented thought, but it slipped away and left only a vague perplexity of loss. She was suddenly heavy with an intolerable sadness. It swirled about her, a visible mist, an opacity that muffled all senses but the overpowering one of melancholy.

"Eeeee!" a sparse voice cackled. "Dreaming again, eh? There'll be none of that, I warrant, when my Dochi takes you to wife! He will keep your feet on the earth, girl! Kelinka! I come to beg that you lend me a butter churn—since my fool of a second son broke mine in a rage. I swear before the gods he was possessed by a demon!"

Even in her first instinctive recoil, Veshti had forced her mouth to stretch into a polite smile, while Kelinka bustled forward with a courteous, "Go gently, Dupken."

Standing in the doorway with the light behind her, Chunor's wife looked like some evil spider. Her emaciated body was hooked into a permanent stoop. Her furs were rolled down and her breasts hung against her ribs like two flat parchment scrolls, upon which were scrawled the purple symbols of some monstrous, unknown suffering. The little desiccated triangle of her face was all but lost beneath a wild mass of matted hair, surprisingly black and vigorous by contrast with the colorless down that sprouted at her chin.

She twisted her hands together and cracked her knuckles and Veshti shivered. It was her hands that Veshti feared, hands growing crooked fingers, like dead brown twigs; and it was her eyes, so black and so bright, and always moving. As they moved now, flicking around the interior of the tent as if seeking some specific thing.

"I saw a stranger ride with Muhlam to the west this morning," she said, and her glance frisked up and down Kelinka without settling. "It is perhaps a trader from another valley?"

Kelinka selected a clean butter cylinder and answered placidly, although Veshti could detect the faint gloss of pride on her voice: "No trader, Dupken, but a traveler from distant lands. From the Han country over the Ta Hsueh Shan. He is to stay with us. He will help Muhlam with the herds."

She saw Dupken's eyes narrow.

"He is a fine boy and brave," Kelinka added, "and he has stories to tell of strange wonders in other lands."

The fitful glance of Dupken bickered now over Veshti.

"Eeee!" she squeaked. "Does this traveler have a *purpose* in coming? He gives his reason for his coming, eh?"

"No, Dupken," Veshti murmured, impaled on those variable eyes. "He . . . he gives no reason. Only that some had told him of the valley's beauty. And so . . . so he wished to see for himself."

"Then do not trust him!" Her fingers clenched down. "Kelinka! How can you be such a fool? How do you know that this stranger is not a demon wandering the earth?"

"Dupken!" Kelinka chided her with a soft laugh. "You are forever talking of demons. Only a little time ago you spoke of your own son——"

"Wandering the earth!" screamed the other woman, sweeping aside the interruption. "Seeking mischief to do! I know! Why, we shall all be rended and devoured in our sleep!"

"You talk nonsense, Dupken." Kelinka was no longer amused.

"Nonsense, eh? Then wait until the priest comes. We shall see who is talking nonsense. Why does a stranger come then if it is not for evil? Has any stranger ever come before without reason? No. Then why should one come now? I tell you——" The hair on her chin shivered and then her ferine face darkened with a new suspicion. "You say he is young—a boy, eh?"

"Of twenty years," said Kelinka calmly.

"Then perhaps it is for Veshti he comes," she muttered spitefully. She crouched toward the girl. "Eh? Do you wish to mate with a demon, girl? Do you? Answer me, child! *Do you?*"

Veshti shook her head helplessly, fighting with nausea and fear.

"Then do not forget you are promised to my son!" Dupken's voice shrieked. "Or the gods will have a terrible vengeance on you. For a thousand lives you will roast in the red pit. Wicked girl! Mating with a demon! Oh, Saintly Buddha, what wrongs have I done to deserve this?"

"Calm yourself, Dupken," Kelinka said sharply. "The boy is no demon, nor is he anything to Veshti, and Veshti has done nothing to merit accusations of wickedness. She is a good girl who honors the gods. And she is free of demons now and always. You and your demons! Calm yourself now, and you shall meet the boy later and see for yourself."

But the madness of Dupken was not to be checked. She shook Kelinka away and screamed her frenzy: "Abomination! Chunor shall know of this, and Yanong shall be told as soon as he arrives. They will know that Muhlam's family consorts with demons!" And, forgetting the butter churn, she rushed from the tent, her skirt flapping wildly about her, her hands clenching and unclenching at her prayer beads.

Veshti clung to the tent pole. The black walls whirled.

"Kelinka," she whispered. "He is not a demon as Dupken says? Kelinka, surely he cannot——"

Kelinka grasped the girl's shoulder and shook her with strong hands and chuckled sourly.

"May the gods forgive me for saying it, my daughter, but if there is any demon in this valley, its name is Dupken! Grasp yourself, child! The boy is a good boy. Can you not see it in his eyes, and on his mouth? Any woman would be proud to call him a son. And surely you must trust the judgment of your father? Would Muhlam have permitted him to stay unless Muhlam was satisfied! Shame on you, child."

They were interrupted by an uneasy cough from the tent door. Two women of the community—fat Naropa and her daughter Maygur—shuffled self-consciously in the slice of shadow.

"We . . . umm . . . we have come, Kelinka . . ." Naropa mumbled in her nervousness.

"As I see," Kelinka replied, irked by the interruption.

"It seems I have mislaid my large copper ladle."

"Not ladle, mother," Maygur muttered. "You told me the small cauldron."

She was silenced by a swipe from her mother that sent her reeling from the doorway. Naropa jellied in embarrassment. "You must forgive my fool of a girl." She twisted her plump hands. "Sometimes I think she is completely witless."

Veshti saw that her mother's eyes danced now with merriment as they had not done for many years.

"Then it is a churn you wish to borrow, good neighbor?" Kelinka asked gently.

"Yes, yes." Naropa wiped her greasy forehead, and started. "A *churn?* No. No. I mean a *ladle.*" She reddened in dismay.

"Veshti, get a good, large ladle for our neighbor. There, Naropa. I think this one will be suitable."

Naropa mumbled her thanks as she took the utensil, and continued to stand there, twirling the bright copper in her hands. The sniveling girl, Maygur, had edged back inside the tent.

"We . . . we met Dupken as we approached," Naropa ventured cautiously. "She was *screaming.* I do not like to tell you this, Kelinka, because as everybody in the valley is well aware I am not an interfering woman, but she swears you are housing a demon." She sniggered tolerantly. "Of course, I took no notice. We are *well* acquainted with Dupken's foibles, eh? But I saw the lad this morning riding with Muhlam . . . umm . . . and that is why . . ." She choked on another snigger and trailed off into silence. Maygur tittered uncomfortably.

"No doubt Kaman will give you a full report on the boy when he returns to your tent at sundown," Kelinka answered evenly. "They are sure to meet at the herds. And now I observe you are impatient to return to your duties, good Naropa. It is difficult, I know, keeping the tent of Kaman tidy. Do not let us detain you idly gossiping."

But before the embarrassed women could mutter their farewells

Renzi frisked between them with her arms full of sagebrush and her face crowded by questions. She dumped the brush unceremoniously at her mother's feet.

"But what happens today?" she asked breathlessly. "As I gathered brush for the fire I saw a party of women—six at least—all coming in *this* direction. What is the matter, Kelinka?"

Her mother's tired mouth was tugged upward, so that for a moment she looked young again, and very merry.

"No doubt, Renzi," she smiled, "a demon has been wandering in the valley, and all the cooking utensils have been stolen. They come to borrow new ones."

Chapter Four

I

THE next few days were the happiest Salom had ever known. It was as if all his previous life had been a tormented journey—and now he had come home to the tranquillity that the old peddler of Ch'eng-tu had so wisely foreseen. Only rarely now did he look up to the still peaks of snow and think of the travail and loneliness that lay beyond—and behind—the Valley of the Dreaming Phoenix. All around him were too many other things.

Each day was a gem of ever-brightening luster. He was enchanted by the beauty of the high pastures: it was loveliness of a quality he had never known before, because its beauty had the frailty of something one knows to be transient. It was the quality of a flower plucked at the supremacy of its blooming. It was a beauty already steeped in its own decay and so made the more beautiful for its promise of ill fate. There were times when Salom, clutching the loveliness to him as a jealous man clutches his mistress, would look back toward the solitary peaks, and then his eyes would cloud with dread. But the peaks would be white and quiet beneath a serene sky, and the valley would fold back in swathes of color tremulous in the heat. The peaks were still unveiled and no blizzard smudged the sky—and winter was far away.

And so his eyes sought more intimate beauties. There were the myriad flowers and bright shrubs whose fragrance was as heavy in the air as the throb and murmur of the insects. There were the fields rolling away, fold upon fold, and each contour bright with some other bloom—fields of the blue poppies that had lapped to the very edge of the pass on the afternoon of his arrival, and fields of red poppies and yellow. There were the smears of gentian and forget-me-not and buttercup and marigold, and the purple asters, and the iris banners standing tall as a man. And there were the jasmine and wild roses twined into the jumbled rocks of the prayer walls, and the downy crowns of thistles, and the pollen wiped thickly on the backs of bees, and the bright tiny gems of nameless flowers that starred the grasses.

It was not only a land of vivid color. It was a land where life teemed as if the intrusion of men had been an incident of little importance. The woods and moors and hillsides abounded in birds and animals, and fish moved, fat and sluggish, in the river and its tributary brooks and creeks.

Because of their religion, the valley people slew no living thing except the creatures that preyed on their livestock. They ate meat only when a bird or beast had come to death without human intervention, and its spirit had presumably wandered off toward its rendezvous with some future incarnation, perhaps human, perhaps animal. Consequently, meat to them was an unusual luxury, and they ate fish never.

Because of this the birds and animals displayed little shyness toward man, for in that valley man was the least harmful of all living creatures—Salom remembered the peddler's indictment of Ch'eng-tu's mankind, and the contrast pleased him—but death and tragedy still stalked the flowered fields or the silent shadows of the woods and the clean clarities of sky and water, for all life that swarmed there was either hunter or hunted. In the hard frost or the dusted snow of mornings Salom would see the dark tracks and pads that showed where a snow leopard or a lynx had prowled, and even in the spongy imprints there was stealth. He would see the delicate arrow points that charted the scurryings of birds, and the heavier markings of pheasants and snow cock and guinea fowl. He would see the ducks and geese plunging in the backwaters and the cranes sedately plodding the marshes and the fish eagles and kites swirling leisurely arabesques high above—and in all this beauty there was only the calculated desire to destroy.

Only man, Salom thought, could be devoid of cruelty. He remembered Ch'eng-tu and knew that man could adapt himself to cruelty, but of all the living, predatory creatures only man had no *need* of it.

II

On the first day Muhlam had taken him to the lower pastures, roughly midway between the tents of Lotor and Kaman and the encampment beyond, which was hidden by folds of crimson hills.

Fed by a hundred streams and cascades, the river, even within the compass of a few miles, had become a broad torrent, urgent and foam-licked above the amber of submerged stones, and even the fords that angled across where the current slackened had whetted razor edges. The horses shied fretfully away from the deceptively smooth lick of the waters.

Along these lower slopes the timber was heavier, but the grass was less rich and the pastures marred by numerous bogs, brown and darkly reeded, where midge swarms shimmered their silent dances.

When the sun was almost at the apex of its climb they cantered back to the tent of Lotor. It was smaller than Muhlam's tent, slumped away from frayed ropes and broken poles, and it was surrounded by litter.

Salom noted the untidiness and Muhlam saw his expression and smiled slightly.

"Lotor has but one real love," he said.

"And that?"

"A stone jar that I swear is never empty."

"Of what?"

"Chang. Barley beer. Lotor drinks too much—but he is a good herdsman."

The men from Lotor's tent, and Kaman's, were with the herds, but Muhlam demanded from Lotor's wife a churn of tea with which to mix his tsamba. Women and children came running and stood around them in a mesmerised half-circle, round-eyed and silent except for reflective tongue-cluckings. Lotor's wife—Salom was never to know her name for she was one of those women who never seem to have a name, and if they have it is always forgotten—was fat and amiable, and although she writhed with her excitement Muhlam made no attempt to explain the presence of the boy, nor did he exchange any conversation with her beyond his peremptory requests concerning food and tea.

Only once did he speak, and then it was to a young, tall girl who sauntered up from the river swinging a vivid skirt about her rounded hips. She leaned carelessly across one of the stay-ropes of the tent and grinned up at Muhlam. There was nothing of deference in her bold eyes.

The headman scowled at her.

"You would do well, Bitola," he said, "to give some attention to the condition of your camp." He gestured contemptuously toward the slovenly tent. "It looks as unlovely as a yak manger at winter's end. Why do you not give some attention to it?"

She laughed. It was a husky sound deep in her throat, and her black eyes danced.

"My attention is occupied by too many other things," she said impudently. She moved her eyes to Salom and appraised him brazenly. Under her insolent gaze, he felt his stomach tingle and a flush creep beneath his skin. This girl was beautiful. She was big and her shoulders were broad and her great breasts stood firm and high. He thought of Veshti's beauty, fragile and elusive—but there was no way of comparing her with this vivid, sensuous creature whose beauty was the beauty of bombast and color and being alive.

Although he was disconcerted by the utter immodesty of her stare it flattered him, and he was a little disappointed when the girl turned away without addressing him and swaggered off to the fields.

They rode back through intense heat. The glare was a pulsation that sucked the pigment from the earth until all the valley was hot silver beneath the throb of the sun. It seemed almost as if the world gasped and palpitated weakly beneath an intolerable burden. But nearing the home thang the light changed as if a filter had been whipped away. One moment it had been the blaze of midsummer; then it was autumn, with the chill of its breath and the color of its decay. The world suddenly strode forward into its dimensions. Hills were sharply outlined; contours that had been trembling mirages a few minutes earlier were clear and without intervening space; the valleys were gulfs of shadow that emphasized the ruddiness of rocks and the glow of timber; and the distant peaks leaned over, white and compelling against the thickening violet of the sky.

The storm caught them before they had made the last river crossing. For an hour it had been massing behind, tossing lurid plumes against the afternoon's flame, clawing higher—and then the clouds erased the hills and rain lashed at them, and they galloped to the tent with their furs tight about them, chilled and drenched and with frozen knuckles numb on the reins. Salom remembered what Veshti had told him. There would be no snow at night if there was a storm in the afternoon. Tonight would be free of snow. He was learning the lore of the Valley of the Dreaming Phoenix.

On the morning of the following day Muhlam permitted the boy to ride the nearer grazing grounds alone, and with the rather forbidding presence of the headman removed he saw a new friendliness awaken in the nomads he encountered. At the first river crossing he met Kaman and Lotor and the sons of Chunor. He suspected that they had been waiting there in the hope of meeting him—and he was pleased.

It was Lotor who began the interrogation. He was clothed like a disreputable bandit, and he had a broad, snub-nosed face pitted by the scars of smallpox. In spite of his ugliness, he had a pleasant manner and laughed easily. Salom liked him.

"What news of the Han country?" he asked impetuously, not one to bother with the niceties of circumlocution. He had never before met any man from China, but he spoke as one accustomed to receiving regular news from countries that to him were almost mythological.

"I bring no news," said Salom. "I was there only a little time and——"

"Then you will know naught but the news of the wine booths and the girls, eh?" Lotor guffawed. "The traveler who passes swiftly sees little else but the bottoms of wine cups and women!" He bellowed appreciation of his own humor, and Salom laughed, caught by its infection.

Lotor wiped his eyes. "Is the chang a good brew in the Han country?" he asked. His voice was serious now, because beer was a subject about which he was loath to trifle.

"They do not drink it," Salom said.

Lotor sat straight in his saddle.

"They drink no beer?" he echoed wonderingly.

"No. They drink wine—from rice and sometimes from fruits—but no beer."

"Then now I understand why the men of Han are so puny." Lotor grinned, and the other men laughed.

One of Chunor's sons leered. "Tell us of the women in the Han country," he said. "Is it true that they are beautiful?"

"Perhaps they are," Salom said. "I am no judge. I was there only a little time."

"A little time is usually time enough," Lotor said.

"I think *you* need not worry about beauty elsewhere. Yesterday I saw your daughter. That should be sufficient of beauty for any man."

Lotor's eyebrows lifted and amusement quirked his mouth.

"You have sharp eyes for a stranger," he said pleasantly. And then his eyes twinkled. "When you came here—was there not anyone to tell you of the dangers of your journey?" He gestured toward the mighty snow peaks. "It could not have been easy."

"Yes," Salom said. "There were many who warned me. And on the way here I met others, and they, too——"

"And they told you nothing of Bitola?" asked Lotor mockingly, and all the men laughed—all except Kaman, who throughout the conversation sat his horse with his head bowed and his lean face drawn in an expression of suffering.

III

Salom's first impressions of the people of the Valley of the Dreaming Phoenix seemed to confirm the opinion of the old peddler. They were simple but kindly, and they were aroused easily to laughter and to hospitality. These were things they understood—and there were so many things of which they had no understanding. Isolation had all but obliterated imagination, and had molded their characters to conform to a standard framework of fundamentals—food and shelter and clothing. These three needs were the template from which all else was fashioned.

Marital relationships developed less from emotional affinities than from a man's need of food and clothing, and a woman's need of protection and physical usage, and the adult need of children to safeguard their old age. That was a pattern of domesticity strongly woven into the fabric of family unity and loyalty. There was even, occasionally, a pattern of affection sharp enough and strong enough to be called love. But such things were exceptional. In general most of the interest of the people was centered in the weather, the condition of the beasts and the pastures, and the presence of predatory creatures. And even all these things were considered mostly in relation to the common denominators of food, shelter, clothing.

Except in the minds of most of the women, little emphasis was placed upon spiritual things, and this was pleasing to Salom because he paid homage to no faith. Even in that he differed from the people of the valley. He possessed no religious belief. But in spite of their superficial lack of interest they possessed unquestioning belief. It was rarely made manifest because the very maintenance of existence against the militant beauty of the land was in itself a problem sufficiently absorbing; there remained little time and less energy to assault dim bastions of theology.

The people believed that at birth they had reincarnated the spirits of men or women who had lived before, and that at their death their spirits would find new abodes in future living things. Some of the more erudite even understood that this continuing stream of life had emanated originally from Chenresi, the Compassionate Spirit, the father of all living. But generally they had no grip upon, nor desire to grapple with, the tremendous thought behind the most naked of beliefs. Such ponderings could be left to the holy ones. They assumed they would find rebirth as cowherds or shepherds, because it was the only life they understood, and they gave little more than formal attention to the fact that if a man sinned too greatly his spirit would wander in the flaming evils of Bado until it found lodgment not in the entity of some future nomad but in the body of some lowly animal. These fears troubled them rarely. They were too busy, and too certain that such punishment was only for others. The priests were paid to worry about the riddles, and deeper spiritual problems could be left to them—and in the meantime prayers could be said and rosary beads fingered and stones carved to give honor to Buddha and also to discourage the demons of whom all were intensely afraid.

Sometimes, perhaps on star-quiet nights, they would be troubled by the whole great enigma of being, and then the eddy of unaccustomed thought would spiral down into dreadful visions of sorcery and monstrous magic, and they would shiver and pull their furs more tightly about their terrors.

There were black shadows in the whirling mysteries of the hereafter, but none so black as the active evils of the present. Through the centuries the pure and reasonable mysticism of Buddhism had become fused with centuries of witchcraft, sorcery, necromancy. And here there were dangers both of the flesh and the spirit. No man in all the valley could truthfully speak of having seen one of the sorcerer priests, the black lamas, who trailed their evil over all the great plateau of Tibet, but there was never any end to the rumors that one had been seen in another valley, heading toward *their* valley—and any season of abnormally severe weather or a disease that blighted crops or other unaccountable misfortunes were usually blamed on the activities of these wandering servants of the evil demons who lived in the white silences of the high peaks.

But in normal times such nightmares were forgotten. Like most people who constantly give battle to nature their memories clung tenaciously to the pleasant things and discarded quickly the moments of pain or fear or anxiety. And they were a sturdy people, and strong.

The men were tall and broad-shouldered and packed with hard muscle; and the women were generally exceedingly comely in youth, although they aged quickly when life had taken them beyond the ripe peak of womanhood. Longevity was not common, and, indeed, the people of the Valley of the Dreaming Phoenix still sometimes spoke with awe of a woman named Pundar who had died two generations earlier at the age of sixty-one. Hardship was the scythe of life. The people were healthy enough, although many were deformed by goiters, there were always two or three people of any given generation who would be blind from trachoma, and the faces of many were scarred by the marks of smallpox, epidemics of which intermittently swept the valley, touching many and killing some. Good health bore no relationship to cleanliness. There were no hot springs in the Valley of the Dreaming Phoenix, and almost every person would be content to travel from the womb to the death cauldron without benefits of washing.

In this way they were essentially the fruits of their living conditions. They possessed no opinion on the subject of personal cleanliness because it was something that never entered into consideration. In summer, the valley from midmorning until midafternoon baked beneath a sun whose rays scorched through the thin atmosphere of fourteen and a half thousand feet. But mornings were cold with hoar frost or wet with the thaw of night snow, and few dusks were not heralded by the tumultuous march of storms conceived in a mountainous funnel that blocked the far end of the Valley of Thunder's Birth. These storms would stride along the chain of valleys leading to the main alpine barrier with such devastating swiftness that they were gone before nightfall in torn rags of scud dissolving against the ice peaks, and the sun would set in serene opalescence. But the valley people knew how chill winds and icy rains driven against knuckles clamped around wet reins, and against contorted faces muffled in fur caps, could rip flesh like a knife wound if it were cleansed of protective oils and filth. So flesh remained unwashed, and, indeed, was made even more malodorous by the application of a crude unguent compacted from soured yak butter and tallow and the marrow fluid of animals. Few of the women used the concoction, perhaps because their comparatively sheltered lives saved them from the constant ravages of the elements, perhaps because of some instinctive and scarcely understood femininity.

If the question were ever raised—which would be most improbable—the nomads would have assumed that such physical crudities as unkempt hair and unwashed bodies could be more than offset by a variety of sartorial splendors.

Clothing was voluminous not only because of the desire for warmth. Three jackets, a pair of skirts, or two pairs of trousers, would frequently be worn when one jacket, one skirt, or one pair of trousers would have afforded sufficient protection. The upper garments were loosely worn so that they could be rolled down, leaving the waist and chest and arms bare during the warm hours of the day. The people had an immense pride in these garments, and the more variety and the greater brilliance of color that could be displayed at any given moment the greater the fillip to the wearer's ego.

It did not take long for Salom to become acutely conscious of his own drab and threadbare garb. The rigors of his journey had done little to improve it. The cheap coolie dye had faded and the cotton had frayed, and beside the flamboyant clothing of the nomads his high-necked jacket and baggy trousers looked cheap and shabby.

"Are all the people of the Han country dressed in such rags?" Lotor asked, and Salom flushed a little, although he was fond of this amiable and picturesque ruffian. Lotor sought as a foil for his rough geniality clothing of almost frightening pugnacity. His black hat, burgundy habit and blue trousers were all trimmed with molting wolfskin. He wore a wolfskin girdle into which were thrust six long knives and an ancient and hammerless horse pistol of unknown origin, questionable history, and indisputable uselessness. A brace of spare skinning knives was thrust into the tops of his boots, and across his shoulder he carried a long-barreled 1896 Mauser rifle, a gilt box of prayer charms, a bandoleer of long-nosed bullets, a leather tinder bag and a flint striker.

"No," Salom said. "Some wear bright silks and rich brocades." He felt a little foolish. In China he had worn Tibetan garments and had been derided. To soothe that hurt he had bought himself Chinese clothes. And now he was being derided because he wore Chinese clothes in Tibet.

"Then why do you wear rags?" Lotor asked.

"Rich silks do not fit well with a hard saddle," Salom said.

"No saddle forces a man to dress like a cloudy day." Lotor grinned. "Look at Kaman." He gestured toward the herd, where the melancholy man was riding. He wore a scarlet jacket with sky-blue sleeves, a purple skirt over black trousers, a pair of kaleidoscopic boots and a floppy felt hat of vivid and poisonous green.

"I cannot see that it makes him happier," Salom said.

"Nothing would make that one happy. I think he must have met some agreeable wench in Bado between his last life and this. It is the truth that ever since he was a child he has looked resentful at having been born. That hat!"

"It is a curious color," Salom admitted.

"It is his only joy. He is more attached to it than to his woman Naropa—a fact which I can well understand, mind you!" The herdsman dragged his useless pistol from his belt and held it in his palm tenderly.

"This is a lovely thing, eh?"

Salom eyed the weapon critically. "But it is broken!" he said. "It will not shoot!"

"Bah! Are all the men of Han mere merchants devoid of souls? Whether it works or not is unimportant. It is lovely! I have known women who could not bear children. I do not remember that it made them less desirable when a few soft furs were spread!"

Salom grinned. "Then it is lovely," he agreed.

"Yet Old Longface over there claims that his hat is a possession of more worth than this beauty of mine. I mention this merely to warn you that you will find here some very stupid people. Kaman is one." He thrust the pistol back into his girdle.

Salom was to discover later that almost every person in the valley carried or treasured one particular possession of specially unique value, theft of which would have been regarded as a crime of the very first magnitude, loss of which would have been felt almost as the supreme woe.

It was Kaman's hat and Lotor's pistol. It was Veshti's beautiful string of prayer beads—a string of amber that Kelinka's grandmother had owned, with every fifth bead a sphere of glowing coral and every twentieth a turquoise. Chunor kept his carefully folded inside his charm box—a sheet torn from an English scientific magazine. He had discovered it one day hooked against a brier and had marveled at the intricacy of its type and illustration without ever marveling at how the flimsy sheet came to be in a remote valley on the roof of the world. It meant nothing to him—and yet he would have felled any person, even his own kin, if they had laid a finger upon it.

Dupken, who by virtue of her own indiscriminate spawning had become self-appointed midwife of the clan (a position she had refused to relinquish in spite of a record of five failures out of the last eight accouchments she had supervised), fittingly possessed a leather casket containing an evil-smelling lotion distilled from the antler juices of a species of deer found in the Tsarung Mountains. It was said that if the cream was rubbed into the abdomen of a women to the accompaniment of appropriate incantations it would certainly prevent her from having children. Its efficacy was never questioned by Dupken, though she had applied the magic oil to her own flaccid belly on several occasions and had still added to her mumbling brood.

With her curiously inverted reasoning she had given another mysterious substance to her firstborn son, Dochi. It was a black powder of revolting odor, kept in a small woolen bag, which was reputed to guarantee a lifelong vigor of youth to the most impotent of men. It had become Dochi's most jealously guarded talisman, but it was far too early to tell whether the black powder would be any more effective than her own treasured unguent.

Renzi's prize had been acquired only recently—a shining Yunnan silver dollar that Salom had given her. Even Muhlam, usually contemptuous of fads and fashions, placed a fantastic valuation on an ancient drinking cup fashioned from the horn of a Burmese rhinoceros which was reputed to sweat out a creamy fluid if any poison was present in the contents of the cup.

It was among these people, seemingly without complexity, that Salom saw his own stifled gregariousness expand and tasted the refreshment of conversation, and in slaking his long thirst for companionship he found the first elements of a happiness he had never known before.

IV

When he sensed the first shadow he did not regard it, in the beginning, as of particular importance—although he was humiliated by its childishness and surprised that it should have been cast by Muhlam. He had known of his probationary acceptance into the family of Muhlam on the very night of his arrival. But it had progressed quickly beyond the formal bounds of hospitality and trial. Within little more than a day the proud and generally taciturn headman, engrossed as he was with the importance of his position, nevertheless occasionally spoke to him with an eagerness to talk, as if he, too, had been a man long starved of conversation.

Admittedly, it was all talk of Muhlam's world, Muhlam's kingdom. He would point out the everyday things that confronted them as they rode between the flocks and herds—the clouds of horseflies that plagued the animals until their eyes were wild and their rumps streaming blood; the golden powder dusted across the black shingle of the river; the shadowed glens where the wolves lurked; the fractured timbers of an old bridge swept away in the first spring freshets; the old spoor of a bear and beyond it the socketed skull and littered bones that were mute testimony to Muhlam's skill as a hunter; the desolate moor beneath the spur, scarred with stunted brush and soiled with the droppings of wolves and foxes, where Muhlam said the old sorcerers had once practiced dreadful rites; the crumbled watch tower gripped in the fetters of brier and bracken that Salom had seen when he first rode into the valley. He asked Muhlam of it, and the headman told him that it had been built four generations earlier as a measure of protection against wandering bandits who had first brought firearms to the valley and ended forever the rule of knife and spear.

"They were wild enough days," said Muhlam, "but they passed. There is no room here for killing."

His words added to the boy's pleasure.

But it was all Muhlam's talk. In the first day or two he had no wish to talk of his own adventures; there was too much to be learned of these new people and this new land, for although it was a part of Tibet it was as different from the world he had known near Litang as China had been. It was a land divorced from the world by time and space, and Salom was content enough to listen.

When he discovered that it would continue in that vein, he learned the first taboo of the valley.

It occurred on the afternoon of the second day. They had been riding at the limit of the herd, scanning the selvedge of gorse below the cypress for signs of wolves. As they turned back they saw a yak bull detach itself from its pit and jolt ponderously toward the herd. It was a huge animal and majestic in the bleached and swinging pennons of mane and tail. With an almost supercilious air of detachment the great beast mounted a docile cow and served her, and Muhlam shook his head admiringly and clucked his appreciation.

"A fine beast, Salom," he said.

"Yes. What name do you give it?"

"Name?"

"Yes. Does the bull not have a name?"

"A name? For a bull?" Muhlam looked at the boy in bewilderment, and then laughed. "We give no names to beasts. To people, yes. But not to beasts!"

"In China," Salon explained, "they give names to their beasts, as they do to people."

"What they do in China is of no concern to us," Muhlam snapped. His face was dark and hard, and before the boy could recover from his shock the headman had wheeled his horse and ridden off alone.

Salom knew now what he had previously only half-suspected, that the headman was acutely displeased at any reference to China, at any reference to a world beyond his own immediate surroundings. On the night of his arrival Muhlam, although obliged to ask the formal questions, had listened with obvious reluctance to any talk of the outer world; the next morning he had rebuked him for mentioning China. Salom rode slowly as he reflected on this attitude, and decided that it was the fruit of the headman's immense pride and assertive arrogance. He was the leader, the ruler, the king of all the world of which he had knowledge. Evidently he had no wish to be reminded that there were areas beyond his own domain and people over whom he wielded no jot of influence.

That day the subject was broached only once more, and afterward Salom accepted the headman's decision.

It was in the late afternoon, and they were riding together back toward the home thang. The shadows were moving swiftly, darkening the low brush and swirling almost liquidly down into the sand pits. The rabbits were swarming and the marmots, whistling shrilly, seemed fantastically large as they stood in alert silhouette against the deepening saffron. Since the earlier incident Muhlam had ridden in a brooding reverie, and even now his mood was somber as the dying day.

He was riding ahead of the boy and he did not turn when he spoke: "You like the valley?"

"Yes. I like the valley."

"And you wish to stay here?"

"Yes."

Muhlam swung in the saddle and the boy was startled at the anger written in the prideful face.

"Then we shall hear no more of China." The words came like chips of ice. "We do not wish to hear of China—nor of anything beyond the pass."

"Sometimes . . . sometimes it is hard to forget, Muhlam," Salom demurred, irritated by what he considered an unreasonable and even childish attitude. "Most of the years of my life were spent far from these parts. All but a few days of my life, and———"

"It gives you no right to talk of it!"

"Why, it is———"

"I say you must cease talking of it!"

"But . . . but why? I do not follow all this."

Muhlam reined his horse and waited for the boy to draw alongside.

"If you wish to live in the valley, boy, you must belong to the valley," he said.

"Can I not belong to the valley and yet still possess what has gone before?"

"No. There can be no other allegiance. This is a hard life. It demands all from a man. *All*—you understand? We people have always lived in this valley. Many lives have been given to it, and from all these lives we have made a way of living. There is no other way to live. Men say this is a hard valley, but it is hard mostly for those who are filled with a foolishness they mistake for wisdom, and in that folly they try to fight against the valley. Bah! The valley wins. Once or twice men have tried—but always the valley wins. *Always!* Not you, not I, nor anyone else, can defeat the valley. So if you would live here then you must forget other places so that you, too, can become a part of the valley. You understand?"

"I understand," Salom muttered, but his voice was resentful because he did not understand.

"Then we shall hear no more talk of these other parts, eh?"

"No. There will be no more talk." There was spite in Salom's quick, vicious tug at the reins.

"It is good." Muhlam was suddenly happy. All his hardness went, and he was instantly friendly with the boy and joked with him as they cantered back toward the thang. And soon Salom's anger had also faded in his joy at the burnished bronze of the beauty all around him. When he dismounted outside the tent the headman gestured to him and rode on toward Chunor's camp. It was not until later that Salom realized he had gone to impart to the others his decision on this new taboo.

It came to him that night, when Chunor and Lotor and Kaman visited at the headman's tent, and around the fire the talk was of hunting and the herds and the sores that were spreading on the back of Lotor's saddle horse, and when the herdsmen absorbed Salom into their discussion the talk became stilted and awkward.

V

Such things, however, were trivial shadows across the brilliance of those early days. After the first sting of its injustice he had even come to accept Muhlam's reprimand with humility, although he remained mystified by its unreasonable vehemence. Nevertheless, he was a mere stripling by contrast with Muhlam. Probably there was a good deal of logic in what the headman had said. He was not so obsessed by the valley's beauty as to regard this idyllic and fragmentary episode of summer as indicative of the valley's real character, slumberous now beneath the sun. There would have to be a pattern of living if the battle were to be won. And a boy should be grateful that a man of such prestige should take the trouble to offer advice, to submit his experience to ease the task of a stranger's assimilation into a new world. Moreover, he liked Muhlam, and respected him. And he liked Muhlam's family.

They had accepted him, and he was grateful to them. He thought of the woman, Kelinka, so kindly and patient and understanding, and surely as gentle and affectionate as any mother could be. And then, there was the child, Renzi. Salom's eyes warmed as he thought of that plump, dirty bundle. Of all the Muhlam family she was the only one with whom he had already developed an association of unreserved intimacy of thought. They responded without reservation to each other's curiosity; they had some intangible communion of restlessness and rebellion against the shackles of convention. And Salom was honest enough to confess that the child stimulated his own egotism. He knew that it was she, more than any other in the valley, who admired him as a man of another world, as a dauntless adventurer, a romantic and even mysterious hero. It was only Renzi that he took to the riverbank, out of earshot of others, so that he could talk about his travels; of the high city of Litang and the booths of the silversmiths in Derge, of the pass that opened onto the choked plains of China, of the forests of the Lolos and the mountains of the panda hunters, and, above all, of the wonders of the great city of Ch'eng-tu. Only Renzi knew the tale of the bridge called Liu Ting Chiao and of his father's heroism.

He had told Renzi of her father's ban on such talk—it would have been both unfair to the child and in all likelihood embarrassing to himself to have been other than frank—and as a result the secret conversations had the sharp and delicious tang of forbidden fruit. And it made Salom happy to have somebody in the valley to whom he could make articulate the things that were in his heart.

He would have preferred to tell these things to Veshti. He sensed that she was the core around which was packed much of his pleasure at being in the Valley of the Dreaming Phoenix—but he was less well acquainted with her than with her mother, less even than with Muhlam. She was always pleasant to him, and friendly, but after the first night of his coming the flash of interest, even of an immature coquetry, that she had possessed was no longer present. She was, in some curious way, detached from him. Sometimes he thought Muhlam might have been right in his criticism—she was too much of a dreamer, too inclined to live in some remote world of her own. It was a detachment not only from him. It was her attitude to the other men of the valley—even to the hulking Dochi to whom she was betrothed. Only once in three days had Salom seen them together, as Dochi rode by on his way to the high pasture, and then there had been a sort of reluctant recognition in her eyes but she had made no attempt to speak to him.

At the thought of the girl Salom's powers of analysis stumbled, because his own emotions lacked any clarity. The physical hunger that had wrenched at him three days before had not returned. It was the mental and spiritual Veshti rather than the physical Veshti that intrigued him now. And she was hard to understand—shy and elusive, like the frail-legged water birds one saw sometimes pecking among the rushes of the high tarns. They seemed so unafraid as one walked toward them, but then, just as one was almost close enough to examine the delineation of their bright plumage and the curved angles of their beaks, they were gone in a shimmer of oscillating legs or a whirr of wings. And the girl was like that. Bright and brilliant and eager, and with something of the frail loveliness of the upland birds, and yet when one approached her so that one's brain could grasp her meaning she was gone. Her head was bent as she became absorbed in some menial task, or her eyes were filmed by some remote thought, or she was looking at one with all the unmysterious insouciance of a child. Her real personality, whatever it was, was visible only as a distant mirage— and was equally uncapturable.

But Salom was young enough to possess impatience and wise enough to curb it. There were many weeks of summer yet, and one day he would know Veshti—and in the meantime there was the sun on a sea of grass rippling beyond his vision, and he had never been happier.

On the evening of the third day of his stay in the valley he sang as he forded the river behind Muhlam. Beyond the ruddy scarp of the far bank he could see the hump of the tent and the smoke smudged blue above it. On the edge of the pasture a gray horse, alien to the herd, was cropping. As they neared the tent Salom saw a stranger standing at the doorway looking toward them. He was a priest, tall and thin and with a shaven skull and a soiled burgundy habit thrown over a gown of yellow silk. He twirled a prayer wheel listlessly.

Salom looked at him and experienced a sudden chill, ominous and yet without reason. It was as if a blizzard had gathered in the sunshine and swept its savage course across the valley in the time that would be taken to blink an eye; it was the shudder that sometimes unreasonably prickles a man's skin and compels him to jest that a goose has walked across his grave.

Muhlam jerked his head toward the priest and looked back at the boy.

"Ah," he said, "it is Yanong. Yanong has come."

Salom dismissed the strange premonition from his mind as a moment of selfish resentment that another should intrude upon his new-found idyl.

BOOK TWO

Chapter Five

1

THIRTY-TWO years before, an impoverished farmer who hoed stunted crops in the bleak glen called the Valley of Thunder's Birth returned from his fields to discover that his wife had been delivered of a child. The event had happened prematurely but without apparent mishap beyond the fact that the baby had been born on the lower floor of the evil-smelling house amid the accumulated filth of generations of animals. The farmer entered to find the village crone who had acted as midwife slobbering incantations over the insensible mother, while the newborn infant squawled its misery from a heap of slime.

The farmer was a simple man, unconcerned by omens or symbols, and neither the squalor of the brat's birth nor the fact that the mother had at her mouth a froth of blood and internal injuries from which she was to die six weeks later could quell his delight. It was his first child, and it was a boy.

After the death of his wife the farmer devoted his energies to caring for the baby. Weeds strangled the untended fields of thin barley, a landslide choked the irrigating channel, two of his sheep were taken by wolves, and his best cow was slaughtered by a bear. The farmer was oblivious to adversity. He kept himself and the child alive for five years, and at the end of that time the boy was dressed in new garments and sent with a wandering caravan of priests to a near-by gompa, or monastery. As a present to the abbot the farmer dispatched a bag containing the silver coins that represented his life savings, with instructions that the boy should be trained as a priest and not be a mere servant of the monastery, untutored and despised.

The old man wept as he watched the column ride away—but his tears were joyful, for he had observed a custom of his country by giving his first-born son to Buddha. And then he staggered back to his desolate farm where, ailing and obsessed, he struggled to support himself for the day when his son should return to him as a lama.

It was fifteen years before the son came back to the Valley of Thunder's Birth. He came in the burgundy and yellow habit of a monk of Kham, his egg-shaped head shaved and encrusted with grime.

At the end of the glen, in a derelict hovel set within a broken farm, the lama Yanong found his father. The old man was an idiot, the spittle drooling at his slack jaw, his mad eyes suddenly aflame with the joy pent up behind fifteen years of misery.

Yanong stayed with his father for five minutes before he struck him to the ground because he had neither gifts nor money with which to pay the temple tithes.

Before the young lama rode out of the Valley of Thunder's Birth his father was dead of a broken heart and the vultures were already settling on his unmourned birthplace.

II

The evil of the lama Yanong was not a clever evil. His was the more dangerous evil of a fool given too much power. His training had followed the unmalleable pattern of religion in the frontier land of Kham, and as a fruit of that training he was no better and little worse than half the rank and file of his order.

His was the White Sect, a branch of the religion dominant in this one area of Tibet and little known elsewhere. It was an order that seldom produced scholars or mystics and which had not the slightest influence on the religious and political policies of the country as a whole—for these were arranged by the ruling Yellow Sect at distant Lhasa and Gyantse, and were generally endorsed by the Red Sect. And neither the Yellows nor the Reds really cared a whit whether or not the Whites observed these theological rulings. They were not regarded as sufficiently important.

The White lamas, however, made a formal pilgrimage to Lhasa once in every twelve years, and although they would walk the Holy Way beside the glittering Potala they would go less to pay spiritual homage than to engage in profit-making trade and barter. Abbots of these eastern highlands were observant enough to see that they were regarded in the capital as uncouth barbarians from the outer darkness of Kham, and when they returned home from their zealous travels invariably they would point out to underling priests and novices that the Yellow leaders of the land were decadent, greedy, materialistic and the perpetrators of unmentionable abominations. They would add that they were reaffirmed in their conviction that the White Sect was the only true sect, and insisted that they could not be induced to enter the Yellow order for all the silver mined in the land. They would then sell to less-traveled lamas some of the goods they had acquired in the capital—for prices from ten to twenty times in excess of the sums originally paid.

Yanong, as we have seen, joined this order at the age of five. He was taken to a small and unimportant monastery built on a high crag overlooking a river. He was taught by rote to mumble, chant, shout and whine a collection of one hundred and eight Tibetan liturgies which were written in swirling script on rectangular sheets of parchment clamped between covers of wood that were carved crudely with an image of Buddha seated upon a lotus.

Between his eighth and twelfth years he spent the hours of every day seated cross-legged in the temple courtyard, beneath the Banner of Benediction, where he yammered his lessons, turning the stiff sheets as if he could read. He still had not learned to read, nor to write—and in his lifetime never would. But he could recite any or all of the liturgies without hesitation or error, and with a faultless imitation of literacy.

In the lamasery, which was devoid of a single man of real learning, wisdom or spiritual integrity, he was taught other things. He was given a smattering of theological history and beliefs, a superficial knowledge of the great mystics of the past, the full details of the inhabitants and geography of the purgatorial phantasmagoria of Bado, through which spirits wandered between incarnations, the mechanics of temple ritual, full instructions for conducting funerary and other specialized mystic rites, and the various methods of dispelling demons with prayer wheels, incantations, long and short trumpets, and devil drums.

He was inculcated with a belief in the superiority of the White over all other sects of lamas, and received specific instructions for identifying and exorcizing the demoniac Black lamas, who occasionally wandered down to East Tibet to practice their occult arts and unmentionable rites of black magic.

The things he never did learn were more numerous than the matters upon which he accepted such painstaking instructions. He knew nothing of simple medicine, of hygiene, of personal cleanliness. He was ignorant of other countries and other peoples and knew nothing of any other religion. His years of training shaped him to be a theological parrot, and to this he added a wordly veneer of crafty practices.

At the age of fifteen he was allowed to leave the monastery for the first time, accompanying a small band of mendicant lamas on a journey which lasted only five weeks but which was sufficient to save him from complete insanity, the fate of more than one of his fellow novices. As it was, the years of parrot-teaching had established inside his egg-shaped skull a clogging and unbalancing morass of mumbo-jumbo. To this he added the animal cunning which he picked up on the road with a troupe of religious charlatans whose only purpose was to suck the blood of illiterate farmers and simple nomads. But beyond this he had come to young manhood having assimilated no wisdom and little knowledge apart from the method of preparing buttered tea for priests engaged in temple ritual, the correct placing of votive offerings and candles, the established prayers for specific occasions, the formula for extracting confessions, and the principles of soliciting tithes, bribes and gifts.

Before Yanong reached the age of twenty, the Living Buddha, leader of the White Sect and its only genuine scholar, visited the monastery to allocate positions. Yanong had hoped that he would be accepted as one of the Living Buddha's attendant lamas—a position he had coveted, aware that there would be rich pickings in such a princely entourage—but his request had never been considered, and, because he had no brain for anything else, he had been appointed mendicant lama along a chain of four unimportant valleys leading to the eastward. The nearest was the valley in which he had been born, and this had been the destination of his first mission. There had been no filial thoughts in his mind as he rode back to the Valley of Thunder's Birth after fifteen years.

Within ten years Yanong had come to enjoy his position. He was largely detached from authority. His territory afforded him pleasant perquisites and a status out of all proportion to his ability. He was revered as a holy man, as a great scholar, as a renowned mystic, as the "superior one" in the Valley of Thunder's Birth (where the circumstances of his origin had been forgotten), in Hammer Valley, in the Valley of Cloud Jade, and in the Valley of the Dreaming Phoenix.

For six months of every year he wandered the four valleys, living as an honored guest in the square houses of lowland farmers and in the black tents of nomads. It satisfied him that families should squabble among themselves for the privilege of giving their hospitality to him. He lived well, received many favors, was looked upon with a gratifying awe—except during the yearly visits of the Living Buddha, when Yanong's importance was eclipsed by the blinding glitter of the leader's glory—and cajoled or browbeat the people of the valleys into giving him a great many silver coins and pieces of jewelry, only a small proportion of which was ever taken from his fat purse and offered to the monastery officials when he returned at summer's end.

During the winters he remained at the lamasery, where he would talk of his experiences and listen to the sly tales of other wandering priests, and when alone in his filthy cell he would sometimes open his swollen purse, and sometimes he would sit before a brazier and think of the girls whose youth was being ripened by another season.

As a novice Yanong had taken the vows of celibacy that a long-dead saint called Tsong-keh-pa had instituted. In that period and for a year or two afterward, the older lamas with whom Yanong had become physically intimate had whispered to him of the ripe, sweet fruit of the valley's women, and their leering tales had given him the correct assessment of the value of his vows. His later travels had illustrated to him clearly the powers he could exercise over frightened farmers and nomads in availing himself of these fruits.

Although sex therefore played an important part in the life of the lama Yanong it was something that could never be separated entirely from furtiveness. The abbot, an old man whose sap had long since dried, talked of sex only in terms of insistence on the vows of celibacy. Moreover, it was whispered among the younger lamas that the Living Buddha, himself a man of impeccable moral character, would banish from the order any priest found to have broken such vows.

And yet Yanong could not remember a life free from this forbidden thing. As a boy, half a dozen monks had taken him to their cells and taught him secret pleasures, and, in turn, Yanong had, as an adult, given his knowledge to other young novices. But in the years of his travels as a mendicant he had abandoned the delights to be enjoyed with those of his own sex and had sought new and more ecstatic pleasures among the comely girls of the country. Again, negotiations were conducted always with sly whispers and arrangements were given the delicious emphasis of esoteric things.

In the four valleys that ran eastward toward the snow barrier the mountain people sometimes talked to Yanong in terms of a tale that no young girl had ever gone to her nuptials unbroken by the superior one. The tales were, of course, exaggerated, for the valleys were fecund and Yanong chose only the best fruits. The people spoke of these things with tongues clucking their admiration, and heads were often shaken in appreciation of the priest's unabated virility and limitless enthusiasm.

Many of these things had been in the mind of Yanong as he had come to the rising trail out of the Valley of Cloud Jade and plodded through the thickets of dwarf rhododendron toward the pass whose stone cairn looked down upon the Valley of the Dreaming Phoenix. He could see the little cluster of square stone houses, and the checkerboard of fields were gold with high barley and vivid green where the corn stood and the peas rippled. But he was anxious to reach the high pastures and he had not stopped at the village to tender spiritual comfort to the old people. He had looked to the eastward, where the valley rolled upward and the distant peaks were only a shimmer of light, and he had mopped his shaved skull and chanted softly as he rode on through the droning splendor of summer.

III

During the evening meal Yanong paid little attention to the young Chinese, and, indeed, Salom seemed to have been almost forgotten by the others. Renzi had been shifted from her position across the fire to make room for the distinguished guest, and she squatted beside Salom, her round eyes following the lama's every gesture, her lips moving as if synchronized with his almost unbroken flow of speech. But she said nothing, and only rarely did she squirm sideways and look up at Salom with a shy smile.

Kelinka and Veshti poked and blew at the fire, stirred at the cauldrons, fussed at the churns, and plied the visitor with buttered tea and tsamba until he threw his arms high in protest. Muhlam sucked at his long pipe of bamboo, nodding his head either with abstraction or impatience at the holy one's observations, sometimes interposing a question concerning herds or trails or the ailments of horses or the condition of the crops at the low fields or in the other valleys.

And Yanong would beam and say, "Back there your barley stands like a harsh forest, and the heads of the grain are fat as pregnant women." Or he would shake his head in scorn and say disparagingly, "There is an ugly blight on the crops at Thunder's Birth." Or, "The sheep are lean in Cloud Jade. Scraggy beasts, and diseased."

Once he smirked at Muhlam and said, "There is no valley to compare with Dreaming Phoenix—not for rich pastures and healthy animals and fine, strong people." Muhlam nodded his pleasure at this and glanced quickly toward Salom, but the boy's face was in shadow and he said nothing.

Salom was content to watch and to listen. He had no feeling of pique that another and more important visitor had robbed him of his novelty. The day's work had tired him and he had little energy for conversation, and in any case the newcomer was an interesting study. The holiness of the man's position had not the slightest influence upon him. Although he had little bitterness in his dislike for the faith of Tibet he gave it no allegiance. The old people who had sheltered him had been simple folk more engrossed in the primitive superstitions of their faith than its spiritual integrity and meaning, and they had been content to allow the boy to think for himself. For his part, he had talked little and watched carefully, and as a result had long since dismissed the priesthood as a brotherhood of parasites who were neither very clever nor particularly scrupulous. Along the northern caravan trails they had always seemed to him vastly more interested in their merchandising than in their mysticism. Some he had liked—bluff and genial scoundrels who had lived lustily but without sham. Most he had tolerated as unpleasant people presumably necessary to the pattern of the country. A few he had detested with a curious cold fury that puzzled and disturbed him.

In the jumpy firelight he studied Yanong, and found him no different from a hundred priests he had known. His face was already gross beyond its years, flabby and soft, with sensuality in its slack mouth and flaring nostrils, and with cunning eyes. His body was that of a man who had lived well and too easily; it was as if his life had been the direct antithesis to that of Muhlam, and the look of the two men underlined the difference. The priest had unhealed sores on his neck, and a furtive habit of brushing his finger tips together as if he were dusting grit from them, and his fingernails were almost chewed away.

In all his conversation there was an inordinate vanity. He talked volubly, but with an air that indicated some hidden profundity in every sentence. He jiggled impatiently when others spoke and invariably interjected his own remarks before they had finished theirs. In speech and gestures he made it clear to his audience that it was especially privileged to be able to hear some of the limitless wisdom of the lama Yanong. And Salom was a little disturbed to notice that both Veshti and Kelinka were evidently impressed and awed and even flattered by the presence of a man who was doubtless a charlatan and a bore like most of his brotherhood. Muhlam, on the other hand, seemed unconscious of the visitor's importance. But Yanong was careful to leaven his oratory with praise for Muhlam, or for Kelinka, and he dressed such tributes in smiles of almost cringing servility.

Salom, studying him, came back to the man's eyes. They were curious eyes, and less clever than the rest of the man, for they frequently betrayed his real feelings. There were hard bronze pinpoints in their black circles, and when he smiled it seemed that they became filmed and cold, and at other times they shifted slyly from one face to the other, calculatingly, and often they gave the lie to bland words and smiling mouth. And then, across the firelight, the thing happened.

Veshti had walked away from the fire and was stooping at the tent wall gathering sagebrush. Her upper body was naked, as it usually was during the evenings, and her robes and furs hung stiff and shapeless around her hips. Firelight was splashed across the curve of her shoulders and the soft swell of her back, and although her face and breasts were in shadow some reflection of the fireglow struck chips of flame from the ornaments at hair and neck and belt.

Salom's face softened as he looked at the girl and then he turned back to the lama, and his heart kicked and a sick chill clamped at his body. For the lama was staring at Veshti, and all the cunning and appraisal had flicked away from the hard eyes and in their place was a new expression—an intensity of lust that was pure animal!

The boy glanced again at Veshti, but she was intent on her task, and when he looked back to the priest the hot lechery had gone from his eyes and the unpleasant opacity was in them as he smiled at some remark of Muhlam's.

Salom's mind spun in a swift and unaccountable eddy of revulsion. He wanted to be sick, and then the nausea passed and he was taut and cold, and he thought of the curious chill that had come to him when he had first seen the priest standing by the tent of Muhlam. The priest was no longer simply a man grouped loosely with his brothers into a category of uselessness. He was suddenly a figure of positive evil. Salom could not know that this was the real beginning of a hatred and tragedy that were to fuse the incongruous entities of himself and the mendicant priest into an indivisible oneness of destiny; he could know only that he was sick and torn inside.

For an hour he sat, numb and wordless, and when the new churn of tea was buttered he accepted his wooden bowl dully. For some minutes Yanong had been silent. Kelinka, perhaps detecting something of the misery in the boy's eyes or his tense immobility, perhaps merely conscious of a measure of rudeness toward him, smiled across and said, "It is good that we have another man now to help us with the cattle."

Muhlam, suddenly jovial, nodded pleased agreement.

"Yes," he said. "And under my eye he improves. He rides well, and is good with cattle."

"Under the eye of Muhlam—" Yanong smirked—"any man would become good with cattle."

Muhlam inclined his head at the compliment.

"He will stay with us, here in the valley," he said.

"So? Then he will be added to my responsibilities. I am glad. It is good to assist people sift the problems that trouble the mind and might imperil the soul."

"Thank you," Salom muttered. "I shall need no help."

There was a moment of oppressive silence, and although Salom's head was downcast he knew that everybody was staring at him.

Yanong smiled. "My son, all people need help in such matters. There are many aspects of the teaching."

"I desire no teaching." The softness of the boy's voice was misleading. He suddenly felt cool, almost aloof from the situation, but in command of it. He lifted his head and looked steadily at Yanong and the priest flushed with quick anger.

"No teaching! Here then is talk from the mouth of an infant! Are you then an abbot or perhaps some learned mystic who knows the answers to all things? There is nothing then in the religion that suggests any mystery to you?"

"Nothing," Salom replied calmly.

"There must be a fine faith inside you if——"

"There is no faith inside me. I have no faith in this religion, nor any other." All the sickness had gone from him now that he had launched the attack. Suddenly, exultantly, he knew what he wanted. He wanted many things, but most of all he wanted to fight against evil. This man was evil. All his life there had been a vague dance around him of half-seen shadows and the shadows were evil. And he had run away. In Ch'eng-tu there had been evil—and he had fled. And now he had identified the enemy and it was time to fight him, for he sensed that this priest could wrench away from him the chance that had been given him to find his own happiness. So Salom looked contemptuously at the priest and said:

"To me there is no mystery in these things—merely stupidity and debasement and——"

"Salom!" The name was a whisper breathed by the startled women.

". . . and a way of maintaining a rabble of priests in sloth and corruption."

It pleased him that he spoke so detachedly. It would have been so easy to lose control, to flame into anger. Now he could savor his own detachment, his own maturely deliberate contempt by contrast with the querulous rage that bubbled from the almost incoherent priest. And then for the first time he saw the effect of his words on the others and the disdain that was his own youth fled from him and he was ashamed.

There was no dilution of the horror in the strained faces of Kelinka and Veshti. Yanong, half-risen, was shaking and sputtering his fury. Oddly, it was only in the stern face of Muhlam that the boy detected any sympathy, any trace of approbation. There was a tightness in the headman's jaw, but his eyes held a new interest, not entirely divorced from endorsement, and for a moment he thought that the giant was about to smile.

"This—this is dog's talk!" snarled Yanong. "By all the sainted spirits I will not—!"

"Enough!" Muhlam's shout throbbed in the smoke. Priest or no priest, he was still the head of his family and of his people. It was time to establish that authority.

"The tent of Muhlam," he said bitingly, "is not for men to squabble and scream like idiot women."

"The dwarf-man is at fault!" squealed Yanong, and at the insult Salom paled and started to his feet.

"Enough, I said!" Muhlam spat the words at the lama. "Who is to say the boy is at fault? Only I. I, the headman! And I say there is no proof that he is at fault."

"But . . . but you heard. . . . The foul heresies . . . the . . ."

"Quiet, priest! The boy is young. Perhaps he is even foolish. But if I, Muhlam, am allowed to think that many of the priests are a litter of babbling loons—which I do!—then why cannot this boy have contempt for them also?"

For a moment the shock of his words stunned Yanong, and then, while Kelinka's gnarled fingers plucked feverishly at her prayer beads and Veshti's eyes probed fearfully into the gloom as if she feared the swift onslaught of all the demons of Bado, the anger drained from his face, and he bowed in ironical submission, although a nerve twitched in his cheek and his hands trembled.

"It will be as you say, Muhlam," he acquiesced sauvely. "As you say."

But as he bowed again he raised his hooded eyes, and in the strange depths Salom saw twin pools of malice, and he knew that this was only the beginning.

The boy pulled his furs about him and walked from the tent.

IV

Outside the chill knifed him. In the sky's bowl stars chinked in the frost and a lopsided moon shed somber radiance across the fields. Beyond the tent was the rhythmic march of the high clouds, mustering their ranks for the downfall of soft night snow. The valley had abandoned itself to an evil, swarthy beauty.

Salom walked to the river, where pale stars floated like the hands of dead women. His anger had gone, his exultation had gone, and nothing remained but a residue of his sickness and a weakness as if in the aftermath of fever, and a shame piercing him that he had betrayed the kindness of Muhlam's family by causing a scene so unpleasant.

Many times before he had been questioned about his refusal to accept the faith of the country, but he had been able to state his case, simply and without spleen, and most people had understood him and let him be. Never before, on any question, had he been whipped to such a pitch of intolerance. Then why had it happened? Why at such a time, when all the demands of wisdom cried out for reticence?

He lifted his face to the impersonal immensity of the sky and the thin light washed over him and he knew the answer. The answer was Veshti—and the look in the priest's eyes as he had studied Veshti.

Yet such a look from a priest was not, in itself, so unusual. He knew well enough that it was a custom for wandering lamas to assuage their inevitable hungers with the women of the valleys and villages. And one had only to look at Veshti to know that men would have a hunger for her.

He closed his eyes and her image wavered under his lids with that same elusive magic. He looked up at the sky and the virginal maturity of her small body was patterned in the stars. He looked down at the river, where the frogs croaked their hollow discontent, and down the current floated her child's face, and it was fragile with something of the beauty of the valley itself.

Well, had he not hungered for her? He kicked at the spiky river grass in a sudden spasmodic embarrassment at the memory of his cravings on the afternoon of his arrival, at his very first sight of the girl. Then how could he tell that in his eyes also had not lurked the filthy thing that crouched in Yanong's? Was he any different from the priest?

He shied away from the question and sought new reasons. Perhaps, in actuality, his anger stemmed from something else, something rooted in deep-buried causes, perhaps some still-surviving prejudice engendered in him in the unremembered and unremembering days of a childhood that was another life, another world, another teaching. How much of the first forgotten years of life unconsciously shaped all the remainder of living? Or perhaps he had been right in that blinding, intuitive moment in the tent when he had seen Yanong as the symbol of all malevolence and himself as the fighter against the dark powers. Was it then merely a fear of another shattered illusion, a fear that here in this tranquil paradise had already appeared the disease that had forced him to flee the high gates and walls of Ch'eng-tu—the disease called humanity?

He heard the soft crackle of boots in the frozen grass, and then she was standing beside him, frail and without substance in the moon wash.

"Salom?"

He turned back to the river that whispered its hurry at the stones. A fish plopped in a tremble of quicksilver and the flurry scored black grooves through the dim images of stars.

"Salom?" She touched him lightly on the arm.

"Yes," he said, not turning, and aware of his churlishness.

"It . . . it is cold, Salom. Come back. It is too cold."

"He—the other one—he remains there?"

"Yes. But it is forgotten. Kelinka sent me for you. She says to tell you it is forgotten."

Then it was only at Kelinka's instigation that she had come for him? He shrugged his indifference. "That? It is of no real importance."

She moved between him and the river, and although he was not a tall man she had to look up to see into his eyes. Beneath him her face was unsupported in the darkness. The nebulous radiance outlined the silver curve of her cheek and he was stung again by the memory of the concupiscence that had flared for a moment in Yanong's eyes.

And he knew with a sudden thankfulness that his own hunger was different from the priest's.

"Salom, why did you say those things?"

"Does it matter? He angered me. The words came before I could check them."

"To me it matters. There was no cause for anger in what the holy one said. He desired only to help you. That was kind and——"

"It was not that. It was something else." He spoke impatiently, as if her words irritated him.

"How else could he have angered you?" she persisted.

"There are reasons that stupid children do not understand," he said cruelly.

He saw the hurt flood her eyes, but she looked at him steadily, and he knew the uncouthness of his words when she said, "I am a woman, Salom. Often women understand more than men believe."

"Some women," he muttered defensively, and then he realized his injustice. "Veshti," he said softly, "you would not understand badness in a man, nor evil. You see, child, you are young, and there are things——"

He broke off inquiringly. There was a strange expression of alarm in her small face.

"Why, what is it?" he asked.

Her tongue ran along her lower lip. "When you speak of evil,

Salom, it is not . . . it is not of yourself you speak? It is not as Dupken says?"

"What talk is this? What does Dupken say?"

"Dupken says——" She smiled nervously. "Dupken is crazed, of course, but she says you are a demon!"

For a few moments he had no words and then suddenly he grinned at her.

"I doubt if I shall ever be very interested in what Dupken says. But what would Veshti say about such things? Would Veshti think of me as a demon?"

She looked at him, and then she smiled as she shook her head. "No. Veshti would not think of you as a demon."

He sat down on the frosty grass and pulled her down beside him. "It is common talk then that I am a demon?" he said lightly.

"Oh, nobody gives heed to Dupken's ravings."

"Yet there must have been some doubt in your mind, Veshti?"

"Well . . ." She smiled at him self-consciously.

"And it explains something else," he said.

"What?"

"Something I could not understand. Yesterday, up with the herd, I was riding past the outer thang and Lotor rode by and burst into laughter. When I asked the reason for his mirth he said, 'Salom, you look less like a demon than any demon I have ever encountered before!' And he rode away in high spirits. I was very puzzled. Now I understand. And even you, Veshti, have heard this stupid talk—and half-believed it."

"I did not believe it."

"But when I said to you that you would not understand evil in a man you asked if it was of myself I spoke. You thought perhaps Dupken had not raved for once, eh?"

She pulled away from him. "And why should I not have doubts? You insult the holy ones. You spurn any faith. You speak strangely of evil things——"

"I had little to say of evil. There was much more I could have said."

"More?"

"Are your eyes useless, child, and your wits dulled?" He, too, was now sharp and impatient. "When I speak of evil it is of Yanong I speak. The holy one. The revered person whom I have insulted." His mouth curled. "He is the evil one."

"Salom!" She scrambled to her feet. "You had best have care of what you say in your ignorance. Yanong is wise and good—and the holiest of men."

The boy bridled. "Holiest of men? Then spare me from holiness! Or perhaps you joke with me? Then it is a better joke than this foolish talk of demons."

"You are so young," she said, with a pity that stung him. "You talk without reasoning. Until today you had never known Yanong—yet now you discuss him as if you were better acquainted with him than I who have known him since I can remember."

"Bah! It is no argument. Perhaps I still know him better than you."

"He has watched me grow from baby to child, from child to woman. He has been a good man and kind and full of wisdom, and always he had helped me with my problems. He is very clever and——"

"I am in no doubt, child, of his cleverness," he interrupted tartly.

For a long time she looked at him, so that he was uncomfortable in his bitterness, and when she spoke her words came with the patient softness of a mother speaking to a rebellious child: "You will grow to admire him as we do, Salom. Wait a little time. Try to understand. Would you care to have judgment passed upon you if we had known you merely a few hours? Would it be fair to you? If Muhlam had turned you away on the day you came, saying you were a man of evil, what would you have thought then? Wait, Salom. You will learn. Already *he* has forgotten what has taken place tonight, and the two of you can be friends."

The boy shrugged. "Let us talk no more of this matter," he said wearily.

"I am glad of one thing, Salom."

"The words you spoke. I am glad they came because of your anger and had no real meaning."

"What words?"

"About having no religion, believing in no faith."

He stared at her in astonishment. "You suppose they were mere words? It was the truth I spoke, Veshti. Only the truth."

She stood above him and suddenly she seemed very tall.

"Then," she said softly, "I am able to feel only compassion for you."

And for the first time since he had known her Salom was conscious of the real Veshti. No longer was she frail and meek, no longer a dreamer hedged off by some elusive mystery. Now he could see the hard core of her validity, the rigid credence she gave to things deeper than dreams and duties. He rose slowly and looked at her, at the tight fiber of her and the calm strength of her eyes, and he knew that he was confronted by a belief strong enough to resist any obloquy.

There was no longer anything to say. He saw himself as a tremendous emptiness into which the flood of melancholy poured. For the first time in his life he knew the hunger that every man without faith must at some time know—the envious hunger of one who sees another who can never lack the comforting food of the spirit.

Still she looked at him, and he experienced again the feeling of brutality that had shamed him as she had looked up from the tea churn and smiled at him and blown a wisp of hair from her face.

He pushed past her quickly and strode back to the tent. The fire was dying and the others were asleep, Yanong curled into his rugs on the grass beyond Kelinka. Salom rolled himself into the furs beside Renzi. The child snored gently. He could not sleep. The tent roof breathed in the night wind and he waited for the whisper of the snow, and in the hissing embers of the fire he could see eyes—the hot eyes of the lama, the calm eyes of Veshti.

It was a long time before she returned to the tent, and Salom was still awake.

Chapter Six

I

VESHTI was foolish in assuming that Yanong would easily forget the incident in Muhlam's tent. For all his unctuous servility, Yanong was a fighter. It was not in his nature to forgive an injury or forget an insult. He fought with the weapons he understood best, and whenever he could, he fought with another man's hand gripped on the knife.

On the morning after his arrival Yanong walked across to the tent of Chunor.

Chunor was a man almost of the stature of Muhlam, but lacking in much of the headman's dignity. Muhlam's weakness was his arrogance, Chunor's his slyness. Where Muhlam was fastidious in his dress and conservative in adornment, Chunor was both slovenly and garish. His trousers were torn, muddy strips hung from his boots, and his furs were split with age and never mended—but his ragged garb shone with jewelry.

Except for the bulging goiter that disfigured his neck he was not an unhandsome man, and, since dirt was normal rather than exceptional, he looked no more unkempt than the average herdsman.

He was well enough liked in the valley, and while he was pitied for possessing an idiot wife he was respected for his cunning and the numbers of his cattle. He would be a good headman, they said, if some accident should befall Hard Muhlam. Indeed, there were at least two rebellious herdsmen who had been heard to whisper that it was a pity he was not headman now. A man could argue and bargain with Chunor and sometimes sway his opinions; but Muhlam was so sure of his superiority that his decisions could never be questioned. Chunor had sternly and publicly rebuked the whisperers, and it had increased respect for him. Muhlam gave no attention to the reports, and his justice was no less impartial because of them. Nor had he commended Chunor for his loyalty—an oversight Chunor had not forgotten.

Chunor was a materialist. He wanted wealth and power, and he was patient. As the property of other herdsmen remained static or decreased Chunor's riches grew gradually, but he was careful that his increasing affluence was not evident. His apparel, and the clothing of his family, remained ragged. His livestock were never so numerous as the headman's flocks and herds. But he was the wealthier man, for a large store of silver pieces was hidden in a secret compartment of his prayer-cabinet, and many amulets and prayer-books had to be discarded and destroyed to make room for the mounting hoard of silver. His wealth had come to him in various surreptitious ways. It had begun six years before when he had been elected to take a wool-laden caravan of yaks westward to the markets of Batang. It was the custom at the end of every four years for the people of the valley to pool all the surplus fleeces and send them on the long journey to a trader in the west, where the wool was sold for sliver. Some of this money was used to purchase woven cloths, utensils and jewelery, and the balance was brought back and shared equally among all the people of the valley.

Chunor had led his weary caravan into Batang to discover that in the previous summer the surrounding valleys had been smitten by a curious disease that had rotted the limbs of the sheep. Thousands of animals had died and the fleeces of those that survived were thin, moulted and almost worthless. The fat, crisply-curled wool packed on his own yaks was the salvation of the weavers of Batang and those of the people who would otherwise have faced a bleak winter in their thin and outworn robes. But Chunor was a business man. Day after day he procrastinated. In the chang booth he talked of moving his freight north to Litang in search of better prices. At the finish, he received for his wool seven times more silver than had ever been paid before to a man from the eastern valleys.

But when he returned home his face was long. He told Muhlam and the herdsmen of the great glut of fine wool that had inundated the merchants of Batang from all the grazing grounds of Kham, forcing prices down to the lowest levels ever known. The people had accepted the misfortune philosophically and the meager store of silver was divided equally among them, and because of his remorse at what he regarded as the failure of his mission Chunor had refused to accept his share, and that had been a little more to divide among the others, and the people were grateful to him.

From that point Chunor had progressed with extreme caution. He rarely did any business twice with the same man—it was usually a matter of lending small sums of money at interest, and preferably for purposes that the borrower would not talk about—and there were long intervals between transactions.

So it was that Chunor's position as the richest man in the Valley of the Dreaming Phoenix was known only to Chunor. Yanong was as ignorant of the fact as anyone else, but he was not unaware of another fact that stemmed from the hidden one. This was Chunor's desire for power.

It was largely on the basis of materialism that Chunor coveted the position of headman. He would then have been able to trade more openly—and much more profitably. And he would also have been able to live at the standard befitting his wealth. He wanted, for instance, the best house in all the valley, and the best house was owned by Muhlam. It was a house of three levels, and Chunor's house was only of two levels and smaller than the headman's. Three years before, Chunor had gathered the stones and begun the work of adding a third level to his own house, but Muhlam has asked his intentions and then had flown into a great rage and had forced him to cease work.

Chunor would have liked the position of headman, but, unprepared to risk any stake on such an ambition, he was willing enough for the position to go to his son, Dochi, when Muhlam, at the age of forty-five, would be compelled by tribal tradition to relinquish his leadership in favor of a younger and stronger man. When that time came Chunor had no doubt who would be virtual leader of the valley. His contempt for his simpleton son contained no paternal leavening. Chunor's fingers itched for the feel of the strings to which his puppet would dance.

At the same time, six years was a long wait for the fulfillment of ambition, and he was never blind to the fact that a chance might present itself earlier. It would have to promise the certainty of success, for even Chunor's wealth would be of no avail against the wrath of Muhlam should the headman suspect treachery. So Chunor waited.

II

He felt a prickle of irritation when he saw Yanong trailing thoughtfully toward his tent. Chunor shared Muhlam's contempt for the priesthood, although he was cautious enough to make the necessary motions of obeisance, both material and spiritual, as a business investment in his future incarnations. But he gave money less willingly than he gave lip service.

His mouth curled as he looked toward the monk.

"Shamble on, Button-skull," he muttered derisively. "I pray your begging bowl is small!"

Yanong called a greeting as he approached. "Does all go well with you?" he added.

"Well enough, holy one," Chunor replied deferentially, making a slight bow. He respected Yanong's cunning, and it was well to keep friendly with such a man. "Although," he added sadly, "it will be a bad season. The valley becomes less wealthy with every year. The cattle are in poor condition——"

"So? I thought I had never seen the pastures so lush, nor the cattle so sleek."

"No, Yanong. Your eyes are turned into your prayer books. It is the worst I have known in many years. And the snows will come early. I can feel it. We shall have blizzards before the next moon is in."

The two men looked instinctively toward the remote peaks, but there was no menace in their unsullied glitter.

"Ah, me," Chunor added, "there will be thin bellies and empty bins in the houses before we see the next snows melt."

"Now I would not have thought that. But then I know not the lore of the mountain as you do. Perhaps then I would be wise if I left earlier for the monastery?"

"You would be wise, indeed. The geese are already moving."

Yanong smiled his gratitude for the advice. "A humble servant of the gods knows little of these material matters. We have other things to occupy our minds. And in many things we are as children beside such wise and stalwart men as you, Chunor."

The herdsman was aware of the reason behind such flatteries. "You will honor us by taking tea?" he asked, anxious to postpone the inevitable haggling over tithes.

Yanong inclined his head and followed Chunor into the tent.

Inside it was almost impossible to see anything for the clouds of smoke and steam that swirled from a half-extinguished fire where the cauldron had fallen from a rakish crossbar, but it was apparent enough that the living space was a shambles. Dupken was crouched over the wet, hissing ashes, prodding ineffectually, muttering incoherent curses.

"Dupken!" Chunor cried in anger, and his shrewd eyes hated her. "Bestir yourself, slut! We have a guest."

"Eeeee!" The crooked shape leaped grotesquely upward, and her eyes glittered over the priest's habit and his benign face. "Ah, so the superior one consents to visit the humble dwelling of Chunor!" She sniggered spitefully. "I had thought we would have been of no importance after the family of the mighty and exalted Muhlam."

Yanong smiled his tolerance. His finger tips dusted lightly together. "My flock are of equal importance in the eyes of the gods, daughter," he said piously. "From the highest to the lowest—all are one. The gods know where true holiness lies. And it is not always with the highest."

Chunor looked up sharply. There was an edge to the priest's words. Dupken's eyes swiveled back and forth between the two men.

"Eeeee!" she muttered. "There cannot be too much holiness among the highest when they harbor demons!"

"Quiet, slattern!" roared Chunor, and raised his hand, but Yanong's eyes narrowed and he peered at her with a new interest.

"What is this thing you say, daughter?" he asked.

"The crone is a fool," Chunor snapped. "Her mind is crazed and she is obsessed."

"Let her talk," Yanong murmured. "Let her talk."

Chunor looked at the priest, and then his own expression altered and he dug his elbow viciously into his wife's ribs.

"Speak up, woman!" he commanded irritably. "Are you dumb as well as mad? The holy one has questioned you. Tell him of your dream."

"Dream? It was no dream!" She spat at him and the white gobbet fell on his sleeve, and he wiped it away. Dupken was rocking herself backward and forward, moaning softly. "It was a vision. A *vision!*"

"Then tell it!"

"A vision came to me, most superior one," she whined. "Chunor calls it a dream because he is an idiot in such matters. It was a vision. In it I saw Minya Konka, the sacred peak. It was quiet and beautiful . . . and then . . . and then upon the white slopes something appeared. A shape, holy one . . . a shape that grew greater and greater in size. . . ." A spasm seized her and she choked and coughed. "And then the shape took clear form and I saw that it was the demon Dorjilutru, and he danced on the ice and he was terrible! Oh, so terrible, holy one! He danced on skulls—and while the skulls were without flesh or features I knew them for the skulls of the people of the valley. I knew them! Clearly I could see the garb the demon wore. Firstly, it was——"

Chunor saw the impatience furrow Yanong's brow and cuffed his wife. "Tell the story then, idiot!" he snarled. "Has the superior one the whole of summer to listen to your driveling?"

Dupken glared her malevolence, but resumed with some sulkiness: "Then even as I watched, holy one, the demon changed in color and his robes were blue now, and patched and shabby. Even his form changed. He became young and fair enough to look upon. He smiled at me and at first I thought his smile was gentle, but then I saw that it was a smile of great wickedness. Eeee! Even in my trance I was chilled to the very marrow. Do you know why?" She peered at them questioningly, anxious to savor the suspense, but Chunor's tight mouth compelled her to continue quickly.

"Because, standing there on the sacred mountain, was the young stranger who is made so much of by the headman and his family!" Her voice squeaked triumphantly and her eyes were everywhere. The wisp of hair quivered at her chin as she clawed toward Chunor with angry hands.

"You laughed at me, Chunor!" she snarled. "You said I was witless. But I know! Dorjilutru is in Muhlam's tent, and that fool Kelinka pets him and makes a great ado about him. Bah! Yet you laugh and knock me to the ground. Oh! I tell you there will be no laughter when all of us are mangled as we sleep——"

She quailed before Chunor's gesture and subsided into spiteful mumbling.

Yanong's expression was difficult to define, but after a moment of thought he selected an area of the floor that was not too deep in refuse and seated himself. Chunor kicked aside a bundle of stinking rags and followed his example.

"This, my daughter, is a very serious thing," Yanong said, rubbing a soiled finger along his oily nose.

"You would be unwise to pay attention to her droolings." Chunor advised contemptuously. "She and delusion are regular bedfellows." He spat into the fire.

"Wait. Do not be hasty, Chunor. I have already made a note of this young cockerel's lack of holiness. The woman here is without doubt obsessed. You will understand I mean no insult to you when I say that there are some in the valley who say her words have no worth. But sometimes the gods select strange messengers for their tidings."

Chunor watched him through half-closed eyes. There was something in the priest's mind that went beyond spoken words. Yanong would know as well as he did himself the folly of attaching the slightest credence to any of the ramblings of Dupken. Far beyond the limits of the valley her demon-obsession was a subject for a crop of jokes, even though such mysteries were by no means the regular material for jests of any sort. There was something more, but Chunor had no intention of declaring himself. He waited.

"Yes, strange messengers," Yanong continued. "And I myself have heard the young dwarf-man openly deride our beliefs." He looked at Chunor slyly. "Muhlam was perhaps not wise in allowing the stranger shelter without more investigation. One would have expected our good friend to have shown more foresight."

"Muhlam is a fine man," Chunor said.

"Indeed. Indeed, Chunor. Nobody admires him more than I. But even the best of us may err."

"Yes." Chunor shook his head sorrowfully. "Muhlam, I think, sees only good in all people. And yet it is, as you say, a strange thing—even a sad thing—that a leader in whom the people place so much trust should take into the community a stranger about whom nothing is known—yes, and about whom Muhlam wishes nothing to be known." He paused reflectively. "I thought it was curious when Muhlam issued his order against the questioning of the boy."

"What order? This is something of which I am ignorant."

"Two days ago—before you came—Muhlam rode over here to forbid us asking questions of the boy concerning his origin or whence he came. He told me to convey his request to Kaman and Lotor, which I did."

"Indeed! That was most curious. Muhlam himself has some startling thoughts about our faith."

"Muhlam is a fine man. He is perhaps too arrogant. That is his fault. But he is a fine man, holy one. It is because of that very fact that my heart is sore for him. We trust him and look to him for leadership. Of course it is also because of that feeling of trust that we do not expect him to expose us to unnecessary peril merely to gratify a whim of his own."

"Of course," Yanong agreed, and there was a long silence between them.

Once Dupken attempted to say something but Chunor said, "Silence, slut!" and she cringed back into the shadows. Chunor decided it was time to drop a pebble into the pool. Only a small pebble, but it might make some ripples.

"There was talk," he said, "of a Black lama heading in the direction of this valley. Perhaps just the usual gossip of the tents, eh?"

Yanong stared at him. Intuitively he knew that Chunor lied, and his was the intuition of another liar. "Perhaps it is not gossip, Chunor," he said. "I heard the tale myself—in Hammer Valley."

Chunor's eyes snapped. The pebble had created ripples. "There is a question I would ask. What if this stranger were indeed a demon, Yanong? What then?"

The priest's gaze fell and for a few moments he was thoughtful.

"In such circumstances," he said finally, "it would be difficult to blame the people if they turned against the headman—and perhaps chose another who would not let pride destroy his sense of consideration for others."

Chunor picked his nose abstractedly and contemplated the end of his forefinger. He said nothing, and in the silence there was only the mumbling of Dupken:

"Eeee! That Kelinka is too big for her boots now that she is headwoman, too. Gay clothes and bright stones—she thinks of nothing else. Bah! I mind her as a girl. She was not so haughty then."

There was a sudden scuffle from beyond the tent, and Dupken looked up hurriedly. Three distorted shadows were crouched against the tent fabric. She darted outside shrilling her rage, and the men heard the sound of cuffing and startled yelps and the woman's voice pitched high and venomous.

"You addleheads! Saintly Buddha, what lives have I lived to

deserve such worthless spawn! Spying on your elders, eh? Eeee!" Another howl, then: "Well, since you are here you had better pay your respects to the holy lama. Get inside!"

Chunor's brow drew down irritably, but Yanong smiled blandly as he chewed on a hangnail. Three of Chunor's sons stumbled into the tent, still dodging their mother's flailing arms.

Chunor stared at them in unconcealed disgust, silently loathing them for witless louts. "Well?" he grunted. "Make your bows and get out! Or are you such dizzards that you do not know how to greet the lama?"

They fumbled and nudged one another, but each made a jerky bow and mumbled a word or two of greeting without any greater disaster than the youngest falling over an up-ended churn and sprawling on the floor.

Chunor jumped up and kicked the boy savagely in the side. "Out!" he said coldly. The boy scrambled, sniveling, to his feet and lurched out of the tent with the second son stumbling after him. Only Dochi remained, shaking his head in embarrassment and shuffling stupidly, while his troubled eyes never left the lama's face.

"Well, clodpoll?" Chunor raised his fist. "Why do you wait?"

The boy cringed but stood his ground. "I want to know about the demon." His voice was muddy with some inner tumult. "I want to know about the Chinese demon. He is after the girl, Veshti, and she is mine." He looked wildly toward his parents, seeking corroboration. "She is promised to me for my woman, to do with as I please. Is it not so? And if the demon touches her I . . . I will *kill* him!"

Yanong's eyes were filmy as he smiled to himself and his fingers stroked his prayer beads.

"Do not be hasty, my son," he said understandingly. "The Chinese will not touch the girl. I myself will see to that. As the earthly representative of the gods it is my personal duty to protect innocence from evil." He smiled at them with great tolerance. "Although you must remember that I have not said the boy *is* a demon. That is yet to be proved. At the same time—" he paused and smoothed his hand across his filthy skull—"it also has yet to be disproved."

Suspicion still lurked in Dochi's eyes. "But she is mine?" he insisted, and his wet mouth trembled. "She is promised to me?"

"She is yours, Dochi," said Chunor, frowning. His crafty eyes flicked a challenge at the priest. "It is my wish, and, for that matter, the wish of our friend Muhlam, that my son should have this girl—and soon."

Yanong made no reply beyond smiling his acquiescence. Chunor spat heavily and rubbed it into the grass with the heel of his ragged boot.

III

Chunor strapped the reins tightly to the horse's foreleg to serve as a hobble and studied the herd. The last laggard had crossed the stream and the beasts had settled down into a slow-moving sea of placid rumination. Apparently Salom was satisfied that the restlessness had gone, for he was cantering his horse carelessly down the flanks of the mob, and beyond the pasture Chunor could see Muhlam and Kaman riding back to the cropped-out thang in search of wayward calves.

The new pasture was a heaving mat, black and shaggy, now that the four herds had been driven in and the low and bleat and snuffle of the animals were as constant and rhythmic as the breath of the wind in mobile grasses. Chunor's eyes watched the green sway of the plumes. It was good grass, fat, and taut and well-juiced. Six weeks of good feed—and all the herds combined for the last of summer's grazing on the last and highest of summer's pastures. Beyond, the green flow blurred into scarred claypans and the clay gave way to a ridge of slate and beyond the slate were the gorse patches and the twist of the timberline and the harsh stubble that prickled up to the rim-sharp pass.

Chunor nodded his satisfaction. He was a fine herdsman, and no fool in his knowledge of beasts and grasses and weather. Even if the blizzards came early nothing could prevent it now from being a fine summer. Never had he seen such luster on the flanks of the cattle, never milk sacs so distended.

He blew his nose between his fingers and stooped to wrench away a clump of dead sagebrush. From a sun-baked boulder his hard fingers scrubbed a fistful of lichen. He squatted and flicked his flint-striker into a pinch of tinder and blew on it until the smoke curled around a tiny red smolder. He tamped this into the moss with his thumb and puffed again, and the flames from the tiny kernel of fire were licking at the eager sagebrush by the time Salom came.

Chunor grinned up at him.

"Well, Han-man," he said, "it was a good move, eh?"

"I thought those two calves—at the stream——" Salom shook his head in self-deprecation.

"No, no. It was good. Your action was wise. I always maintain it is best to let them run when they lose the ford. They swim. No matter how swift the water or deep the pools—they swim. Calves never drown, not in clear water. In mud, sometimes—but never in clear water."

Salom dismounted. Although his self-criticism had been the mere formality demanded by custom, and he was well enough aware that his handling of the animals had been above reproach, he was still pleased at the herdsman's approval. Chunor had never before displayed more than a perfunctory interest in him.

Chunor nodded toward the fire:

"We will take tea, eh? I have a small churn in my saddlebag—and butter. It has been a strenuous afternoon, and some tea will be good."

"It will be good," Salom agreed.

When they had consumed the last of the greasy beverage Chunor took a long pipe from his jacket and filled it with coarse tobacco and offered it to Salom, but the boy shook his head.

The blue smoke dribbled from Chunor's mouth and into his half-closed eyes. "Do they not smoke the long pipe in China then?" he asked.

"It is not permitted to talk of China," Salom said warily.

Chunor laughed softly. "You mean Muhlam's order? It is one of his obsessions. But there are no others here, and you and I, Salom, are traveled men. Muhlam has never traveled and so he resents those who have. It is his pride. When I returned here after my travels he was the same. He would have no talk."

"And to where did you travel, Chunor?" the boy asked, his eyes cautious. There was something behind the big man's friendliness that he distrusted.

"West of here. To Batang."

"I know Batang. Each year I used to travel with a caravan to Litang and down to Batang."

"Oh? It is six years since I was there."

"Six years?" Salom thought for a moment. "I was there six years ago. I remember it well. It was the bad year. We went down to buy skins but there was nothing to be bought. There was nothing of anything to be bought. It was the year the plague swept the flocks and killed them."

"No, no," said Chunor quickly. "You must be wrong in your years, boy. Six years ago was the year of the fat flocks. There was wool such as I have never seen—and from all the parts of Kham."

"I thought——"

"You are a year out in your counting perhaps," Chunor said blandly. "I recall now that the merchants did speak of a bad season the year before, of threadbare fleeces and a disease that smote the flocks."

"Perhaps it was seven years," Salom said. "It is easy to lose count of a year."

Chunor lolled back on his elbows. "They tell me," he said conversationally, "that there was a difference between you and Yanong in Muhlam's tent."

Salom looked up sharply. "So you heard of it?"

"A whisper, nothing more."

"It was of no importance. I have forgotten it."

"But has Yanong also forgotten? He is a cunning one, that priest."

"It is forgotten."

"Of course." Chunor smiled amiably. "In any case, I pay no attention to the gossip of the thang. If I did I would be eating malice and whispers with every mouthful of tsamba. If I even gave heed only to the tales brought me by that draggled trull the gods saw fit to burden me with as wife there would be no time left for the flocks and herds. Do you know—" his expression sharpened— "the fool came to me with a story that you were a demon?" He laughed and smacked his fists together, as if in appreciation of a well-pointed jest.

"I know," Salom said quietly. "Veshti told me."

"Only an idiot would pay attention to Dupken's drivelings. You must take no notice."

"I take no notice. I am merely sorry that Dupken——"

"Oh, she is mad. It is only my regret that it has to be *my* woman who is the laughingstock of all the valley, who is the one to offer insults to a distinguished traveler." He stared at the ground and sighed softly. "Yet once she was beautiful. She was happy and she sang and she was beautiful. Her madness came in giving the first child."

Chunor's eyes were looking far beyond him, beyond the humped and slanted contours of the valley, beyond the peaks, back into some remote point in time when an agony had come to him.

Salom suddenly felt sorry for this man in the ragged robes. His face was strong and sorrowful with a hidden dignity, and its shallow amiability had gone and in the dark eyes there was a deep weariness in the place of the usual slyness, and then he looked back at Salom and grinned and the brief thread of sympathy snapped. Salom felt unaccountably embarrassed in the other's company. He wanted no more talk with him, no more of his superficial friendliness, nor his oddly disturbing attempts to push forward some kinship of common interests. He scrambled to his feet.

"You are not going?" Chunor asked. "Come, sit for a while and you will tell me of your journey from China."

"No. I am to meet Muhlam by the second ford. My thanks for the tea, Chunor." He nodded and walked to his horse.

Chunor's hard eyes watched the boy ride upstream.

He had wanted to talk more to him. There had been other things he had planned to say, other questions to ask. Yet even such conversation as had passed between them had not been profitless.

There could easily be some moment in the future when Chunor might find it convenient to be able to say that it was he who had warned the boy against Yanong, he who had pointed out to him the worthlessness of Dupken's ramblings. And if that moment did not arise in the future then it was equally easy to forget such a conversation.

Chapter Seven

I

SALOM was never able to say with certainty when the first uneasiness had come to him. It was like the beginning of a ground mist, furtive, groping, scarcely visible. By the time he was consciously aware that a shadow had darkened the serenity of the valley the vague uneasiness had developed into a hostility which, for all its uncertainty, was inescapable.

It had been synchronized with the coming of the man Yanong, and yet in the beginning there was no evidence to suggest that the priest was directly responsible. He had expected repercussions on the day after the argument in Muhlam's tent, but it had been a day like any other. There had been too much to do in moving the herds to the new pasture, and, indeed, the only incident of any note had been the reverse of hostile—it had been the friendly overture of Chunor, the second man in the valley.

More than a week passed before the hostility had become clearly manifested, and in the intervening period the subject of the quarrel had never been raised.

For a time, of course, some measure of embarrassment had been unavoidable, particularly when Yanong was present in Muhlam's tent, but the monk, with a tact that surprised the boy, spent the greater part of his time visiting the other tents, and riding between the two upper encampments on an industrious campaign of stipend-collecting.

For a day or two a new gleam of interest had lingered in Muhlam's eyes. The presence together of Yanong and Salom seemed to stimulate him, and he was pleased to be particularly genial to the boy, while rebuffing the sycophancy of the monk. He abandoned the sport when he realized that it had no effect on the attitude of the holy man, who was as bland and obsequious as ever. Such exchanges were not lost on Kelinka, and because they disturbed her she directed most of her energies toward the entertainment of Yanong and she filled the difficult silences with artificially eager questions about the most trivial things.

So far as Salom was concerned, only Renzi was articulate on the subject of the dispute. At the first opportunity she dragged the boy to the riverbank and in earnest words made it clear to him that she ranged her plump little body squarely alongside his in this new and exciting iconoclasm, and, while he realized that her grasp of the situation was, at best, limited, he was oddly touched by the knowledge that not ten thousand demons nor the prospect of wandering for a hundred lives through the sixteen dismal hells of Bado would shake her loyalty by a hairsbreadth.

Veshti made no reference to anything that had happened. She was friendly enough to him, but the elusive nature of her personality was intensified. Occasionally, when she strode across the flowered fields, he was conscious again of the strength and dignity that she had displayed beside the riverbank, and he knew that he could not talk to her of the things that troubled him.

He was happier, in the long bright days, with the bawdy companionship of the herdsmen—until that companionship, too, began to change. At first it was only a sudden silence that hovered awkwardly about a group as he approached. It was a pair of eyes quickly averted when he looked around. It was a whisper behind his back, never quite heard. It was a crone groping for her prayer beads as he passed by one of the encampments.

The herdsmen still visited the tent of the headman and talked and laughed and gossiped, but he found himself imagining that there was a taint of artificiality in their manner. Seldom did they speak to him, but this could be explained in more ways than one. There was Muhlam's ban on talk of the outside world. It was obvious from Chunor's words that most of the herdsmen would have heard the tale of his argument with Yanong, and some would naturally give tacit support to the monk. And probably it could have meant nothing more than that he had ceased to be a novelty and was being relegated to his proper status in a gathering of older, wiser men.

II

It was warm on the high trail. Salom wished it was Lotor who was riding with him, for he was hungry for cheerful talk. Kaman's normal taciturnity had given way to complete silence. His long, sad face was steeped in its customary melancholy and Salom's few remarks were answered only by dolorous grunts. Constrained by this cheerless companionship, Salom began to sing lustily a song of his childhood. Although now scarcely remembered and without real meaning it was one of the few fragments that had lingered in his memory from a forgotten Chinese infancy. The foreign words were now nothing more than a rhythmic gibberish and he would never remember the mother who had crooned them to him. It was a song that Chinese herdsmen had sung fifteen centuries before:

> Who says you have no sheep?
> Three hundred the flock.
> Who says you lack cattle?
> Ninety are the black-lips.

It was tuneful and it had all the essence of bravado, and even if it meant nothing it at least saved him from another attempt to make conversation with the dour one.

Kaman's reaction was curious. For a little time he listened intently to the words that were no more intelligible to himself than to the singer, and then an odd expression of fear took command of his face. He reached furtively toward his throat, where prayer beads hung against his furs, and deliberately dropped back until he was far behind the boy.

Salom did not realize he was alone until the sheep, frightened by the dive of a lammergeyer, bunched foolishly and began to swing toward a stony gully where wolves lurked.

Salom turned quickly and started at seeing the man so far back on the trail.

"Kaman!" he called. "They go toward the wolves! We must turn them!" But Kaman merely pivoted his horse and galloped away down the slope, leaving the boy to block the animals alone.

After his anger had subsided, Salom almost persuaded himself that Kaman has not heard his call—although the man was not blind and could scarcely have failed to see the terrified swirl of the flock—and he would have thought nothing more of the matter except for the disquiet that existed by now in his mind, and because of another incident that happened next day.

Not far from the tents pitched by the lower trail was a Mani Wall—the customary lopsided prayer cairn consisting of hundreds of boulders, slates and pebbles each carved with the enigmatic supplication "Om Mani Padme Hum." Such monuments to spiritual belief had never aroused in Salom any emotion other than a faintly scornful amusement, except when a line of script beautifully carved or the flowing formalism of a graven Buddha appealed to some inherent aesthetic sense within him. But he was well enough acquainted with the country's lore and he knew that all prayer in Tibet adhered to an inflexible pattern of clockwise movement. A prayer wheel was spun in a clockwise direction; to reverse the spin would be to unsay all the prayers so laboriously written and packed within the charm cylinder of the wheel. Water wheels erected at brooks and cascades and festooned with prayer flags had to conform to this pattern of movement (a fact which gave the diabolic Black lamas endless amusement as they reversed the wheels under cover of darkness); trails and paths and roads invariably divided into two branches to circle any cairn or wall of prayer stones, and custom was rigid in its insistence that all horsemen or pedestrians should pass to the left of the stones lest the countless prayers be nullified—to the dire peril of the community whose spiritual security was pinned to the protective strength of such strong talismans.

In spite of his skepticism, Salom always observed such customs of the country, but on this occasion he was engrossed in thoughts of Veshti and he rode to the right of the pile of stones; indeed, he was not consciously aware of his action until he was startled by a piercing scream. He wheeled to see a dirty, gaudy woman standing by the trail, watching him as if petrified. Then she gathered her ragged skirts around her and ran, stumbling toward the tents.

That afternoon he returned earlier than usual to Muhlam's tent. Kelinka was squatted outside the tent door, her skirts bright around her, her furred and trinketed head nodding in the sunshine as she stitched at one of her husband's saddle cloths. She started as Salom's shadow fell across her.

"You return early, my son," she said, with no real surprise. Kelinka was not frequently surprised by anything men did. Salom tossed his shapeless old hat into the grass and sprawled beside her.

"Yes." He watched her hands and the sun streaking on her silver rings. He liked watching Kelinka's hands. They were callused and none too clean, but they had strength and courage and patience and tenderness. "Are you alone, good mother?"

"All alone, Salom. Veshti has gone to the milking. Renzi is——" She smiled at him. "Nobody ever knows where Renzi is. Muhlam is not back from the high thang. And Yanong visits his flock."

Salom plucked a grass stalk and chewed on it, savoring the acid on his tongue.

"Kelinka, I . . . I am troubled."

"Tell me of it."

Her busy fingers did not hesitate, he noticed. There could not be anything very wrong if Kelinka's hands never faltered in their multitudinous tasks.

"It is difficult to tell, Mother. Perhaps I read too much into things that happen, things that are not as important as I think."

"Yes, my son?"

"Well . . . it seems that people avoid me, and whisper as I pass. Yet I cannot tell."

He remembered the analogy that had come to his own mind.

"It is as if a shadow is spreading across the valley," he explained. "When I came here first I was happy, but now it seems that a cloud has driven across the sun, and I am chilled."

And now her hands were motionless and her eyes steady on his. "Are you sure, my son, that the cloud is not in your own heart?"

"My heart?"

"Your eyes are searching out for reasons that might be found inside yourself."

"No, Kelinka. Men are talking together and laughing, and then I approach and there is silence. I turn suddenly and people are watching, and before their expressions change I feel that they dislike me. There are whispers that I never quite hear. Things like that."

"And what else?"

"Well, let me tell you what happened today. I rode the lower trail past the prayer cairn, and because my thoughts were on other matters I did not see the stones and rode to the right of them. A woman—I do not know what woman—ran into the fields screaming. In itself, I suppose it was nothing, but there have been these other things—and it troubles me."

"It is what I meant, Salom, when I asked if the cloud was not in your own heart." Her head was nodding. "See, my son, if you had a rug that you treasured above all other possessions, would it anger you if a stranger stamped across it with muddy boots?"

"Yes, I suppose it would."

"Then you, too, must be careful where you walk. We have a treasured thing. It is a faith in our beliefs. To many of us its value is more than life. It is not good that you should trample down this thing."

"But, Mother, it is not *my* belief!"

"Salom, you are young. You are free to believe or not to believe, as you will; but you must grant the same right to others. You insult our priest whom we admire and respect. It is now forgotten, but it should not be allowed to recur."

"It was not the belief I was angry with—not so much. It was the priest himself. I am tolerant enough of this faith or any other faith—but it is this—this priest."

"My son, there is a proverb in this land that runs: 'The only way to reach the gods is through a lama.'"

"In any calling, Mother, there are bad servants as well as good."

"That may be. But there is this other thing. You know well enough the ruling concerning prayer walls. Even if you care nothing for the many patient hands that cramped over the carving of these stones, you must show respect for their devotion. Perhaps it was foolish of the woman to scream, but it was a bad thing you did and the woman was not to blame. Perhaps, Salom, you are a little ashamed—and that is the cloud across the sun, eh?"

Her weathered face nodded gently.

"I say these things," she added, "only because in many ways you have become as my own son."

Salom looked away. Here was Veshti's faith again, but wiser and more deliberate.

How could he tell her the fears and doubts and suspicions that were only flutterings at the edge of his mind? How could he throw against the rock of this kindly woman's belief the froth of his own imaginings?

Among all these things there was only one certainty and that was the certainty of the evil of the lama Yanong, and it would be useless to disparage the priest of Kelinka. And so there was nothing he could say that would not merely serve to emphasize his own uncouthness, the crude intolerance of youth, stupid with youth's pugnacity.

So he said: "Thank you, Kelinka. I never had a mother. At least I cannot remember—she died so long ago. When I was young she died."

The woman touched his hands with her rough fingers.

"It is well you came to us, Salom," she said.

"At first I thought it was well. At first it seemed that the old man was right."

"Old man?"

"The peddler. I spoke to you of him. The one who told me I could find happiness only in this land. Now I do not know whether he spoke the truth or not."

"Salom! Salom!" She chided him gently. "For you it is not yet time for melancholy. That is only for the very old—or the very young. We have another proverb in this land."

"And what is that?"

"He finds no tomorrow who dawdles to pluck the coat of yesterday."

He glanced at her sharply and then he grinned.

"It seems I am always seeking the advice of others."

"When you are twenty it is wise, Salom."

"Then I will take your advice if you will give me more advice."

"What about?"

"About Veshti."

She looked at him curiously. "Veshti? What do you seek to know, my son?"

"I seek to know Veshti," he said simply. "And yet I cannot. She is friendly and kind to me——"

"Then—what else do you——"

"She—she puzzles me."

"Perhaps she puzzles herself, Salom. She is young."

"Perhaps. But she is so hard to understand."

"She is no harder than any other of her age. She is no harder than you. Veshti and you are much alike, Salom."

"Alike?"

"Of course. In many things. Both of you are dreamers who do not understand their dreams."

"I do not think we are alike." He spoke firmly, and yet as the words came he suspected that the woman's observation might possess more wisdom than he thought.

There was little enough evidence. If there were a kinship between the girl and himself it was a subconscious, unspoken thing. Although of all the people in the valley it was Veshti to whom he most wanted to talk, he had talked to her very little, and then mostly on everyday matters. But once or twice he had sensed a deeper thread between them. It was as if she, too, did not quite belong to this place or these people. She was something isolated, apart from the valley and the rough lives of its nomads. Where all the others were oblivious to the beauty of the setting in which their lives were cast she possessed an elusive quality of poetry that had revealed itself to him in a few chance remarks, and he had been warm in his knowledge that only the two of them could see the beauty beyond the beauty of utility and feel no inner shame in seeing it nor self-consciousness in talking of it. They had been fragmentary moments but he had hoped that one day he could talk to her of the little things that stirred him through the turn of seasons and the move of days. He had hoped that they could share the indefinable wonder as dawn crept in the scarves of hung mist, the uncontrollable impulse to lift one's face to the first thin wash of warmth poured through the gray, the exultance of striding down-valley arm in arm with the storms of afternoon, the nostalgia of smells, of smoke and snow and earth and the sun hot on the mud of the reed-dark tarns.

"I do not think we are alike, Kelinka," he repeated stubbornly.

"So? Veshti is very young, as you are. Moreover, she is a deeply religious girl, for which I am grateful. Doubtless, you hurt her deeply with your harsh words to Yanong. And I think she believes you have only mockery for her faith. You see, Salom, she is too young yet to have learned tolerance. And it seems, my son, that the same might be said of you."

Salom shrugged and turned the conversation to domestic matters. The discussion had drifted far away from the problems he had come to discuss with Kelinka. True, she had given him some comfort in her assurance of her own affection for him, but there were issues upon which they were not mentally compatible, and she had done nothing to resolve the doubts that nagged at him. Elucidation was to come from an unexpected quarter.

"I will hobble my horse," he said to Kelinka. "It will snow tonight."

III

The thought fumbled into Dochi's mind as he looked down from the high ford and saw the home thang bleached in the evening drift of smoke from the cooking fires. His big hands were folded on the curved wood bow of the saddle and the veins were corded hard on his brown skin and the muscles of his body were taut against his soiled sheepskins.

He grappled with the thought but it eluded him again, and so he savored the strength of his body and knew that he could kill if it were necessary to kill. With one of his great hands he could kill! With one hand! And yet was there need to kill? This was the question that danced away from him, that mocked him, tantalizing as the flame and flicker of the night lights above the bogs. His face clouded and there was a muddiness deep in the black studs of his eyes.

For Dochi was not a killer. He had no desire to kill. In this there was nothing ethical, nothing of morality: it was merely that in the valley man did not kill man. They killed the bear and wolf and sometimes the leopard, and when musk was needed they slew the ungainly deer for his pod, and if a herdsman coveted the glow of red fur on his garb a fox would be hunted. And all around there was killing—a savage and endless slaughter that continued night and day. It was the arrowfall of the hawk and the swift plummet of the eagle and its upward arc with the glint of flapping silver at its claws, the ripped lamb and its torn guts swelling, the hammer of the black bear's paw, the hurry of a wolf's shadow in the night, the gathering of the naked-necked vultures like black-cloaked sorcerers around the death shudders of an aged hare, the voracious shuttle of the ants between their nests and the vultures' spurned scraps. Death and killing were things that were easily understandable, but there was something that said men did not kill men. And now Dochi wanted to kill a man.

He crossed the ford and rode down slowly, the blunted fingers of his brain fumbling at the unaccustomed and terrifying thing that had come to him. He wanted to kill, and yet he had no wish to kill, and there was nothing that suggested that one should kill. As he rode his big head shook stupidly.

But all of Dochi's thoughts were not stupid.

At times he had periods of sharp perception, just as in the fuddle of his mother's mind there were moments of clarity. In their character there was something of balance, as if each had sacrificed as much and suffered equally. Dochi's had been an agonizing gestation and a tortuous birth that had shattered Dupken's mind and destroyed her beauty. Only in the brief periods of near-sanity did Dupken rue that birth and all its aftermath and wish that for her sacrifice she had at least been repaid by a son intelligent and comely. But in the more frequent spasms of her madness she was maliciously glad that her child, in destroying her, had himself been destroyed. The shattering of her own organs in that bloody torment of birth had battered at the formlessness of her son, so that he too was stamped with the ugliness of his idiocy—and for this Dupken was glad.

But Dochi had not remained all of Dupken. In the beginning he had inherited nothing from Chunor but a body destined to become massive and strong; but through the misted years he had still been the son of his father and had ridden with him in the pastures and worked with him at the milling stone and sat with him in the slovenly house and assisted him in the combing away of the yak hair and the fleecing of the sheep. This daily environment had given him more of his father's cunning than either of his parents realized. He was a fool—but he was not so great a fool as they or anybody else imagined.

There was a Dochi who was not the idiot to be jeered and derided. Mostly he found his sanity when he thought of Veshti or looked at her. In his fumbling way he had taken one or two girls of the valley—but he had never touched a finger of his own betrothed, and he had talked to her only infrequently, and even then uncomfortably, in stumbling monosyllables. For Veshti was the only precious thing that Dochi possessed, and the only beauty. It was a possession that overawed him so much that the girl had become almost unattainable, as if she were a goddess remote from him. But she was real, and the gods were only vague shadows in his mind. She was his only loveliness, his only treasure, the single glint of all the other beauties engulfed by the black ooze of his mind. She was all he had.

And now even this loveliness had been tarnished. It had begun when he had overheard the conversation in the tent between his father and the priest, because it had been almost a confirmation of the almost unheeded things his mother had muttered to him. So the suspicion had come to him, never quite clear, never absent. It had not been allayed by any reassurances given by his father or the priest. Perhaps his mind had been abnormally sharp because the conversation had concerned Veshti, but he had left the tent with a distrust of the priest and an unsureness even of his own father's protective value in such a situation.

It was not until later that it had come to him—clearly and without misgiving at first—that he would have to kill the stranger. There were many things beyond his understanding, but he knew his own tremendous physical strength; he could snap the slender neck of the small stranger with one twist of his wrists.

He rode on to the thang, and at the edge of the cropped grasses he could see Salom making fast the hobble to the foreleg of his gray horse. As he approached the boy he observed that the thang was empty of others, and then his horse whickered and Salom turned and smiled, with friendliness and with the fleeting touch of an unspoken sympathy that he unconsciously had for Chunor's son.

"The three blessings on you, Dochi," Salom said. He jerked his head toward his own horse. "There will be snow tonight. I do not want him to stray far. I have no love for long tramping in the cold dawns." He turned away and pulled tight on the buckle.

Dochi watched him silently. His head still swung slowly from side to side, and his long arms hung slack and his body was rigid.

Salom slapped the gray's rump and stretched as he grinned at

Dochi, and then he became aware of the other's tension and the trouble that lurked deep in the peering eyes.

"What is it, Dochi?" he asked. "What ails you?"

Dochi shook his head dumbly.

He had no wish to kill this one. He was friendly. He made no jeers, nor did he laugh at him. In that way he was different from all the others. Never did he deride him. Up at the cropping grasses he had always spoken to him as he did to all the others; he did not adopt a different voice and simper and posture as he spoke. Dochi rubbed his great hands into his eyes. No, he did not want to kill this one. He did not want him to take Veshti, and yet he had no wish to kill him.

"What troubles you, Dochi?" the boy repeated.

Dochi groped for words. "Tell me . . . tell me . . . it is not true . . . not true . . ."

"What?"

"It . . . it is not true, the thing that Chunor and Yanong say? It is not true? If you tell me it is not true I will believe you."

"What is not true, Dochi? What do they say?"

"If you say it is not true then I will have no need to kill you," Dochi mumbled.

Salom's eyes widened. "Come, Dochi," he said patiently, "what talk is this?"

"It is not true that you are a demon?"

Salom laughed. Here it was again! "No." He chuckled. "I am no demon, Dochi. It is a crone's tale that travels fast and far."

"And there is no truth in it, eh?"

"No truth at all, Dochi. It was something your mother, Dupken, imagined and—why—" he grinned—"why, even your own father laughed at the tale, and told me to disregard it. He made apologies to me because it had been his woman who said these things."

"Ah, now you tell lies," snapped Dochi, his eyes sharp with cunning.

"Lies?" Salom stiffened.

"Yes. Lies. Chunor would not have said that thing."

"I tell you——"

"It seems that what Dupken says is true, eh?" The veins coiled on his clenched fists. "You are a demon and you came to this valley to take Veshti." He lurched forward. "Tell me this thing truthfully, and then I must kill you."

"Stop acting foolishly!" Salom spoke with sudden anger. "I will say two things to you truthfully. I am no demon. And I did not know of Vesti when I came to this valley." Dochi had paused and was shambling uncertainly. "Do you believe these things, Dochi?"

Dochi nodded. The fog was settling on his mind. He was relieved that there was no need to kill, but beyond this there was only a whirling bewilderment.

"Then there will be no need to kill you," he muttered absently, and began to walk away to his horse, but Salom was alert and moved in front of him.

"Wait, Dochi. There are other things to say."

Dochi shook his head and began as if to push past him, but the boy's hand was like steel on his arm.

"Dochi, what is the thing that Chunor and Yanong say about me?"

"You mean the thing they said in the tent?"

"Yes."

"I told them that if you tried to touch Veshti I would kill you, but they said they were watchful and there would be no need for killing."

"Watchful?"

"They gave warning to the other herdsmen that you were under suspicion."

"Suspicion of what?"

Dochi sniggered. He was happy. The troublesome fog had cleared from his mind. "They are crazy. They watch you because of the fear that you are a demon. Now there will be no need for this. I will tell them that I have talked with you and you are no demon, nor did you come for Veshti."

"No, Dochi, it would not be wise to talk to them. It is best in these cases to say nothing. Now listen to me. Are you sure that Chunor, too, gives heed to this talk?"

"Yes." Dochi seemed surprised. "Although perhaps he does not think you are a demon. Perhaps a Black lama. There is talk of one in these parts."

"I thought Chunor——"

"Oh, he is less concerned with you than with Muhlam's behavior in this thing, and——"

"Muhlam?"

Dochi grinned. "Muhlam, the headman. Now that we know you are not a demon he is still headman. But if it had been shown you were an evil visitor then the people would have sought a new headman. Now it is all right."

"Yes, Dochi. Now it is all right." Salom nodded thoughtfully, and when Dochi shook off his restraining hand he made no effort to halt him. Dochi shambled away contentedly, and then he turned, a grotesque shape against the golden throb of evening.

"I am glad there was no need to kill," he called.

"I, also, am glad, Dochi," the boy replied.

For a long time after Dochi had gone he stood amid the trampled grasses.

Then there *was* justification for the doubts and suspicions that had worried him. The pieces were falling together. There was a reason now for the strange atmosphere that had developed, for the moroseness of Muhlam (who must have sensed something of it), for the willingness of people to give heed to the fantastic delusions of an idiot woman, for the reluctance of Veshti to share his company. It was absurd that such importance should have been attached to the ramblings of an imbecile; and yet so much importance had been given them that apparently even the overthrow of the headman could be considered.

There was no logic in it—unless there was some deliberate machinery working to foster the fantasy. And Salom thought of Chunor and his friendly words. He had no doubt of Yanong's enmity. But with Chunor it was different. Chunor's shadow was more menacing, because his enmity was less understandable.

IV

When Veshti reached the edge of the field Maygur and Bitola were already at the milking. Maygur's method of milking was as slipshod as her appearance. She sniffed constantly and wiped her nose on the back of her hand and squirted milk over her clothing and the surrounding grass.

Bitola employed her strong brown fingers with easy grace. She looked vital and handsome as she squatted comfortably beside the shaggy beast. On such a menial task her aggressive beauty was as obvious as when she swaggered her hips for the benefit of appreciative tribesmen. There was no setting that was not Bitola's setting—except possibly a gathering of the valley gossips, who showed unflagging interest in Bitola's unconcealed liking for men—particularly lusty men. They whispered, but there was no need to whisper. Bitola was the most honest person of her tribe, and she never hesitated to proclaim her appetites.

Veshti paid no heed to the gossip. She liked Bitola for herself and admired her for her forthrightness and her bawdy humor, even though she was occasionally shaken by the other girl's complete lack of reticence on those subjects usually discussed in sniggering whispers behind women's hands.

"Ha, Veshti!" Bitola grinned. "It is good you come, little one. Maygur has been in and out of the bracken three times already since we arrived. She is very excited, you see. And she can scarcely milk, as you will observe from the state of her dress. It is thoughtless of you, Veshti, to be late and so keep Maygur in such a state. Is it not so, Maygur?"

Maygur flushed. "You tell lies, Bitola! As if I care what Veshti does! If she is foolish enough to dip her head in water as Renzi told my sister—" she shrugged, and the milk splashed across her boots—"why should it concern me? I only hope she does not die of it. Naropa says she has never heard such foolishness. Naropa once knew a woman who died because she watered her hair!"

Veshti chuckled. "Have no fear, Maygur. I shall not die. It was very pleasant. All the head tingles, and when the hair dries it is smooth to touch, and light. It makes you want to dance. I shall do it again. And you should, too."

"Your hair looks no better for it." Maygur sniffed. "And I will certainly not attempt to copy such stupidity. Naropa would thrash me for it. Naropa says if you water your hair you will not have any children!"

Bitola rolled her eyes. "Oh-oh! This is a thing more women in the valley should know. Then Dupken would have little use for her belly lotion!"

Maygur ran her tongue over lips and giggled nervously. "You know about such things, Bitola. Is it true that——" She glanced sideways at Veshti and leaned over toward the big girl to cup the whisper in her hand.

"Maygur! Maygur! If you are so curious about these things why do you not ask Dupken? Or perhaps Veshti will be able to tell you after she is married to Dochi."

Maygur covered her face in her hands and snickered. "Bitola! You are without shame!" She looked slyly toward Veshti. "I warrant there are some surprises in store for Veshti when she is wed. Maybe her hair will need watering more frequently."

"But then you would know more about it than I," Veshti said placidly. "Perhaps you have some firsthand knowledge."

Bitola chuckled: "And if she has not, then it is not for the want of trying. Eh, Maygur?"

Maygur flushed and another stream of milk hissed over her sodden skirt. At that moment the cow began to relieve itself. Maygur quickly grasped a small wooden container and collected the liquid, which she decanted into the milk pail.

"Kelinka forbids me to do that," Veshti said, glad to divert the conversation. "She says it spoils the flavor of butter and cheese."

"Nonsense! Kelinka is quite wrong. It improves the flavor."

"I tell you Kelinka has tried it both ways. Muhlam prefers the flavor without it."

"Well, since it is you who have raised the subject, Kaman has often said that never at Muhlam's tent do the butter and cheese taste quite right. He says the taste is flat and without interest. One night he came home and said to my mother, 'Well, Naropa, you might not be headwoman, but at least you know how to make a good cheese!'"

"I fail to see that it makes much difference whether you add the urine or not," Bitola offered amiably.

"Of course it does!" Maygur snapped. "How can the milk curdle properly otherwise?"

"That I do not know. Does it really matter how the milk curdles, or whether the milk curdles at all?"

"Kelinka," said Veshti, "insists that the milk should be allowed to curdle naturally, and I have never heard any visitor, *including* Kaman, complain of my mother's cheese or butter."

Bitola yawned and slapped the cow on the rump. It jolted away awkwardly, and Bitola stood with her hands on her hips looking after it.

"Well—" she grinned—"at least the cow does not care if the milk is curdled or how it is curdled or why it is curdled, so long as she gets rid of it. And, for that matter, I do not care either."

"You are a strange girl, Bitola," Maygur said. "I fail to understand how you can show such little interest in these things. Naropa says no woman should be allowed to wed unless she knows how to feed her husband properly."

Bitola tossed her head and laughed until her big, round breasts quivered. "If the man I marry thinks about food more than twice a week I shall be greatly disappointed. No man will be marrying me for my cheese-making!"

She swaggered off toward the herd, and Veshti smiled as she watched her. "I think the man who wins Bitola will be very lucky."

"He will walk a road that many have trodden before him." Maygur sneered.

"He will still be lucky. She is easily the most handsome girl in all the valley."

Maygur's eyes held a curious expression.

"I would have thought you would be the last woman to say that." She giggled nervously.

"Why?"

"Oh—nothing. But I could tell you something about Bitola that would change your opinion." Maygur wriggled on her haunches. "And it would serve Bitola well if I did." She laughed on a high, excited note, and there was malice in the laugh.

Veshti's small fingers squeezed rhythmically and the thin white streams lanced into the pail. "It would be better, Maygur, if you kept your gossip to yourself. I have no wish to hear it."

Maygur sneered. "You *are* strange," she said. "I thought you would have been glad to know something that affects your family."

"If it affects my family I have no doubt I shall hear of it at the proper time," Veshti said evenly.

"Oh, all right then! But do not say that I made no offer to tell you."

Bitola sauntered toward them, prodding another cow in front of her. Veshti savored the sensual magnificence of the girl.

"Ah, me!" Bitola sighed. "No pause to a woman's task. Sometimes I wonder whether it would be so bad, after all, to be reborn as a yak. It might be good just to roam among the fields and let others solve your problems."

"And get milked twice a day?" Maygur tittered.

"Bah! That is nothing to what will happen to you twice a day if Kaman ever catches you behind the bushes with Chunor's sons! Although why in the name of Buddha you should choose Chunor's sons will forever baffle me! If you had come to me I could have given you the names of ten men better than any one of them—or all of them, with Chunor himself thrown in for good measure!"

"Bitola!" Maygur's anger flared. "I do not know why the gods do not strike you down for such wickedness!"

"Come, Maygur." Bitola's eyes danced. "Do not play the innocent with me. We have much the same tastes, you and I, except that I have no great regard for skulking behind bushes!"

"You . . . you should be filled with shame."

"Shame? And where, pray, is the cause for shame in the natural things? I might have shame if I were like some women in this valley who are forever cheating and lying and showing malice toward their neighbors!"

Maygur squirmed and rubbed the back of her hand against her dripping nose. "You will be shocking Veshti with such talk," she muttered.

Veshti flicked her eyes over Maygur and continued with her milking. "I agree with Bitola," she said. "There are no sins greater than lies and cheating and malice. The other——" She shrugged. "Well, I suppose the other is a matter of taste. If it does not happen to be *my* taste, then is not that a good thing too? For think now, if the gods had given every woman as much interest in the subject as you and Bitola—" her eyes crimped—"all women would suffer, because every man would be flying beyond the mountains for safety!"

Bitola laughed. "Ah-ha," she spluttered, "it seems to me that if it has done nothing else watering the hair has brightened Veshti's wits." She was convulsed with mirth.

"I wish you would stop talking about my hair," Veshti said, suddenly impatient. "It is not such a very strange thing."

"Well, it might not be strange to you, little one," Bitola said. "But I have lived for nineteen years, and you are the first I have heard about—excepting, of course, Naropa's acquaintances, and as they are almost certainly some more of Naropa's lies, then you are still the first I have ever heard of."

"In China all women do it. It is considered a very good thing to cleanse the hair. To cleanse the whole body, also."

Bitola looked at her sharply, and then her eyelids drooped a fraction. "Your knowledge of the outside world has improved a good deal."

"And what is wrong with knowledge?"

"Oh, nothing. Nothing." Bitola grinned. "But it is more pleasant to learn from a handsome stranger, eh?"

Maygur sniffed. "The Chinese? Well, I for one do not think him handsome, and——"

"He is all right," Bitola said. "His face is good, but his body is a child's. He would be good enough if there were not huskier men about. He would be good enough for Veshti. They are of a size."

"For such a puny, sickly creature he has far too many airs and graces." Maygur sneered. "And he has no wealth. Why he should think himself so wonderful is a puzzle to me!"

"And have you no other standards than wealth?" Veshti snapped, and she was surprised at the vehemence of her anger. "Is not courage as important? Or kindliness? And why must you label as airs and graces the natural superiority of one who has traveled a good deal farther and seen a great many more wonders than any person in *this* valley? You would do very well to think a little before you proclaim your judgments, Maygur!"

"And *you* would do well not to let Dochi hear you praising the Chinese so fervently." Maygur spat. "It is not seemly for a girl betrothed to one man to display quite so much interest in another."

"Bah! There is nothing unseemly in being just." Veshti's eyes were cold with displeasure and she was Muhlam's daughter.

Maygur shrugged. "Well, you know your own business best. But it seems strange that you, who are supposed to be so religious, can openly side with a man already proved a blasphemer. I would have thought you would be more careful in your friendships if you value the opinion of the holy lama as much as you have always pretended. And there are frightening tales about this young stranger with whom you are so friendly. I will tell *you,* Veshti, a few truths since you are so high and mighty. Kaman says the people of the valley do not trust this Chinese who sings his devilish songs, and Kaman also says that your family would do well to remember it!"

"How dare you!" Veshti was shaking. "How dare *you* tell the headman's family what they should do! It is a fine thing when the actions of the headman, and the headman's family, are open to the criticism of one of his herdsmen! And Kaman would do well to remember *that!* If the people of the valley believe such as Dupken speaks then the people of the valley are fools. They would be proving their holiness better if, instead of condemning the boy, they showed him friendship and understanding, and so led him into the true path of faith."

"As you, doubtless, are doing?" Bitola inquired, with one black eyebrow lifted.

The angry words rising in Vehti's throat were instantly dammed, and she flushed at the realization of her own insincerity. What right had she to condemn the attitude of others? Her own behavior had been no more reasonable, no more understanding. She had half-heeded all Dupken's accusations. She had been intolerant of beliefs that differed from her own. She remembered his tight face as he had pushed past her on the riverbank, the bewildered pleading of his eyes since, her deliberate avoidance of him.

Her chin lifted as she looked at Bitola and her eyes were proud.

"As I have not done," she corrected. "But as I have every intention of doing."

"A pleasant way of earning merit," Bitola murmured.

"Oh, undoubtedly Veshti will be reborn as an abbess for such noble self-sacrifice," Maygur jibed.

"At least she will not be reborn as a yak—which is likely enough to be our fate!" Bitola chuckled and Veshti was grateful to her for edging the conversation onto firmer ground.

"I still do not think it fair to Dochi." Maygur sniffed.

"Bah! Dochi—Salom! Dochi—Salom! A pair of hairless boys with no more strength in them than a couple of chirping sparrows!" Bitola's eyes flashed. "They are not worth squabbling about."

Veshti and Maygur looked at Lotor's big daughter expectantly, silenced by her unusual intensity.

Bitola flushed as she caught Veshti's eyes and bit her full lip. "There is only one man in the valley," she muttered defensively, and shrugged as she turned back to the cow.

Chapter Eight

I

MUHLAM left the boy at the edge of the forsaken moor and cantered to the higher ground where the gorse laced the valley to the pass. The herd was restless.

There was an unusual atmosphere in the day. In the light wind he could see the slow drift of leaves from the birches. There was a new frenzy in the noise of insects: in the strident impatience of the crickets, in the clicking of dragonflies across the weeded ponds. It seemed as if the restlessness of the cattle was only a fragment of a much more extensive restlessness. Salom knew that animals often were more highly sensitive than men, and he played with the thought that already the creatures of the valley had smelled the end of summer. Salom knew nothing of Chunor's forecast that the blizzards would come early; and there was no single thing that he could grasp with certainty as proof that the wheel of the seasons had turned again. Yet the clouds gathered above the southern hills were torn into swirling feathers by high winds, and on one summit was a veiled edge that told of dusted snow wind-driven over the crag's lip.

Nevertheless, there was a lull, a suspension, a great sighing inhalation all about him. It was as if the world had filled its lungs and was holding its breath, waiting for the assault. In the brooding quiet the soft wind that touched his cheek was heady with a new smell, as if a strange wine had been spilled, and he knew the smell for the odor and ferment of death—the decay of old grasses beneath the sun, the pulping of mosses and the rot of leaves—and the warm air itself seemed colored with autumn's gilt.

And yet the air was warm, and it caressed Salom like a scented voluptuary.

But he was infected by the melancholy of decay and change, and he tried to rid himself of it by riding down to the desolate moor that had fascinated him ever since he had heard Muhlam's words: "The Pon sorcerers used it for abominable practices, and our people shun it in darkness." The move did nothing to lessen his despondency.

The pastures, vivid with iris and poppy, curved down only as far as a serrated ridge of slate, and beyond this the gaunt heath folded toward a line of low scrub, malformed and without color. The heath undulated in regular waves and the juiceless grasses grew sparse and close to the soil. The moor was scarred by the clawed squats and burrows of rabbits and by the untidy earth cones of moles, and made the more repugnant by the droppings of wolves and foxes and by a litter of bones. Between the slate ridge and the scrub line it was as if a great bruise had been hammered into the beauty of the valley.

Salom shuddered at the desolation and looked up toward the herd. The restlessness had passed. The beasts were grazing placidly. He tugged at the reins and walked the horse back toward the herd. He had almost reached it when he heard the distant slap of a rifle shot.

He looked up quickly. The topmost fringe of the herd was swirling inward. The shot had come from the spur beneath the pass, where Muhlam had gone. Salom drove his heels into the gray.

The animal labored up the slope in long, rhythmic strides, its breath rasping, but Salom kicked into its flanks again and lashed it with his reins. He could see Muhlam now, a small black figure on the ridge, clear against the white gleam of the peaks beyond. He had dismounted and was moving cautiously on foot just above timberline. Salom rode as far as he dared but when the ground roughened he dismounted, dropping the reins, and ran ahead quickly, his body crouched against the ascent, his hands fumbling for his rifle. Once or twice, as he blundered through entangling undergrowth, he could see Muhlam high above—motionless, tensed forward as if waiting for something.

He was still there when the boy burst through the low timber. The headman was now not more than a hundred yards away, peering toward a limestone spur and a cave partly choked by withered vegetation. And then Salom stopped and his breath sucked in.

A bear, black and shaggy and monstrous against the skyline, lurched from the brambled lair and lumbered toward Muhlam. The headman stood his ground, legs straddled, and leveled his rifle deliberately, but there was no report, and then Muhlam seemed to cringe away and suddenly he turned to flee—but as he did so he tripped and fell to the ground with his arms thrashing.

The grotesque figure was curved over the desperately wriggling figure as Salom's finger squeezed. The movement was almost mechanical. He had no memory of having put the weapon to his shoulder, and he was startled at the unexpected jar of the recoil against his collarbone, and the roar of the discharge was like a slap across his face, and his eyes closed against the acrid whiff of powder smoke.

The black mess thudded upon Muhlam's flailing legs, and Salom could feel iced fingers squeezing at his belly, but then he saw that the bear was motionless. Muhlam was dragging himself from beneath the animal's weight. Salom experienced a strange wonder as he scrambled up the spur toward Muhlam.

II

The headman drove his knife again into the carcass with vicious and unnecessary force, and dragged the blade back with a smooth, sweeping motion, and then he took one side of the pelt in each veined hand and pulled toward himself so that the fur peeled free to expose a pulpy mass of red and purple entrails corded and clotted with seams of fat. The carcass steamed and the autumn fragrance had been dispelled by the rank sweetness of hot blood and the sick odor of guts scarcely dead. Muhlam's knife lunged again at the misted belly. His arms were crimson and dripping to the elbows, and his face and chest were blotched with the blood that had spurted against him. He wiped his face against his upper arm and grinned up at Salom.

"Soon we shall have it off," he said. "It will be a fine rug for the tent."

Salom nodded. He looked down at Muhlam's right leg. The felt boot had been ripped open and blood welled slowly from a deep gash in the calf where the great sickle claws had gored him as the monster fell.

Muhlam completed the skinning, and grunted as he dragged the fur clear—one side of it sleek and ruffled, the other a hideous bloody mess. He tossed it into the burned snow grass and plunged his knife two or three times into the soil to cleanse it. He kicked the animal's head over, a head horrible and grotesque now with the eyes glazed and the great mouth fixed in a grinning arc of curved fangs, and the scalp gone in a shambles of bloody flesh and hanging sinews.

Muhlam knelt beside the skin and fingered it expertly.

"A summer fur," he said critically. "But a good one. It will make a fine rug."

He hoisted the warm and sticky mess and threw it, dripping its redness, across his shoulders. As he clambered down the slope, limping only slightly, the blood trickled down his back in thick, serpentine chalk lines, and the trophy swung from his broad shoulders like the cloak of a ghoul from the shades of Bado.

When they reached timberline Salom looked back, and the vultures were spiraling low over the untidy mound of steaming offal.

"I saw it first in the thickets above the herd," Muhlam explained, when they had returned to the cattle. "It was a poor shot the one you heard, but aim had to be speedy and the range was far. I should have killed." He grunted contempt for himself. "I merely wounded."

"They are ten times as dangerous when merely wounded. It was a great risk for you to follow it alone."

"Perhaps," Muhlam admitted. "I should still have killed it with the second shot had not the rifle misfired. I had no fear of that. I have shot bear before."

"Rifles frequently misfire. It was dangerous for you to have gone alone."

"From where did you shoot, Salom? Tell me of that." He was obviously eager to evade further talk of his own rashness.

"I had just broken through the scrub line. Perhaps a hundred paces." The boy shrugged. "It was not a difficult shot and the beast was clear against the sky."

"Ah, if my first shot had been in such a way!" He shook his head ruefully, but almost immediately became aware of his own ingratitude. The boy, regardless of whether the task was easy or not, had quite certainly saved him from death. He could not have lived fifteen seconds beneath the scything of those claws.

"Nevertheless, it was a fine shot, Salom," he said. He tapped his hand beneath his armpit and then against his heart. "Right in the heart. You killed him instantly. Pouf! He was dead like that! But for that—well, but for that the people of the valley would be seeking a new headman tonight. I owe you a debt."

"It was an easy mark, Muhlam." The boy mumbled in his embarrassment. "Even a child———"

"Not so easy, my son. It was necessary to kill instantly. No other shot would have done. I had no more than a few seconds to live when you fired. A few seconds, no more! I say it was a fine shot!"

He slapped the slim youngster on the shoulder and Salom inclined his head silently, but pleasure and a vast pride rested in his eyes. "My son," Muhlam had said. It was the first time the headman had said such a thing.

III

He knew that he would never see Muhlam in better spirits, never find him more disposed to reasonable and friendly conversation, never again have him so free from the pride and dignity and arrogance of his position. And yet he found it difficult to broach the subject.

All the way down from the upland herd Muhlam had unbent until his conversation had reached almost a point of friendly equality. He was no longer wrapped in the black cocoon of his own aloofness—but already the home thang was in sight, a-shimmer with evening and still Salom was silent.

He gulped. If he remained mute now he might as well bury and forget all the thoughts that troubled him. He licked his lips and said:

"Muhlam, there is a question I would ask."

"Of course. Ask."

"Are the people of the valley loyal to you?"

"Loyal?"

"All of them?"

"Of course." The shaggy eyebrows lifted. "This is a strange question, Salom."

"All of them?" Salom repeated.

The headman was puzzled, but he humored Salom by smiling thinly and saying: "It would go hard indeed with any who were not! But I do not understand why——"

"Yanong, then? Is he, also, a friend of yours?"

"Yanong is not of the valley. His loyalty, I suppose, is to his abbot—if he possesses loyalty, which sometimes I doubt. Of his friendship with me——" He pursed his lips. "Oh, he is friendly enough. I had not thought of it before. Why do you ask these things?"

"Because . . . because I believe people are plotting against you . . . people here in the valley. There are things . . ."

"What is this? *Against me?*" Muhlam's eyes were wide, and then laughter erupted from him.

The coughing guffaws stung the boy so that he glared: "It would be well for you, Muhlam, to listen to somebody in the valley who has no need to be overawed by your position, and who owes allegiance to nought but your hospitality."

Muhlam choked on his laughter and reined his horse to a standstill. By the time Salom had pulled his own mount back the headman's face was serious and his narrowed eyes surveyed Salom quizzically.

"There is something that troubles you, eh?" he said softly. "Perhaps it would be better if you cast aside riddles and spoke bluntly." He leaned from the saddle and with a thumb pressed against his nostril cleared his nose. "Speak, boy."

Now that the time had come Salom felt curiously uncertain. He was flustered by the intensity of Muhlam's stare, and he suddenly found that his thoughts lacked coherence. Facts that had seemed clear enough in his mind became vague intangibles when he attempted to form them into words, as when a stone is cast into a pool's reflection to shatter its veracity.

"It . . . it is hard, Muhlam, to depart from riddles. It is not that I really *know* these things. More, perhaps, that I feel them in my mind, and now it is time to talk of them they become hard to express."

"Then of whom do you think when you talk of disloyalties?"

"Of Yanong . . . and . . . and I think of Chunor."

Muhlam stared hard at him. "Of Chunor?"

"Yes. I think he covets your position as headman."

"Well, what of that?" Muhlam grunted. "He is the second man here—and all men covet the position of headman. But Chunor is not headman, nor will he be."

"But I think he and Yanong plot against you. I . . . I think I am the cause . . . doubtless because you have given me shelter and taken me into your family. There is whispering about me . . . and . . . and it is damaging to you. I do not know for certain but it seems . . ."

"Bah! This is fool's talk, Salom, and utterly wasteful. What I chose to do is the decision of the headman of the valley, and therefore is right. My actions are not questioned. Yanong? He is a mawkish monk with no blood in his veins. Chunor?" He gestured disdainfully. "Chunor knows his position. By all the gods, he would not dare flout my authority!"

"Some men discover the existence of the assassin only by the knife that parts their ribs," Salom retorted sententiously.

"All this talk is idle, I tell you," Muhlam said, with a flurry of impatience, but then understanding spread across his hawk face and his eyes became softer. "I think I am aware of the thing that troubles you, Salom," he said and his voice was kindly. "I hear the tales of the thangs as well as the others. It is because of the argument in the tent with Yanong, and the gibberings of the zany, Dupken, who claimed that I was harboring a demon." He chuckled. "But by the sixteen pits, even if it were true I would prefer to give shelter in my tent to a thousand demons than to one Dupken! I say these are the reasons for your troubled thoughts, but your thoughts are a muddle. The matter with Yanong is forgotten—even by Yanong himself. The tongue-dung of Dupken is well known in this valley. Only a stranger would be troubled by it."

"No, Muhlam, there is more than that. It is not only——"

"Enough! I am weary of such fool talk. Now, let us hasten to the tent and tell the story of the slaying."

He slapped his fist against the soggy crimson mass laced behind his saddle. And nothing more was said.

IV

Salom had gone to the river with Veshti, and inside the boy was a giddy warmth that was partly a reaction from the boisterous praise lavished by Muhlam, who had recounted the tale of the bear's killing in increasingly exaggerated repetition, leaping about the tent in grotesque travesty of the attack and its failure, spinning into minutes of anecdote incidents that had taken only seconds of time.

Salom was warmed also by his consciousness of the unsaid gratitude of Kelinka, by the adoration of Renzi, and by the pleasing softness in the eyes of Veshti. In the flush of this exciting stimulus all the fears and doubts that had nagged at him had been dispelled.

In the tent only Kelinka remained. Muhlam, his audience reduced, had marched off impatiently to gather new listeners in Chunor's tent, and Renzi had gone with him, for it would be long before the child's appetite for the tale would be satisfied.

Kelinka crouched beside the fire with her chin cupped in her hands, and her face was thoughtful. Except in an indirect way her thoughts did not concern Muhlam, nor the peril he had mercifully escaped. They were of Salom and of Veshti, and mostly of their faces as they had walked from the tent. She knew the expression well enough because she had seen it, so many years before, waxing in the eyes of Black Muhlam, and she had known that once it had betrayed her own feelings. She was aware, with a precise and troubling clarity, that Veshti and the boy would soon be conscious, if they were not already, of an overwhelming need for each other. And it had happened so suddenly. It was only a few days since the boy had come to her and spoken of his troubles, and he had told her how little he knew of Veshti. Then, in the last two days, it had changed. Had it been her own words to the boy that had caused the change? Whatever the reason, it had happened. They talked much together. Mostly it was serious talk, but sometimes they laughed, and there was a loveliness in Veshti that she had not seen before. And then tonight the look had been on their faces. And soon they would have longing and need for each other.

This was a growth that was swift; it was a growth fecund and devouring, as complicated as the entangling embrace of the vines wrenching at the stones and soil that gave nourishment, and destroying the tree trunk that offered support.

It was not that she was unsympathetic; on the contrary, in the unmaterial corners of her generous heart she could imagine no better alliance. But there were terrible problems that could not be pushed aside or overcome, and there was no precedent to ease her sorrow for them, and there were chilling premonitions.

She started guiltily at the rustle in the doorway.

Yanong stood there, stooped into the entrance with his habit slung from his shoulders so that he resembled a gigantic vulture, with the shaved, naked head pushed out from hunched shoulders and his black eyes holding the opaque fixity of a bird's glance. His grubby fist was pushed into his mouth as he gnawed at his nails.

She bowed respectfully and motioned him to enter.

"You are alone, Kelinka?" he asked with a show of surprise, although the question was obvious and it was evident that the absence of others pleased him.

"Yes. Muhlam visits with Chunor."

"Ah." The monk brushed his fingers together in satisfaction. "I am glad that you are alone. There is a matter I wish to discuss with you—and it is one best talked of in privacy."

"With me?" Kelinka made no attempt to dissemble her surprise. It was not common for holy men to desire speech with women. Unless—her heart skipped—unless there was some trouble, some terrible happening. She fingered her prayer beads.

"Yes." The monk nodded profoundly. "It is best to discuss this thing with you. With you at first—and later, of course, with Muhlam."

"What does it concern?" she asked, still fearful.

The monk lowered his head with a gesture of deep piety and did not look at the woman.

"I suppose it concerns Veshti," he said softly.

"Veshti! Why, what has she done that—?"

Yanong raised his hands in quick remonstrance.

"It is nothing harmful, Kelinka. Veshti is a fine girl, and full of goodness. Perhaps that is why the gods have decided to select her. No other woman in the valley——"

"The gods! To select Veshti? Yanong—you must talk openly!" Her voice was agitated and her head shook.

"Perhaps it would be better if I told the whole tale," Yanong agreed gently.

Kelinka tried to conceal her anxiety, but her hands were twisted into each other and the veins were hard knobs.

"I do not think that in all the four valleys that are my province there is a girl more saintly or more true in spirit," mused the monk. "Consequently it is not surprising that the gods have chosen her before all others——"

"For what?"

"For the everlasting blessing of the gods. Before coming here, Kelinka, I was vouchsafed a vision. It was a spectacle of unparalleled beauty and holiness. Ah, if you could but have seen its splendor! During the vision it was conveyed to me that the gods desired, as a tribute I suppose to piety and goodness—which, alas, is far too rare!—to grant the supreme benefaction to the girl Veshti. It is a great honor to the girl, and, of course, Kelinka, to you as the girl's mother."

She shook her head with the tilted, nodding motion that served merely to accentuate her bewilderment. "I . . . I still do not understand, Yanong," she whispered.

His sharp eyes peered at her with sudden fanaticism. For a moment he had the appearance of a madman.

Then he said slowly, "Very few women, Kelinka, are granted the privilege of mating with the gods. Very few. It is a guarantee of splendid future lives. It is worth whole lifetimes of toil and labor in the gaining of merit. It is——"

"You . . . you mean . . . ?" It was impossible to finish the question. She knew, and so she could not ask. Her stomach had stirred and now it was cold and knotty and by contrast her skin was flushed unbearably.

But he could see the unspoken question in her eyes and he nodded profoundly.

"The vision was clear, Kelinka."

"But how?"

"The only way to reach god, daughter, is through a lama."

It was the very proverb she had quoted to Salom, and at the thought of the boy she was seized with a trembling nausea.

"Speak, Yanong," she said. Her face was turned from him.

"It is customary on such rare occasions for the eternal and merciful spirit of Chenresi to inhabit for the brief period of ecstasy the physical shape of some humble mortal chosen by the gods for———"

"You?" she breathed, while the pain clutched her and her mind reeled.

He nodded reverently. "I am a servant of the gods," he said diffidently. "The vision made it clear."

"You?" she mumbled again, and her eyes darted beyond him, helplessly, as if seeking succor, but there was only the lozenge of purpling light that made the tent door a somber jewel.

"Yes, Kelinka. It is naturally a source of immense pride to me that the gods should consider my work sufficiently meritorious to grant this honor, and . . ."

His words trailed off. He could see that the woman was heedless of him. He lowered his head submissively and his stubby fingers moved with mechanical calculation along the polished spheres of his rosary.

Kelinka's knuckles rubbed tiredly at her closed eyes as if she were weary of an attempt to erase a vision that defied obliteration. It was an image of twenty summers before, and yet she could still feel herself cringe away from the memory of holy hands that had pawed her, and every fiber of a body now prematurely withered could still jangle with the pain and shock and uncomprehended violence and sickness of a summer evening that had been rolled back by so many other summers. Her shaking fingers dragged down the furrows of her face. She turned to the monk. He was still bowed in pious contemplation. And she knew that the will of the gods would have to be observed—knew it with an implacable certainty that numbed her and chilled her and gave no particle of compensation in religious fervor and exultance—and yet she was compelled to ask the question.

"And if Veshti is unwilling?"

Yanong did not look up from his beads.

"The gods would be most displeased, of course," he said, but his words were gentle and understanding.

"Yes. The gods would be displeased," she echoed, and stared

beyond the slow curl of the smoke beyond the gently moving walls of the tent, beyond the slow, creaking turn of season and year, season and year, back to a night of never-explained terrors. She had once given herself to the gods so that the gods should not be displeased with her. And in what coin had the gods made repayment?

"I shall discuss it tonight with Muhlam," she said absently.

"Of course. Perhaps it would be better if you were alone, if I were not here? I will sleep in the tent of Chunor."

"It would be better."

"I understand, Kelinka. You are a good woman, and with the gods you have much merit, daughter."

A shadow of a smile touched her mouth painfully but did not reach her tired eyes. "You will go now," she said. "I will talk to Muhlam."

It was a long time after Yanong had gone that the tears came.

V

In the days that followed Kelinka was never able to explain to herself with any satisfaction why she should have told Muhlam in the presence of the others. In the beginning as they had sat in the fire flicker she had hoped the boy and Veshti would go again from the tent, that Renzi would sleep, that only she and her husband would share the gloom and the sharp incision of words. But the others sat there, talking drowsily, and after a time she had not cared.

Many times the words were formed in her mouth, statements molded and glossed and careful in their import and balance, but each time she shied away and the fabric of unspoken speech had crumbled and collapsed again into the chaos of her mind, only to be reformed with agonizing labor. Perhaps she had wanted the others there as a bulwark against the torrential fury that she knew would come from Muhlam; perhaps she was powerless to circumvent the implicit justice of announcement while Veshti was present, and—because of the expression that had glowed in his face—while Salom was present also. And perhaps it was a yearning back into her own youth for the comfort of others that she had lacked in her own travail.

The words that she had assembled and polished with such precision vanished as she spoke, and the words came bluntly through her dry lips.

"Yanong desires Veshti," she said, and although she looked at nobody her wide eyes flared in the firelight.

"For what?" Muhlam grunted without interest.

"No, no!" She stumbled. "It is . . . it is not Yanong. Not really Yanong. Not really Yanong . . . the gods . . . perhaps Chenresi himself . . . it is a great benefaction upon Veshti. . . ." But the words failed and she looked up at her husband pathetically.

"What drool is this, woman?" Muhlam glared at her impatiently. The others were looking at her in bewilderment.

And suddenly the whole verbal edifice was erect again, and while her gaze rested on some unseen point in space she narrated with simple fluency the tenor of her conversation with the monk. She spoke without embellishment, without concealment, and when she had completed the story, as if the caressing flow of speech had calmed her into some serene detachment, she was able to lower her eyes and look into each face in turn before the cataclysm broke about her.

She saw fear rising like a slow tide to engulf the perplexity of Veshti, the dazed incredulity of Salom, the puzzled curiosity of Renzi, and then her eyes met Muhlam's and her own gaze faltered beneath the storm.

Muhlam was on his feet, his face contorted, his fist clenched at his side.

"That—that egghead!" he shouted hoarsely. "Why, by the ragged teats of Dorje Phagmo I shall find him now and break his crooked back across my knee like a dry twig!"

"Muhlam! It is the gods' wish. It was a vision he had——"

"Vision! Bah! The guts of a wolf's bastard for his talk! No slobbering priest weaned on urine and with his rotten heart soiled by filth will mate with Muhlam's daughter if it be the desire of Buddha himself!"

And Salom was on his feet, shouting: "It was as I told you! As I told her! It was in his eyes! He lies when he talks of the gods! It was in his eyes———"

Muhlam whirled on him. "Staunch your tongue, boy! This is no time for the prattle of children!"

Salom recoiled as if he had been struck, and then the blood went from his face and in its haggard pallor a cold fury gleamed.

"My tongue was staunched before," he spat. "Always it is staunched when I have truths to tell. You will not listen. I said he was evil! I told you———"

"Quiet!" roared the headman. "I want no help in the forming of my decisions. No babbling, nameless child who does not even belong here shall hurl his talk at Muhlam!" He was oblivious to his cruelty, blind to the lacerating whiplash of his words. And although Salom winced he did not flinch from his stand.

"I have a right to talk," he said, and for a few moments the intensity of his expression held Muhlam in check. "If Yanong speaks truth—which he is incapable of doing—then what are these gods that I am not permitted to decry? If he speaks lies then was I not right on the very night he came? I tell you it is as I said. It is madness to believe him. He is all evil!"

"Enough, boy!" Muhlam strode across the fire and towered above Salom, his massive arm raised in threat.

"These things are of no concern to you. I am the headman. Are you such a ninny that you cannot understand? It will be time for you to speak when my people decide that they will be led by an undersized brat with the mother's milk still slobbered at his mouth! What happens to Veshti is nothing to you. What happens to Yanong is also nothing to you. But whatever happens there will be only one man who will decide such happenings—*and that man is Muhlam!*"

"What concerns Veshti is———"

"Get out, boy!" Muhlam rasped his impatience. "Out! This question will be settled by the family of Muhlam. We need no advice from strangers. Now, *out!*"

VI

For a long time he squatted on the frost-hard grass beyond the tent. He could still hear voices—mostly the voice of Muhlam, muffled now by the tent fabric if not by any measure of restraint; occasionally the placatory murmur of Kelinka; never the voice of Veshti. And then there was a silence—an aching stillness that spawned the black shape of Muhlam, breathing heavily, who strode past the boy and was gone in the direction of Chunor's tent, his footfalls harsh.

Still the boy made no move, and after a time the light lanced at him from the swinging tent flap and Kelinka came to him. She stooped over and her hand was soft on his shoulder.

"Salom?"

He looked up at her.

"Salom, I understand," she whispered.

"Understand what?"

"About Veshti and you—what you feel. I know. My son, you say you saw something in the eyes of Yanong. But I saw into your eyes, too, and——"

"Mother, it was different!" He grasped her wrist. "I tell you, Kelinka, it was different!"

"But you have a fondness for Veshti. I saw it. Is it not so?"

"Yes. But with Yanong——"

"Let us not talk of Yanong, my son. Not yet." She looked at him dully. "Or perhaps it is time to talk of Yanong."

"What is Muhlam's decision?" he asked urgently. "What does he say?"

"What he says now is of no account, my son," she said sadly. "He goes to order Yanong from the valley. It is what he says." She shrugged. "But finally it will be as the gods desire."

"But he cannot——"

"I know Muhlam. He will call Yanong from Chunor's tent, because he will not declare himself on this thing in front of others. He will storm and rage and insist on receiving the respect he regards as his due, and for a time Yanong's spine will melt. But Muhlam will not win. He could have only one chance of winning."

"What chance?"

"He could win only if he had affection for the girl. He has little real affection for Veshti. And, even if this were not a decree of the gods, Yanong is cleverer than Muhlam. I know, Salom."

She dropped to her knees beside him and her eyes were on the brittle chips of stars that swirled above the black arch of the hill. "I know, because twenty summers ago I was Veshti."

"You were Veshti?"

"It happened to me, Salom. With a monk whose name I think was Kano. Yes—his name was Kano."

"And your family? They permitted this—this—?"

"They knew nothing of it. Or at least they never spoke to me of it."

"And you believe that the gods had asked—?"

"Of course. Kano explained."

"He also lied, Mother. The priests are all the same. They are animals!"

"Please, Salom." Her censure was gentle. "You know little of our land or our customs. You can know nothing of our faith if you are unprepared to accept anything of it. And your opinion on such matters can be of little worth. The monk Kano told me the gods would be pleased."

"And were they?" Salom edged the question.

"A year later I was the wife of the headman. No woman in all the valley stood equal to me. And Veshti, too, will be the wife of the headman."

He turned quickly, and even in the pallid light he could see the scars of suffering and weariness on her kindly face.

"And you have been happy, Kelinka?"

"Yes, Salom," she said truthfully, "I have been happy."

"Always happy?"

She spoke the lie calmly: "Always happy."

It was a long time before either of them spoke.

"Why do you say that Muhlam will not win?" Salom said.

She looked at him blankly, her eyes still on the past. The boy repeated the question.

"Nobody, not even Muhlam, can defeat the valley and its customs, Salom. Muhlam knows the strength of these things, things that are stronger than himself."

"He is still the headman, and surely his command is law, at least in this valley?"

"If he defied the command of the gods and the people heard of it there would be trouble. The herdsmen would whisper against him——"

"I think perhaps they do already."

"Perhaps. It is the more reason why he must be cautious. Moreover if he defied such things the gods themselves would be angered. He would become a solitary man standing against everything else, both material and spiritual. He is not so strong as he thinks. When he has calmed a little he will realize that such a fight would end only in disaster for Muhlam and perhaps for all the people of Muhlam."

"But Veshti! It is not fair to her."

"Salom, Veshti is not so important as that. Not to Muhlam. She, too, must be woven in the pattern of the valley."

"The valley!" he spat. He shook with a sudden rage. "The valley, the valley, the valley! Always it is this talk of the valley. It sickens me!" Misery welled up in him. "It is what Muhlam told me. He will not let me talk of things beyond the valley. To him nothing exists beyond the pass."

"But he told you why?"

"Ah, I know. It is his arrogance. He says that a man can have allegiance only to this place. Bah! It is nothing but his intolerance. Nothing belongs that does not belong to Muhlam!"

"It is not only that, Salom. He told you nothing of Janbor?"

"Janbor?"

"His brother. His younger brother. I think he gave to him love such as he has given to nobody else—not even to me."

"You speak of something that is past?"

"It is past. Janbor was a dreamer. Perhaps it is from him that Veshti inherits her dreams, although Muhlam never thinks of this. One summer—it was many years ago—the weather acted strangely. The thaw came late and there was almost no summer, for by August winter was raging in the valleys. It was a cruel season. We lost many sheep and cattle and the grain bins were empty, and some died of hunger and some of a strange fever. Toward the end of summer Janbor saddled his horses and rode up to the Pass of White Watching. Muhlam argued with him, but the boy was firm. He said he would ride out beyond the pass to find another valley—a better valley. He never came back. The blizzards on the pass that night were the worst any could remember. Janbor never returned. And Muhlam never forgot. From that moment, I think, he hated everything that was beyond the valley. It is strange he did not talk to you of this."

"He said nothing."

She inclined her head. "Someday I think he will talk to you of it. Perhaps it will give you some understanding of his intolerance. At heart he is not an unkind man."

"Perhaps," the boy admitted doubtfully. His voice sharpened: "But it will not give me tolerance for such evil as Yanong proposes. In this there is more than Muhlam to consider. Whatever he does I tell you I will not allow——"

"You speak with rashness. What can you do?"

"I can fight against this thing!"

"For what, my son?"

"Why . . . for . . . for Veshti."

She shook her head sadly and her long earrings caught the white glint of the moon.

"It cannot be, Salom. It can never be."

"Only weaklings accept the impossible, Mother."

"It can never be. I must say things to you. Answer me a question, Salom. Is Veshti snaring your heart?"

"Why, I cannot——"

"Answer me, Salom."

"Yes."

"Then you must saddle your horses and ride on. For she cannot be for you."

"But why?"

"In the first place she is already bespoken to Dochi. That union cannot be broken. In the second place you are poor. You could not pay the required wealth for her. In the third place you are not of our people. And in the fourth place Veshti herself would refuse to wed you." She paused. The boy was silent. "You do not ask why. Perhaps in your heart you know. It is because you have no faith, Salom. Veshti is fond of you—that is easy enough to see. But there are deeper things. She would not mate with a man who did not possess her own belief. It is as important to her as it is to me. You understand, Salom?"

"I understand," he muttered.

"It will be easier for you if Yanong carries out the will of the gods. And someday you must saddle your horses and ride to other parts. Perhaps somewhere your destiny waits, Salom. But not here."

"But what of Veshti, Mother?" he pleaded. "She is not a yak or a votive bowl to be——"

"Veshti will accept the will of the gods, Salom. She may have grief, but she will accept their will."

The slowly spoken words hung between them like a thin veil, and Salom, his head bent, said nothing. And after a time Kelinka rose and her gnarled hand fluttered across the boy's shoulder in a vague motion of pity.

"I must return to the tent, Salom," she said gently. "The girl weeps. Twenty summers ago there was none to comfort me."

Chapter Nine

I

THE moon and stars were plunging down the sky before Salom returned. It was very still in the tent. Yanong had gone, and in the darkness there was the slow pulse of breathing. He curled into the rugs, and although none stirred he sensed that all were wakeful and conscious of his return. For an hour or more he stared at the slow drift of smoke and stars across the roof aperture, and then, aware that he would not sleep, he draped the rugs around him like a shawl and went quietly out into the night. Again the silent figures in the gloom gave no indication that his restlessness had been observed.

Dawn came as he shivered by the river's bank. He thrashed his arms and stamped his feet to bring warmth back to his body, but the damp chill clung in his bones. He strode downstream, away from the tent of Muhlam. The sound of the river was loud in the dawn hush. On a hillock beyond the far bank a herd of gazelle was grazing. He counted. Thirteen animals, and all does, and he stared around for the buck. He saw him, like a statue cast from bronze, amid some broken ground, and the glitter of sunrise was on his antlers. Wild goats were foraging on a gaunt rock face that overhung the trail. A toad hissed as he skirted a patch of oily bog, and a snow cock whirred into the morning paleness. Beyond a coppice of spruce the marmots were whistling. Life was astir again in the valley. He stared back to the thang. A thin ruled line of smoke stood above the tent of Muhlam. For a long time he watched it, until it wavered and became a drift in the morning wind, and then he saw two small figures come from the tent and walk toward the river. He tossed the rugs across his shoulder and strode back.

Veshti was crouched at the water's edge, and Renzi stood behind her with the pail. As he called to them Veshti looked up quickly. He could see the flash of light across her face—and then she was gone. He stopped and watched as she fled, leaping the tussocks of the bog, her arms outstretched, speeding across the flat grasses with her hair a banner and her boots bright against the frost. She did not look back. Soon she was only a darting speck beyond the thang.

His arms fell loosely to his sides, and the sick pain almost made him incapable of movement, and when Renzi came he still stood there.

The child's face was troubled.

"She was *weeping*, Salom," she said, but he brushed her aside and without looking at her or speaking he flung his rugs to the grass and hurried away down-valley. Renzi's mouth quivered as she watched him go. "Perhaps she did not want you to see her weeping," she whispered, and then she blinked her eyes and walked slowly back to the river, a lonely and bewildered little figure.

II

The sun was almost at the peak of its climb before Salom rested. To skirt the lower tents he had deviated from the rough trail and climbed the foothills, but as he looked down upon the vivid plain where the smoke hung he knew that he had returned to a familiar loneliness, because he spoke his thoughts aloud:

"Lotor, though, is a good man, and friendlier than most. He will let me have barley and meal and tea, and maybe a cheese or two—enough to take me to a distant valley."

He clambered across a spur of wet clay. A big hare, its ears alert and nose twitching, hopped unconcernedly from his path and looked at him as he plodded past. Salom paused and stared at the creature. "And where shall I go, animal?" he asked. The hare wrinkled its nose and nibbled at the grass.

Where would he go? He could not waste time in indecision. If he were to return over the Pass of White Watching there could be no delay. Within six weeks, perhaps within a month, he would have to be clear of the snow and beyond the gossamer-draped country of the Man-tze if he were to see China again. Even now it would be too late if the blizzards came early. Well, he could leave tomorrow. As soon as he had obtained food from Lotor and seen to his horses. He would ask no favor of Muhlam.

Or should he head west to the lower valleys? He would pass some encampment or village or monastery where men could tell him the way that led westward to the city of Batang, and he was well enough acquainted with the trail that curved north from there to Litang. There would be less danger along those lower trails. Even in bad weather there was no particular hazard for a traveler in the lowlands. There would be gales of dust and bitter nights— but no avalanches, no overwhelming storms of snow and ice, none of the perils that lurked in the shadowed silence of the lost forests. He dismissed the thought. Why should he seek the safe way? He remembered the squalid mud village beside the Lhasa Trail where he had spent most of his life, the grubby shops of Litang, the villainous bandits who roystered at the inns. No. He would return to China. And since there was no longer reason for prolonging his stay he would leave without delay.

And then he thought of the old peddler, the seller of dried vipers, the one who had set his feet on this unrewarding path. When he returned to Ch'eng-tu he would seek out the dotard. It would be a different conversation from the last one! There would be some questions which the old man would find trouble in answering, and no solutions to be found in the books of the apothecaries, nor in the directions scribbled across his packets of dried herbs. It was a great shame that the old philosopher had not traveled with him! Salom waved his arm contemptuously.

"Why did you not come with me, oldster?" he said aloud. "Then at least each of us would have had a shoulder upon which to weep!"

He clambered down to the level ground, and shuddered at the stab of icy water as he waded across the ford.

But the peddler had been right in one thing. Why had he warned him against seeking his future in China? Not because the streets were narrow or the trees filmed by dust; not because the houses were falling down or the streams sluggish. No. But because of the cruelty of laughter, the cutting whiplash of derision. In short, because of humanity. Yes, up to a point the old man had been wise enough, but his wisdom had not traveled four months across the hard mountains. "Peace," he had said. "Happiness," he had said. But what he had not said was that there was a disease on this valley, too, and the disease was humanity.

A mile beyond the ford he rested, and it was then that he saw the approach of a brilliant cavalcade. He moved off the trail and climbed to a ridge of slate where he would be screened by the stunted pines. He had no wish to be seen by other men, nor to be engaged in conversation; and yet he was curious, for it was a bigger caravan than he had seen in many months.

He could discern the flash of bright robes and steel, and the tossing of horses' heads. The column was strung out as it skirted a red hillock. He could count fifteen riding horses and twice as many pack animals, both mules and horses, and before long he could hear the melody of bells. Most of the riders wore red or yellow. Salom's mouth curled. Priests! They were close enough now for him to see the red and gold tassels below the horses' necks from which brass and silver bells were slung, and the wool saddle rugs woven into patterns of dragons and demons, and the shine of silken garments.

Two lamas in red habits plodded ahead of the column swinging their prayer wheels. Behind them, on a brilliantly caparisoned white ambler mule, rode a prodigiously fat man in handsome robes. He wore a hat of yellow lacquer shaped like a pagoda, and it shone in the sun. His boots were red and his apparel glittered with jewels. His face, flabby and tremulous, even with the easy gait of the mule, was set into an expression of bored and contemptuous arrogance. At a respectful distance behind him rode a pack of attendant lamas, voluble and grimy, and in the rear of the cavalcade were the pack animals, heavily burdened with rugs and drums and trumpets and vivid blankets, with black tables and cooking utensils, and with what appeared to be a folded tent fashioned from fine material in stripes of the five mystic colors.

The parade passed, but the noises of voices and drumming hoofs and tinkling bells had been lost in the murmur of the wind long before Salom climbed down from the knoll.

He knew that the fat man was the Living Buddha, the religious leader of these people. They called him the Tulku, and the talk of the herdsmen lately had been very much concerned with the imminence of the great man's annual visit to the last outpost of his spiritual dominions.

Salom was glad that the visit had come at this time. There would be enough hubbub and excitement now in the valley to ensure that an unwanted Chinese could take his leave unnoticed.

He turned to the east and walked back along the trail now scarred by the hoofs of many animals.

III

Afternoon was ebbing by the time he reached the upper thang. He was weary and hungry. He saw that the Living Buddha's tent had been perched on the edge of the field, about a hundred paces beyond Muhlam's and the home pasture was crowded with hobbled animals and priests who bustled backward and forward burdened with dung and brush for fires which were already thickening the air, with rugs and furnishings, with cooking utensils and food bags. Circling the striped tent like a demented person was the Tulku himself. He was wearing a high, arched hat that apparently had ritualistic significance, and he brandished two prayer wheels as he gyrated and leaped and pranced, and his obese body jellied through his robes as he robustly dispelled the evil spirits from his camp site.

Salom walked resolutely to Muhlam's tent.

They were all inside, and they looked up quickly, almost fearfully, as he pushed aside the black flap. Muhlam turned away as if unwilling to meet the boy's eyes, and Salom knew that in the headman's mind the decision had been made. Except that his face tightened, there was nothing in the boy's expression to reveal his feelings. He looked from one to the other steadily.

Renzi was two eyes beyond the smoke, and Kelinka smiled a timid welcome, and Veshti put the blowpipe to her mouth and stooped to coax the flames higher, although the fire was bright enough, but before she stooped Salom saw that her eyes were inflamed, and he wanted to take her hands in his.

"You will be hungry, Salom," Kelinka said. "Come. Tonight we have dumplings and a stew of ku-zeh with fine beef from a young yak."

Salom smiled. "I shall be able to eat my share, Mother."

"You were not with the herd," Muhlam said gruffly.

"No. I walked. I walked to the low pastures."

"So? Sometimes it is good to walk—if there are no other duties." He spat into the fire. "Kelinka, go loose the dogs. The herd today was troublesome to handle alone, and I am tired. Veshti will help you with the calves. But first loose the dogs. They will keep those whining priests away for the night. Tomorrow there will be no work done. There will be bowing and mumbling, and they will be on us like a plague for tea and food. The worth of a week's grazing will dribble away in a day! Then let us have peace tonight. Go, Kelinka."

His wife nodded and stooped through the door. She turned, her arm restraining Veshti, who had risen also. "There is no need for Veshti. I can manage the calves."

She went, and Salom immediately rose to follow her.

"Where do you go, boy?" Muhlam barked.

"To Kelinka."

"Have you no ears? She needs no help."

"I have a thing to tell her," Salom said evenly, and pushed through the door.

"Kelinka," he called. She turned, and in her embarrassment her head was shaking in the stupid way that had become a habit with her.

"Kelinka, I have a thing to say."

"Say it, my son."

"Tomorrow I take my leave of you."

"Ah!" She looked at him for a long time. Her tired face was drawn. "It is best," she said finally. "It is best, Salom."

"You mean——?"

"Yes. It was as I said."

"And . . . it has happened . . . it has happened already?"

"No. Not yet. There will be a concession to Muhlam's pride. Maybe a few days. But already he talks as if it is a fitting thing that the gods should select only his daughter." She shook her head uncertainly. "That is the truth, of course——"

"And Veshti, Mother?"

She looked at him silently.

"Ah, she agrees to be another that the evil one has broken, eh?" His words held no bitterness, no criticism, only wonder.

"She says nothing, Salom, but she will bow to the will of the gods."

He shrugged. "I will ride tomorrow. I plan to ride back to the east, and so I cannot delay."

"No. You will not want to delay."

"I will get food from Lotor, and——"

"Food? But we have ample food, Salom. We can——"

"I will get food from Lotor," he insisted firmly, and then he lowered his gaze uncomfortably. "Mother, there . . . there is nothing I can give you in repayment for what you have done . . . nothing. You know I have no wealth, and . . . and so I can make no repayment. . . ."

"Salom!" Her voice choked. "Salom, it is not you who should talk of payment. You . . . you have paid us by being with us. It is we who should make repayment . . . and we cannot."

She turned swiftly and hurried toward the calves, and there was none to see the hot tears that blotched her face.

Salom went back into the tent.

IV

By sunset five more tents had been pitched on the thang, spreading a half-circle from the garish tent of the Tulku almost to the home of Muhlam. The air jangled with bells, the outcry of the mastiffs, the yell and yammer of priests, the raucous blare of their demon trumpets. Even when the general din had subsided, a group of lamas continued to hammer with human femurs against the taut skins of their devil drums, and the throb came to the headman's tent in a maddening rhythm.

Around Muhlam's fire there had been little talk, and it had been only between the headman and Kelinka. It was talk that came in spurts, like beads strung on a long, strained cord of silence.

Salom stared into the red glow of the coals until his eyes ached. Through the night he had not spoken, nor had he looked at the silent Veshti. To the fitful words of Muhlam and Kelinka he gave no heed. But he looked up when the headman's voice sharpened in sudden impatient anger:

"Do these priests plan to play with noisy toys all through the night?" he snarled. "I no longer marvel that half of them are mad!"

Kelinka said nothing.

He strode to the door and wrenched back the flap.

"Enough!" he thundered into the darkness. "There are others here who would sleep!"

The only response was a burst of laughter muted by distance, and the pulse of the drums quickened.

"Muhlam!" Kelinka reproved fearfully. "Muhlam, you must not offend——"

"Offend? Who is doing the offending? Is it I who am fouling the night with noise, or is it the men of wisdom?"

"You will offend the Tulku, Muhlam."

"Bah! The Tulku shall be told tomorrow that his lackeys are offending Muhlam!" he retorted, but he tugged the flap back and returned to his rug.

"Why we should be pestered with a horde of sniveling fools is something I do not understand," he muttered.

"Muhlam!" Kelinka seemed almost angry with her husband. "How can you talk like that of the Tulku? It is——"

"Quiet, woman! I shall talk how I like of whom I like. And in any case I was not referring to the Tulku. He is a good man, and the cleverest in all of Kham. Except in one thing."

"What thing?"

"The crowd of jackals he drags at his heels."

"It is his position, Muhlam. He must have lamas in attendance. It is his position."

"You talk nothing but muck, Kelinka! How does a man look to his position by trailing around the land with a pack of mongrels yapping at his heels?" He punched a fist into the opened palm of his other hand. "By Dorji's guts, I have had a bellyful of it! I shall settle this caterwauling now!"

He strode from the tent, brushing away the imploring hand of his wife, and when he returned the night had gone back to its silence. Without further words the headman wrapped himself into his rugs.

V

Salom knew that he would not sleep, but he underestimated his weariness. He had scarcely pulled the furs around him before he was sleeping. He awakened long before sunrise. His mind was smooth and cool as carved jade, and his thoughts, poised a hairsbreadth above reality, moved with unimpeded precision.

It was dark. The fire was cold, and in the snow-hard air distant sounds came to him clearly. He could hear the lament of Chunor's dogs, disturbed by the presence of strange horses on the thang; and the desultory ringing of many bells; and there were the more familiar noises of a nightbird's chuck and the disquiet of some prowling wolf. But the drums were silent and no sound came from the lamas' tents. The night owned the valley's equivalent of silence—a stillness of many small sounds stitched haphazardly to the grumbling undertone of waters.

Salom tossed restlessly. What profit was there in this endless turntable of thought? It was like a Chinese juggler drawing from the brocade of his long sleeve an interminable riband of variegated colors and then waving his hands and there was left but the empty walnut shell between his fingers. It was the same—the same overbright ribbon of thought, and then, at the end, nothing—nothing but the empty walnut shell of finality.

What was the sense now in thinking of futile "ifs" and "whys"—what profit in deceiving himself, in wondering what would have been had Muhlam done this, or Kelinka said that, or Veshti shown rebellion? It all ended the same way. Again he was the man from outside, the man whose coming had not been sought and whose going would be of no more importance than the riffle of wind on pond water. He did not belong here. Then where did he belong? Perhaps he belonged nowhere. That was it. Everything else belonged somewhere—the rushes in the soft mud, the hares in their burrows, the wolves in their briered dens, the nettles amid the prayer stones. There was a place in the valley for all these people—for Muhlam, Kelinka, Veshti, for Dochi and Dupken—yes, even for Yanong. But there was no place for him. Only he, the Han-man, did not belong, as he had never really belonged to the old couple near Litang, as he had not belonged in the streets of Ch'eng-tu.

Kelinka had put it to him in another way—in terms of wealth and race and precedent. But it meant the same thing. He did not belong.

The night was moving now. The dawn wind was astir and it

came in bitter, nagging flurries, whining at the tent ropes, jabbing at the uneasy fabric of the tent. And the wind stabbed its bitterness into him.

What chance had they given him to belong? Who had been willing to talk to him, to give him counsel? Not Muhlam, with his pride and bigotry; not Kelinka, with her faith ready to support any vileness if it were clothed in holy robes; not Veshti, because of far too many things that were beyond his grasp. Even Kelinka's kindness had held injustice. She had condemned him for his intolerance—yet what tolerance had been shown to him? He had been called a demon on the evidence of a yammering fool, condemned as intolerant because he had raised his voice against evil, forbidden to mention a past that was the greater part of his life, scorned as an interfering upstart because he had stood against Muhlam's wrath in his demand for justice. Was this tolerance? If it was, then tolerance, too, was an empty walnut shell.

He rose to his feet stiffly and walked from the tent into the whisper of the snow. It was very light snow. The thought came to him as he looked along the curved line of strange tents to the spectral gleam in the darkness that marked the sleeping place of the Living Buddha. The thought came with the echo of Muhlam's words: "He is a good man, and the cleverest in all of Kham." If this man in the yellow hat was wise and good then why should *he* not listen? He pondered the thought for many minutes. He had nothing to lose. He would be leaving the valley. Why should he be overawed by the importance of a man who was merely the leader of a faith that meant nothing to him?

At the very least it would be good to talk to some person in the Valley of the Dreaming Phoenix before he took his leave of it. Probably he would gain nothing, but then there was nothing he could lose. He smiled slightly. In some ways it was good to be a pauper in all things. There was nothing one could lose. Only those with wealth feared thieves.

His mind was easier when he returned to the darkened tent to wait for morning.

VI

Outside the great man's tent the trampled thang had the appearance of a colorful fete. Lamas shuttled between the six tents of the initiated, their mulberry-colored robes flapping about them; bright-tasseled horses and mules cropped beside the more workmanlike beasts of the nomads. Standing apart was the hobbled white mule of the Living Buddha, its mane decked with red and gold and blue ribands.

Almost all the people of High Valley were there, decked in their brightest raiment, and there were people strange to Salom, but as they spoke to Chunor and Kaman and Lotor and the others with an easy familiarity he assumed correctly that they were from the lower camps, come to continue homage to their spiritual leader.

The Tulku was still eating, for the lamas trotted in and out of the striped tent, bearing platters of barley-meal cakes and steaming bowls of soup and fat spheres of cheese and ladles of warm curds. Then most of the priests disappeared into the big tent, and in the lull the valley people clustered outside, impatient and silent.

Salom stood apart from them, although Veshti and Kelinka and Renzi were there. They were talking to Bitola, who appeared to be the only person unimpressed by the momentous occasion. Only she did not lower her voice to a reverent whisper, nor did she waste time, as the others did, in gaping at the mystic frieze that hung above the doorway of the tent. She talked loudly, laughed brazenly, and flaunted her gay skirts and firm hips.

Salom saw with some surprise that Yanong was not present; nor had he seen him, he recalled, in the company of the other lamas. He was less surprised that Muhlam was also absent.

A chubby-faced priest hurried to one of the lesser tents and returned with the high-crowned hat of yellow lacquer, and then two more priests came from the Tulku's tent and stood on either side of the doorway, heavy brass trumpets in their hands. A shiver of anticipation ran through the watchful people. Salom walked forward slowly and took up his position at the end of the line, next to Lotor. The herdsman squirmed and averted his face, and then began to pick his nose nervously.

There was an expression of ineffable boredom on the Living Buddha's face as he came to the door. He was wiping the food from his lips with the back of a flabby hand, and then he belched and yawned. With complete disregard for the patient people, he walked slowly across to where his mule was grazing. His bare arms, soft and almost white, quivered and his chins shook with the ponderous labor of his gait.

For a few moments he studied the beast petulantly. With a weary gesture he summoned one of his lamas to his side.

"The hobbles are too tight, dolt! Loosen them. Is the beast to be lamed because of your stupidity?"

The displeasure remained on his face as he sauntered back to the reverent line of worshipers, who, at his approach, dropped to their knees in the melting snow, some swiftly, some clumsily. He stared distastefully at them, and then he belched again, and walked slowly along the vivid, uneven rank, occasionally placing a listless hand on the head of some tribesman in the form of blessing.

Dupken had flung herself full-length across his path, mumbling unintelligibly, but when he came to her he placed his heavy red boot beneath her body and gently kicked her aside. He did not look at her. Dupken's eyes blazed with insane joy because the great man had touched her, and her fingers scrabbled to reach the hem of his robe, but he had passed, and he was heedless now of all who crouched in obeisance before him.

There was a curious expression on his face as he looked at Salom. Of all the people only Salom stood erect.

The boy's mouth and eyes were rigid as he waited.

Beyond the ponderous approach of the massive figure he could see a dwindling arc of faces, all turned up to him; and in all the faces there was fear and horror and fascination, and in an instant of exaggerated clarity he could see the imploring eyes of Veshti.

"You do not kneel, boy?"

"No. I do not kneel."

He could hear the hissed intake of many breaths. The Living Buddha lifted both faint brows.

"Why?"

Salom gulped. His face was flushed, and the words he had planned had gone, and his tongue was dry and swollen.

"There was a question asked, boy. Why do you not kneel?"

"I . . . I did not come to pay homage," Salom muttered.

"So?" the Tulku's fat lips pursed and his gaze rested on Salom's blue jacket.

"You are not of our people."

"I am from China."

"Then they have altered the teaching in that land, eh?"

"Teaching?"

"There was a time in China when they taught respect for authority and reverence to those who were older."

The shame burned at Salom. He lowered his head.

"Why did you come then if not to pay homage?" the deep voice continued remorselessly.

"To speak with you." There was no defiance in the statement.

"So?" The arched brows snapped down imperiously, yet Salom had an uneasy feeling that he was being mocked.

"I came to speak with you," he continued doggedly.

"Are you insolent, boy, or merely stupid?"

"Neither. I came to speak with you."

He glanced nervously beyond the great man, and he could see the people of the valley, grotesquely immobilized, down on their hands and knees like fantastic animals in the soggy grass, and all their eyes were unswervingly upon him.

"You are impertinent," the flabby man observed gently. "Impertinent."

"No impertinence is meant, Tulku." The boy's forehead wrinkled. He looked at the Tulku pleadingly.

"You do not kneel because you do not follow our faith. Eh? Is that it?"

Salom nodded.

"Then what is your faith? Confucianist? Buddhist? Perhaps a Taoist, eh?" There was amusement lurking somewhere in the oiled silk of the old man's words.

"I follow no faith."

"So? Then you will be able to tell me something that has puzzled me. Why is it that unbelievers are always so—so—" he waved his flabby hands as if to conjure up the right word—"so—*belligerent* about their unbeliefs? It is a distressing thing that they should always be so belligerent."

"I did not mean——" He did not end the sentence. He was acutely conscious now of his youth and uncouthness. He wished he had never had this insane idea. And then he heard a muffled snigger, and other stifled laughter bubbled along the crouching, absorbed line beyond the Tulku. Salom lifted a shamed face and stared quite steadily at the fat man with the mockery in his eyes.

"I seek your pardon, Teacher, for wasting your time," he said firmly. "I realize now that I do *not* desire to speak with you."

He turned and began to move away. Although he held his head high, his heart was heavy and his belly sick with his own foolishness.

"Boy!"

He spun swiftly.

The Living Buddha was beckoning him. "Come here, boy!"

Salom stood before him awkwardly, while the old man shook in obese amusement.

"But you see, boy," said the Tulku gently, *"I desire to speak with you."*

He turned and glared along the crouching line.

"Away!" he shouted suddenly, and in his bellow there was a repugnance for all these things. "The lama Nunskar will arrange audience for those of you who wish to see me on spiritual matters. Now go! This morning I will be fully occupied with the man from China. Off to your tents now!"

He nodded a perfunctory acknowledgment of their bows and looked after them with contempt as they scuttled, whispering, from his immediate presence. But they were too enthralled by this unrehearsed drama to entertain the thought of leaving it. As soon as the Tulku turned back to Salom they stayed their flight and turned and squatted watchfully. And then a great hiss of astonishment came from them as the Living Buddha placed his hand on the boy's shoulder and ushered him inside the mystic tent, through the door where the devil daggers hung beneath the frieze of bright symbols that spelled certain destruction to any importunate demon.

Dupken's eyes snapped like those of a hunted beast.

Lotor swaggered across to her, his thumbs hooked into his wolfskin girdle. His usually amiable face was dark and sardonic.

"And what of your demon now, witless bitch?" he sneered. "Should he not be writhing on the ground, impaled by the sacred knives? For a demon he is on surprisingly good terms with our holiest man, eh?"

Dupken whirled on him, hissing and spitting like a horned toad, and as she squatted on all fours with the saliva froth at her mouth and her black eyes flicking she had the very look of some loathsome swamp creature.

"It is what I said!" she screamed. "This is no *ordinary* demon! This is Dorjilutru himself! This is something more powerful even than the Most Excellent One!"

"Wipe the filth from your tongue, crone! If I listen longer my guts are in strips!"

"Eeee! Fool! You would not recognize wisdom if it struck you across the face. If there was a fine grain of it in your body you would understand the deadly peril that faces the Tulku at this instant—with that—that *creature* in with him!"

"It is as I said." Lotor grimaced and clasped his belly in comic pantomime. "My guts shred already!"

He looked at the others dryly.

"Then you will follow Dupken, eh?" he called. "She will lead you into the tent to inform the Tulku that he shares his mat with Dorji. The Tulku will be grateful for this information. He is a dull person, a simple clod. He will be glad of the benefit of

Dupken's great wisdom." His eyes jeered, and a few of the others laughed, and Bitola smiled at her father appreciatively.

"As for me," Lotor continued, "I have other matters. There are three jars of chang in my tent. If anybody has need of three empty jars he will find them outside my tent at sundown. But do not disturb Lotor. He will be asleep, trying not to dream of Dupken!"

He laughed and sauntered away. But then he turned.

"If you go to the Tulku's tent," he called, "send the crone in first. I swear the sacred knives will fall on her—if there is any worth in their magic!"

Chapter Ten

I

THE Tulku's tent was divided by curtains of brocade into several chambers, the largest of which was hung with six thankas, or religious paintings. Five were painted in smoldering colors on tanned human skin stitched to silk and stretched between gilded scrolls. The sixth hung against the brocade behind the Tulku's dais. It depicted a complacent Buddha reclining in the heart of a lotus and fondling a naked girl who was curled voluptuously at his feet. Its placid sensuality was in direct contrast to the other paintings, which were unlovely portrayals of hells and demons and monsters, of flayed and mutilated bodies, of a goddess with wolfish fangs drinking blood from a human skull, of tormented writhings and a variety of obscene tortures.

Salom averted his eyes quickly from these repellent studies. The Living Buddha grunted as he began to climb to his throne, a high platform of folded rugs and boxes draped with bright saddle cloths. A gaudy rug was spread before the dais in the form of a table, and upon it were utensils such as the boy had never seen before. There were tall urns of beaten silver, a gem-encrusted teapot of great size, and food bowls carved from jade so milky that it looked like porcelain. Ivory platters were heaped with cheese, butter, brown sugar, roasted walnuts, dried peas, crushed nettles and azalea leaves, and many sweetmeats made from tsamba brightly banded with cords of dyed butter.

Four lamas with expressionless faces sat cross-legged on each side of the rug, all twirling prayer wheels, all looking blankly toward their leader. A ninth attendant stood in the corner beside a shallow drum. His right hand clasped a curved drumstick fashioned from an animal's rib. He stared expectantly toward the Tulku as if awaiting a signal. Salom's eyes followed his, and for an instant all his tautness passed and he could scarcely suppress a smile.

The Living Buddha was making the last stertorous effort to mount his throne. There was nothing to be seen but his boots wriggling from beneath his brocaded gown and his vast buttocks quivering beneath the silk. And then with a final grunt he clambered up, twisted around awkwardly, and sat cross-legged in the attitude of contemplation.

"Ahhhh!" A relieved murmur breathed from the squatting priests. The man beside the drum rapped out a vibrant tattoo with fanatical fervor, clapped his palm to the drum to mute its resonance, and shuffled from the tent.

The Tulku squirmed himself into a more comfortable position, broke wind, scratched his swelling belly absently, reached for an ivory prayer wheel, and closed his eyes.

He seemed to have forgotten Salom's presence; the lamas were whispering among themselves and gave no attention to the boy. Salom licked his lips nervously and stared beyond the Tulku to the holy picture.

It was framed with an inch-wide strip of scarlet paper, then a strip of gold, and then a wider band of dark-blue silk. The scrolls at top and bottom were of ebony or some very dark wood, and ornate embossments of silver guarded the projecting ends. A rectangle of sumptuous brocade was sewed below the picture. But it was the painting itself, and in particular its subject, that held Salom's attention, and troubled him. The artist, whoever he was, had been hampered by no lack of skill. The draughtsmanship carried a fluidity that was almost musical, a rhythm so sensitive that its full beauty could not be absorbed in a cursory glance. Most of its beauty was of line and rhythm and balance, for if there had once been any color in it the hues had faded now into colorless tones. There was nothing left of the smolder that still lurked in the demon pictures. And yet for all their hideousness Salom almost preferred the horrors. At least they were honest in their obscenity. This had a quality of slyness, of prurience. It was pornography leering from a mask of saintliness. It was—his heart hammered at the realization—it was Yanong and Veshti; Kano and Kelinka; it was the never-ending lasciviousness of evil men posturing in holy robes! The thought chilled him, and yet it bound him in morbid thrall: the surrender in the wanton body of the girl, the slack ripeness of her mouth, the eyes half-closed and heavy-lidded with a sensual ecstacy, the indifference on the face of the Buddha and the delicate grip of the girl's left nipple between his tapering fingers, the flowing abandon of her limbs.

"You are quite wrong, boy," the Tulku murmured, and Salom looked up to him, startled. The eyes were still closed into wrinkles of fat. "Quite wrong. It is not a sensual picture, nor an evil one. Only those who have wrong things in their own hearts will see wrong things in it."

"But . . . but . . . I said nothing!"

"And for those who see evil in it because they possess evil in themselves there are other pictures to be studied. For those who ponder too much on fleshly desires there are penances and punishments."

"I said nothing! I do not understand this!" Salom looked around wildly, but the lamas were spinning their wheels unconcernedly, as if they had heard nothing, and the Living Buddha's face was rapt and unseeing.

"Let me explain, boy." The old man's voice was weighted by boredom, as though he had said these words many times before: "The lotus is the symbol of divine birth, the woman the symbol of the purity of the spirit, the Enlightened One the symbol of compassion. That is all. Purity, compassion, the belief in a divinity of impulse. There is nothing more to be read into it."

There was a dryness in Salom's mouth, and his voice shook:

"But . . . I . . . I said *nothing!* How can you hear things that are only in my mind?"

The Tulku opened his heavy-lidded eyes slowly. He looked at the boy as if he saw him, and yet saw far beyond him also.

"Because we have been over these matters already. We have said these things before. You understand?"

Salom shook his head dumbly. He wished he had not come. He felt muddled and afraid.

"No," the fat man agreed thoughtfully. "No, perhaps you would not understand. Then let us call it a dream."

"It does not explain——"

"Enough!" The Tulku flourished his hand impatiently, and acidly surveyed the double line of his attendants, all of whom were now peering toward him expectantly.

Distaste dragged at the old man's mouth as he looked back to Salom.

"We will talk in Chinese," he said. "I say the language well, and it is one of the million things upon which these oafs of mine are ignorant. Buddha himself regarded ignorance as the most heinous of all sins—and look at these——" He gestured his contempt toward the priests, who sniggered appreciatively and beamed up at him.

"But I speak no Chinese," Salom said ashamedly. "You see, I was there——"

"Of course. I recall now. Most of your life was spent in Tibet." He gave no indication that he had observed Salom's bewilderment. "Then we shall dismiss this pack of cretins." Again the priests sniggered happily, but at the disdainful gesture of their leader they scrambled to their feet and began to file from the tent. They went cheerfully, nodding their nubbled skulls in relish of their leader's wit.

"Hurry!" he snapped. "The stench of your brainlessness overcomes me! And return in an hour with tea and bowls of curds for the visitor and myself. With sugar. Now go, else I vomit!"

For long moments the Tulku glared at the doorway.

"I am——" he sighed heavily—"the reincarnation of a saint who lived in a most uncomfortable cave near Koko-nor seven hundred years ago, and yet there are times when it is scarcely credible."

Salom was still bemused; he waited for him to continue.

"It sometimes surprises me that the reward for such saintliness should be the worry of administering fourteen monasteries crammed with nincompoops, and then being cursed with a train of piddling lackeys who barely warrant reincarnation as gnats!"

"But . . . but are they not specially chosen?"

"Chosen? Bah! What choice is there when the whole litter is warped? There are seven hundred priests under my authority, and if I dredged the lot, and sieved them, and then skimmed the scum from the whole odious mess I doubt if I would find one with the brains of a louse, the spirit of a tick, or the integrity of a village rat! And *that* is the reward for seven hundred years of holiness!"

"I also have no high opinion of the lamas."

"So? And what difference does that make to me? Is the sorry brood your responsibility or mine?"

"I expressed only an opinion. Any man has the right to his opinion."

The Tulku's heavy eyelids drooped slyly. "Unless he is an unbeliever who expresses opinions on beliefs he is not prepared to understand or tolerate. Intolerance waives the right of opinion."

"I do not think——"

"Ah, the truth at last! You do not think. Then is it not time, boy, you began to think?"

Salom was suddenly angry. He had been mocked and humiliated long enough. "I came here to talk . . . and . . . and you twist my words so that . . ."

A rumble of laughter shook the silken mound of the saint's belly. "I thought I had made that clear, boy. *You* came here to listen!"

Salom bit his lip. He had an almost overwhelming desire to leave, to take his horses and ride quickly away, to put the great white shafts of the mountains between himself and this repellent old fool who merely played with him and mocked him.

"Go if you desire, boy." There was a yawn half-stifled in the words. "But if you saddle your horses and leave the valley you will have accomplished—what? Nothing. Nothing at all."

"In any case I have accomplished nothing."

"So? There is still time, you know. It has taken me seven hundred years, boy, to learn that there is always time. But let us not talk of accomplishment. It is one of the illusions that chain men to their futile rounds of lives. And in each man's mind it has a different meaning. So let us talk of faith, boy, for that also has a different meaning in each man's mind."

"I have no faith."

"So?" The Tulku had closed his eyes, but even through the thick white eyelids Salom could feel, uneasily, a glint of mockery still lingering. "Then in your stumbling fashion, boy, do you think you could tell me *why* you have no faith?"

"And have you mock me again?"

"I do not mock. Do you think you could tell me?"

"I do not know. Perhaps. Unless you . . . you twisted my words again."

"Talk then, boy."

And Salom, after a moment of indecision, talked. The words came hesitantly at first, for he was absorbed in the face of the Living Buddha in his eagerness to assess the effect of his words. But the eyes of the old man soon closed, and he rocked gently from side to side, and his lips moved as if he were talking to himself, while his pudgy fingers rippled with astonishing dexterity along his prayer beads. After a time even that activity ceased and the Tulku appeared to be sleeping.

Salom said nothing of Veshti nor of Yanong, but he spoke of his childhood and the mercenary monks he had seen, of his journey into China and the disillusionment he had experienced, of the meeting with the old peddler and of how he had learned his father's story, of the peddler's advice and his journey to the Valley of the Dreaming Phoenix. His tale faltered when he came to the more recent events. What purpose would be served in talking of the shadows that had fallen across the serenity of the valley? And, in any event, the old man was certainly not listening. He was asleep. A thin thread of spittle dribbled from his open mouth. The boy fell silent. He could hear the heavy breathing and see how the silk across the huge stomach wrinkled and tightened. He lowered his head despondently.

"But this does not tell me why you are planning to leave this valley," the Tulku murmured sleepily, his eyes still closed.

"Your pardon, Tulku. I thought you did not listen."

The old eyes half opened. "But in any case you did not intend to tell me of the girl or the monk or the other things." A smile hovered at the thick mouth. "Eh?"

Salom stiffened. This was magic! But how? Could this grotesque old man read thoughts as a scholar would read a book? Or were there spies in the valley who reported the actions and thoughts of people? Yet how could thoughts be spied upon?

"I have no spies, boy." The Tulku was looking at him steadily now, and there was a strange look in his eyes, as if their focus was an infinite range of vision. "No, I have no need for spies. We have said these things before, you and I." Even the man's voice was different now; no longer bombastic, petulant, mocking. It had a blurred quality, a misleading softness, the quality of steel wrapped around and around with many layers of silk. "Already, boy, I know more than I need to know. More than you know, more than the monk knows, more than the girl, or the headman—more than any of the others. You see, my son—" he paused wearily—"I know how the story ends."

Summer sounds drowsed thickly in the silence, and the silence drowsed on in an endless moment, and a pulse throbbed in Salom's throat.

Then the Tulku yawned and scratched his belly and thrust out a petulant lip. "I am hungry. I will call for food and when we have eaten and the fools are dismissed I will talk to you." He smiled amiably and joggled on his seat as though he was very pleased with himself. "And this time *you* will listen," he added.

II

The last of the priests had gone from the tent with the empty bowls. Salom had eaten little, but the Living Buddha had attacked his food with relish, smacking his lips and rolling the sugared curds on his tongue. And now he eased out his silken girdle and belched and allowed the mass of his flesh to settle ponderously back into the attitude of contemplation. A beatific smile gently rolled back the soft white cheeks. He closed his eyes.

"I am a saint, boy," he murmured happily. "I am a *very* wise man. I know many things."

Salom had a sudden hysterical desire to laugh, but the Tulku opened his eyes a fraction, and there was something in the sly, dark slits that forbade laughter.

"You may laugh if you wish," the old man said. "Many have laughed before. Let me tell you something. Four summers ago I journeyed to China. There was fighting in the land—it seems in that land they never tire of fighting!—and many soldiers tearing one another like wild beasts. I saw nothing of these stupidities, although the market places were full of talk, because the fighting was taking place in remote districts, and there were more important matters demanding my attention.

"I, too, traveled to Ch'eng-tu, for we have a monastery there, on the outskirts of the city, and there was a matter of an abbot who had been untrustworthy and who had trodden paths that Buddha had forgotten to include in the Middle Way. After the abbot had been dealt with I found time hanging on my hands, for there was a delay in the assembling of my caravan for the journey back.

"There were many Western people in the city, come from lands far distant because of the attraction of this killing that had crazed the land. You have seen these Westerners? No. They are ugly in appearance, although often of good build like our people. But their faces are thin and hideously red, and the skins of them like the flesh of a flayed rabbit, and their bodies covered with hair. They follow a strange religion. A meaningless pap, with easy rewards and childish punishments and most convenient repentances. A thing that can be swallowed and digested at a sitting, like tsamba by a child just weaned. To the thinking man it has no challenge. No challenge at all. But I suppose the Westerners do not desire a belief any more challenging than this, since it gives them much time in which to plan and build the magic machines they love, and to make money, and to indulge their fleshly appetites."

He paused for a moment and reflected, and when he continued there was a trace of bewilderment in his voice.

"Mind you, they are clever enough. They sought me out to make pictures of me with a black casket that breeds a likeness without color. And then they showed me wheeled carriages that run across the land faster than the hawk drops, other articles that carry voices over vast distances, boxes that contain music and laughter and talk and noise to be released at the twist of a handle, great rooms in which shadow pictures of people sing and dance.

"These things I could not understand. Never had I seen such marvels, and when I admitted my astonishment they piled new wonders upon new wonders until my brain staggered. And then they laughed at me. They laughed at me because I could not understand."

The striped canopy breathed in the summer wind, and the light that filtered through the fabric played over the Tulku's fantastic figure in wavering patterns of the mystic colors, until he seemed to melt into and become part of the hideous pictures all around him. Salom opened his mouth to speak, but the Tulku's lifted hand silenced him.

"Wait, boy," he said. "The tale is not yet finished. To you it might seem irrelevant, but it is not yet finished. Before I took my leave of Ch'eng-tu some of these Westerners came to visit me at the monastery. They came with gifts and pleasant words, and with requests for me to inform them of my faith. It is a subject which cannot be encompassed in a mere afternoon of talk, but I spoke to them, although I knew that they had really come for some vulgar display of magic. Still—I spoke to them. I tried to explain to them that ours was the faith for the intellectual man, for the scholar, for the thinker, for the individual. That a man in search of the Absolute Truth must be prepared to devote a hundred successive lives, perhaps many thousand of years of living, merely so that he could find the last answer and his own release from the Wheel.

"I could see their skepticism—as plainly, boy, as I see yours—but I told them of the lives I had lived, back for the seven hundred years I can see behind me. I told them a little of the next life I would have. One man asked me if it was as easy to see into the future as to look back into past lives. I explained to him that it was not so easy, but it was quite possible to do it, although the training was harder. And do you know what happened, boy? They laughed. They were convulsed by laughter! And so I became angry and bade them go.

"But when my anger had subsided I began to think about the stupidity of these people. They were of a race that for many hundreds of years had devoted almost all the energies of its brains to fleshly and material things. I had seen the fruits of those energies in their wheeled carriages and picture caskets and machines that snared voices, and I had marveled at them.

"Now, here is my point, boy. *My* people had devoted all their mental energies for as many years—perhaps for even more years—to reflections on matters as far removed as possible from material things, on matters hidden in the expansive realms of pure thought. Yet those Western buffoons could only scoff. They expected me to believe their accomplishment, even though they were beyond my understanding. And they derided my accomplishments only because they were beyond *their* understanding!"

Salom's head was lowered, and he sat very still beside the brilliant rug, turning the Tulku's words over in his mind. As he looked up a slow flush crept under his skin.

The fat man nodded gently and smiled. "Ah, you begin to see, eh? You begin to see that you are perhaps not unlike these Western barbarians. You are contemptuous of things you do not understand, quite intolerant of beliefs that are not of *your* mind." He stroked his chins reflectively. "True, you are more considerate. But that is merely that you are a man of the East, and men of the East are born with more courtesy than those of the West will acquire in a lifetime. Later, of course, you must lose it. In most people acts of intolerance, rudeness, arrogance, are the notches of the years. But now you have much to learn—if you are willing to learn?"

Salom nodded with a new and sudden humility.

"Yes," he said. "Yes, I think I am willing to learn. But first I wish you would tell me how it is that you can read my thoughts."

The Tulku jiggled impatiently upon his rugs. "Bah! I think I waste my time with you! It was so with the Westerners. All they wanted was magic. I am not a magician at a fair, boy, to amuse you with little deceits! I am a Tulku! Have I spent a hundred lives on the mystic path—and many of them not nearly so comfortable as this one, let me tell you!—merely to perform tricks for a stupid Chinese boy? This thought-reading foolishness! It is so unimportant that it is not even a separate study." He frowned peevishly. "It is a long path, and tiring, and there are many things yet to do. I wonder why I waste my time with a Chinese boy and a lecherous monk and a silly little maid who does not know her own mind! We have said all these words before, and all the words that have yet to pass between us—and still the outcome will be the same."

"Then if you know these things," Salom said harshly, "why do you not take action against this priest? It is a transgression against the priestly vows, and——"

The pudgy hand waved contemptuously. "It is not important. And, in any case, it is written. The ability to foresee events and to read the writings gives nobody—not even a Tulku—the right to alter them."

"Then I see no need for further talk. Tomorrow I leave this valley—and these people."

The portly saint looked down at him with renewed interest.

"You do not like them, eh?"

"Let us say that they do not like me."

"It is as I said, boy. People are always sympathetic only to the things they themselves understand. They do not understand you. So they are unsympathetic, and that will lead to hostility. Because they do not understand you, and do not want to understand you. That is all."

"But at first I was happy here——"

"Until you met people?"

"Until I met *certain* people." All his misery was welling up in him again.

The Tulku appeared to have lost his peevishness. He had settled back more comfortably upon the dais, and he smiled faintly as his fingers flickered along the polished spheres of his rosary.

"And do you think it will be different in other places?"

Salom did not answer. "Boy, there is only one peace to be found," the old man continued, "the peace of the spirit—the absence of all desires—the cessation of all the mental struggle that creates illusion. Running away will not bring you peace. You will only go from people to more people, and wherever people are there also is a conflict of mental activity creating many whirlpools of desire and distraction that will pull you this way and that. It is the same. Wherever people are it is the same—and with *all* people it is the same."

"Then if people are so bad why are there people?" Salom asked. He was puzzled by the Tulku's words. And yet, while he was wary of further mockery, he was impressed against his will by the fat man's sincerity.

There was no trace of mockery when the Tulku went on:

"There is a chain that binds man to existence until he can find that which breaks these fetters. A long time ago a man lived who was very much wiser than I. He was Gautama, the Buddha, the Enlightened One. He formulated the four Noble Truths. Now, boy, listen to them: Existence is sorrow; sorrow is caused by desire; to conquer sorrow a man must annihilate the thirst of desire and the attachment of life; to attain this cessation he must follow the path."

"But . . . but what is this path?"

"It is the way that leads us beyond the limits which we assign to the Self, before we realize that the Self is compound and impermanent and does not exist. Some have tried to attain the supreme enlightenment in one lifetime. It is as if instead of following the road which goes around a mountain, ascending gradually toward its summit, one attempted to reach it in a straight line, climbing perpendicular rocks and crossing chasms on a thread. It is very dangerous, and such an adventurer falls into spiritual abysses and gains nothing." He pursed his mouth. "That is why even for such a wise man as myself there are many lives to be lived—still to be lived. It is the price of faith."

"And if a man has no faith?"

"No man is without faith. Some men *say* they have no faith. Bah! They are children whistling to dispel the shadows of a windy night. *All* men have faith."

Salom's smile was lopsided: "Even such a faithless one as I?"

The Living Buddha looked bored and belched. "Your questions are extremely stupid. You yourself told me you had a faith. Think before you speak. Your thoughts are as shaggy and uncombed as a yak!"

"I have never said I possessed a faith."

"And what of the word, eh?" the fat man asked craftily. "What of the word, boy, that your father left you?—that the peddler told you? *Undefeated.* There is your faith. Ha!"

And Salom, bemused and angry at the garish old man's ridicule, was still forced to admit that there was wisdom embedded in the boasting and mummery and gibing that comprised most of the mystic's conversation. Mystic? But was he really a mystic? Or merely a cunning old man with a good sense of stagecraft? He had never before met a mystic, but he had heard many tales of them, and this man tallied with no description he had ever heard. He fidgeted beside the rug and wished he were older and more experienced and with some learning that would help him to understand this man and to parry his thrusts. He felt now as if he were groping in a muddy stream for some bright article he had dropped. When he had thought of talking to the Tulku he had not planned that it would be like this.

"What you plan, or what I plan, does not matter, boy." The old man spoke with a kindly intonation. "The end of the story is the same."

Salom again experienced a sudden humility. "Teacher . . . please do not mock me . . . if you really know these things. . . . You say you know how the story ends. I do not know what you mean . . . but . . . but will you not advise me?" His voice pleaded. "Will you not tell me what to do?"

The Living Buddha sighed and reached for his prayer wheel and he watched the smooth spin of the ivory cylinder with eyes that were old and tired, eyes that looked almost as if they *had* watched the puny struggles of humanity for seven hundred years.

"Am I a soothsayer to be bribed with silver?" he asked softly. "Am I an astrologer selling horoscopes like bags of meal? No. There is only the one thing I will tell you, boy. You have a faith that is a good faith. Keep it. The end of the story will be the best ending, the only ending, for each one of you. For the maid, for the headman, for the monk—and for you. Life, boy, has a way of meting out rewards and punishments." He paused significantly. "My son, do you know the last words that were uttered by the great Buddha himself? Eh? Of course not. I would not expect you to. He said: 'Decay is inherent in all living things; work out your own salvation.' "

The wind knuckled at the tent and the ripples were transmitted to the heavy silk of the thankas, and in that taut, oppressive silence it seemed to Salom that the devils and imps and monstrosities squirmed in a sinister dance, and the naked girl smoothed herself against the detached caresses of the Buddha.

Salom stared at the painted figures. "You say my faith—my faith in a word—is a good faith. Does it not matter then that I believe in nothing of . . . of this?" He gestured toward the thankas.

"Everything is in the mind, boy. Gods, demons, heavens and hells. All spring from the mind, and sink back into the mind."

"But . . . but if all this is . . . is *illusion*—?"

"It seems that you do not yet grasp what I have told you, boy. All life is illusion, and religion is part of life because religion is fear. And as all people have fear, then all people must have their religion. It matters not whether it is the pap of the Westerners or the challenging thinking of our people. They must have it."

"Then I do not understand what you mean by faith." Salom's face was puckered with concentration. "I cannot see where the difference——"

"Faith is that which takes the spirit for a time beyond the unrealities of Self. Religion, whatever the charlatans say, is that which *fetters* the spirit to Self. Can I make it more simple than that? Listen. Religion tells a man that he is somehow immortal, that his Self will be perpetuated in some manner in another life, on and on, everlastingly. Bah! It is his terror of the things he cannot understand. On your journey here you traveled past the high peaks, eh? You were afraid? To many people when the world was young these peaks were the old gods of the world. Today some are still regarded as sacred. But in the beginning it was fear that gave them what is called divinity. Man could not conquer the peaks. So he worshiped them. In the same way he could not defeat death. And yet he was loath to worship a thing so inevitable and all-effacing. So he placed figures at its portals and chambers and gardens beyond wherein he could live forever. Only the more thoughtful of us saw that the ultimate goal was final extinction, release from the long tyranny of living. Religion, boy, has become the terrified wail of the mob against the unseen beasts that lurk beyond the darkness. But faith always has been, and always will be, the inner cry of the man alone."

Salom pondered the words, clutching at their elusive meanings, and then he said slowly, "But there is still a thing that is not clear. *You* follow a religion. You are the leader of a religion. And yet you speak like this. This is a thing I do not understand."

"*You* do not understand! By the reincarnate spirit of the Black

Hat Dancer, boy, do you *expect* to understand?" He glowered down. "After seventy decades of saintly living, and the garnering of a wisdom that I assure you is singularly lacking in this benighted land, *I do not understand either!* It has been a long path—and sometimes appallingly devoid of comfort—and yet I have not passed beyond the stage of having to administer to a pack of ninny-hammers. That is the Wheel, boy! We are all chained to the Wheel until we can find extinction. And if I were not a saint I would be—what? A herdsman? A silversmith? A harlot's pimp? Does it matter? Except that I would rather be a saint. It is more comfortable."

He closed his eyes suddenly, and his soft white hands stroked a fold of his gorgeous robe. Salom waited uncomfortably for an opportunity to bring the conversation back. He waited for a long time before he realized that the conversation had ended. The prodigious and resplendent figure breathed with a heavy rhythm. Salom coughed, and then he squirmed into a more comfortable position and coughed louder.

The old man's eyes opened sleepily, and then hardened in irritation.

"Are you *still* here, boy?"

"I thought——"

"Off with you! Go! Do you think a man as important as I has all the summer to waste on fatuous children? Now be off with you!"

"There are still some things I had to say," Salom suggested nervously. "I wanted——"

The Living Buddha jerked upright, his flesh quivering.

"Before my sainthood I must have lived some uncommonly vicious lives," he grumbled, "to be pestered by dolts for seven hundred years. Now, be off with you, boy, before I begin to show my displeasure. Away!"

Not until Salom had left the tent did the Living Buddha relax again—and then the annoyance left his face and he sank back on the bright rugs. His eyes were open. They were old eyes and wise eyes, but somewhere within their age and wisdom was an older, troubled bewilderment.

III

Many of the valley people were still assembled on the thang when Salom came from the Tulku's tent. They had formed a silent and attentive arc about forty paces away.

He looked toward them without interest, and stood for a few moments in thought before he walked toward them. Only then did he realize the effect his audience with the Tulku had created. All the people nodded toward him respectfully, and some bowed, and Naropa jerked an absurd and involuntary curtsy.

In the attitudes of one or two of them there was so much of unwitting caricature, such a travesty of deference, that his mouth twitched: yet there was something pleasurable in the realization that the mere fact of having been closeted for so long with the holy man had greatly enhanced his own prestige.

But it was later that he discovered its full implication.

He had almost reached Muhlam's tent when he saw Yanong. The monk was standing midway between the tents of the headman and Chunor. He was stooped a little and he chewed nervously at his fingernail. The hostility toward the priest gripped Salom instantly, but then he saw with some surprise that Yanong, too, looked toward him with an unusual deference. Salom stopped. For a little time they faced each other indecisively. At first he thought the priest intended to speak. But nothing was said, and Yanong cringed a little, as a man would fearing violence, and then he shook his head quickly and bounded away, clutching his greasy habit about him.

Salom looked in amazement at the absurd picture of burgundy robes whipping in the wind, the shaved skull nodding ridiculously, the thin arm thrashing as if to ward off a plague of venomous insects.

When he next saw Yanong the monk was astride his hungry-looking horse, riding rapidly into the sun. His sleeping rugs and food bags were strapped behind the saddle and his booted heels kicked viciously into the beast's thin flanks.

And then Salom's bewilderment passed and laughter gushed from him. He shook with laughter, and he choked and spluttered. He laughed until his sides caught with a stitch. There was an element of hysteria in his mirth, and there was relish, too, of the extravagant parody of flight created by the terrified monk.

For Yanong had gone! And it was he, Salom, who had driven him away! And it was all so simple! So magnificently simple! For Yanong must have believed that he had told the Tulku of the priest's designs on the headman's daughter, and he had fled in panic from his leader's retribution!

His guffaws brought Renzi running from the tent with questions in her eyes.

"Salom!" she piped. "Salom, why do you laugh like this?"

He wiped his eyes and seized both the child's hands in his.

"Nothing, Renzi," he spluttered. "An old man told me something today, and I have just seen what he meant." He stared toward the Tulku's striped tent, and then he smiled down at the child.

"Come, Renzi," he said. "Let us see what fine broth simmers in the cauldron for tonight."

BOOK THREE

Chapter Eleven

I

Veshti slept late. It was a sleep without dream or movement. There was a smile on her mouth and one arm was flung wide in an unconscious gesture of supplication. Kelinka nodded to herself as she prepared the first churn of tea. Muhlam stretched from beneath the panda skin, and his face hardened as he saw Kelinka engaged on Veshti's task, and Veshti sleeping.

"What fool's play is this?" he mumbled, but his wife's gesture silenced him, and he went from the tent muttering.

When Veshti awakened there was the clatter of wooden bowls and the sense of morning already well advanced. For many moments she teetered on the slender bridge that separates sleep from wakefulness, unwilling to accept the day and the unprecedented problem of bowls already clattering. She closed her eyes.

"Come, Veshti," Kelinka said. "Wake up, child. The tsamba is ready."

She jerked upright, questions tumbling in her bemused eyes, and Kelinka answered them gruffly.

"You needed the sleep. Now come, or the day will be gone. There is much to do."

Veshti took the bowl that Renzi offered and sucked the warmth of the beverage into her, and then she saw, from across the tent, the happiness on Salom's face, and she understood. There had been a gift made—a gift of time. Yanong had gone. She was unsure of the reason, but Yanong had gone, and although Salom had told her nothing she knew that it was Salom who had made him go. An almost uncontrollable impulse gripped her. It was a desire to shout and to sing and to dance. And then the feeling was touched by a trace of penitence. It was surely not right that a girl should rejoice because a benefaction of the gods had been withheld? Surely not? This was a heresy in her mind—and yet it was not only that one thing; it was a mixture of many things, and Salom was in all of them. And, in any case, the rejoicing in her heart would not be stifled—no matter what feeling of guilt her mind held!

"Where is Muhlam?" she asked.

"Gone," Kelinka said. "Gone to the herds."

"Then?" She looked her inquiry at Salom.

"Oh, I go now," he said. He wanted to tell her that he had stayed only to see her waken. Instead, he said diffidently, "There is little for me to do today. I may return early."

Veshti understood the unspoken question that interlaced the statement, and answered it to herself: I am glad you return early. Yes, I am *very* glad you return early. I shall be here.

"Then you are not leaving the valley today?" she asked aloud. "I thought——"

"It is changed now. I think I will not leave."

Veshti had forgotten the presence of her mother and sister. "Then it is . . . it is because Yanong has gone that you have altered your plans?"

"Yanong? No. He is of little importance." He spoke airily. "No, child," he continued with deliberate casualness, "it was because of what we discussed—the Living Buddha and I. We talked about it, and decided it would be best if I remained. For a time, anyway."

He saw on her face the thing he wished to see, and he whistled as he unhooked his bridle from the tent post.

Outside, the mists had gone and the hills rumpled back with the soft green pile of a fabulous carpet, and little baby fists of flowers curled open in the sun. Salom grinned at the surly mastiffs.

"It is a fine valley you live in," he informed them. "A fine valley, indeed!" He laughed at himself as he swung into the saddle.

As he followed the dwindling river uphill he could scarcely quell his elation. He had a new-found sense of power, of resolution, of confidence, of a buoyancy that lifted him on a tide of strength and joy. Life was as immense and brilliant as the day itself.

On the high thang he parried the herdsmen's questions on his interview with the Living Buddha with such aplomb that he left them with the impression that perhaps it was Salom who had granted audience to the Tulku.

Nevertheless, he accepted gratefully their overtures of friendship, and the evidence of a new respect, even awe, for him.

Lotor, whose eyes were very bloodshot, rode up to him. "Within an hour," he said, "I ride back to my tent. It is a curious thing, Salom. Today I have a thirst upon me such as I cannot ever recall before. You and I know that it is always bad after one has slaked yesterday's thirst, but this time it is worse than ever. And yet yesterday I was moderate enough."

"What did you drink, Lotor?" Salom smiled.

"Drink? I merely sipped. Two jars, no more. I had thought there were only three jars, and I planned to keep one for the thirst of today. But that Bitola of mine has a man's taste for the brew herself, and I find that the cunning bitch has hidden two other jars beneath a bale of skins. Salom, I tell you the man who trusts a woman treads a thin rope across a chasm! Still, now I have three jars remaining instead of merely one." He chuckled. "And I have hidden all three beneath a pile of saddle cloths that have been waiting all summer to be mended. Bitola will never look *there* for them!"

"Then you should have no worries about this thirst that torments you."

Lotor grinned. "Why not ride down with me to the tent?" he suggested. "Come. It is a long time since you have been to my tent. And we shall drink like men, eh?"

Yes, Salom thought wryly, it is a long time since I have been to your tent, but it is an equally long time since I have been invited. He stared down beyond the curve and slant of the valley. The mystic's tent was a speck of white, but he could see it all—its garish stripes, its silken pennons, the heavy thankas breathing against the wall so that the demons writhed. Old man, he thought, I thank you. Whether you be mystic or charlatan, wise or only cunning, I do not care. You have done me a great favor, a very great favor. You do not know just how great a favor. Or perhaps you do. But, anyway, I thank you.

He turned back to the herdsman. "Yes, Lotor," he said. "I will come."

Lotor squinted at the sun. "Good. In an hour's time then. Meanwhile I will ride up and tell Chunor that the herds can chew their cud unwatched today for all two herdsmen care." He paused and looked at Salom seriously. "Oh, there was something I meant to ask you. Something important."

"What?"

"Are you a staunch drinker, Salom? Where you come from, did they regard you as a man redoubtable with a drinking cup?"

Salom laughed. "No, Lotor. I had no such repute. I have done little drinking in my time."

'Ah, then it is time you were instructed, eh? But it is best to go gently at the beginning. Two jars for me—and one for you!"

He rode off chuckling. Chunor was on the rising ground beyond the fringe of the herd.

"The beasts are quiet today," Lotor said.

"Yes. Fat-lazy with too much food." Chunor growled toward the animals.

"You and Dochi can watch them. I am so parched I fear I will be taken with a seizure. I must return home for some chang. I have asked Salom to come with me."

"So?"

"Why do you look like that? Is something amiss?"

"Nothing," Chunor said pleasantly. "So long as you are certain you would be wise in asking the Chinese."

"And where would the unwisdom be?"

"Perhaps there is no unwisdom. You are free to choose your own companions. But after the tales that are told about this Chinese——"

"Bah!" Lotor scratched inside his furs. "I swear there are some different tales being told today." He grinned self-consciously. "To speak the truth, Chunor, I am ashamed to have listened to them in the beginning. Demons!" He guffawed. "Can you see the most respected Tulku honoring a demon with two hours of private audience? No. We have been unfair to the boy. All the time while I listened to the tales of harridans—and I am man enough, Chunor, to admit I *did* listen—I had a feeling of shame and guilt. He is a good boy, that one. And Lotor is not a man so stubborn as to refuse to make known his mistakes."

"If you are certain that it is a mistake. Perhaps it is that I am just a little more cautious than you. There are old tales—you and I have heard a score of them at the knees of our mothers—of demons more powerful than any Tulku. Why, there are demons, Lotor, who are almost as powerful as the Buddha himself. And you would not suggest that any Tulku would have so much power as that. Still, if you are certain . . ." Chunor shrugged.

"Listen, Chunor." Lotor wagged his forefinger earnestly. "I say that this is a good boy. So I invite him to drink chang in my tent. And any other man who wishes to come will be made welcome, and I say this even knowing that the thicker the company the sparser the drinking. But this is so that we shall all be good friends again. It is happier in the valley when we are all good friends. I have no liking for these tales and whispers and suspicions. The gods meant men to drink together, to laugh with one another, to be happy."

"True enough, Lotor. But the evil ones often mean things that the gods do not mean."

"I would have thought you a man too clever to give attention to the whisperings of a crazed bedmate. And yet——"

"I give attention to no whispers but those that come from my own heart, Lotor. I do not say I am right or wrong. I am a reasonable man, willing to hear both sides of any argument. And so I merely say that the suspicions are not quenched in *my* mind. I am content to wait. And in the meantime I will continue to show caution."

"Bah! If the boy is good enough for the tent of the Tulku he is certainly good enough for the tent of Lotor!"

"Well, I suppose you could be right," Chunor admitted thoughtfully. But when Lotor rode away Chunor looked after him, and his eyes were hard as the rounded agates of the streambeds.

II

At the edge of the pasture Renzi squatted cross-legged on a mound of saddle cloths. She was engrossed in a new game. An inverted copper dish was balanced precariously upon her head; four of the altar bowls from the tent were set on the grass before her; her hands were crossed piously above her outthrust belly. Her dirty little face grimaced toward a cow and two knock-kneed calves that grazed placidly near by.

"See now, witless one," she said. "Must I tell you again that I am the Tulku, that you are nothing but my attendants? Do you not have enough sense to know who the Tulku is? Eh? Do you think of nothing else but chewing? Oh-ho, it will go ill with you in your next lives if there is not a little more reverence shown me! I am a great saint. I have the ear of the high ones. And I will see you confined in the sixteen pits if——"

"Renzi!" The call was clear and high in the thin air. Kelinka stood in the doorway of the tent.

"Here, Kelinka! Here!" Renzi tumbled from the platform, pulling a sour face at the apathetic animals. "Go then—chew, chew, chew! I do not care! I have better things to do than to amuse stupid animals who have not the wits to appreciate it!"

Kelinka walked slowly across to her.

She smiled. "And what game is this, child, that you must remove half the furnishings of the tent to play it?"

"I was being the Tulku, Mother, and these—" she gestured her contempt at the animals—"these were my lamas. But it was not a good game, for such things are too stupid even to play the parts of attendants well!"

"Renzi, child!" Kelinka sighed. "Renzi, how many times must I tell you that you must not make games of sacred things? Suppose the Tulku himself had seen you?"

"Kelinka!" The child grinned unrepentantly. "Now, how could he see me? When he left the valley this morning?" She jiggled her head wisely. "And he is kind enough, that holy one. Did he not place his hand on my head in blessing, and tell me I was a fine child, and smile at me and wish me well?"

"So? I did not hear him speak to you, child."

"Oh, yes. Of course, he spoke very softly. The words were only for me."

"Of course, Renzi." Her mother's eyes twinkled.

"And is he not a friend of Salom's, who is my best friend? And as Salom cares little enough for these holy things I do not think it matters if I play the Tulku." She put down the copper bowl and smoothed her hair. "I like that Tulku. He made Salom stay with us."

"Yes, child, he made Salom stay with us." Kelinka began thoughtfully to fold the saddle cloths across her arm.

Renzi looked at her sharply. "Kelinka—because the Tulku has gone—that does not mean that Salom will wish to go now?"

"It is hard to say, child. . . ." Kelinka's voice trailed away, and then she shook her shoulders, as if to shake something off. "Come, hurry now, Renzi, and take these things to the tent. There is a task for us. I want you to come with me to gather azalea leaves."

"Azalea leaves? But why do we gather azalea leaves?" Suddenly her eyes sparkled. "Oh, Kelinka—is it for a *feast?*"

Kelinka smiled and touched the child's head. "It is for a feast, child. There will be a feast tonight, and the leaves shall be burned for incense."

"Why?"

"Well, we must mark the visit of the Tulku fittingly."

They started back for the tent. Renzi bounced at her mother's side, twirling the copper bowl. Her bright boots thudded exuberantly on the flowers, and her child's eyes were full of the day.

"Kelinka?" she said, suddenly puzzled. "Why do we have a feast for the Tulku when the Tulku has gone?"

Kelinka surveyed the trampled thang and the droppings of many animals and the litter that marked the place where the Living Buddha's entourage had camped these last two days.

"He has gone, Renzi," she said slowly, "but such men often leave good thoughts behind."

And although Renzi nodded, the woman knew that she had not given her child the true reason. Because she had not given her *all* the reason. She was not certain that she herself knew all the reason. It was often the custom to celebrate the departure of the leader with suitable ceremony and feasting, as if to mark the end of the summer's spiritual season. But there were other things in her mind—other reasons beyond this—matters that were concerned less with the Tulku than with Veshti and Yanong and Salom. They were things in her mind, vague fears, thoughts that lacked coherence and in any case could not be explained to a child. It was almost as if she sensed dimly that the Tulku's visit was an interlude in a story that had not yet ended. She had fingered the fabric of the story in those few moments of solitude before Yanong had come to the tent to tell her of the god's wishes. That fabric had not been changed by the Tulku's coming. Perhaps it would have its effect on the final weaving of the pattern, perhaps even on the fabric itself. She groped for something more explicit, but it eluded her. She knew only that it was the time now, tonight, for feasting and talking and laughter. It was the time now, before the story went on.

She smiled down at the eager face of her child.

"And where do *you* think we should find the best azalea leaves, Renzi?" she said.

The child's face puckered for a moment, and then she squeaked her delight. "I know, I know! Below the ford, Kelinka, at the bottom of the red cliffs. I saw them when I was seeking the nests of birds. Such bushes you have never seen! Oh-ho, there will be sweet incense burning for our feast! Kelinka, I love feasts!"

III

"I wish it were always summer," Veshti said. Again she dipped her small, silver-weighted hand into the black shingle. The fine grains trickled through her parted fingers and drifted down her arm into a little mound in the crook of her elbow, and on the brown skin a fine dust of gold was left sheening. She twisted her arm to catch the sunlight.

"It was what Renzi said to me—" Salom nodded—"on the first morning I was here."

"I wish it were always summer," Veshti repeated, as if she had not heard him.

Salom squirmed onto his belly and squinted up at her.

She squatted as the herdsmen squatted, with the full weight of her body supported on her heels, and her arms hung forward from her knee, but with her there was no ungainliness in the position; only a delicate balance and poise, as if she might stretch her arms and dart upward, quick and brilliant as the kingfisher who skimmed his blue iridescence through the furred plumes of the bulrushes behind them. There was nothing studied in this grace she possessed, in the rhythmic curve of her tapered back, in the full drop of coral-tipped breasts tugged downward by their own ripeness, in the eager tilt of the flat-planed face with its crown of heavy, oil-dark braids, in the movement of the gold-dusted arm.

"I wish it were always today," Salom said, but she smiled away from him and said nothing.

Always today, he thought. Always and forever today. Always to feel the sharp, exciting roughness of hot shingle against hot skin; always to have the senses tightly wound like this, so that they vibrated to every sight and sound and smell. Yet, it was more than seeing and hearing and smelling: he felt these things right through him, as if they were part of his blood and bone, and he part of their tang and texture. He felt the primitive roughness of the broken bridge that lurched into the stream, the hot dryness of its chipped timber, and the damp brown crumblings where the ants were busy. His blood coursed to the wild thrill and leap of the current that ripped the even center from the river. His skin drowsed to the half-heard joy of the stream's contented chuckle in the slow eddies near the shore. The sweat beneath his shoulders was the dampness of the russet cliff face that shouldered above the trail. He wanted to shout his exultance. He was alive, and he was a part of everything.

He looked at the two little islands, softened by their own frill of rushes, that forced the racing water to fan out in a sweep as wide and beautiful as a pheasant's tail. He could see the gray hover of a fish eagle high above, and the stiff, excited scurry of the self-important little birds that pricked their arrow trails through the hot mud from which the reeds sprang.

The world was alive, and he was alive, and his was the essence that made all things!

And then Veshti smoothed her hair, and he had that feeling, too, as if it had been his own hand in caress upon the thick blackness.

"Veshti?" His fingers prodded into the shingle.

"Yes?"

"Tell me something. That day—the day I came—you had cleaned your hair, and yet you were ashamed when I spoke of it."

"Yes?"

"You told me it was not the custom here."

"Nor is it. I . . . I can tell you . . . if you will not laugh."

"No, child, I will not laugh."

"Well——" She flicked a quick glance as if to make certain that he was not teasing her. "Well, it was—oh, it is hard to tell, Salom! I do not think I know why it was. But once—— Now! Look quickly, Salom! See? The raven."

He followed her pointing finger. The bird floated out of the sun, and there was an aureole of light about it, and then it turned and paused and fell in a curve of infinite grace to the river. It ruffled its plumage in the water.

"You see?" Veshti whispered.

"I see the bird, yes. But what has this to do with your hair?" He looked at her. She was crouched forward, intent on the riffling creature and the blue-black sheen of the water along its wings. And then he remembered the thought that had come to him in his last moment of wakefulness on his first night in Muhlam's tent. He had likened her hair to a raven's wing.

"Veshti," he said softly. "You cleaned your hair to make it like the raven's feather?"

She nodded quickly, her face bright at his quick understanding. "Yes. The bird was there in the water, like that one, and so—and so it came to me." She smiled timidly. "You do not think it was a stupid thought?"

"Stupid? No, child, it was a beautiful thought."

"And there was what Muhlam had said once," she added, with a defensive insistency.

"Muhlam? Surely he did not tell you to——"

"No, no. It was two summers ago. Muhlam does not possess much tenderness. But he looked at me, and he put his hand on my head and said, Veshti, your hair has the blackness of a raven in it. It was what he said."

"And do you remember what *I* said to you?" He smiled.

"About the custom in the Han country? About washing *all* the body? Of course I remember. I told Bitola and Maygur."

Salom pressed his chin into the sharp, hot gravel, and he was content. The sun's heat flowed beneath his skin, and he closed his eyes to make louder the music of this most splendid of all days.

"Will you *show* me, Salom?" Her voice was a whisper and part of the music.

"Show you what, Veshti?" he murmured sleepily.

"This custom of the Han country."

"You mean——?" He glanced at her in surprise.

She nodded. "I would like to . . . to do it, Salom. To do as your people do. And . . . and there is a great beauty today in the river."

She spoke the truth. There was gold misted on the water, and the sun made little leaping whorls of light about the pebbles.

"Let us go into the river and bathe ourselves as the Han people do. Now, while the sun is hot."

Already she was pulling at the thongs that made fast the dull jade buckle of her girdle, and her face was eager. She loosed the wide skirt and its bright braiding fell away into a rumple of color at her feet. And then she reached up to her hair and pulled the wooden combs, and the fat black braids snaked down, blotting up the skin-heat peeled from the sun. She kicked off the big, vivid boots and he saw that her feet were small.

Except for the weighted silver of her collar and the gems that glittered at her ears and wrists and fingers she was utterly naked. Her face and hands were stained to the glow of new-axed timber, but the rest of her body was a slim column of warm honey. The sun caressed her and polished her. Her skin was ivory-smooth, unblemished by hair or down, and flecks of mica glinted against the deeper gold of her body.

She smiled down at him and cupped her hands in invitation. "Come," she said. "Show me."

Salom undressed slowly, looking at her, conscious that she was studying his body with curious frankness. He wished he were bigger, stronger.

Then she smiled at him and he knew that his body pleased her.

"Hurry, Salom," she said.

Now? He could take her now. He could feel the warm young skin vibrant beneath his hands, he could eat the sunlight from the smiling mouth. Yes, he could do it now. . . .

"Hurry, Salom." She laughed between white teeth. "You are so slow."

No. Not now. There would be time for such things, but not yet. For this day—this perfect day—let her eyes be still the eyes of a child. For he knew, instinctively and surely, that when he took her there would be new things in her eyes, and he would never see her like this again.

He reached for her hand.

"Come then," he said gently, and led her down to the river.

IV

"Oh! You did not tell me that it would be so *cold!* Oh! Ten thousand knife points stick into me!"

She struggled with the fastenings of her skirt, and spat a strand of dripping hair from her mouth. Little globes of water were beaded on her cheeks and shoulders. She wriggled into the skirt and pulled the bodice tightly around her.

"But it was good," she admitted cheerfully. "Now, here is something to tell Bitola and Maygur! Their eyes will open, eh? But, oh! Salom, how my skin smarts!"

"It will be better in a moment, Veshti. You will begin to glow with warmth. But you liked it?"

"Yes, yes. Now I think I liked it . . . but then . . . when I was in the water . . . it was very cold. And when my head went under the water I had a terror that I would not come up again."

"But I was holding your hand, child."

"I know. It is why the fear left me."

She squatted and reached for her boots, and then she turned the bright felt distastefully, and wriggled her toes into the gravel.

"My boots do not seem nice now," she said, with a trace of surprise in her voice. "I think I would like new boots to put on." And suddenly she smiled. "Oh, Salom, it *is* a day of great beauty!"

"Then the day suits you."

"Suits *me?* What meaning is this?—the day suits *me?*" She looked at him through the dark fans of her lashes, and he was suddenly shy at the warmth in her face.

He reached for her hand, and turned it over in his, tracing with his finger a pattern on the palm of it. "You said it was a day of great beauty. And you are a person of great beauty. Therefore the day suits you."

She pulled her hand away quickly, and then wished she had left it in his. But it was strange, this thing his finger tip had been saying in her palm; curious and exciting and perhaps even dangerous. She began nervously to braid her hair.

"It was a fine display the Tulku's caravan made when it left," she said.

"It was a fine display the Tulku made altogether." Salom grinned. He rolled on his back and closed his eyes against the sun. "Veshti, you should have seen the inside of his tent! Ah, he is a wise old one, that Tulku!"

"I think he is the holiest of all men, Salom. You do not realize how lucky you were to be granted such an audience." She looked at him with slightly bewildered respect. "I have never known it to happen before. Never. And you have not told me what you talked about." She glanced at him shrewdly. "You seem different since you talked with him. I do not know how—but you *are* different. Perhaps the Tulku talked to you of the religion, eh?"

"Yes. We talked of religion. But I still think religion is a stupid thing—the terrified wail of the mob against the things they do not understand." He paused and flushed. "It is all in the mind. Gods, demons, heavens and hells. They all come from the mind, and sink back into it." He opened one eye and looked at her. The sun made him squint. "And the Tulku agreed with me that this was so," he added.

"The Tulku said that religion was stupid? Salom! He did not say that!"

"Well. . . . Well, not in those words, perhaps. But there was no doubt of his meaning. We talked on the subject a long time."

"What else did he tell you?"

"Oh, many things. Religion we talked about, and faith, and— and intolerance. Many things." Again he squinted at her. "On most matters we were in agreemeent."

"Wait. I cannot understand this thing. You told him you were without faith. I heard you. Outside his tent you told him, and——"

"Inside his tent I told him again!"

"And what did he say to that?" Her eyes were round.

Salom wriggled on to his side to face her. His fingers scraped at the gravel reflectively. "He told me that no men were without faith," he said softly. "He said it was something few people understood rightly. He showed me that I *do* possess a faith." He smiled at her, but there was a guard over the expression in his eyes.

"I am glad. What did he——?"

"Veshti," he interrupted urgently, "some other day we can talk of these things. I will tell you all that the Tulku said, and I will listen while you tell me of the things that are in your mind. I promise you I will listen, and I will try to understand."

"You have changed, and I am glad you talked——"

"Yes, yes, Veshti." He clasped her hand tightly in his, and she made no attempt to withdraw it. "I am changed, and everything is changed. But we shall talk of it another day. Today——" he pulled her fingers apart and curled them over against her palm—"today is for other things—things to be said about *us*—about you and me."

"What things?" She leaned toward him. Her hair hung loose and shining over her shoulder in two long plaits, and as she moved the plaits fell against her cheeks. Again he had the illusion of feeling their cool thickness against his own skin.

"The things that concern people like us, Veshti. You see, child, there are feelings that people have for each other, feelings that can be very strong—stronger even than feelings about faith or religion. Do you know what I mean, Veshti?"

She turned her face away from him and her free hand stroked one wet braid.

"Yes, Salom, I think I know."

She trickled some gravel through her fingers, and dusted the residue of golden powder down her arm. "It . . . it is a hard thing to put into words," he said.

"That I know, also."

How well she knew! It was the answer to all those wild and lovely thoughts that had gone spinning and bursting and flitting elusive from her grasp every time the snows thawed. It was the thing unsaid in the words of men, yet spoken by their eyes. It was the faint nausea that would seize her sometimes when Bitola and Maygur talked of secret pleasures and longings. And there had been a longing in her own heart when Salom had stood beside her, brown and thin and beautiful in his nakedness, and she had known no sickness, only a great hunger to talk to him, to touch him, to feel the hard warmth of him, to have him always there beside her. There had been strange stirrings inside her that she had never known before, and suddenly the ugly things about which Maygur whispered were not ugly any more, for they were part of her, and part of Salom, and part of this shining day.

"Salom?" she said softly. "Will you help me?"

"I will always want to help you, child."

"Is it right . . . is it proper, Salom, for a girl to hunger for somebody? To need somebody? Not for just a little moment, or for a day or a month. But always to have this . . . this thing?"

"Yes, Veshti. Yes, I think it is right." He turned her hand and twisted at the heavy silver ring. "There are things one cannot weigh on the balance as one measures out barley meal. This is such a thing. It is of the heart more than of the mind——" His words trailed off.

"It is of you I think, Salom, when I say these things," she said quite calmly. Her fingers tightened on his, and the trivial gesture carried a disproportionate weight of trust and acceptance.

He closed his eyes so that she would not see the hunger he knew was in them. He said nothing.

"And yet," she continued anxiously, "I am betrothed to Dochi. To Dochi." She repeated the words, almost as if she were rolling them on her tongue, savouring their flavor. "I am betrothed to Dochi."

The words struck at him, sickening him. He had forgotten. He had pushed aside all the things that Kelinka had told him. Kelinka was wise. Kelinka had seen all this. And this was nothing to do with Yanong. If Yanong did not exist this thing would still be the same. *It cannot be. It can never be.* That was what Kelinka had said. Veshti was already bespoken. A penniless Chinese could pay nothing for the girl, and even if he could he was not of her people. *If Veshti is snaring your heart, Salom, then you must saddle your horses and ride on, for she cannot be for you.* Yes, but what of Veshti herself? What of Veshti's heart? He looked at the girl dumbly, and he saw that her face had clouded.

She turned and gripped his shoulder and shook her head. "Why must I marry Dochi?" she cried. "I do not want to marry him! Why? Why? *Why?*"

"Kelinka . . . Kelinka told me . . ." He faltered. "Kelinka said it cannot be changed." He looked at her miserably. But she was staring toward the plumed rushes.

Yes, it was what Kelinka had told her, also, when she had asked the question in the tent on the morning after Salom's arrival. Kelinka had said that the wise woman did not question her destiny; she accepted it and earned merit by her humility. And at the time she had bowed to this, because it was an established thing, and all her life she had clung to the established things. They were the shelters of life, the palisades against change and disturbance. But now there was something different. She no longer wanted to cling to these sureties. Indeed, how could she be certain any longer that they were sureties? There had been other beliefs she had clung to with as much assurance. She had been so sure of the retribution of the gods against those who erred. Until Salom came she had never known anyone who questioned the gods. She had heard Muhlam's bluster—but always it had been a tempest whirling in a small pool, and always it had been directed against the priests, never against the mightier things for which the priests stood. There was no excuse in Salom's alien birth; the gods could not be doubted even by people living in distant lands. When Salom had uttered his cold, blasphemous words it had seemed to her that the words themselves had spiked discordant circles about his head, and she had waited for the venegful flames to engulf him. And what had happened? Nothing. Nothing had happened. Nothing had happened since—except that the holiest of all men had taken Salom into his tent, had chosen him before all others in the valley for private audience, had eaten with him and shared words of friendship! Then where was the certainty of these established things? It was another such established thing that said she should marry Dochi. And yet still another established thing was that the wrath of the gods should smite her and annihilate her even for expressing fondness for a heretic who derided the established things of the spirit. Her mind was bemused by it all. She turned to him.

"Salom," she said, "what of Dochi?"

"Dochi?" he said. "I do not know."

He remembered Dochi on the edge of the pasture with the madness on his face, and he had a deep pity for the poor, broken fool. But he looked again at Veshti, and the radiance of her, and he was sick at the picture of Dochi fumbling at her body, pressing himself against her clean, warm beauty.

"You are not for him!" he said harshly. "Whatever is done or not done—you cannot be for him!"

Veshti smiled in acceptance. She immediately was content. Salom would know more about such things than she. Salom had shown that he could defy these established things, and she was secure, at least, in her certainty of him.

"Then I will not be for him, Salom," she said. "I will be for you. No matter what happens, I will not be for Dochi."

He squeezed her hand tightly. "But there is another thing, Veshti," he said soberly.

"What other thing?"

"Yanong." He mouthed the name slowly, hating it, and hating the shadow that darkened the girl's face.

"But he has *gone,* Salom! You made him go!"

"Yes, but he will return, little one. When the Tulku's caravan has cleared the valley I think he will return."

It was odd, he thought with a detached curiosity, how even the speaking of Yanong's name could scar a day of beauty. The light seemed less golden, the sun less warm on his back, and the tall rushes shook their plumes against a whip of wind. He shivered.

"Let us not fret about it." He smiled, shrugging away the chill.

She curled her legs up, and pulled the bright skirt down over them, as though she also had felt the chill. Her head was bent. All the pleasure had gone from her expression. She was so small and forlorn and defenseless. He felt an overwhelming tenderness toward her.

"If he comes back, Salom, what will happen?" she asked anxiously.

"I do not know, child. But something will happen. It must. And besides—the Tulku said it would."

"The *Tulku?* But, Salom, you did not tell *him* of this thing?" Her eyes were wide.

"No. No. I did not tell him," he mused, looking past her to the tossing rushes. "He told me. He is a wise old man, that one. *He* told *me* of you and Yanong, and of many other things." Again he shivered with a sudden coldness.

"The Tulku spoke of *me?*" Her voice was breathless, and in spite of the coldness in him, Salom was amused by her childlike awe. "But he does not know me! How could he know me?"

"He seems to know many things, Veshti. He knows of things that have not yet happened. Or so he claims. But he told me something, little rabbit. He told me that this tale of ours would end in the best way—the only way—for you and me." He stood and reached down his hands and pulled her to her feet. "We must not have doubts, Veshti. It will be well. The Tulku says it. Life gives its rewards and its punishments—that is another thing the old man told me. And I do not think this Yanong speaks with the words of the gods, Veshti. The Tulku and Yanong cannot both speak with the words of the gods, for each says different things. And I swear that if there are gods then the Tulku is closer to them than Yanong."

He tipped up her face and the fear was gone from it, and there was only an accepting trust and content in the obliquely tilted eyes. He closed his arms around her, and his fingers moved gently along the smooth runnel of her spine, and his mouth was pressed against the thick, wet-smelling hair.

"Salom?"

"What is it, little rabbit?"

"It *will* be well, Salom? It must be well, eh?"

"It will be well, child."

She moved inside his arms. "I am cold."

For the first time he noticed that the sun had gone. The rushes crackled their plumes in a silence suddenly oppressive. Everything was steeped in a strange green light.

"Look!" Veshti pointed.

The western end of the valley had vanished. The lower slopes were obliterated completely by a wall of rain that strode toward them swiftly; and to the zenith the sky was packed by wildly swirling storm clouds. Distant lightning cracked the boil of black and gray and purple. Contour after contour was drowning in the tide: the big bluff that overhung Lotor's tent had been sucked into it: now it had slashed beyond the red cliffs at the ford, and the cliff was swallowed; and they could see distant trees tossing rebelliously for a moment and then bowing subjection to the wind.

"Come, Salom! It will be a bad storm, this one! Come, or we shall be soaked!"

But he clung to her hands and laughed at her.

"And in the river, little rabbit, were we not soaked?" He flung wide his arms. "No, Veshti. Let us wait. This is a thing I have thought about. To hold your hand and to feel the rain hit us, and the wind!"

"No—come now! To wet the body all over once in a day is enough for me. Let us run for the tent!"

But even as they ran the wind hurled spears of rain at them, and in a moment they were crushed by the deluge of wind and water, and it battered the breath from them so that they were scarcely able to struggle to the shelter of a twisted pine.

For an hour they stayed there, and then the downpour eased a little, and they began to run, laughing and with their hands entwined, toward the billowing tent.

But when they had almost reached it they saw Renzi racing toward them, and in her streaming hair and waving arms and urgently twinkling boots there was something that checked them and chilled them. Instinctively they began to run toward the child, and then they could hear her sobs and see the horrified misery of her face.

"Quick! Quick!" she choked. "Come quickly!"

"What is it, child?" Veshti's face was strained.

"Kelinka! Oh, *quick!*"

"What has happened? Speak, Renzi! Say what———"

"The cliff! Quickly!" She grasped Salom's hand as if to drag him with her. Her small body shook.

"Renzi! Say what has happened!"

"The red cliff!" she gasped. "There was an avalanche. The rain came—and we were gathering azalea leaves—and when the rain came we went to shelter beneath the cliffs—and then the storm—and the cliff fell down—and———"

"And Kelinka?"

"Yes. It fell on her! She is down there now. All the stones and mud—and there is nothing but her head. You can see only her head, Salom! And—oh, Kelinka!"

"Salom!" Veshti turned. But the boy had already gone, racing ahead of her through the rain and wind toward the distant ford.

Chapter Twelve

I

HALF the cliff face had dropped forward, although most of the mass of debris and ooze had fallen on either side of Kelinka. Salom could see her face, unnaturally white and quiet. Her head was still protected by a jutting spur of limestone which was now holding back a mound of slime that bubbled thickly and sighed at the slowness of its movement away from the broken wall of red rock and clay. But the mud was piling higher on the spur and he knew that it could not resist much longer the mass that pressed down from above. Great clots of debris slithered from the naked rock face that was scarred with runnels of melted clay like broken arteries. Although her head was clear the rest of her body was buried beneath a sucking mass of rock and mud.

He waded into the still-moving ooze, felt it dragging at his legs, heard all around him the frightening sounds—the plop and suck and hiss of moving clay, the whisper of the rain, the creak of smaller trees crushed by the inexorable forward pressure. He struggled ahead until the mud reached to his chest, and then he flung himself forward, tearing with his hands at the yielding mass. He did not know that Veshti was with him until he heard a sudden cry of pain, and he turned quickly and saw her sprawled a little behind him, clawing at the muck. Mud was clotted thick on her face and arms and clothing. He could not see what had caused her cry, but his own hands were torn and bleeding, for the mud was studded with broken rocks, jagged and sharp as knives.

They were almost within reach of Kelinka now. He scoured with his legs to find foothold. For a moment he slid back, and then he felt solidity beneath his feet. He pressed against it and scrambled upward desperately, and his hands clutched at Kelinka's shoulder as the first greasy flood began to slide over the protecting spur. Again he thrashed with his legs and wrenched at the limp form. And then he felt a movement beside him. It was Veshti.

The rain and the clay were in his eyes, and he could see nothing for the blinding yellow screen that crashed down upon him, and he cried out to her, "Go back! Go back, child! It is all coming down!"

But the squirming, slimy mud wriggled closer to him.

He spat the grit and water from his mouth and tugged again, sobbing at the pain and the effort. But this time the mud slobbered, and then Kelinka's dead weight was thrusting down against him. He pushed at Veshti and lunged away, and even as the limestone spur was swallowed the three of them rolled and slithered down the slope.

Veshti, her hands bleeding, helped him drag the insensible figure clear of the solidifying fingers of mud. He clawed the viscid mask from Kelinka's face, and groped in her clotted bodice.

"She lives!" he croaked. He swung toward Renzi, a trembling, sobbing figure with her plump hands wringing. "Quick, Renzi!" he shouted. "Go for Muhlam! My horse grazes near the tent. Take it. But ride, child! Ride quickly!"

When she had gone, streaking across the fields, he looked up at Veshti: "She is sorely hurt. Perhaps inside she is hurt, but there is no blood at her mouth. I will carry her to the river so we can wash this filth from her. And then we will see——"

"I will help."

"No. I can carry her."

He stooped and settled his arms beneath the slack, sodden body. But as he began to lift her a shudder ran through him, and he lowered her unsteadily.

"Salom! What is it, Salom?"

"There is something—her legs. There is something wrong."

"Ah! She is bad?"

He nodded. "I think she is *very* bad, Veshti. Come. We will take her to the river."

Salom stumbled beneath his burden. He tried not to think of his right hand, and the warm, sickening pulp that squelched against it.

II

There was no summer in the wind. It lashed at the tent, slapping the rain in petulant discord against the lament of the storm. Inside the shadows lurched. At the entrance the rain cracked and giggled into the spreading puddles. In the uneasy splutter of the light from the fire and the butter lamps Kelinka seemed to tremble convulsively. But it was a trick of the shadows, for she lay without movement, silent and falsely peaceful. There was movement in her, but it was only the slow, almost imperceptible, rise and fall of her stained bodice. Her eyes were closed and her mouth hung open a little, stupidly, and on her face streaks of mud had dried white against the soft leather of her skin.

Salom swallowed at the hardness in his throat and wished he could look away. Kelinka's head was propped against Muhlam's high saddle, and her gaunt figure was stretched along the panda skin, but where her limbs rested the luster of the rich fur had gone. It was black and matted, and the hair was sticky and twisted, and in some places it was smeared with a bright red glitter, but mostly it was black and dull around where her limbs rested. Her skirts had been cut from her, and the firelight splashed without pity across her legs. From the knees down there was almost no recognizable shape. The left leg was crushed, but the clay had been washed from it, and it was less revolting than the right leg, which was a shapeless mess of raw pulp and mud through which the blood bubbled occasionally with a faintly audible hissing. But such wellings, which had at first been rhythmic as a slow heartbeat, were becoming more infrequent. The bleeding had ceased on the left leg, and its redness seemed covered by a static film of water.

Salom listened again for the tiny whispered hiss that showed that life still moved somewhere within the mutilated body, but there was nothing to be heard above the swish and scurry of the rain, and the spite of the wind, and the crackling spit of the fire, and the slow breathing of the others.

He closed his eyes, and there was more to be seen than when they were open. The rain glaze across heaving mud . . . the slow drowning of the limestone spur . . . the writhe and split of tortured trees . . . Veshti, with the gold of the river dusted on her arms . . . and then a host of meaningless things flickering across his brain—yet all fused somehow to sounds and smells. His hands clutched at his head, the fingers flexing. There was some meaning in all this ghastly fantasy. It was as if it had happened before . . . as if he were reliving his part of an incident that had occurred in some scarcely remembered past.

He opened his eyes. The tableau was unchanged. He looked entreatingly into the hissing whirl of the roof aperture. In the red flicker of the fire he could see the rain like lines ruled fine across the restless night.

The rain! The rain had some connection with this thing. Yes. The rain and the grunt of the river and the storm-anger. *The rain and the river* . . . and the blood. The wet glaze that was across the crimson pulp. The smell of it. The sick warm smell of blood. Yes—it was in these things! If he could only think! Somewhere it was in these things! *The rain and the river and the smell of blood* . . .

His mind clutched for the reality, but it was gone again, and there was just Kelinka stretched on the panda skin, and the serene, dignified face that only emphasized the bloody horror of her limbs. In the gloom Renzi stifled a cry, and Muhlam moved clumsily so that the light etched the anguish deeply into his face. He looked over to Salom, and in the drowned eyes the boy saw all the suffering that Kelinka could not feel.

"It . . . it cannot be much longer," Salom said. His voice was toneless.

Muhlam shook his head.

"She has lost much blood," Salom said.

"Yes. But she suffers no pain. She . . . she knows nothing." The headman gestured ineffectually.

"She will die," Salom said.

"She will die." Muhlam echoed the words. He shook his head quickly, as a man does who comes from beneath water. "No, perhaps she will not die. See. The bleeding has stopped. And she is a strong woman. A good, strong woman."

Muhlam's eyes burned at him, pleading for reassurance.

Salom turned away and said nothing.

Muhlam jerked his thumb toward the inflated bear's stomach that was suspended above Kelinka.

"There is time!" he said vehemently. "There is time for it to accomplish something. Such things do not work instantly. It must take time for the strength of the bear to be transmitted to the sick one. Always it takes time."

But still Salom looked away from him and said nothing. There was nothing to be said.

It was a whole lifetime ago that he had sat by the river with Veshti and known happiness. The river? The ghosts of memory romped in his brain again. The river! *The rain and the river and the smell of blood.*

"Yes, boy, she will die." The headman had crept back into the shadows, and his voice was no longer the voice of Muhlam.

"She will die," Salom muttered. "She will die, unless . . ."

Unless? What followed after that? There had been words on his tongue, and now they had gone. The storm wailed at the tent, and then the gusts sobbed away down distance, and there was a breath of silence, and in the silence the river roared in his eyes. And it was as if the sound had riven a wide cleft in his mind, and the light had rushed in so that he could see! He could see! It was all clear to him now! *The rain and the river and the smell of blood!*

He was a child again. With a clarity of vision that surpassed reality he could see a stream snarling at a black cliff, a stream yeasted at the obstructing rocks and laced by foam, and this he knew for the water near the bridge called Liu Ting Chiao. On the black wall of the gorge were the men in fiber cloaks—the grotesque and faceless figures he had always been able to see—and across their clawing figures the rain ruled fine lines. In the rain the black rocks shone. But now he was able to see so much more than he had ever been able to see before! Flame darted and flickered along the far bank, where the machine guns chattered. He had been able to see that before, but here was a new thing: there were people huddled beneath a camphor tree so dense of foliage that the grass beneath was dry. And these people had faces—tense, watchful faces that had seen much of pain and privation. One was a tall, taut man who wore a khaki cap. His hand was firm on a long knife. In the dryness beneath the camphor tree some of the others huddled round this man, and in their hands were burning pine brands, spluttering and resinous. There was wetness on a patch of grass, but this was not the wetness of rain. It had drained from an immobile man whose legs were mangled. The man in the khaki cap knelt and cut deftly at the crushed flesh, working above the red ruin of skin and bone and sinew until finally the leg was severed; and then a shabby woman brought long lengths of brown cloth steaming from a cauldron; and two other men tied leather thongs above the rawness where the knife had chewed; and with a small billet of wood they twisted the thongs until they bit deeply into the hale flesh. For a little time the blood swelled against the wet cloth, surprisingly pink, like a delicate rose, and then there was no more blood. The man with the khaki cap nodded to the others as if well satisfied. He smiled around him, and his smile was weary, and he said something in the tongue that Salom no longer remembered.

But now he knew! This was the thing that had been in his brain! This was the thing that had happened before!

He looked quickly toward Kelinka, and the horror struck him so that the vomit clogged his throat. But she could still be saved. That was what this thing had told him!

In China he had seeen beggars and peddlers and mountebanks,

and even merchants in silken gowns, with but a single limb, walking well enough with strange supporting props. So such things *could* be done. And perhaps only Kelinka's right leg would need to be severed; by contrast the other limb was not so bad. Strips of cloth would be needed . . . and if the leather thongs were passed around both her thighs to staunch the bleeding . . . ? But the bleeding had ceased anyway.

His fingers writhed at his hair. What if this thing were attempted and it failed? What if this tangled memory of his was all a delusion? Or, if it were no delusion, then what if something of it had been distorted? The thongs? The steaming cloths? It had been so long ago.

But it could not fail! This thing he had suddenly, almost miraculously, recaptured . . . it was too vivid, too certain. No, it could not fail! And he would do it, and his fame would resound in the valley, and he would be accepted.

"Muhlam!" he whispered in a queer, high voice. "Muhlam, she will die unless something is done!"

The headman nodded, and then gestured stupidly toward the bear's stomach. "Maybe . . . maybe; it takes time," he mumbled.

"Something *can* be done, Muhlam!"

"We must wait. It takes time——"

"No! It does nothing. It is a hag's tale. But there *is* something! I tell you I know!"

"What?" Muhlam's head swiveled slowly, but there was no curiosity in his eyes.

"Where the leg is destroyed—we must cut it away. It can never mend. Not like that." He looked shudderingly at the red mass. "Not when there is nothing remaining that is good."

"You mean—you mean—*cut* the leg? Altogether?" Muhlam stiffened.

"Yes. I have seen it done. I can do it. The destroyed part is cut away. And where it is cut cloths soaked in warm water are wrapped tightly about it. Many thicknesses. And then above where the knife works leather thongs are twisted—twisted very tightly so that the blood is staunched."

"Are you *mad,* boy? You mean that there is only half a leg remaining? How can a person live with but half a leg?"

"I tell you I have seen such people. In China. I have seen many of them. They fashion a stick for support, and they live well enough. It is better than dying."

Muhlam groaned despairingly. His massive head swung from side to side.

"No," he said hoarsely. "No, this is mad talk! Give the talisman time. Give it time, I tell you! It *must* work! The strength of the bear will be imparted to her. It takes time."

Salom moved toward him. A dreadful excitement shuddered through the boy.

"Muhlam," he whispered quickly, "you have no belief in the magic of a slain bear's guts. No real belief. You *know* she will die. Answer truly, Muhlam. You *know,* eh?"

In the long silence there was nothing but the sounds of the storm's fret, and then Muhlam nodded. "I know. She will die."

"Then let me try," Salom cried. "If we do not try she dies anyway."

"No. If she dies—if she dies—— No! I will not give way on this."

Salom licked at his dry, bitter lips. "With every minute she grows weaker, Muhlam. There is nothing we can lose."

And then, as they crouched toward each other, they were held rigid in an endless moment.

"Muhlam." It was a flat, croaking whisper from Kelinka herself. The two men swung toward her. Her eyes were still closed, but her lips moved in an ashen face drawn now into a mask of incalculable suffering.

"Let him try, Muhlam," she whispered.

And then a spasm wrenched her, but after a moment of writhing she fell quiet again. Muhlam leaned across her. The breath still came, but faintly now. The false serenity had gone and her face was locked into the awful mask of anguish.

Salom's fingers trembled as he smoothed them along the edge of his hunting knife.

III

Salom lurched to the tent flap and pushed it aside, and as he stumbled into the darkness the rain struck him.

She was dead. The words rang like a slow knell, like the brazen booming of a temple gong. She was dead. The gong vibrated to the ponderous beats. She was dead. Once, on the road to Ch'eng-tu, a gong had called sullenly to him from a temple hidden in the pinewoods. But it had spoken different words. They had been words of challenge to a youth whose feet were set to a beaten pathway. The gong had said: "Turn back; turn back!" but he had gone on, and only long weeks afterward had he found that the cry of a hidden gong had been a cry of wisdom. But now the words were different.

She was dead. *She was dead.*

He was oblivious to the storm. Scud raced at the moon's face, and the whine of the wind had fury in it, and the rain hammered him.

She was dead.

He stumbled to the river. The river had changed. Everything had changed. This was not the golden stream where he and Veshti had bathed. The current tossed in racing black hummocks and the wind sliced silver from the running mounds and scattered it downstream. The wind half-choked the river's roar, and the night sang with storm.

She was dead.

She had been kind to him. A kind woman. A warm woman, human and generous. A woman of patience, and a woman content to give more of love than she received. She had been so kind to him, this woman whose flesh he had hacked with a dirty hunting knife. And now she was dead.

The welling sickness filled his mouth, and his body was torn with the violence of his retching.

Veshti came in a sharper flurry of rain, and found him still vomiting into the river. She shivered as she held his head down, and when the spasm had passed she pressed against him and clung to him, shuddering, and there was an unknown terror in her whisper: "There is no blame———"

For a moment they stood clutched tightly together, as if they would be held together eternally, locked and shaken by the horror of this thing he had done, and she had helped to do.

"She would have died," he muttered angrily into her wet hair.

She wiped at his face with her cold, wet hands. "Yes. Oh, yes, Salom! She would have died!"

"Muhlam knows she would have died."

"Yes. Muhlam knows."

He shivered. His arms fell slackly to his sides.

"Veshti," he whispered. "I . . . I thought the bleeding had stopped. And then . . . then, when I cut, the blood was like a flood. When I cut . . ."

She held his head down while the sickness poured out of him. The storm howled at them, and neither was conscious of it.

After a time he wiped the sour filth from his mouth and looked at her in silent misery. The rain sliced between them. Veshti's face was a blur that wavered in the darkness.

"Salom, there is no blame. Not for this thing. There cannot———"

"I should have saved her," he muttered, and then his voice rose, gruffly. "I should have! It was so *clear!* I tell you I could *see* it! I knew what I had to do. *I could see it!*"

"There is no blame."

His hands clenched painfully on her thin, soaked shoulders. "She knew nothing!" he insisted fiercely. "She slept and knew nothing. It is true, Veshti! I swear she knew nothing!"

"No, no, Salom! She knew nothing. Nothing!"

But for both of them the air throbbed with that one bubbling scream of unutterable pain that had filled the tent when the knife bit.

"I had to do it!" He shouted the words, and the girl knew he was trying to drown that frightful sound.

"Understand, Veshti," he continued pleadingly. "I *had* to do it. It was . . . it was as if everything in my life had folded back to show me this thing. There were things I could see that I had never been able to see before. It was as if . . . as if I had been *given* this thing to do . . . and . . . and when it was done she was dead."

Veshti shivered. "Come back now. It is done. So come back to the tent. It is best, Salom."

IV

There were many people in the tent, and among them Muhlam was incongruously insignificant. He was crouched against the pack saddles, his swarthy face loose.

The scene was dominated by Chunor, who gestured with a strange new authority to those who hovered around the heavy sheepskin that covered Kelinka.

When they saw the boy standing at the tent entrance, motionless beside Veshti, their mutterings ceased abruptly. Salom could see their faces swelling and sinking redly in the swell and sink of the red flames, and he could read the accusation as clearly as if the words had been shouted at him. All the faces were turned to him, all silently shrieking the words.

But nothing was said, and then Dochi shambled in from the night, slapping his soft hands against soaking robes, peering eagerly. His flattened head was tilted a little; his nostrils twitched as if sniffing at the strange atmosphere.

"At last!" Chunor muttered angrily. "It took you long enough to get here."

The faces had turned to Dochi, and Veshti pulled Salom into the darkest corner of the tent. His feet dragged and his full weight was upon her. His legs felt like melting butter, and he let them flow away from him, and then his head dropped down into his icy hands. Voices oozed thickly through the fug.

"It was the storm," Dochi protested surlily.

"Spare me an idiot's excuses! You should have been back ere sundown. You were needed."

"There was trouble. Down lower the storm struck early. There was terrible trouble."

"Bah! Are you such a fool that you cannot ride through a little wind and rain? Must you skulk like a child in some sheltered tent when you are needed here?"

"It was not *that*. It was the Tulku——" Dochi tittered pleasurably.

"The Tulku? Tell it then, dolt—what of the Tulku?"

Dochi's laughter hiccuped. "His caravan was caught at the third ford. Half the animals were swept away. Ho! Such a whirl of animals! And the Tulku's mule missed its footing, and the Tulku was taken downstream. Like a great golden bladder. Ho! It took much time and trouble to get the Most Excellent One to the bank again——"

"Cease your laughter, clod, lest I break your neck! Was Yanong with the Tulku?"

"No, but the Holy One in the water was very funny—like a bladder of gold! No. I do not know where Yanong was. But Pangtok was there, aiding the Holy One, and Yanong had spent a night in Pangtok's tent. Pangtok told me that—but—but the Tulku in the water!" He spluttered and choked on his mirth.

Chunor hit him across the mouth.

"Enough! There is more riding for you. Get your beast now—and hurry!"

"*At night!* But I do not wish to ride," Dochi sniveled. "I am cold and weary and the day has been hard, and now you have hurt me."

"You will be hurt more, clown, if I put my boot to you! Muhlam desires that you ride. You will do as the headman orders."

"But why do I ride at night?"

"You ride to find Yanong. And you had best find him with all speed. You will tell him that Kelinka is dead."

Kelinka is dead. Dead. Dead.

Salom opened his eyes. Dochi was leaning toward the sheepskin bundle, a fantastic figure of grotesque surprise, and then he stooped clumsily and picked up something and turned it over, and then tittered stupidly as the stain came away on his hand. He wiped his hand on his trousers.

The mist was across Salom's eyes again. He was spinning down into a red pool that bubbled with unutterable pain.

When his senses returned to him the tent was full of brilliant firelight, and the shadows were only meager blotches on the billowing fabric of the roof. Muhlam sat motionless against the pack saddles, staring blankly into the flames, and Renzi was hooked against him, but the child slept. The others had gone—all except Dupken. Dupken was busy, and Veshti was helping her.

He looked curiously at the big black cauldron that had been mounted now upon a flat dais of folded rugs. That was odd. Kelinka had cleaned the cauldron that very morning for the feast. Now there would be no feast. That was very odd.

He swung his eyes back to Dupken. The hag was enjoying herself. Her eyes flicked and sparkled, and the thin hair of her chin shivered as she crooned her incoherencies, and she hopped around with the looseness of a toad, and her flat breasts slapped softly against her ribs.

"Where . . . where are the others?" he asked hollowly.

Dupken's eyes flicked him like a lash.

"They have gone to Chunor's tent," she squeaked maliciously. "There are things to discuss."

He nodded wearily. There was something behind the crone's words, but he was too tired . . . too tired. . . .

The sheepskin had been pulled away from Kelinka, and the clothes cut from her body, and Veshti was selecting her mother's most resplendent robes and glittering jewelry with which to deck the corpse.

He could look at the rawness below Kelinka's knees now without any sickness, but he felt angry that she should have to lie there for all to see, in her gaunt and pitiable nakedness, with all dignity stripped from her by the hands of an evil old woman who had always envied her, and hated her. And then he thought that once Kelinka's nakedness must have been like Veshti's nakedness, round and smooth and honey-colored and with the smell of youth. *Decay is inherent in all living things.* That was what the Buddha himself had said. His eyes filled, and he blinked them wearily.

The preparations continued. It was not the first time he had seen the funerary rites of the country.

The people of Kham believed that the dead person's "double" continued to inhabit the body until it was released by a priest for its journey through Bado to its rebirth. Until that time there was always danger that the double would escape and wander unshepherded in a familiar environment made bewildering. Such a double could become filled with malignance at its impotence, and, in its rage, destroy; and it could even desire to take known companions with it on its hazardous journey into the shadowed beyond.

And so the rites were always conducted with great haste, and then the body was taken away to a desolate area to be cut into fragments and scattered for the wolves and foxes and carrion birds, and for the fairies who lived on the odors of the dead, so that all vestige of mortality was gone, and there was no longer danger of the spirit wandering back to its old abodes in some earthly guise.

Even though she worked quickly it was near dawn by the time Dupken nodded her satisfaction.

Kelinka was dressed in her finest scarlet skirt and blue jacket embroidered with gold and silver threads in a pattern of lotus flowers and gazelles, and on her head was placed the jaunty fur cap she had loved so much. But all the garments had been placed upon her back-to-front, as an additional assurance that the spirit would not retrace its steps to its mortal dwelling. Her apparel was made the more brilliant with her finest jewelry—rings and bracelets, neckpieces and earrings. Silver, jade, coral, amber, turquoise, lapis-lazuli winked and blazed with life on flesh that was cold and dead. The double would have no need to return for some treasured trinket that had been forgotten.

She was trussed in a sitting position in the big cauldron, and her jaw fell open over her gaudy necklets, as if in surprise that she should be in such a place, and there were lamps lighted and placed at the front of the cauldron, and a bowl of tsamba to staunch the hunger of the double, and buttered tea to quench its thirst. Smoke curled from a smolder of azalea leaves. Except for the votive offerings yet to be fashioned from butter and barley meal, Kelinka was ready for Yanong's ministrations.

It was finished. Veshti rocked with fatigue and wiped her hands against her mud-clotted skirt. Renzi was asleep, her small nose flattened against a clenched hand. Muhlam stared into the fire glow.

Dupken patted the corpse. "Eeee!" she cackled. "It is well done. You will thank me, Kelinka, for a task so well performed, even though you have given me little enough of thanks in your day!"

"My thanks also, Dupken, and my father's." Veshti sighed. "And now the day is here and you will wish to sleep."

Dupken pulled up her furs. Her eyes darted slyly around the tent. "Eeee! There will be no sleeping for me, girl. There are things to be done—and things to be told."

She looked directly at Salom, and on her face was a strange mixture of terror and triumph and less easily definable things. She twisted her prayer beads through her fingers ostentatiously. "It will be well when Yanong comes," she muttered. "There will be things he must be told, also. I knew! I *knew* there would be blood on the grass. And you would not listen, Kelinka!"

She prodded at the corpse and laughed shrilly, and then she tugged back the tent flap. The storm shrieked in with such violence that she reeled, and then she lunged out into the darkness awhirl with madness.

Dawn brought no abatement of the tempest's violence. All

through the wild day the wind strengthened until the grasses were flattened and torn clumps of sagebrush tumbled and skittered, and the birds battled with the monster until they surrendered and were tossed downwind like leaves. The rain, which had been a torrent at dawn, eased by midday, but the gale screamed the louder. Sometimes watery sunlight filtered through the racing, shredded clouds. Once a rift appeared to the east, and Salom could see, framed in a cold and startling blueness, the great peaks that stormed the sky, and there was no clarity to their contours. The nearest of the summits streamed a long banner that he knew was powdered snow. Then a squall swept a smudge across the scene, and the howling grayness pressed in around the valley. The cows faced downwind, lowing plaintively, and dogs and horses cowered beneath the onslaught.

On this day there was no glow of sunset, nothing of the brightness that had punctuated the ends of days. There was only a gradual soiling and extinction of light.

Salom knew that the first of the blizzards had struck.

Chapter Thirteen

THE night came again.

Outside, the taut ropes thrummed and the straining fabric tried to bound away from the spiteful tugging so that the whole tent bellied and swayed and shook in a frenzy. A harsh, spattering gust of rain slapped the tent, and inside the flames twisted and writhed to escape the heavy drops plummeting through the central aperture. The tent heaved like a sea.

"What was that?" Veshti whispered.

"Nothing, Veshti. Nothing." Salom patted her arm gently. "It is only the wind talking. Nothing but the wind."

He, too, had heard sounds that were not human sounds. Sometimes, he thought, it was easy to understand why these people believed in their spirits and demons. Monsters could ride tonight on the lash of the storm, evil beings could lurk in the noisy wet, spitting and hissing. It was on such a night as this when the Delogs, the living dead, could rush blindly through black chaos; when sorcerers could summon to abominable rites the dancing corpses of the dreadful Rolang, or bloodthirsty ghouls attend the macabre feast of Chod.

The smoke contorted into strange patterns and the swaying bladders pulsed with a queer luminosity. The light trembled and flowed and leaped in torment, and on the bellying wall was a silhouette of a black form in a black cauldron, and the figure moved with the slow gyrations of a witches' dance.

The wind had voices and the rain had voices: voices that shrieked and whispered, that hissed and muttered; and it seemed that feet trampled outside, and that there was the flap of many garments tugged by the wind.

"Muhlam!" A lost voice cried the name.

The wind piped the sound away, sobbingly.

"Muhlam! We would have speech with Muhlam!"

It seemed that the wind growled low with many sullen voices.

"Muhlam! Where is the headman?"

And then Salom knew that it was not the wind, for Veshti had risen and was shaking her father by the shoulder.

"Muhlam. Someone wishes to speak with you. Outside, someone calls."

The giant looked up at her, uncomprehendingly, and shook his head vaguely.

"There are people outside," she said, shaking him again. "They call for you."

Muhlam came to his feet unsteadily and stood for a moment looking down at the cauldron. He was massive in the crazed jump of the light, with his shadow flung above him—massive, and, to Salom, somehow pitiable. Veshti nodded understandingly and took his place beside the dead. Renzi crept across the tent and muzzled against Salom, and he put his arm tightly around the child.

"We want the headman!" The cry belonged to the wind, and yet it was imperatively human.

Muhlam straightened and looked around the tent with disdain. All of the old arrogance was in the jerk of his head as he pulled back the tent flap.

Outside, in the lee of the tent, his people were gathered: a thick clot of men and women glued together by rain and darkness so that faces were indistinguishable. The black group was hammered down by the wild immensity of the night, by the rain that appeared luminous in the jet, by the slide of black shapes across the meager islands of stars. They shuffled when Muhlam came, and their angry muttering sank to sullen whispers that were torn and shredded by the storm.

"Well?" Muhlam stood wide-legged. "Speak!" The wind whipped the word from his mouth and flung it at them.

Again the group wavered, shuffling, as if the people were cowed by his strength, and they hung their heads and nudged one another, and every person waited for some other to speak, until the dark wet ranks were clawed apart by a hooked figure whose rain-lashed garments flapped with the intensity of her own malevolence.

"Cast out your demon!" The voice shrilled, and wavered into silence.

Muhlam stood unheeding, as if Dupken were not there.

"Speak!" he repeated.

The people growled in the darkness. It was the sound of an animal, but it unleashed stifled feelings, and for a time Muhlam stood against a torrent of words that beat at him:

"We want no demons in this valley!" . . . "Who killed your woman, headman?" . . . "I saw the body—no human hand held that knife!" . . . "Cast him out, Muhlam!" . . . "Who brings the blizzards six weeks before pasturing is done?" . . . "You give food and a sleeping rug to Dorji, fool!"

The great howl of accusation and invective slobbered into silence. Still the headman stood there, magnificent, contemptuous, wordless.

A small voice slimed: "We want no headman who consorts with demons, Muhlam!"

Another: "Do you care nothing that an attempt is made to drown the Tulku himself?"

"Or that my best bull wastes of a strange sickness?"

"Or that the prayer flags are torn down and the wheels reversed in the brooks? Why do you not answer, headman?"

And again the small voice slimed: "Why? Because he knows the truth. We need a new headman when our leader consorts with demons!"

Inside the tent Salom pushed Renzi away from him. He began to rise, but Veshti shook her head fearfully and motioned him back.

"Let it be, Salom," she whispered. "Muhlam will answer them. Let it be."

And then they heard the ringing cry of the headman's words:

"Enough! Let there be an end to this mad clamor. There was

a time in this valley when my people would have shown more courtesy than to come to a house of sorrow screaming in their madness. I see that the time is past. If there is something to be said, say it then. But let one say it—and then go! Or by the great Buddha himself, I shall throw you from my grasses with my own hands! Now let *one* speak!"

There was a pause now in the wind's sob, and in the fragment of silence they could hear the sucking slither of many feet shuffling uncertainly.

"Well? Does none speak? Why, a moment ago I thought there was much to be said!" His contempt was withering. "Ah, do I not see my good friend Chunor skulking behind the women? Surely Chunor will speak, eh?"

The wind came again and with it a sharp hiss of rain.

"Speak, Chunor!" one shouted, and there was a mumble of support.

Chunor pushed from the shambling group and faced Muhlam squarely in the shelter of the tent wall. He shook his head deprecatingly and spread his hands:

"This is not my wish, Muhlam. I would that some other should speak for the people."

"They have asked you to speak," Muhlam snapped. "And so have I. Now speak!"

"I shall say what is in their minds, but only because you and they have asked for it."

"Tell it!"

"Your people have grievances, Muhlam. You see they are all here. It is not just one man or one woman, or even an aggrieved pair. If I speak, then I speak for all the people of the valley." He paused, and endorsement growled from the black clot.

Muhlam looked at them, and his face was tight. He spat.

Chunor shrugged. "As you will. Muhlam, this is what your people say——"

"Do you, too, say it, Chunor, or are you standing apart from the people?" Muhlam asked curtly.

"I said *with* them in this. Since the dwarf-man of Han came to this valley there have been many strange happenings, and——"

"By Dorji's guts, and did nothing happen, then, before the man of Han came? Am I the headman of a pack of weak-boweled children dirtying themselves with fear at the tales of old women?"

He peered scornfully through the whining night, and there was surliness in the surge and shuffle of the wet shadows. "Well enough for *you* to talk!" a thin voice sneered.

"If it were merely the tales of old women your people would not have listened, Muhlam," Chunor continued suavely. "But it was Yanong himself who warned us, and many have agreed that the priest did well, since there have been happenings here for which one finds it hard to see a human origin. It is not just that Kaman's bull wastes and will assuredly die. Nor that the prayer flags are torn down——"

"Someday, Chunor, you must make me some prayer flags that stand against a high wind," Muhlam jeered.

"Then what of the prayer wheels that are reversed in the brooks, headman? Do not forget the wheels!" The voice screamed at them, and Chunor nodded.

"Yes, Muhlam," he said, still speaking with calm and reason. "I have yet to see a wind high enough to spin a prayer wheel back-to-front. And I myself have seen the strange blue growth that spreads on my woman's cauldron——"

"Eeee! And in the shape of a serpent!"

"Yes, Muhlam, but it is not just these things, although even for them no explanation can be found——"

"Bah! I could find an explanation soon enough for the filth of your own slut's cauldron, Chunor!"

"But it is not these things of themselves that have made the hearts of your people sick with fear. It is these things coupled with other things. Muhlam, this is not idle chatter. You are the headman. And yet these people are here to stand against you! Would they do this if there were not sufficient reason? Has it ever been done before in your time as headman, or your father's time? No. Then you must hear what the people have to say."

A pool of rain caught in the tent roof spilled over and giggled down the fabric. The wind shrieked along the ropes. Muhlam said nothing.

"Will you hear these things, Muhlam?"

"I will hear them. But I am the headman, and when the tale is read I will make the decisions—and what I say will be obeyed—and whatever is said or done there will be stern punishments for this disturbance of a house of sorrow. Now tell all you have come to tell."

Chunor inclined his head. "You have heard of the prayer flags and wheels, Muhlam, of the serpent growth on the cauldron, of the sickness of Kaman's finest bull. There are other things concerning this man who says he is from the Han country. He sings strange songs in a tongue none can understand. Now this is a strange thing. It cannot be the tongue of Han because he confesses he knows it not. But let that pass. Now this man has been seen to skirt the prayer cairns in defiance of the gods and to laugh as he did so. He has derided our own most respected priest, scorned our beliefs, openly blasphemed even before children. Although I have not seen it myself, Naropa swears to seeing a footprint on the trail to the sorcerers' heath—with no other footprint before it or behind." Chunor coughed. "Now, you have asked me to speak for your people, Muhlam. I speak. Your people say this: there is a demon in your tent, perhaps even Dorji himself!"

A sob of terror shrilled up behind him, and Muhlam spat again and laughed shortly.

"Ay, Muhlam, you laugh in your pride and sneer at your people as weak-boweled children. Yet your same weak-boweled children will stand here in the night, whipped by storm, that this matter shall be discussed and straightened now. *Now!* And yet you laugh, and in your mind you will ask them how they know that this is Dorji, or some other malicious demon. But they say this—how do *you* know he is not? How do you know? Listen, Muhlam. Their priest, the servant of their gods, has warned them against this stranger in blue garments. The people have heard things and seen things not seen nor heard before in this valley. Listen again,

Muhlam, for these are stout enough words seeing that we know the demon is in earshot and could wreak a vengeance on us! The dwarf? What do we know of him? He comes from nowhere. He comes with no good reason for his coming. He has been with us three short weeks. Must I list again the signs of sorcery plain for all to see?"

"No need, Chunor," a voice cried from the pack. "No need. You have spoken well."

"They say I have spoken well, Muhlam. Like you, I laughed at this talk. I dismissed it as the chaffer of the crones, until there was too much evidence for me to disregard any longer. I have spoken of the signs and the marks of the demon pressed upon our lives. Now let me talk of happenings that are closer to us all. Look above you, Muhlam. Open your nostrils and smell the wind. Stride across the thang and feel the blows of tempest about your shoulders. Go to the river's edge and harken to its song. Stand on the flank of the herd and listen, not to the words I speak, but to the words the rain tells. When day comes, bend your eyes to the eastern peaks. What do these things say to you, Muhlam? They say to you that the blizzards come. Perhaps within a few days we must muster our cattle and move from High Valley. Six weeks of fat grazing have been devoured, Muhlam! And cast back your memory to the last occasion when summer was so swiftly swallowed. Do you remember? It is a long cast for memory, Muhlam, because it was eighteen summers gone. But *you* should remember, since it was then that your own brother Janbor was seized by a mad impulse and rode away, never to return. And the plague was heavy that year on corn and kine. Do you remember, Muhlam? Now the blizzards come again in August. Is this not proof enough? And if even more proof be needed, was not the Tulku himself almost drowned but yesterday?"

"Eeee! Did I not say it? Did I not say that this one was more powerful than the Most Excellent——"

"Quiet, slut!" Chunor snapped. "This is talk between men."

He turned again to the headman, and his voice was lowered until it was only a deeper hissing in the hiss of the rain. "And there is this other matter, Muhlam. This thing I have not raised before, because I feel for you. But ... have you looked at the death cauldron, Muhlam, and laughed at *that*, too?"

"And I said it!" Dupken keened. "Oh, I said it! Blood on the grass! I foresaw it!" She stumbled forward and thrust her streaming face to within an inch of Muhlam's and burst into shrill laughter. The headman's unwavering eyes looked beyond her.

"And where is Kelinka now?" she cackled. "Where? Where is the headwoman?" Her mad laughter rioted high above the wind, and in the darkness the people sighed on a long, shuddering note of fear.

Chunor swung in a fierce frenzy of rage, and his clenched fist struck his wife's open mouth. There was no control in his action, none in his words:

"Who are you, foul slut, even to mention the name of a good woman?"

He shivered in his anger, and Dupken whimpered, but Muhlam still said nothing, and none could tell from the black silence of that massive shadow what his thoughts were.

For a long time he was silent. Then: "You are all fools," he said, quite evenly.

There was a silence singing with storm, and a mounting anger that was greater than fear. A voice sneered: "So we are fools, eh? Not so much fools that we cannot guess you were glad enough to get rid of your woman. Perhaps it was good to have another see to it, eh?"

The unknown voice seemed to spur the people into a fury that knew no restraint. For a moment Chunor remonstrated, but his voice was drowned in the ugly, insistent clamor that rose high above the noises of the night.

"Did you help him with the deed, headman?"

"Be rid of the demon murderer if you value your position!"

"Cast him out, or get out yourself!"

"Is it good to have your woman removed—the useless woman who could spawn no son?"

"Are Bitola's loins warmer than those of your woman?"

"Yes! He covets another———"

And suddenly the clot of figures was rent apart, and a figure stumbled away from the fretted ridge of upraised arms, and Bitola stood there, her hands on her hips and her head flung back. For a moment her blazing magnificence daunted them.

"And if he does? And if they are?" Her voice was a taunt. "Then I, for one, am proud! *Proud,* you milk-suckers! He is still a better man than any of you yapping curs who have lusted vainly."

"Dirty bitch!" Lotor said coldly, and struck her so that she lay still in the sodden grass and the rain beat upon her.

"You, too, Lotor?" Muhlam said softly.

And then the tent flap was dragged aside, and the light poured out. For a moment the grotesque tableau was frozen by the ruddy gleam, and all the figures were garish puppets immobilized before the swinging black silk that was the movement of the night.

Salom sucked in his breath. He could see Dupken on her haunches with her head in her hands, sniveling quietly. The rain drummed against the sodden, muddy garments of Bitola, sprawled in the wetness with one leg crooked. The others stood behind the unconscious girl, crouched a little against his coming. As he stared at them they fell back a little, and no face was other than a puppet's face, masked by a still mask of terror. His fingers unclenched and the tent flap fell behind him, and the darkness rushed over the memory of the light, but it seemed to him that the puppets' faces still grimaced through the blackness.

"Out here there are things being said." Salom spoke softly, and in the hiss of rain and wind perhaps his words were inaudible to them, for none answered him.

"There are things being said," he called, "and I wish to hear them."

Still the silence hung between him and the people. He turned to Muhlam.

"They say things of me, Muhlam. Is it proper for me to give answer to them?"

The headman looked at him sadly. "They have a high tally of

things to say against you, Han-man," he said. "And, for that matter, against me. If you wish to give answer, then speak."

"Do not heed his silver tongue!" a voice shouted.

"Enough!" Muhlam cried. "Did I not give heed to *your* case? Then let the boy answer."

Salom turned to the people and grappled with his thoughts. He knew the immeasurable importance of this moment. It was well enough for him to dismiss as fantasy these things that had been said—a whole fabric of fantasy woven round a mad woman's words. There were some things that he could not explain even to himself—the single footprint, the reversed prayer wheels—but they could have been bred in the fogs of Dupken's imagination. But all the other things—the moldy cauldron, a sick animal, prayer flags torn down by the wind, the mishap to the Tulku, the avalanche that had cost Kelinka her life, the early arrival of the blizzards—none of these things needed a supernatural explanation. They were things that had happened before and could happen again. They were part of the warp and weft of the valley itself.

But in the eyes of all these people every happening had been attached to Dupken's ill-reasoned claim. Even the brief prestige gained by his audience with the Tulku had been turned against him, as proof of the power of his malignancy. Everything that had happened had been distorted, exaggerated to fit the diabolical picture of him assembled in their minds.

A pulse hammered at his temple. For the first time he was conscious of the strength of the thing he was fighting. Yanong had done this—Yanong and Chunor. They had been clever. Muhlam? Was Muhlam clever? But Muhlam had been right: they did have a high tally of things to say against him. And Chunor had been plausible; Chunor was clever. He had spoken the tally and it had seemed reasonable, complete, unanswerable . . . no, it seemed stupid, childish, unreal. . . . To him, yes—but what of the others? He had heard their screaming. They had been convinced. Convinced or frightened? Both. And whatever one thought it would be no use pleading fantasy or imagination against this tale that

Chunor had told! Chunor—two faces and two tongues. Already even Muhlam was half-convinced that there was something in what Chunor had said; he had seen it himself, seen it in the headman's eyes! And what if Muhlam would not stand beside him? Who else was there? Kelinka was dead. Veshti? It would need Muhlam, it would need the headman—and already the headman was possessed by doubt.

There was a rising inflection of impatience in the sullen mutter of the mob. They were waiting for him to give answer.

He stepped forward slowly, and again they dropped back a pace.

He would say the words. Words? The words would not be for them: nothing could sway them; in their minds he was condemned already. No. He would say the words but they would be only for two people: the headman who already had a doubt in his mind—the man who stood gaunt and black before his own tent—and his daughter who crouched within.

"I will not hold you long in the rain," he said calmly, but there was an intensity in his words that held the people silent and suddenly still. "I speak to you not as a stranger befriended by the headman, nor as the demon you say I am. I speak as the man from the Han country, as one who does not belong here."

He paused. The silence held. He knew, with a hard satisfaction, that they were caught in the spell of a brief power he had somehow acquired.

"I speak first to Chunor," he continued. "Chunor seeks little enough—merely that Muhlam steps down from the leadership and allows him to occupy his place."

There was a sharp, hissing intake of breath. He waited. Again none spoke.

"Chunor speaks smooth words. I thought he would have come here before this with his smooth words. Perhaps it took him longer than I had guessed to collect the people about him, and to whisper to them, and to thread the lies and idiot's tales and accidents and everyday happenings into a truss for the headman and a gallow's rope for me. He has been planning this thing for a long time—he and the priest called Yanong. They were disturbed when the Tulku came..."

He had made a mistake! Bringing in Yanong and the Tulku had been an error. These people were caught in a strange web of supernatural fear, of holiness; the priests were their only champions against this unknown thing. His argument was collapsing.... He could hear the swift upsurge of muttering, and he swept on more rapidly:

"... and they were angry. Yanong was more than angry. He was fearful." It did not matter now. He was committed and he would say all he had to say. "Yes, Chunor, he was fearful—very fearful. He thought I would have some stories to tell the Tulku, and so he ran down-valley, Chunor, and his tail was dragging like the tail of a whipped cur." The mutter had grown into a roar and the sound beat against him, but he pitched his voice higher and shouted at them: "But he is the wisest of men, that Tulku. He gave some wisdom to me, too. It might seem to Chunor that all has happened as he wanted it, even to the Tulku's own mishap. You will be wrong, Chunor! Wrong, I tell you! For I know how this sorry story of yours will end. I know! As I know that everything you say could have happened to anybody. It is for your own vile purpose, Chunor, that these things have been hammered into the brain of a half-witted crone."

"Listen no longer to this filthy blasphemer!" The cry shrieked above the howl of the mob. His brief moment had gone. A great wave of words ... other people's words ... the words crashed over him ... incoherent words ... invective and fury.

"You fools, fools, *fools!*" he screamed. "Will you be led like sheep against your own headman by a liar and a hypocrite, and a prancing monk dirty with his own lusts? Will you—?"

And then there was a sudden searing pain across his head. He reeled back and clutched a stay-rope for support. Faces and figures and the great din of their cries were a black whirl in his senses. His eyes cleared. He put his fingers to his head. The blood trickled warm across his hand.

"Stone him!"

"Kill the demon now!"

"More stones for the blasphemer!"

The roaring wave engulfed his senses again, voices mad with killing hunger. The mob heaved forward. He shook his head and spat the blood from his mouth. He could see clearly now: the blur of white faces . . . open mouths . . . the slide of rain and stars . . . wild eyes . . . he could hear a high-pitched screaming fused into an unbearable singing ribbon of sound. . . .

Then Muhlam was in front of him, lashing at the black wave with his fists. The wave broke and fell apart. Muhlam turned and pushed violently at the boy so that he fell full-length inside the bright improbability of the tent.

And then there was blackness and the yell of voices, and through the bedlam he could hear bells jangling . . . little bells . . . the ridiculous melody of horse-bells. The boiling sea of noise was suddenly calmed. A cold horror folded over him as he heard the voice—the unctuous, servile, hated voice:

"Come, come, my children. What happens now? Is this fitting conduct before a house of sorrow and bereavement? The gods will be displeased."

The voices ceased. There was a whisper and mutter of many voices, but again the hush fell.

"Let it be for now, my children. Let it be. Differences between the living can be settled at a more fitting time. This is a time for the dead. For Muhlam's dead."

Yanong walked into the tent.

Chapter Fourteen

I

BY MORNING the storm had spent itself, although its scattered forces were regrouping among the high mountains. The valley was scoured and cold, and mists clung to the peaks.

Slopes which two days before had been dark with vegetation now glittered beneath snow, and new brooks and cascades had appeared on the nearer hills. The river was a yellow tumult that pushed exploratory fingers across the flats and drove the swamp insects from the marshes. Everywhere mud banks were sliding silently into the diligent runnels of opaque water, and the runnels carried an endless freight of leaves and twigs and draggled feathers and the battered nests of birds.

The air was calm but there was still wind in the sky and the balmy odor of decay had been swept aside by a chill, wet smell that had in it the harsh presage of winter. The gale had stripped the birches and almost overnight a clump of willows had become a burst of flame in the cool glitter of fields and hills.

Within the comparatively brief span of the storm other things had happened. The swallows had fled south, and now the sky was stippled with harsh-crying arrowheads of cranes driving urgently in the wake of the smaller emigrants. Crowds of ravens and magpies swirled impatiently around trees already overcrowded by birds that had swept down from the northern plateaus on wings of tempest. Everywhere there was a raucous, chaffering restlessness.

The swollen lagoons swarmed with ducks and geese. Life streamed across the valley endlessly, skein after skein of honking geese, the black drifts and smears and flecks of smaller fowl.

To the new sad music of the morning was added a clamorous urgency that sometimes almost stifled the diapason of the river.

On the rising ground that lifted toward the pass into the Valley of Cloud Jade the Tulku halted his mule and looked back along the Valley of the Dreaming Phoenix for a long moment before he shrugged and rode on with his mud-spattered cavalcade.

In the tent of her father, Veshti's voice was flat: "They will be coming soon. For the rites. I shall prepare the ku-zeh."

"Prepare nothing!" Muhlam said. "There will be none coming."

"But, Muhlam——"

"There will be none coming," the headman repeated harshly. He looked at Salom. "They will be afraid to come."

"Yes." Salom's face was strained, and the clotted gash stood livid on his forehead. "They will be afraid. Of me."

"Dorji's guts! They will be more afraid of me before this tale is run!" Muhlam spat. "There will be some soreheads who will long rue the doings of last night. They will learn that it does not pay to forget who is headman." He clenched his fists and shook them violently, and then, as if conscious of the ludicrous surprise on the dead face of Kelinka, his arms fell slowly. "They will not come," he said.

Salom shifted his body wearily. "Perhaps it would be better if I left the tent while the rites are conducted," he suggested.

Muhlam shrugged. "Leave if you like, boy. It makes no difference. In any case they will not come. If you stay there will be but the three of us, and the child—and Yanong."

"Yes—" Salom's smile was twisted and ugly—"and Yanong."

"The priests must do something to earn the silver that pushes their purses out of shape!"

Salom looked at Veshti.

"Then I will not leave," he said. "You do not care if I stay?"

"I do not care what you do, boy," Muhlam said dully, as if his mind were occupied with larger matters.

"Then I stay. Kelinka was a good woman, and kind to me."

II

Yanong and Chunor nodded at each other in understanding and fell again into thoughtful silence. Yanong turned to Dupken. She was kneeling by the fire fashioning barley-dough funerary offerings into the shapes of chortens and formalized yaks.

"The dough on that one is too soggy, daughter," he said sharply. "Here—give it to me." He kneaded at the paste deftly and regarded the result with satisfaction. "There. Now you may add the red symbols, and the green."

Dupken muttered at the implied rebuke, and prodded at the dough.

"Hurry, woman!" Chunor snapped. "The priest and I will wish to go soon."

"Eeee! It is well the priest is with you. His prayers will need to be powerful." Her hands left the dough, and the twiglike fingers fluttered into the tangle of her hair. She held her head, rocking it from side to side, chanting: "Blood, blood, blood! And there will be more before this day is out. I see it all. I always see it all. You are a fool, husband, to set foot inside that accursed tent. The evil is not yet finished——"

"Shut your mouth," Chunor said automatically, "and bestir yourself with the offerings."

"Let me take them, Chunor," Yanong murmured. "You may follow when you are ready. But are you sure you are wise, my son, to enter the house of Muhlam? There will be none of the others——"

"I have no fear of Muhlam, nor of his demon," Chunor said. "The anger of the headman matters little, since he will be headman only for another day or so. And I am certain, good Yanong, that your incantations will be powerful enough to restrain the dwarf throughout the ceremony." There was a taunt in his words that Yanong did not fail to notice. "Afterward, when the people have dealt with this matter, there will be no need for fear among any of us. No, I shall attend the rites. None will say that Chunor turned pale. Besides—" he stared toward his sniveling wife, and his face was sad and puzzled—"besides, I had a regard for Kelinka. She was a good woman."

III

Lotor's ugly face was contorted and his eyes were muddled.

"And I say you will *not* go, bitch!" He looked toward his daughter, and his woman fluttered helplessly and his children whimpered their fear at this new anger on their father's face.

Bitola adjusted the jade buckle of her belt. She said nothing, but when he raised his hand she looked at her father evenly, and her bruised mouth twisted with contempt.

"Daughter!" Her mother looked at her unhappily. "Listen to your father now," she pleaded. "Do not go near that wicked tent. There is much badness spoken of you already—oh, I do not know what will happen!"

Again Bitola was silent, but she patted her mother's head awkwardly.

"You will not go! I say you will not! If I have to beat you to a pulp—no flesh of mine is going to be mixed up in this thing! Mixed up in *killing!*" Lotor screamed the words and struck at her and the blow crumpled her.

Bitola rose unsteadily and wiped the blood from her mouth. She swayed a little and looked at the back of her hand curiously, and then she walked from the tent.

Her father's face worked as he watched her go, and then he put his head down into his hands so that his woman and his children should not see his tears.

IV

In Kaman's tent, Maygur sniffed and rubbed the back of her hand against her nose, and her fingers shook as she strung up another wooden dagger point-downward over the tent entrance. "What . . . what will happen?" she whispered. She looked toward her brothers, busy fastening mystic symbols to the wall under Kaman's direction.

"Nothing!" Kaman snapped. "Nothing will happen to us. I had these symbols blessed by the Tulku himself. I knew there would be trouble. I knew it when the bull began to waste. If they had listened to me—but nothing happens to god-fearing people who are cautious. Now I say that not one of you will venture from this tent until the rites are finished. If we stay here nothing can happen. What happens in Muhlam's tent is no concern of ours."

"Buddha be merciful!" Naropa mumbled fearfully. "Oh, how well it reminds me of a tale my grandmother told me. There was a death in a family she knew, and it was as this case of the headman's. The family had unknowingly harbored a demon. And after the rites, when my grandmother went to pay her respects, all the mourners were mangled to death, and the corpse still sat there—but it was untrussed from its bindings!"

Kaman licked his lips nervously. "Nothing will happen to us, woman," he said impatiently. "I have told you. We will stay here until the rites are finished—and then the matter will be settled so that no decent people will have further cause for fear."

Kaman's face was grim and courageous and determined, and he knew his family was grateful to him for his strength.

V

Even on the high pastures the day was different from all other days. It was the day of the funerary rites. Dochi crooned contentedly to the beasts. It was a wordless song of his own contriving that he sang to the cattle when he was lonely or when pleased or sorry. Today his feelings were mixed, but mostly he was pleased, even though he wished he had been given permission to attend the funeral instead of being sent with the herds. But his father had been firm against his pleas. And he had told him to be very watchful, for the storm would come again and the animals were restive.

Dochi sighed. He liked funerals. They were exciting. And this one promised to be more exciting than most; and if he had gone perhaps he could have seen Veshti. He could have watched her, and perhaps she would have spoken to him, and then he could have whispered to her the fine joke that only he knew.

He rocked in his saddle and sniggered.

Why were there so many stupid people in the valley? Why, when he had returned last night with Yanong he had laughed to himself until his sides ached! What a hubbub there had been! All the people of the valley standing there in the wind and rain and screaming that the man from Han was a demon! Idiots! Such idiots! He sniggered again and clapped his hands together. Only Dochi knew that he was not a demon. Only Dochi! Oh, such idiots they were!

His face clouded. But what was the use of being the only one to know a joke if there was nobody to tell it to? No, he was no longer content. It would have been so much better to go to the rites in Muhlam's tent. Veshti would have been pleased to know that her betrothed was the only clever one of the valley.

He stared down toward the home thang and sighed.

VI

Chunor came to the headman's tent as the butter lamps were being lighted.

Muhlam rose slowly and stared at him.

"Why do *you* come, Chunor?" he asked softly.

"I have some homage to pay to the dead."

"There is homage enough here. We need no more."

"I still owe the dead some homage."

"There was little enough of it last night! Did I not hear voices shouting that Muhlam's dead would pass through Bado unmourned and unrespected?"

"You did not hear my voice, Muhlam." Chunor's eyes challenged the headman, and then moved slowly and meaningly toward the upturned face of Bitola. "Kelinka was a better woman than most," he added and walked inside the tent.

Yanong frowned as he motioned Chunor to a position.

The monk was hideous. He had donned his robes loosely so that his arms were bare. His hands and face were smeared with soot and rancid greases, and in this mask of filth his eyes were rolling circles.

To Yanong, as to most of his order, dirt was a symbol of fighting strength, and in the funerary rites a priest was in need of all his courage if he were to vanquish the creatures of the shadows. Yanong was sure of his courage, sure of his power. Strength surged through him as sap through a tree in springtime, and he was possessed by the strange ecstasy that always came to him when he prepared to do battle with the hidden forces. For in this thing, at least, Yanong was sincere.

Bado was a real territory to the monk, a familiar region that he had studied and traveled a thousand times, threading through its maze of diversely colored paths and byways, greeting radiant beings and misshapen monsters almost as well-known to him as his fellow monks. Had not the reality of Bado been hammered for years into his half-crazed mind by his ecclesiastical teachers? For countless thousands of times he had chanted the inventory of its inhabitants, pored over maps of its territory, studied in a hundred thankas the pictures of its gods, genii, monsters, fairies, demons and imps, listened to descriptions of every hall and corridor in the court of Shinje, the Judge of the Dead. And finally the hammerblows of instruction had beaten into his brain an unquestioning acceptance of the reality of this weird phantasmagoria that embodied the witch-ridden fancies of the old Shaman sorcerers and the cluttered folk tales and demonology of centuries.

He could mock secretly the laws of celibacy of his order, and yet could possess absolute belief in the existence of the dreaded Towos, who feasted upon the brains of the dead. He would rob his own abbot of his rightful tithes; yet there was no limit to his respect for the Lahmayin, who battled with the gods in Bado, or the Yidags, with heads as large as clouds and necks thin as string, who howled through the shadows seeking consecrated water with which to slake their everlasting thirst.

In his necromantic ecstasy Yanong could achieve a dignity that he lacked utterly in the routine of priesthood. The strangely anchored life after death, the shadowy world between death and rebirth—these were firm truths in the mind of Yanong; these were the worlds wherein he marched with the power and the majesty of the initiated. With each venture into these dark mysteries his powers grew; and as his powers increased so did his longing to master newer mysteries and accept more perilous challenges in the world of fettered corpses, ghouls and possessed spirits.

He looked behind him at the half-circle of frightened faces that swam in the sacred lights, and he was filled with triumph.

What power had they—these puny ones? Could the contemptuous headman lead his dead wife into her next incarnation? Could the blaspheming dwarf-man pass unharmed across the lakes of fire or the lairs of the Towos? Could sly-eyed Chunor say the words that unlocked the courts of Shinje? No! They could only sit, helpless, afraid, malleable as the dough of the funerary offerings to be kneaded between Yanong's fingers. They could only wait for him to show the way. There they sat, helpless as the dead one herself, terrified of the things they could never understand.

Who now was as powerful as Yanong? Yanong, the initiated. Yanong, the servant of the gods. Yanong, the guide of the dead.

So you do not scoff now, Muhlam! You sit with fear in your face and plead with me to guide your woman safely. Yes, I will guide her safely, Muhlam, for she was a good woman.

And you, arrogant dwarf, who laughed at my powers—I see no laughter on your face. You pay for that laughter, eh? And you know the payment is not yet ended?

And you, girl—you who were reluctant to mate with the servant of the gods—you thought you had concealed your reluctance, but I saw into your eyes, and now I see another thing in those eyes. You feel my power, eh? It is greater than the power of the comely dwarf? You feel it? But you have felt nothing yet, girl. Wait a little time, and see all of my power—and then grovel at my feet and beg me to confer upon you the benefaction of the gods. Wait!

He turned slowly and faced the cauldron.

The battered holy book had been taken from its wooden coverings and wrappings of cloth, and its oblong sheets were opened at the liturgy for the dead. True, Yanong could not read one word of the flat-topped script, but he had no need to read. Every word was a symbol stamped indelibly into his brain. And he rejoiced in the words. He rejoiced in the ponderous, rhythmic chant that had lost all meaning except the meaning that he, Yanong, was one with the gods; more powerful than the living, more powerful than the dead.

His eyes were hooded, and spittle bubbled at the corner of his slackly working mouth.

From the half-circle behind there was no movement.

It was as though the brooding inevitability of the words had cast a spell upon them, and under this spell they were compelled to sit through all eternity watching the lights falter and flicker over the still, mute woman who listened with an air of ludicrous surprise to the words that told her she was dead.

The chant ceased. Yanong sighed and called for tea.

Veshti filled the bowls, moving with the deliberation of a sleepwalker. As she followed Yanong's command and placed a second bowl in front of the cauldron, Salom saw with sudden foreboding that her face had some of the content of sleep.

Yanong sucked thirstily at the bowl, and when it was empty he wiped his hand across his mouth, streaking the soot into a barred pattern that made his face even more repulsive.

He leaned toward the corpse. There was insanity lurking in his expression as he muttered, "Drink deeply, Kelinka. You will need all your strength for this journey. It will be a journey of fatigue and perils. But you must trust in me. Now—drink deep, daughter."

Salom's breath choked in this throat and strangled the cry that was rising. For a moment he thought the corpse had moved! It was a delusion of the light. Of course, it was a delusion. He glanced quickly at the spare bowl. The level of the liquid was the same. The wisps of steam had cleared. He could see the fat congealing, thick and white, on the cooling surface of the beverage.

But Yanong indicated his satisfaction. His head was tilted and his attitude intent, as if he were listening to words, inaudible to others. Then he seized the bowl and tossed the liquid across the grass. His hooked finger summoned Veshti, although he did not divert his attention from the dead.

"She enjoyed it," he whispered. "She desires another bowl, and also tsamba." Then, more loudly: "It is being prepared, daughter. You are wise, Kelinka. You will need all your strength so there will be no need for you to return here. There must be no return, you understand? No return."

A fresh bowl of tea and a kneaded cake of tsamba were set before the cauldron, and Veshti slid back into the shadows, her boots dragging.

It was a long time before Yanong spoke, and in the tautening silence the strange tableau became, to Salom, finally divorced from reality. It almost seemed as if he had become bewitched in the Tulku's tent and had walked into one of the thankas on the walls. There was the same smoldering light, the same play of shadows, the same horror in the rigid figure.

The noise of the outer day came with the drowsing clarity of summer sounds heard when eyes are closed.

"Ah, I see you are ready, Kelinka."

Salom jumped. Against his will, against every vestige of reason he possessed, he was being drugged into a half-belief in this fantastic mummery. He shivered, and glanced furtively at the others. All were strained forward. In their faces, even in the face of Muhlam, there was unquestioning belief and a deep fear.

"Then we will go, Kelinka," Yanong droned, rocking himself from side to side. "Here. Take my hand. I will lead you. The path here is rough. You can trust in me." He stretched his filthy hand toward the cauldron.

Salom's scalp prickled. His mouth was dry and acid. He had almost expected the richly garbed arm of the dead woman to burst its bindings, to reach down toward the offered hand of the priest, but the only movement was the play of light across the gleaming eyeballs and the hanging jaw.

"Ah, it is well, daughter. You are surprised that you walk so easily? But those broken limbs were merely illusion. Your legs are firm, Kelinka, firm and robust—yes, even the one carved from you by him whom you trusted and gave of your kindness. Come."

Salom looked at his hands.

"But do not worry, Kelinka, about such earth-bound evils. You and I are to meet many demons and monsters and fairies. The trail we take will be well-peopled. It is a well-worn trail this, for all men have trodden it, and all will tread it again. But have no fear. Rest your hand firm in mine and have trust in me and I will guide you. And there will be beautiful things to see also. Look—to the right of you—do you not see that lovely grotto? No, not yet, daughter. Later you may visit it. Later. First we have two high summits to cross, and the lakes of fire, and ere nightfall we must be through the pits where the fiends wait. Come, daughter, we must not be distracted——"

The priest's voice trailed away. His body rocked from side to side, and his face was loose and yet obsessed. He seemed in a trance. It was perhaps half an hour later that his eyes opened wearily. He turned to them.

"Tea, child," he said listlessly. "I am parched."

Muhlam knuckled at his eye sockets.

"But it is not yet finished?" he asked gruffly.

"No, no! I have left her for a moment. She waits with many others outside Shinje's court. She is quite safe there for a time." He brushed his finger tips together and peered at Muhlam slyly.

"There will be need," he purred, "of a fee for the keeper of

Shinje's halls. A silver piece." He rummaged in his purse. "I have one here that will serve. Perhaps you will recompense me later?"

"You will be paid for your services, Yanong. But let us press on with the rites."

"Of course. But now you must all leave for a little time. I must be alone with the dead. It is time for the word to be uttered."

Muhlam nodded. The ceremony was familiar to him. He sought no elaboration, and he was irritated that Yanong should make explanations. But the monk's eyes were on Veshti as he spoke:

"There is a magic formula to be uttered before Kelinka can go before Shinje—a word that is only for the dead, and for those powerful enough to be initiated into the secret mysteries of the beyond. It is the word that separates the spirit from the husk, and any others who heard it would be made dead by its very sound. It is not a word for the living."

Bitola reached for Veshti's hand and began to lead her from the tent, ushering Renzi before them. The expression on Veshti's face was not lost to the priest. He smiled benevolently.

"Muhlam has seen such rites many times before, my child," he said seriously, "but you, most fortunately, would have had less experience. You see, child, Kelinka's spirit is still connected with her earthly form. It is like a long thread that has been unraveled between here—" he gestured toward the cauldron—"and the court of Shinje. When the magic word is uttered the thread is snapped and the spirit flies away through the top of the head. It cannot return. It is finally released for its travels into the next of its rosary of births."

"These matters are common knowledge," Muhlam snapped. "Come, continue with your task, priest!"

Yanong bowed obsequiously. "You are right, Muhlam. We shall continue. But even the headman must leave his tent."

Salom had been the last to rise. He went slowly toward the door and there he hesitated, as if about to speak to the priest, but Yanong was leaning over the cauldron whispering into Kelinka's ear. Salom hurried outside, trembling.

He blinked in the false, scoured brilliance of the day—a gray, metallic brilliance in which wind and the sheen of wet things compensated for the absence of direct sunlight. The thang was untidy with crushed flowers and swirled and flattened grasses.

The others clustered nervously in the tent shadow, as if reluctant to move into the unreality of the day. Bitola talked in an undertone to Veshti. Muhlam and Chunor stood in silence, their hands clasped behind their backs, their heads bowed. Beyond the little group Salom could make out the figures of Dupken and two of her sons standing on the thang and looking up toward the tent of sorrow.

He walked uncertainly toward the little clot of mourners. They turned away from him, and although their actions were not deliberate he stopped and stood apart awkwardly. From within the tent he could hear rustling, and then the sound of sharp, chipping blows. A few minutes later Yanong parted the flap and smiled toward them.

"It is done," he said. "Now, will you all come back and take up your positions again?"

Salom shuffled uneasily. Nothing would force him back inside that tent. Nothing! He had a swift and uncontrollable abhorrence of the tent, of its grisly inhabitant, of the smell of smoldering azalea leaves, of the magnetism of the monk who smiled at them from the doorway.

The others were beginning to move forward in response to Yanong's beckoning finger—almost, he thought, as if they were marionettes moving to the jerk of his hands. How would they take his refusal to re-enter the tent? Would they regard his absence from the rest of the ceremony as a slight against them?—as further proof of his unholiness? Or would they care at all? He could explain to Veshti. She would understand. Later, when the time was more suitable, she could explain to Muhlam. And if these two understood, what did it matter what the others thought?

He intercepted her a few paces from the doorway. She still seemed bemused.

"Veshti?"

"Yes?" Her eyes slid away, and he could see her knuckles whiten on Bitola's arm.

"I . . . I am not going back . . . not in there. I have no belief in all this. I do not think it proper that I should."

He halted lamely. Veshti was looking away from him. She was silent.

"Come, child," Yanong's voice purred. "We are waiting."

"Yes," the girl whispered. "Oh, yes, holy one."

She pushed past Salom, seeming to shrink from him, and then she was gone into the rustling gloom.

For a moment he stared stupidly at the gently swinging cloth of the tent flap, and then the full implication struck him.

She was afraid of him. She had gone from him. Gone! Yanong had tugged at the threads and she had been dragged away into the dismal, half-understood jungle of her beliefs. He had seen it happening in the tent, when he had watched her carrying the tea to the priest. He had seen the awe altering her face as Yanong mumbled his holy mendacities. And now he had seen the respect with which she had obeyed his summons to the continuance of the gruesome rites. He had even seen her cringe away from him as if fearful of contamination! The smell of some burning leaves, the flicker of a few lamps, the chanting of a charlatan—these had destroyed the other Veshti, the Veshti of the river, as surely as the rock and mud of an avalanche had destroyed Kelinka! And the real Veshti had gone, the Veshti of the golden body and the laughter and the sand dusted on her skin, the Veshti who had watched the raven, the Veshti whose hand had fallen so trustingly into his. She had gone as if she had never existed outside a wistfully recollected dream. She had gone!

He could hear Yanong's chant rising on a crescendo, vibrant and confident.

Salom strode across the thang to his horse. There were things now to be thought about. He would ride. He could think better when he rode. He would ride until he had decided these thoughts; ride until saddle-weariness numbed his body and mind; ride until he had obliterated the picture of something that had gone from him.

VII

When the others had reassembled in the tent Yanong took up his position beside the cauldron. He smiled tolerantly, like a showman about to present in person the finest juggler of his troupe.

A long straw, fashioned from a dried stalk of wheat, had been inserted into the top of Kelinka's head. It added the final caricature to her death. This was the straw through which Kelinka's spirit would escape into the beyond.

Yanong stared at them and savored his power. Never before had he experienced a feeling of confidence so superb, so overwhelming, so ecstatic. There was no task beyond his capabilities! Today he linked hands with the great mystics, with the saints and giants and heroes of long ago! Today he straddled two worlds and held both of them in thrall!

"There will be the ritual of the cutting of the thread," he said, "and then the girl Veshti shall prepare a good meal of the best meats, for the last offering to the fleshly form of that from which the spirit has gone—and to her guide and guardian—must be a fine offering. And then toward evening I shall take this ugly shell to the high ground and there disperse it so that it will not return."

He looked around, and the awed faces looked up at him silently, and he nodded.

The remainder of the ceremony was carried out without further audible conversation.

Yanong stood behind the cauldron now, stooped over so that his mouth was at Kelinka's ear. His right hand, with its chewed fingernails outlined in grime, rested on the dead woman's shoulder. Even in the filtered daylight the tent was not without gloom, and the long row of butter lamps cast against the wall a wavering spectral outline of the bizarre scene—and Veshti closed her eyes against it.

It was a strange thing. All her awe and reverence had drained from her, and she was fearful. She was fearful of filth and unclean intangibles. It was the monk's fingernails, the dirty embrace in which he clasped her dead mother, the sinister madness in his eyes. Her hand tightened on Bitola's. Why had not Salom come back with them? Why had he stayed outside? She needed him here. She needed to look toward him, to see in his clean eyes the unspoken answers to her own unspoken questions. Why had he not come back? Before, there had been a sense of security in knowing that he was here also; that fear was in his eyes, too. She closed her eyes against the grimy fingernails. Now, if she opened her eyes she would not see Salom; she would see only other eyes—the eyes of the lama; the frozen eyes of her mother. . . .

Yanong was whispering his final instructions to the spirit, but the words were only an uncomprehended hiss as meaningless as the splutter of the tea cauldron that simmered on the fire.

Bitola breathed out in a long, shuddering sigh.

Sweat furrowed lighter grooves through the blackened face of the priest, a clown's face now with its streaked finger marks and melted soot. His arms jerked spasmodically as his fingers pointed, directed, beckoned, retarded, cautioned. And then he took a great gasping, breath and flung his head back. His eyes were puckered tightly. His body trembled as if in some terrible labor. His arms stretched outward slowly, strainingly. The hooked fingers quivered. It seemed that the whole tent shuddered, and the air with it, and the onlookers trembled as if linked to the throbbing tension of the transfixed figure. And even as the terror sobbed from Renzi, a strange, high-keyed scream bubbled from the priest's throat, and the straw flicked from Kelinka's head and fluttered lightly into the fire. Veshti tried to look at the priest's fingernails, but her gaze returned to the burning straw. It flared and twisted and sagged softly into a black thread curled against the coals. It was the passing of her mother—the weary dissolution of a broken straw. Veshti's tears welled slowly.

"Ahhh!" The sigh whispered from the others, and there was

fear in the sound, and the unspoken hope that this was the end of the ritual.

Yanong turned his back and tottered to a sheepskin rug tossed against the far wall. He lowered himself slowly and lay there for a long time, his head hooked within his dirt-stained arms.

At length he looked up and spoke exhaustedly:

"Tea. It is over. Bring me tea."

"There is nothing more then?" Muhlam asked.

"Nothing. The last feast must be prepared. The rites are done. So let us have the finest dish you can conjure from the food bins, girl."

"And . . . and Kelinka?" Muhlam asked awkwardly.

"The woman's spirit already adventures newly in another life." Yanong gestured disdainfully toward the trussed figure. "This is a mere envelope dressed in gaudy rags, containing nothing. I will take care of the few formal matters remaining. They will be done on the high ground far from here."

"And Kelinka will be no more." Muhlam murmured the words with a sad wonder, almost as if he were talking his thoughts aloud.

"Already Kelinka is no more," Yanong said sharply.

"And nothing more remains?"

"Nothing—apart from certain related matters. There will be the question of a fee to discuss, of course, but that———"

"There will be no discussion. There will be no haggling over this. Name your fee, priest, and it will be paid."

"The fee is not for me, Muhlam. You understand that? It is a final gift on Kelinka's behalf to the keepers of the inner temples. In the winter to come there will be many prayers cylinders spun for her. In the barrel of each cylinder there will be ten thousand well-scribed prayers———"

"Name the fee, priest!"

Yanong pursed his lips and stared at the ceiling.

"For the purposes of discussion, shall we say . . . ummm . . . three silver pieces? And, of course, the extra piece for Shinje's attendant?"

Muhlam thrust his fist inside his jacket and drew out his leather purse. As he loosened the thong Yanong wished fervently that he had suggested five. But he smiled gratefully as he caught the four coins that were tossed to him.

"You say the silver is for the temple prayers?" Muhlam asked suspiciously.

"Of course." Yanong jingled the coins. "With this, prayers will be uttered all winter through."

The headman's hard fingers groped into the bag again. He tossed three more coins onto the grass before Yanong.

"Then prayers will be uttered a whole year, you understand?" he snapped. "This was a worthy woman."

"A worthy woman indeed!"

"And now the matter is discussed and the business done." Muhlam turned fretfully to Veshti. "Hurry, child, with the food! You are laggard in your duties. There will be heavier tasks now for your hands—and no time for your dreamings!"

Bitola took the dish from Veshti's shaking hands, and stared at Muhlam until the headman's eyes wavered.

"Harsh words will not speed the girl's fingers," she said reprovingly. "The girl worked through the night and saw no sleep. She has had no easy task this last day or two, Muhlam. Sometimes it would do you good to consider that there are others beside yourself who know suffering. *I* will prepare the food."

Muhlam glowered into her insolent face as if he would strike her, then he lowered his head, ashamed, and turned away.

Yanong sidled up to him.

"There are one or two other matters," he whispered slyly. "Perhaps we could talk outside?"

His finger tips rubbed together as he followed the headman through the doorway.

"Come then," Muhlam said impatiently. "What are these other matters?"

"There is the matter of Veshti," Yanong said suavely. "The matter that we discussed some days ago. And there is the question of the stranger who says he comes from China. This second matter, in particular, is one that cannot be long postponed."

Muhlam glared at him. "It will be discussed, priest! As will a lot of other matters concerning the behavior of my people. As will the matter of Veshti. As will the charges laid by the boy against Chunor and also against you, holy man! But nothing will be discussed until my woman reaches her own finality. Nothing, I tell you!" He gestured angrily toward the tent. "There is something in there, Yanong, that must be taken away. Tonight, when you return with your duties done, all the people will be here, and the Han-man will be here, and I shall hear all this evidence and these idiots' tales, and I swear by the holy cloak of Sakya himself there will be some other finalities!"

"Yes, but———"

"But nothing! There is another thing, priest. During the rites I did not care for your remark about the boy's action in severing my woman's leg. It was I, Muhlam, who told him to cut the leg."

"But the talk said———"

"Bah! The talk! There has been too much of it already. The rest of the talk, priest, is for tonight. But first there is a thing to be done."

And the headman strode back through the doorway of the tent to stand beside the effigy of the woman who had failed to bear him a son.

Chapter Fifteen

I

SALOM unbuckled the bridle and loosed the horse, but it was too weary to forage, and it stood with hanging head and twitching tail. He clambered up the uneven ground to the Pass of White Watching.

Until he reached the crest, the snow summits beyond were obscured by the rough rise of blackened grass. It was curious, he reflected, that it was only here, when the mountains were so close, that they could not be seen at all. But then, as he clambered higher, crag after crag reared majestically from the gulf until the barrier shouldered aside the pale sky. It was immense and beautiful and awesome—and yet, even at this short distance, it was as remote as when it had been a mere bleaching of a distant skyline.

Salom went thoughtfully to an overhanging spur from which all of the alpine range was visible, and looked to the southward along the funnel that twisted beyond the twin glaciers.

The ravine, he decided, was still negotiable, although the white lick of the stream appeared intimidating even from such a height, and the high snows had pressed down below timberline. The noise of the cascades that sprang from gullies and glaciers to form the river was the voice of living waters. There was no song of larks.

"It can be done," he said aloud. "With hard riding it can be done."

The highlands directly across from him were more forbidding. Beyond the immediately confronting ridge of rock and ice and snow stretched a shining blanket rumpled by lesser peaks, receding until it was lost in the luminous throb of snow blink. Within that white sea lay hidden trails he had known, and the passes that had opened the way from the solitudes of the Man-tze to the Valley of the Dreaming Phoenix. Those same trails and passes could lead back again.

The bleak and inhospitable country, cold and quiet, revealed no dark traces to show a traveler's way—yet he knew the trails would still be there. It did not follow that the passes would be insurmountable. Snow in itself was not an invincible enemy. It would not yet be deep enough to form a bastion that could not be assailed. Not yet. But what would it be at the end of the three or four weeks he would need to reach the critical gateways of the lost fastnesses?

He squinted into the glare. The sky was polished like a plate—a chill, blue-gray glitter, devoid of blemish, but which spoke certainly of snow.

"It can be done," he said stiffly.

Again the focus of his eyes changed. He studied the peaks that had pushed aside the sky, and his face was troubled. The ragged range he had remembered, with its clean, clipped-out purities, had gone. Ribbons of mist, swirled at the crags; wadded knots of cloud blotted some out altogether; driven snow blurred the contours of the others. The extreme limit of the Ta Hsueh Shan was not visible at all, for a storm stood against it, sheeting its final buttresses in a dirty whirl that flickered sullenly.

"It can be done," he muttered, but he spoke as a stubborn man attempting to justify himself.

He stumbled down from the spur and seated himself on a tussock of stiff grass, wrenching a stalk from it to chew upon.

The resolve went from his face and bitterness hardened it. Then this, too, passed. He gazed at the silent peaks, and their very majesty absorbed him.

After a time he rose to his feet slowly, like someone inexorably drawn into motion by an unseen force. His eyes were fixed on the highest of the summits as he spoke softly:

"You have seen it all," he said. "Over and over again you have seen it all."

He stared across the chasm as if awaiting an answer, but there was only the muted song of movement and change. But he nodded his head wisely, almost as if he had been answered. And when he raised his eyes to the peaks again they were almost the eyes of the Living Buddha.

"You have seen it all," Salom repeated. "And it all means nothing. Nothing."

He was thinking of the Tulku, and in his mind were the disturbed outlines of words that seemed to be spoken from distances beyond reach. Gradually the random words knitted into a pattern, and spoke to Salom of illusion. Illusion, and sorrow, and decay. The words boomed at him: *All life is illusion. Illusion, illusion!* The words jeered at him. *Decay is inherent in all living things,* the words cried. *Sorrow is caused by desire, and desire is illusion ... Illusion.* The words shrieked at him.

And suddenly his upturned face was alight: the face of a man who had found illumination at the end of a long quest. All his life had been a quest, but until now he had never known what he had sought. And now he knew! Now he had discovered humility, and, in its finding, the worthlessness of the other, brighter shadows he had pursued.

His mind was clearer now. Doubts no longer troubled him, nor fears. For he knew. *He knew!* He even knew that he would fail, and that his dreams would vanish as certainly as the ground mists cleared, but the realization possessed only a gentle sadness. Many people failed. Most people failed. Yet there was room in the world for the whispered account of failure. As much room, surely, as for the pompous struttings of the victors?

Even in failure this journey would have its reward. It need not end in nothing ... the last nothing ... finality ... the empty walnut shell held between the fingers of an adroit juggler.

He would return to the valley and he would face the people, and he would tell his words so that they might ring a long echo in some ears. There would be some who would remember his words, and know why he had failed. And then he would take his animals and ride back to the eastward, and perhaps he would be overwhelmed as Janbor was overwhelmed—for the season was far enough advanced—but like Janbor, at least he would have tried. Or it might be that he would succeed, and in China, with his eyes newly opened, he could seek again the things he had fled from before.

And then—would it matter that he had failed in the Valley of the Dreaming Phoenix?

The people of the valley would drive him away and consider that they had vanquished him. Fools! Only he had seen humanity in this valley and known what he had seen. He could even see his own posturings, so childish, so futile, so ridiculous.

Within the span of a few flat fields and their encompassing hills he had seen all humanity!

He tried to think of Veshti, to explain her. Well, in the last summing-up, did it matter that he should hunger for the girl any more than that Yanong should covet her, or Dochi? Each, in his own way, sought something. But by itself each something meant nothing, for there was nothing in life that stood by itself.

This was what he had learned: life was a stream, ever-flowing, ever-broadening. Here was the only immortality. *Living* was immortality. All these people—even the Tulku—were wrong in their fears. They did not understand that living itself was the only immortality. And life as a whole, great, streaming river—not merely a pretty ripple or a passing wavelet upon that river!

When one had this knowledge, what did it matter if one struggled and failed? The value was not in the accomplishment. It was in *the attempt to accomplish!* And the lessons that others might learn from that attempt. Beyond that, life mattered no more than the darkening of a lampwick pinched between fingers.

Someday perhaps one man would discover the ultimate wisdom, and then all the innumerable lifetimes of puppet-play would attain a meaning—the squalid as well as the radiant, the good with the bad, the strong with the weak. His own struggles would be there, and Muhlam's, and the hypocrisies of Yanong. Veshti would be there, and Kelinka, and all the rest of them.

They would all be parts of this onrushing stream pouring through the ages to that point in time when somebody would know its meaning.

Salom shivered. Between him and the glittering flanks of the impassive pinnacles a V of geese drove urgently southward. Suddenly he stiffened.

"Yes!" he cried. "Then you will have seen it all! All of it! Everything! And then you will know you were wrong to think it meant nothing!"

But only a thin echo wavered back to him, and with it the distant melancholy of the birds.

"I am nothing!" His shout rang against the loneliness. "Yes, I am nothing—but there is meaning in me! You will see!"

The thin, inhuman voice throbbed across the void as if the old white gods mocked him.

He turned on his heel and crunched back across the burned stubble to his horse. An oncoming storm was draped across the distant slopes, and the Valley of the Dreaming Phoenix appeared to him as a desolation devoid of beauty.

II

He rode slowly and with increasing melancholy, so that it was dusk before he reached the gloomy aisles of the birches. The valley ahead was black with night and storm, yet the clouds seemed static and ten shrouded miles stretched between him and the darkness.

He knew that both the storm and the night would overtake him long before he reached the tent of Muhlam, yet he had no impulse to hurry.

The exaltation of the spirit that had gripped him for a time on the pass had gradually burned itself out and all that remained were the ashes of his own mortification. He flushed and chewed at his lower lip as he thought again of his conduct, of his puny screamings at the lifeless mountains. At the thought of it he sank deeper into misery and self-pity until he was sick with shame.

Beneath the birches the light had almost gone, and on the slender trunks fungus glowed with eerie, ugly fire, and the glowworms danced in the vaulted shadows. In the undergrowth was the rustle and whisper of small, nameless creatures. He looked nervously to either side. A night bird clattered in the branches. He was suddenly afraid of the moving gloom. He shouted to his horse, and his voice and the familiar tattoo of hoofs comforted him.

But when he had cleared the wood he felt another twinge of shame. He spat bitterly. So he was a coward, too? He was afraid of trees in twilight? He halted the horse. These were only the idle terrors of fancy. He could prove it. He could ride back into the wood and show whether he was scared by birds that called in the darkness. He turned his horse. But he made no attempt to ride back.

A halved moon was sliding above the peaks, and the naked branches of the trees clawed upward like fleshless fingers struggling from the pits. From the undergrowth between him and the woods two bright eyes flickered and vanished, and he could hear twigs crackling secretly.

He jerked the reins and galloped away from the wood. His heart hammered and his skin prickled. In the silver of the moon wash, the valley had a new and haunted quality that filled him with terror.

For several minutes he rode blindly, and then he pulled the horse in.

He felt sick again, but this time with contempt for himself. He was stupid and weak and cowardly. He knew now the reason for his lofty thinking on the high pass, for his lordly self-eloquence. He had been too weak to admit even to himself that he had been defeated. He had tried to justify and excuse this failure by tortuous delusions and by shouting his foolishness into the air. To his shame, he had almost convinced himself that he would return to the tent of Muhlam and confront those who were implacably opposed to him, and intimidate and subdue them! Bah! He was a fine hero!

Then he would deceive himself no longer. He knew now exactly what he would do. He would return to the tent, gather up his paltry goods, and steal away as quietly as possible. And in China he could forget the stupid dreams and find some niche for himself in a city that could be no worse as a city than he was as a person.

By the time he reached the edge of the sorcerers' moor the moon had ridden clear of the range, and the bleak heath flowed with liquid silver. He remembered Muhlam's warning: "It is shunned by our people in darkness." He headed for the rising ground that skirted well clear of the wasteland.

III

The storm had arched high overhead. Drifts and tendrils scurried from its ragged edge. The cloud was a great hand clawing down the stars, and beneath it the forsaken moor crouched in a half-gloom.

When he first saw a movement within the play of shadows, Salom felt only a momentary disquiet. It was a trick, an illusion of light and atmosphere, a lingering of the panic that had seized him in the wood. The hush that preceded a storm was breaking into little chips and streamers of sound, and the valley was moving. A timid ground wind sighed against the gorse, nudging the shadows this way and that; and somewhere above him a higher wind piped.

His eyes roved back to the forlorn expanse, seeking reassurance. But he saw the movement again. A dark shape had stirred near a clump of dead trees that marked the beginning of the sorcerers' heath. He tugged at the reins, but the horse was restive. By the time it had come to an unwilling halt the movement, if there had been a movement, had ceased. For a long time Salom stared toward the twisted trees. Nothing. Nothing but the nebulous ripple of shadows. As he rode ahead again he whistled softly.

Perhaps it had been some prowling night creature. He smiled slightly. He was working himself into a fine state—fleeing from tree shadows and the call of a bird and the movement of some frightened beast in the undergrowth!

But his eyes went back to the contorted grove. And this time he could not control the quick terror that leaped within him. This was no deceit of the night! No vagary of moonlight and shadow!

There, undeniably, was the figure of a man—tall and thin and black: a man who circled slowly on the unhallowed ground, now a clear silhouette against the dull silver, now sucked into the spongy shadows of the trees.

Salom's heart raced as he reined in the horse and dismounted slowly. His skin crept and every instinct urged him to flee, but he conquered his weakness and bent cautiously and tethered his animal to a low shrub.

He straightened slowly, reluctant to look again toward the trees, and yet desperately eager to see some tall stump, some pattern of shade, that would prove his imagination had misled him. No. It was there—the figure of a man, bent over now and still circling in and out of the shadows.

But who could have business that would bring him to this desolation in darkness? To this wasteland that Muhlam had assured him was forsaken by all people during darkness? Or was it a living thing? The wind fluttered at him and he shuddered in the sudden piercing cold. Was it a living thing?

He knew the Tibetan tales of Delogs and familiar spirits and monsters that wandered in the lonely places, but had always dismissed them as stupid fancies. And yet—and yet how could one be *sure* of such things?

He moved forward stealthily. His hair bristled and in spite of the chill of the night there was a film of sweat across his face.

On such a night one could be unsure of almost everything, for all realities had been drained from the world.

The pallid ebb and flow of the moon's light, the overreaching clutch of the storm, the very loneliness of the moor and the night, and the flurry and sigh of the ground winds—there was evil in these things. Nothing real remained in the world except himself. He was the only reality crawling through a world of shades and vapors, for in the drench of black and silver the solids of earth and vegetation had become vaporous and something of their substance had gone into the clouds and stars and sky.

He was screened by a belt of low brush, and he crept to within ten paces of the gnarled trees before he halted finally and crouched within the shadow of the ragged hedge.

Now he could hear the other person. He was chanting in a low monotone but the words were unintelligible. Salom raised his head cautiously. The figure was only a darker blotch of shadow beneath the trees. The chanting ceased.

For a long time Salom waited. And then the darker blotch loosed itself from the clinging darkness and moved beneath the pallid radiance of the moon.

It was Yanong! For an instant Salom was stunned, and then he felt an overwhelming relief. He was about to cry the priest's name when he checked himself. The questions flooded back, and he crouched lower into the shadow.

Why was Yanong here? What was he doing?

The priest was shuffling now in the narrow circle, his head lowered, his hands clasped in a gesture of piety. His pace slowed until movement became almost imperceptible, and finally he stopped, swaying hesitantly, and mumbling to himself. A strange, humorless laugh squawked from him. But he relapsed again into the same shuffling uncertainty. Then he bounded ahead again, and in the hush of the night Salom could hear the thudding of his boots on the freezing earth as he leaped about, flinging his arms wildly and gibbering his high-pitched chant. But again his frenzy drooped into awkward hesitancy.

Salom was locked in a rigid fascination. What *was* Yanong doing here? And suddenly he remembered Kelinka.

This would be the last ceremony of Kelinka's death rites. He strained his eyes toward the dark trees, and imagined he could see the huddled shape of the dead woman amid the shadows.

A surge of wretchedness swept him—and grief for this woman so soon to be abandoned to desolation and the whimpering wind.

Yanong would mutter the incantations and dismember the body and scatter the fragments across the earth so that the wolves would eat of them, and the foxes, and what remained at sunrise would be fought over by quarrelsome birds, and then the sun would whiten the bones and the snow cover them.

He shuddered, and in his revulsion he felt a fierce resentment toward Yanong. Why had the bastard priest brought her here, to this unholy midden? Kelinka had been a good woman, a warm woman and kindly. Then why should her last resting place be this foul moor, cold, cruel, bewitched, and shunned by everybody as unclean?

Yanong had ceased his gyrations and was crouched almost to the ground. He was peering toward the shadows beneath the trees. Moonlight flecked his robes with tarnished silver and brushed a dull glaze across his egg-shaped skull. His arms, hooked in front of him and with the fingers spread, stretched toward the shadows. And behind the malignant silhouette the clouds swirled blacker grotesqueries across the whining sky.

Then Yanong spoke his first intelligible words. His voice was quavering, shrill, almost demented: "Come, Kelinka! We shall see who is the stronger. Come now. Come!"

The priest moved forward, mincing, still in the attitude of some clumsy animal. His fingers clenched and unclenched.

Salom's skin crawled. He stared in anguish toward the shadowed trees where the cadaver was hunched, but nothing moved.

"Come, daughter." Yanong's voice was pitched lower, wheedling. "It will not take long. It is a fine night for the Rolang, Kelinka, and the headman's wife shall dance as merrily as any other. So come, daughter!"

The blood surged across Salom's eyes in an endless, throbbing ribbon, and the sweat streamed at his face, and his heart was a huge bladder pressing his chest outward, outward, outward. . . .

The Rolang! What devil's play was this? How many times as a child had he shuddered at the bare mention of this accursed sorcery—the dreadful thing that older people had talked of in whispers around the fires while their eyes implored reassurance from the painted religious symbols on the walls? *The Rolang!*

Once, in Litang, a naked mystic had been pointed out to him as one who performed the Rolang, and the people had nudged one another nervously, and fingered their beads and their amulets, and skirted wide around this man of frightful powers. But this one had been an old ascetic, a fanatic whose very life had been devoted to solitude and the hidden arts. But Yanong? Yanong was not such a one as this. His brain was deficient of such powers. How could he hope to challenge with his meager knowledge this Thing of darkness—to pit his limited wits and strength against the very Beyond itself? Great mystics themselves had been killed in attempting the Rolang—this practice of breathing life back into the dead, and then challenging the writhing, thrashing corpse to a contest in which only one could conquer. Surely not *Yanong?* And yet he had heard the other stories of stupid monks who had perished in unseen agonies on lonely highlands for attempting the weird magic in defiance or ignorance of the dire penalties meted out to those who invoked powers beyond their own. These were monks suddenly made drunk with an unbalanced confidence in their own secret lore. They never lived long enough to realize their incompetence or to talk of their deeds. Or so the tales went. And as none lived, who was there to say the tales were true or false? And how else was there to be an explanation rendered for the mangled bodies of priests found in the fastnesses? There were skeptics who talked of wolves and leopards. These were the explanations that Salom had always accepted. But most people held trembling fingers to their prayer beads and spoke in hushed tones of the Rolang.

And here was Yanong attempting this black endeavor . . . and with the broken shell of Kelinka . . . and Yanong was a fool, drunk with his own power.

"There is no time to waste, daughter," the monk's voice throbbed. "Come then."

The red film cleared from Salom's eyes. His whole body shook as he stared, horrified and yet curiously engrossed, at the shape scarcely seen in the blackness. Still there was no movement. Did he expect it to move? It seemed as if his whole being had been stretched out, endlessly, into a spinning thread, and the thread was a soundless scream, but he knew that if anything within the tree shadows moved the sound would come and the valley would be rent by it. Still there was no movement. The mincing silhouette of the monk had almost reached the shadow fringe.

The thread snapped in a spasm of fear and horror, and whirled into a thousand bright lights, and then the bloody film was across his eyes. The scream came as he lunged forward, seeing nothing.

He tripped on a curled root growth and sprawled headlong. The shock of the fall tore away the red veil. He looked up into the mad eyes of Yanong.

The monk had swung toward him. But he retained his crouching position and his long arms were still extended in front of him. He was motionless and the moonlight glistened in his demented eyes. In the timeless second as they faced each other Salom saw other things.

The harsh grasses were curling away from a blustering wind that had risen. Scattered flakes of snow twirled and drifted between them. The storm had struck the foothills behind and the ramparts of the valley had disappeared in the jet chaos. Even as Salom scrambled to his feet the snow hissed at him in a thick flurry. He flung himself toward the priest.

IV

Salom scooped the snow into his cupped hands, and drew the blade of the knife through its chill softness. He did it several times until the dullness had gone, and in the faint light that came from the dancing flakes he could see the steel gleaming. Only then did he return the knife to its sheath. The knife that had killed Kelinka. The knife that had killed Yanong!

He groaned and climbed stiffly to his feet and looked down at the body sprawled so awkwardly and already dusted with a gray film of snow. He turned it with his boot. The limbs moved jointlessly, and the head fell to one side with the tongue lolling. Salom was glad he had killed!

He was tired. His mind was jumbled with words that others had said to him: Muhlam, at the crumbled watch tower—"There is no room here for killing!" Kelinka, seated outside the tent with the sun glinting on her jeweled fingers—"The way to the gods, Salom, is through a lama." Veshti, soft in the river's moonshine—"You will grow to admire him, as we do." The Tulku on his resplendent throne—"It will be the best ending, the only ending . . ."

He wiped the snow absently from his face. He was glad he had killed!

He could recapture everything so clearly now. He remembered his surprise at Yanong's solidity when he had first hurled himself at the crouching figure. Until then, in that strange nebulous light, all things, even Yanong, had seemed devoid of substance. But the shock of the impact had knocked the breath from his own lungs and bruised him, and when he recoiled his stumbling feet had caught in a marmot's hole, and he had gone to the ground with the priest on top of him.

And then everything had been a bewildering tangle. There had been the wet swish of the snow and the thrash and thud of limbs that writhed and hooked . . . blackness . . . the heat of the priest's breath on his face. He could feel his boot driving into the priest's side, hear the cry of pain . . . he could feel beneath his hand the greased skull and the flat nose; he could savor again the immense, cruel pleasure he had known when his thumb had gouged hard into the bulging eye, and Yanong's anguish had sobbed into the night. Yes, he was glad he had killed.

Yet he had not thought of killing until he had seen the glitter of the priest's knife—the narrow, pointed blade coming from its black sheath with the silver embossings. It had been like that day when he had shot the bear as it charged Muhlam. Then he had not known that his rifle was at his shoulder until the report startled him. And he had not known that his own knife was out until Yanong thrust at him and the blade had rung against steel. He could have killed him then, for the deflected impetus of the stroke had unsettled the priest and he had blundered past, and he could have lunged the knife in, but instead he had driven his boot smashing into the lurching figure. It had been later, as the priest's blade ripped past his head, that he had driven his own knife down with all his strength. Not once, but many times. Again and again and again; until the blade had been robbed of its sheen; until the monk's cries had faltered into a sob, into a whimper, into a long, bubbling sigh; until there was no sound left in the world but the wind's lament and the swish of snow. And so he had killed him. And he was glad.

He looked down again. The sprawled figure was losing its contours beneath the imperceptible rise of the snow. Salom dusted the flakes from his shoulders.

Well, the Tulku had been right in one thing. The end that had come to Yanong had been the best ending for him. But what of the other prophecies? He knew that what he had done created the definite finality. He would have to leave the valley. In the valley there was no killing. And yet he had killed. He had killed one whom the people regarded as holy. It would be the final, irrefutable proof of Dupken's accusations!

He would have to leave the valley immediately. He turned and stared anxiously into the sky, closer now and moving with a white rhythm. The wind was still rising, and the snow was heavy. He would have to take the chance. He could return to the tent and call Veshti, and she would fill the food bags for him. He would muster his other horse and ride up toward the pass. He could shelter from the storm in the old watch tower, and then when the weather cleared he would set out for distant China.

His head drooped. So this was the ending—the best ending? It was curious how it had worked out. Yanong had been the factor that most prevented him from belonging to the valley, and in ridding himself of that barrier he had forever denied himself the right to belong. But perhaps the Tulku had been wise. Perhaps this was the best ending for all of them. Yanong had found his punishment. By his own departure from the valley the position of Muhlam could be retrieved. The girl would no longer have to bow to the will of the monk: she could marry Dochi, and live the life she would have lived if a Chinese stranger had not entered the valley. Unless . . . unless she would come with him? His pulses hammered—but he cast the thought from him. No—her life was the valley. That was what the Tulku had meant. This was the ending of the tale.

He turned wearily toward his horse. His feet dragged as if he were bearing a great burden. And as he passed the grove he could see the huddled shape of Kelinka through the snowflakes that wavered across the broken clots of shadow, and it seemed that her eyes were darting at him. He stumbled toward his tethered animal.

As he flogged the horse downhill through the blinding whip of the storm he was no longer glad. He was numbed, and he moaned softly, gripped in a clamp of insensate fear of what he had done.

Chapter Sixteen

I

THE snow was gentle. It drew long frail lines of white on the night's mute thickness, and the night curved down secretly over the bewitched valley. With a delicate reticence the snow piled stealthy flake upon stealthy flake to meet the downward curve of the night.

Through the roof aperture of Muhlam's tent a few flakes fluttered, twisting like leaves, settling on the dark bent head of Veshti. She stirred at the stew boiling in the cauldron which, a few hours before, had held the body of her mother. She stirred vigorously at the steaming, sucking mess, as if the activity would afford some release from the turmoil of her thoughts. Her small, anxious face was darkly pink and beaded with globules of sweat from the heat and her own exertions.

"Help me, Renzi!" She turned irritably toward her sister. "Come—there is still the tea. You could do that instead of sitting there and crying." Her face softened. "Oh, forgive me, Renzi! I am sorry, child. I do not wish to be sharp. But there is so much to do, and now that Kelinka has gone both of us must do more."

Renzi gulped and wiped her sodden face on the hem of her skirt.

"But it is so strange now." She sniffed. "It . . . it is not like home any more. I . . . I try to think of Kelinka in Shinje's court . . . but . . . but I can only see her churning the butter . . . and—" her voice rose shrilly—"and Salom has *not* come back. It is dark and he has *not* returned!"

"But it is still early, child."

"You said he would return by dark, and now it *is* dark, and he has not come back."

Muhlam looked up from the sheepskins he had been bundling together in preparation for the trek back to the far end of the valley, and spoke for the first time in hours.

"He will return," he said. He paused and straightened the cramp from his back, and rubbed his hand across the fringe of black hair. "Although perhaps it would be better for him if he did not. He has brought little but sorrow and trouble to the house of Muhlam, and to this valley—and yet——" His forehead crinkled. He spoke softly, almost to himself. "And yet no man could say he was without courage. He fights, that one." The headman nodded. "Yes, he will return," he said explicitly, and, again lapsing into thoughtfulness: "It is an odd thing, but I have a strange liking for this troublesome man of Han."

"And what will they do to him if they find him guilty?" Veshti's voice was tight with control, her eyes rigid on the suck and bubble of the stew.

Muhlam's laughter cut her like a whip. "*If?* They have *already* found him guilty, child! And I do not know what they will do. But, by my wife's dead flesh, I know what they will *not* do! They will not dictate to Muhlam! And they will not break Muhlam! A thousand Chunors plotting ten thousand plots could not break Muhlam. And if this charge of the boy's is found to be true, then Chunor will be sent from this valley, and there will be no betrothal of the headman's daughter to a plotter's son. Heed that, child!" He thrust his thumbs into his girdle and his chin jutted at Veshti, and he thundered his defiance: "By Dorji's guts, they will discover that Muhlam is *still* the strongest man in this valley!"

And in spite of her father's confidence, for the first time in her life Veshti could feel only pity for the gaunt giant whose seed she was. In some ways he was like Salom. He underestimated the strength of the things he stood against. For a moment her heart had leaped at her father's words. There *was* a way out of her betrothal to Dochi! And then she had realized that it would not happen; that it could not happen. The forces against these two were so much stronger than they knew. Muhlam might bluster and Salom might condemn—and even she herself might feel such sorrow as could scarcely be borne—and yet what would it all mean? Nothing. They were all as nothing. She had realized that when Yanong had taken her mother's hand and led her safe from the maze that went to Shinje's court. These were the real things. The gods were everywhere. She had felt their presence, and they were there. Sorrow would not alter that, nor weeping, nor Muhlam's cursing, nor Salom's arguments. Nor would pain alter it—that pain that pressed against her heart when she remembered that once there had been a golden day, and a boy and girl had shared it, and laughed in unison with the river's laugh. For the boy and girl who had laughed together were as nothing. Nothing at all. The road to the gods did not skirt that river. Kelinka had known that—Kelinka, the wise and the understanding and the loving; Kelinka, who had been led through the shadows to the jeweled courts. And the Tulku had known it also. He had told it to Salom, and Salom, in his ignorance and youth, had misinterpreted the wise words. The Tulku had said that the ending would be the best for all. He had not said that it would end in happiness for them all. Happiness was only an illusion, and only the gods were real. It was so necessary to guard against the illusions. Even during the ceremony, after Salom had gone, she had longed for him to be there. That was the strangest part of it all. She had been *with* the gods; every fiber of her body had been under the holy man's spell—and yet there had still been a something, a knot of desire that did not belong to such sacred things. For she had wanted the presence, the companionship, of an unbeliever! Well, that was the folly of illusion. Better to cling to the certainties of faith, the certainty of Yanong's wisdom and holiness. And to be humble. "The wise woman does not question her destiny—she accepts it and earns merit by her humility." Wise, wise Kelinka!

"Veshti!" There was urgency in the cry from outside the tent.

She jumped to the doorway and pulled aside the flap. Salom's face was a white blot against the dimmer whiteness. There was snow crusted on his head and shoulders and his breath snorted in fuzzed clouds of steam. His horse stamped beside him, tugging away from the boy's grip on the reins.

"Veshti!" he hissed. "Come here, child. Here—close to me."

She moved hesitantly for a few paces and then stopped.

"Closer!" he whispered angrily, and then he jumped forward and grasped her arm roughly, pulling her toward him with such force that she uttered an involuntary cry of fear. There was a strange, terrifying wildness in the convulsive clasp of his arms around her shoulders, and his body shook as if with a fever. He bent his head down to her. Even in the darkness there was a strange looseness upon his face that appalled her.

She tried to pull away from him.

"You are hurting me!" she choked. "Let me go, Salom!"

He peered at her stupidly, as if he had not quite grasped what she had said, and then his grip slackened. She wriggled free and stepped back.

"Come inside, Salom," she said nervously. She half-turned toward the tent. "It is cold—and you are covered with snow. Quickly. Come inside and warm yourself before the others arrive. Come, Salom."

"No, Veshti! No!" His voice was urgent and high-pitched. "I must ride now. I must ride away. Tonight. I must leave the valley tonight."

"Are you mad?"

"Perhaps I am. But I tell you I must go—at once! Before the others come! Veshti, I tell you I must go now!"

"Something . . . something has happened," she said slowly. She peered at him through the gentle drift of snow. "Something has happened."

"Yes, something has happened. And I must leave now. Veshti——" He stumbled toward her, his arms outstretched. "Veshti, come with me! Ride away with me! We can be happy."

"Something has happened," she repeated dully. "What, Salom? What has happened?"

"We will go to China, Veshti." He hurried on insistently. "You will like China. I will show you marvels such as you have never even dreamed, Veshti. Cities and towers and gardens and palaces. And you will wear a silken gown———"

"Oh, tell me, Salom!" she breathed. "Tell me what has happened?"

"———and slippers of silk for your feet. And there is a temple of your faith outside Ch'eng-tu. The Tulku told me, Veshti. So you can follow your own religion if you wish, and I will never try to change it if you do not care to. Veshti—you said by the river that you had a need for me. Not for a little time, but for all time. That is the important thing, Veshti. Nothing else matters. Veshti—?"

"Is that you, boy?" Muhlam called. The headman's bulk was a blurred silhouette against the light that leaped inside the tent, and he peered at them through the snow.

Salom retreated a little and stared down curiously at his hands. They had been cupped imploringly while he had talked to Veshti. There was a little cone of snow in each palm.

"Yes, Muhlam," he said softly. "It is I."

"Ha! I knew you would return. Come inside then. I wish to talk with you before they come. They will come soon, and Yanong will be back from the uplands."

Salom turned his wrists. The snow cones fell with a small plopping sound. He wiped the wet palms against his furs. His movements were very precise. And then he brushed past Veshti and followed Muhlam into the bright warmth. Renzi jumped at him like an eager puppy. He patted her head and pushed her aside gently.

"Yanong will not be coming, Muhlam," he said evenly.

"Of course he———"

"Yanong will not be coming."

In the moment of blank, inquiring silence Salom was conscious of many small things: the tentative pause of a snowflake before it fluttered down to become a tiny worm, wriggling and hissing down the curve of the hot cauldron; the bundle of ragged sheepskins, half-packed for the journey to the other end of the valley; a small pink blister, round and transparently thin, on the back of Veshti's clenched hand; the hot savory smell that steamed up from the cauldron, almost stifling the faint linger of the azalea's perfume. His belly reminded him that he was hungry, and a small compartment of his mind wished that he could stay for a little and eat.

"Why do you say Yanong is not coming?" Muhlam's eyes were quizzical on the boy, and his voice low, as if they were conspiring together.

"Because Yanong is dead."

There. The words were out. His mouth had opened and his lips and tongue had moved, and the words had rolled off so easily. Simple little words—one pushing the other off his tongue as if it were a game they were playing—one word tumbling off after the other until all four were there, all joined together, but now instead of being in his head they were loose in the tent, advancing from his mouth toward the three people who stared at him, swelling terribly as they advanced, growing enormous in size, tremendous in volume—gigantic, unbelievable, impossible words, filling the whole tent, splitting the valley, engulfing everything.

"You killed him." It was a statement, flat and uncompromising, and Veshti made it.

"I killed him."

"*Why?* In the name of Buddha, boy—*why?*" Muhlam stumbled toward him, his head shaking, his attitude that of a man suddenly buffeted by forces he cannot understand.

"He had to be killed," Salom said, "so I killed him."

Muhlam's mouth opened, but no words came. He ground his knuckles into his bulging eyes and sank unsteadily to the bundle of skins. Renzi's boots slithered as she inched back toward her father. Her dirty hands were tight on her prayer beads and her eyes never left the boy's white face. For a long time the four of them were held in a wordless, uneasy spell, and then from outside came the impatient whickering of Salom's horse. The sound seemed to break Muhlam's trance.

He rose slowly and went across to the tent flap, stumbling a little as if his legs were weak. He peered into the darkness, and then turned and faced them.

"All right," he said harshly. "We have a little time. Now tell it, boy—and tell it speedily!" He was regaining his control. His body was stiff.

Salom told him. He could listen himself to the precise clarity of his words, but he was perplexed even in this detachment. For they were merely words—and what relationship did such bloodless things have to the dark happenings on that unhallowed moor—to the unclean thing that had moved there—the scarcely comprehended impulses that had moved in his brain? Could words describe that red blindness he had known? Or the evil he had breathed until his very soul had shrieked? Could words present a finality as clear and as clean as the silver slice of a knife in moonlight? He could still smell the warmth that had spouted into his hands, and he could still see the snow drifting down, light and lovely as the laughter of happy women, until it had shrouded the black obscenity of the night—and how could words tell of these things?

But the others listened to these words, spoken so slowly and with freedom from all emotion, from all the artifices of excuse and condemnation. Only once—when he spoke the word "Rolang"—did their attention falter. For Muhlam's face blackened and Veshti choked on a cry of terror—but they heard him out. And when he had told it all there was an anguished silence that was broken finally by the headman's whispered question:

"There was no mistake? It was the Rolang?"

"He spoke the words. I heard him. There was no mistake."

"And he did this with my woman?"

"No. He did not start. He was about to start when I killed him."

"Ah!" Muhlam turned away. His head hung and his arms fell loosely from his sagging shoulders. He did not look at Salom as he spoke. His words were flat and heavy:

"Which way do you ride, boy?"

"East."

"Back to the Han country?" Muhlam turned and looked up to the roof aperture, and the white drift that was across it.

"Oh, I can take shelter in the old watch tower until the storm clears."

Muhlam swung to face him. His fists were knotted and his stern face drawn, and his eyes implored the boy to understand.

"You know why this is?"

"I know why." Salom nodded.

"There . . . there never has been killing in this valley, my son. You understand?"

"I understand, Muhlam."

The headman nodded quickly, and averted his gaze from the steadiness of the boy's eyes.

"You will not need to delay then," he said gruffly. He swung toward Veshti. "Fill the food bags. Hurry, girl!"

Veshti moved swiftly enough, but her actions were almost automatic. She still felt stunned, and there was only one way to fight against the daze and that was to be very careful in her task. Firstly, there would be need for barley. He would want plenty of barley—and butter. How long would the butter keep? He would be riding for weeks, perhaps months, before he met people again! And tea. It would be cold . . . there would be little shelter on the trail. There must be plenty of tea . . . there was warmth in tea. What else? Dried peas . . . yes, peas . . . and some strips of smoked beef. Oh, yes. She had almost forgotten! Salt. He would need salt for the tea . . . A cheese would be good. . . . Yet it did not seem to be very much. Then he should have a good hot meal of the ku-zeh before he left. No—there would be no time for that. He had killed Yanong, and so he must flee before the others came. He had killed Yanong because Yanong had attempted the Rolang! It was strange that Yanong should do that—and now Yanong did not exist any more—and who was there to lead Yanong to Shinje's court? Ah! Now it was all ready. Five leather bags. Barley, butter, salt, tea, beef, cheese, peas. Barley, butter, salt, tea, beef, cheese, peas.

These were established things—barley, butter, salt, tea ... And now where were all the other established things? Like Yanong? Yanong had been an established thing, and now he did not exist. And in a moment or two Salom would not exist. In a moment he would not exist any more, just as Kelinka did not exist any more, just as Yanong—and what did all this mean? Barley, butter, salt ... But there was no time! No time for him to eat a bowl of ku-zeh. No time for talk, for explaining these things, for the sifting of feelings and emotions; no time for deciding wrongs and rights, no time for deciding anything. But later there would be time ... all the time until the end of her life ... and it would be so empty because Salom would not be there. In a moment he would not exist any more, because he was waiting only until the food was ready, and now it was ready and the thongs were being pulled tight by two brown hands, and the hands were hers. Three more thongs ... two more thongs ... one more. ... There! Five leather bags. Barley, butter, salt ...

"Hurry, girl!" Muhlam rasped.

She nodded quickly and scrambled to her feet. The two heaviest bags were in her hands.

She looked at him, so slim and proud and hurt, standing there. Less than a moment now, and his brown eyes were consuming her, drawing her into him.

"It is time, Salom." Muhlam rubbed at his chin. "Get your horses."

The horses! She had forgotten. Then there were additional moments remaining—while he caught the pack animal and made the five bags fast to the wooden saddle.

"I will help," she mumbled, and ran quickly from the tent. At High Valley it was still a snow-soft night, but the wind was rising. It was a fretful wind, and the snow was uneasy. The pack horse was humped dejectedly at the edge of the thang, and she grasped its wet mane and tried to pull it to its feet. And as she panted with the effort she was seized by strong arms and twisted around, and Salom held her in an embrace that was fierce and possessive.

"You are mine, Veshti," he whispered.

The wild tears came as she nodded. No time now for words, no time for anything except the circle of these clamping arms and the certainty that she belonged inside them.

"You will come?" His voice was hoarse.

She clutched him.

"You will come?"

"I will come, Salom."

"Then quickly——"

He kicked the animal to its feet. Through the new agitation of the snow they could see the blur of lights moving toward them from Chunor's tent. Together they slung the food bags across the wooden bars, and hitched the trailing rein to the lead horse.

"There will be no farewells."

"No."

No farewells, no time. The moment had slid past them like a chip dancing down a river. No time for anything. No time to say anything to Renzi. No time to make Muhlam understand. No time even for herself to understand.

But his arms were around her again, and she was lifted to the saddle, and there was the firm pressure of his body against her back. He kicked the horse and the animal reared and plunged forward and behind them the pack horse snorted.

II

Salom felt it first. He pulled Veshti closer against his body and knew that he had been waiting for it. Ever since the snow had fallen like a wall across the rise toward the spur, and even before they had reached the grove of birches, he had been waiting.

It was a silence unlike any other silence—wide and deep and round, stretching outward, stretching in beautiful taut curving lines, stretching into timelessness, stretching out of shape, stretching and stretching until it snapped with a low, cold, humming sound . . .

and then it began to contract, whirling inward, hissing inward, becoming smaller and smaller and smaller.

He heeled into the horse's flanks and the beast plunged upward desperately.

"Salom!" Veshti cried his name in the white dark, and her voice echoed his own premonition, and he knew there was no need for her to say other than his name. He knew her fear.

III

Muhlam felt it as he crouched in the pungent warmth of the tent, breaking with sadness. He had driven the others back to their tents, and now he was alone with his fear and his loneliness.

And when he felt it he lifted his head, and his nostrils flared, sniffing the silence.

The smoke hung without movement above the fire, like a carved, soiled column; and Renzi's drowned eyes were suddenly, fearfully, still.

As the tent ropes began to thrum, first with a whispering sound, then growing louder and louder into a muted growl, he stumbled outside. The long, curved lines of drifting flakes were beginning to waver, to writhe a little, and he could no longer see through them. And the padded silence was disintegrating into a thousand scurrying whispers, wild and evil.

He attempted to calculate the length of time that had passed since they had ridden away. And then, knowing what was to come, his pride crumbled. With his dreadful face turned blindly toward the high pass he wrenched at the tent ropes in a savage impotence, and from his contorted mouth came an incoherent prayer.

IV

It came in waves, borne on a drawn-out sibilance that hissed up unseen gorges and rose shrieking through the wadded air. As the first wave crashed over them, burning and stinging, Salom slid from the frightened horse and dragged Veshti down beside him.

"There will be more shelter this way," he shouted. "It will ease soon. Then we will get to the watch tower."

The words were wrenched from his mouth and hurled away into the seething white eddies.

Veshti clung to him silently. Her breath was quick and hot on his cheek, and he could feel the snow melting down his neck, trickling beneath his furs. The wind screamed louder.

He put his mouth to her ear and shouted: "No! We will try to get back!"

He lunged up against the weight of the wind, and the mad whirl drove lances into his eyes, and instinctively he loosed his grip on the stirrup to rub away the pain. The shuddering horse whinnied its fear and reared away from him, dragging the pack animal with it. Salom plunged forward, his hands groping, but he was caught and tossed on a curling wave that stung him and grazed him. In the white madness he could not see the horses. He could see nothing! And now panic had blinded him also, and he groveled through the buffeting flood, screaming Veshti's name. There was a roaring in his ears. And then he felt her hands scrabbling for him, and he caught them and dragged her into the curve of his side. A convulsed sea of snow boiled over them, spinning and heaving. It tossed them about as rapids would in a flooded river. He held her body close to his, and tried to make his eyes see through the blizzard the way they had come. But he could see nothing—nothing but the white shafts driving down at them, striking them with gigantic, icy blows.

His body was braced to shield her as he half-carried, half-dragged her forward.

It seemed an endless time they had spent in stumbling and falling and scrambling to their feet, and sometimes they had fought into the roar of it, and at other times they had been hurled back by it, and now their breathing came in terrified gulps that tasted weak and watery in their mouths. Their eyes were streaked and destroyed now by the white blindness so that sometimes they reeled against old stumps and the skeletons of trees which still stood against the tempest; and sometimes they seemed to be struggling up unfamiliar slopes; and sometimes they were falling down into soft pits that seethed and hissed at them. Once they fell across two lumpy, snow-encrusted shapes still faintly warm, and they knew with a sick fear that they would never ride the horses again.

But still they battled against it until suddenly Veshti was only a dead weight dragging against his numbed arm, and as he peered down at her through his blindness she slid along his arm and crumpled into a mounting drift. He went down on his knees beside her. It was like sinking into a soft and unbelievably warm cushion. It yielded gently to his bruised weariness. It was warm and quiet and it promised peace. Always he had sought peace—and this promised peace. It wadded the blizzard's shriek to a muted hiss, a whisper, a sleepy sound that promised peace. . . .

He forced the white weight off his eyes and felt for her face and rubbed the snow from it and chafed her hands between his own. He bent very close to her. Now he could see a little. Her breath was only a faint streaming above her parted lips. He could feel it on his hand. He slapped at her cheeks until her eyes opened.

"Salom," she whispered. The same promise was in the languorous whisper—the promise of peace and sleep. "Salom . . . we will rest a little time, eh? We will go on . . . but let us rest first. I am very tired. So tired. And it is warm and pleasant here . . . and . . . I am . . . very . . . tired."

He heard the slow words fuse with the gentle, formless murmur of the snow. "Peace," the snow said. "Sleep," it said. "Rest," it said. The whiteness was billowing over him again, but its touch was gentle. It yielded to him. It laved the pain and the weariness. It caressed him, so gently, so very gently.

He shook her and slapped her face harder.

His fingers struck at her urgently. "Veshti, if we rest there will be no going on. You should know this. We must go on now.

Now! If we do not go on there will be no returning to the valley, and no setting out from it again. Come, little rabbit! We must go on—if we are to live."

But she squirmed beneath him and pulled his hands away from her face and held them tightly.

Above them the monster ravished the night, but here it was warm and soft and full of peace, and there was a deep soothing tenderness in the touch of the snow, and she was content. Snow shredded quietly from the top of the drift. And Salom, too, felt the peace stealing over him, white and whispering.

"Salom." The dreaminess had almost gone from Veshti's voice. "Listen now, Salom. We will speak to each other the truth in our hearts." Her fingers tightened upon his hands. "Already we drop from weariness. We could not go on. This I know, Salom—and this you know. We will not reach the watch tower, will we?"

"Who can tell? It might be very close and———"

"Salom, we speak the truth in our hearts, remember."

"No, Veshti. We will not reach the watch tower. But we can still go down. We can follow the curve downhill, and so we must———"

"We are speaking the truth to each other, Salom. We know we will not reach the watch tower. And I know I have no wish to go back. For me, Salom, there can be no returning, for if I returned there would never be a setting-out again. This I know, Salom, and this is the truth." She stroked his arm gently. "And this I think you know, too."

"But, Veshti, why should you not——?"

"There are many reasons. But let us say, Salom, that the flowers would twine around my feet and chain me to the meadows. I would hear the music of bells and the laughter of the river, and they would deafen me to the truths you tell. I would be afraid. And there would be the words of my father and my people———"

"But these would not be good reasons, Veshti."

"They would be all that would matter. You see, Salom, I have made the setting-out, and since I have closed my ears to the river and the bells and the wind in the grass, and to the words others speak, there can be no return. Can you not understand this, Salom?"

Salom saw her words like a great slice of light curving between them and the hissing madness above, so that the madness recoiled and created a screen upon which many images danced. Everything was there: Muhlam and Yanong and Kelinka, Veshti and himself and Dochi; everything and everybody were there; and the Tulku's words were there, strung one to the other like an endless necklace, and linked with the peddler's words; and in all these things there was a meaning. The meaning of it all was *now*. One no longer had to search for meanings. *This* was the meaning!

The screen broke and the madness shrieked back above them, and yet the madness could not touch them. Drift flakes floated and paused and turned and sighed over them. It was warm and peaceful.

Salom shivered and clasped her to him fiercely.

"You speak the truth, little rabbit!" He ran his mouth over her icy face, half-seen in the white dark. "I, too, have known this. But is there no bitterness in your heart then that I have led you to this? Is there no fear?"

"There is no bitterness, Salom," she murmured against his mouth. "And there is no fear. Only gladness, Salom."

Her small hand fell into his, and it was as on the golden day by the river, for it was an accepting hand and utterly trusting.

"Yes, Salom," she added, "I am glad we are setting out together. Wherever the journey should take us—I am glad we travel together."

For a long time he held her. It was curious that it was so warm and quiet. He knew that the pressure against the drift was increasing. It would not last, but now it was warm and quiet and peaceful—so peaceful. As he held her, his mouth warmed her small chilled face, and as he clasped her close to him the world seemed to expand in broad, undulating bands of white that gathered into themselves oddly shaped columns of spinning snow. The columns leaped and fell and sprang up again to twist anew into ever-changing fantasies, and as the world swelled outward the seethe became louder and louder, gathering strength, humming a deeper and deeper note.

Veshti stirred in his numbed arms and rubbed her face against his.

"I had no wish to become Dochi's wife," she whispered.

"I know it, little rabbit."

"But . . . but, Salom, there is something that is hard for a woman to say. . . ."

"Say it."

"I would wish to become your wife."

"Veshti!"

"Yes, Salom. I . . . I think there is not much time."

The humming was deep in his ears, deeper and deeper, and then it burst in a wild peal of bells.

His frozen fingers fumbled clumsily with the fastenings of her jacket.

"Help me," he whispered.

And so the story ended.

With her naked body burning under his, the long, white waves curled upward into a shouting, tumultuous column, and the old majestic gods leaned out from the Ta Hsueh Shan and gathered the columns to themselves, and ended another summer in the Valley of the Dreaming Phoenix as they flung themselves forward and inward, and the columns burst with a wild and triumphant roar into a million seething balls of snow, curving inward, hissing inward, growing larger and larger and larger.

The blizzard wailed its fury over the Pass of White Watching and the drifts mounted with a secret silence until even the trees were drowned beneath the slow white flood.

Epilogue

THERE was no precedent for such a thing.
    That was the strangest part of it. It had never happened before. And the villagers who clustered in their square stone doorways recalled that most of them had even forgotten to make their bows, and, although this was a shameful thing, it could be excused, surely, by virtue of the fact that such a thing had never happened before?

Long after the bright cavalcade had passed the little settlement they had stood open-mouthed in the new mud of the thaw, staring after it until the pennons were only tiny specks of fluttering color and the horsebells tinkled back on the wind with the frailty of fairy bells.

Dupken was the first to throw aside the fetters of this unique enchantment. She bounded across the slushy alley to where Muhlam and Bitola stood before the largest of the square stone houses.

"Eeee!" she squeaked breathlessly. "I know what it is. The Tulku must be on the trail of a demon to ride toward the valley when the snow is still to thaw on the uplands. Is it not so, Muhlam? Why else would he come so early—or ride through the village without stopping? Eeee! Mark my words—a demon! I know it! Take care, Bitola, lest your unborn child be marked with a serpent."

"I have no fears for my son." Bitola grinned contentedly, rubbing her heavy belly. "There will be the mark of Muhlam upon it, Dupken, and that should be sufficient to make any demon quail." She smiled at her husband with lazy affection. "Still, it is a strange thing that the Tulku comes so early to the valley—and that he rides without pause toward the high pastures. He could have stopped at least to greet the headman."

"He will be back," Muhlam said shortly, and turned and went into the house.

Lotor lounged over to a group that included Chunor and Kaman.

"How about a jar of chang, my friends? We must celebrate this."

"Celebrate what?" Chunor asked.

"Why, the Tulku! True, he did not stop—but is that good reason why we should not celebrate?"

Chunor spat.

Lotor grinned. "Then if you do not wish to pay your respects to the Tulku I have a fine assortment of other reasons worth drinking upon." He began to tick them off on his fingers: "There is the Tulku, there is the coming of spring, there is a fine stock of weaving done, there are the bins filled with new-ground barley, there is a fine stack of fleeces for someone to take to Batang, there is my wench's big belly. Come, let Lotor entertain! Now that I am related to the headman—and, mark you, if Bitola's bellyful turns out to be a son there will come a day when Lotor will be the headman's grandfather—then I think I should live up to my position. So come—drink with the grandfather of a headman! Never have I possessed a throat so parched. Let us all drink to the Tulku—or to something!"

Kaman shook his head glumly. "I do not like it," he said. "No, I do not like it at all. Neither the coming of the Tulku or other things. I do not care for a season that begins so strangely. I looked in the manger again this morning, and it is as I have feared all winter long. That fine cow of mine has the look of wasting upon her. The same look that came upon my bull after Yanong had put the black blight upon him. You can jest, Lotor, but I tell you there is another strangeness afoot."

At the mention of Yanong, Lotor's face had clouded:

"This time when the new priest comes let us have sense enough to realize whether he is a good man or not. We want no more monks who love the black arts."

"You speak truth, Lotor, but I fear this will be another such year."

"It is the Chinese boy I feel for," Lotor continued seriously. "I would trade a winter's brewing of good chang to meet him again and apologize for my part in driving him from the valley. He was a good lad, that one."

"As I always maintained." Chunor nodded.

"Not I," Lotor said regretfully. "I turned against him. You know, Kaman, it is a strange thing. He must have been riding away at the very time Yanong was being destroyed. Uggh! I tell you I needed more than my share of chang this winter to clear my eyes of the picture of those two bodies on the heath. That bastard priest! I am glad he was destroyed in the Rolang! It was a fitting end!" He spat in revulsion. "I must have a drink else I vomit!"

Chunor rubbed his chin thoughtfully.

He rather wished he was riding with the Tulku's caravan—since he thought he had a shrewd idea where it was going. The Tulku would have heard the report of Yanong's death in the Rolang, and he would be riding up to High Valley to examine the bodies. Well, Chunor would have liked to examine the bodies, too, before the snow thawed completely and they decomposed or were torn by the beasts.

When Muhlam had led them all to the heath after the blizzard had ended there had been so much jostling and such a fantastic hubbub that nobody had been able to make a close examination even if they had cared to. And all the loose-bellied idiots had tured around completely and screamed about the dead priest's sorcery, and lamented that they had accused the boy unjustly and perhaps sent him to his death—and there had been no way for a sensible man to deal with such a hysterical rabble. Yet, even at the time, he had smelled something suspicious about the whole affair. There had been the disappearance of the boy, and with him the headman's daughter who had been betrothed to his own son. It had all been too convenient for the headman. Chunor cleared his throat of its sourness. *Very* convenient for Muhlam—especially as the headman had fined him six good head of cattle. And all the disloyal fools had acclaimed Muhlam's judgment, and approved the sentence, and sworn a great tissue of lies to prove that they had been deceived by Chunor. Well, there was one who would not easily forget these things, and there would be some interesting inquiries to be set in train once they had reached the summer pastures again. Meanwhile, it had passed, and even without those six head of cattle he was still a richer man than the headman. He smiled crookedly. It was as well Muhlam did not know the contents of his prayer chest, otherwise the fine might have been increased by some pieces of silver.

Well, there was work to be done. Chunor hitched at his girdle and strode toward the milling wheel. Still, he would like to look at those bodies again.

Dochi had trotted behind the cavalcade for a little time, expecting that it would stop and set up a camp on the outskirts of the village, but it had gone on without heeding his cries, and now he leaned on the wooden bridge that spanned the river a short distance beyond the village.

He felt very miserable. It was a feeling even worse than the anguish that had sat beside him all through the slow run of winter, for the anguish was still there and this new misery was added to it. Tears trickled slowly down his cheeks. Oh, why had the Tulku ridden straight on, without stopping? Such a wise and holy man would have talked to him, and listened to his tale, and then he would look at the wise books and be able to tell Dochi where Veshti could be found. Chunor had told him she was dead. How did he know that? And if she were it would not matter. Even if she were in another life the Tulku would surely know all about it, and he would tell him where to look for her. There was no loveliness left in all the world, and no loveliness could return to it until he had found Veshti.

"Do not weep, Dochi." He turned quickly, his face working. It was the little girl, Renzi. She also must have trotted down the slippery trail in pursuit of the vivid column. The child leaned beside him. "Why do you weep, Dochi?" she said.

"I . . . I thought the Tulku would have stopped. And he rode straight on. I cried out, but they paid no attention to my calls."

"They say he rides to find the body of the evil one. Is it for that you weep, Dochi?"

The boy's face shook miserably, but he said nothing.

"I know why you weep, Dochi. You weep for Veshti. But it is no use weeping, Dochi. All winter I have wished to weep. Because of Veshti also. And Kelinka, and because of Salom. Salom was a good man and kindly."

"Yes." Dochi sniffed. "He was good and kindly."

Renzi blinked and smiled timidly at him. "You must not be sad, Dochi. Look, now the spring is here, and soon the last snows will go and we will be riding again to the valley. And you like the valley, don't you, Dochi? You will feel happier when we go there."

Renzi rested her face on her chubby fist and stared up-valley. Her expression was oddly mature, as if the passage of a season had given her more than her tenth year, more than a season's wisdom.

One day, she thought, she would ride farther than the Valley of the Dreaming Phoenix. One spring when the birds sang loud the great mountains would beckon her. And she would ride away, ride to China—to Salom's land of palaces and moats and walls, of great cities and of men who sold dried vipers in boxes of red silk, and she would find Salom and Veshti, and they would saddle their horses and all ride together throughout the land, and if there were any lands beckoning them beyond China they would travel those lands also, and learn of the whole world. And, even if she did not find Salom and Veshti, she would ride alone—and somehow Salom would know of it, and he would be glad to know that his little friend had listened well to the words he had told her.

But Renzi was wrong, as Chunor was wrong, and all the others. For the Tulku's cavalcade rode past the sorcerers' heath on the uplands as it had ridden past the little village. And the fat man who whipped his mule through the soft, clinging drifts, and who flayed his fearful and bewildered attendants with the lash of his scorn, spared no single sidelong glance to the forsaken moor or the white mounds beneath a tangle of twisted trees.

He rode on, almost to the edge of the spur that folded up to the Pass of White Watching. The contours of the land were unfamiliar, for in some areas the snow had gone, and in others great drifts glittered in the soft sunshine, and the air rang with the music of liquefying snow.

Suddenly he shouted a command. The column halted. The Tulku grunted as he dismounted. A broken watch tower thrust from the whiteness, and about forty paces away from it was a buttress of snow from which a twisted tree protruded. For a long time he stared toward it, and his lamas stood in a silent circle around him, and although they fidgeted in their bewilderment they were silent, because they were afraid of this thing they could not understand.

"Dig," the Tulku commanded quietly, pointing. "Dig there."

A dozen cowed lamas crouched over the drift, scrabbling with their hands into the clean snow.

They recoiled when the wet furs were dragged clear, stiff and hard, and the sodden garments, and looked imploringly toward their leader, their eyes entreating him to discontinue this thing they could not understand.

"Dig!" he said.

And when it was done the priests shuffled back behind him, and their limbs shook with the horrible enigma of it all. But no single pair of eyes could be loosed from that which had been uncovered from the snow.

"We will camp here," the Tulku said tonelessly, not turning to them. "My tent will be set up for the funerary rites. I will conduct the rites myself."

As if released from a spell, the monks scurried thankfully back to their animals. Only Nunskar, the Tulku's chief attendant, stayed behind with his master.

For many moments his wide eyes darted between his leader and this thing the snow had revealed—the boy and the girl, naked, locked together, like carvings in marble, and yet with a color, even a life, that no stone possessed.

He turned timidly back to the Tulku.

"You knew them, Most Excellent One?" he whispered.

"Yes, I knew them." The Tulku nodded. The sadness that was in his eyes made his face the face of a saint.

"Ah!" Nunskar shook his head regretfully. "It is a great shame that they were defeated by the storm and the snow."

He cringed away as the Tulku whirled upon him, stumbled back before the darkness in his master's face. And then the Living Buddha flung wide his arms, and tears flooded his eyes, and yet in his thunderous face was a titanic contempt and an overwhelming pity for the blindness of humanity.

"Look again, fool!" he muttered. "They were the *undefeated!*"